PLAYING BY THE Rules

BETH BOLDEN

CHAPTER ONE

THE WORST DAY OF Davis Abernathy's life started at two thirty-eight in the morning.

His agent exhaled, the sound sharp and dreadful, before he began to speak.

Davis' stomach clenched tight and refused to let go.

"The Condors," he said, "just traded for a new quarterback."

Sure, not everything was perfect between Davis and his team. But they were *his team.*

Except not anymore.

"Tom Taylor," his agent said, after hesitating long enough Davis knew it had to be bad.

And it was.

His agent kept talking, but Davis could barely hear him.

The Condors had given up a first-round and two second-round draft picks, and signed a new contract with Taylor for almost two hundred million dollars, guaranteed money.

Davis had known that the owner of the Condors wanted to win a Super Bowl. *He* wanted to win a Super Bowl, and they'd gotten damn close, a handful of times.

But clearly, the owner had gotten tired of waiting, and not only had they spent next year's draft, and all that money, they'd given it to someone currently fighting multiple counts of spousal and partner abuse.

By the time Davis got off the phone, he went straight into the bathroom, and threw up.

The bad day had only gotten worse from there.

Everyone around the NFL—all the media pundits, all the players, the personnel managers, even agents—in shock at the sudden trade, had searched for a reason why the Condors, previously enamored with Davis, would give up on him so easily, so suddenly.

The Condors answered this speculation with reasons.

Davis was a problem in the locker room. He couldn't win games, not with regularity. He couldn't be counted on in tough situations. He wasn't *their* quarterback. The insinuation was that he'd never been their quarterback.

It was all bullshit, but it didn't matter what was true and what was not true, because the media believed. The NFL believed. Even the fans, who Davis had always assumed would stay loyal and love him no matter what, believed.

By the time the Condors released him a few weeks later, they'd done such a good job annihilating his reputation, there'd been not a single trade offer for him, and for a year, nobody had called.

He'd gone home to the coast of Carolina, and licked his wounds.

For fourteen long, interminable months. For those fourteen months, his phone stayed silent. And then, one morning, that all changed.

The best day of his life started early too, but this time it wasn't his agent calling.

"Davis? Davis Abernathy?" the man drawled on the phone, sounding even more deeply Southern than some of Davis' own neighbors.

"That's me," he said, his voice rough with disuse. Some days there wasn't anyone he talked to.

It was easier that way.

"It's Asa. Asa Dawson. I'm puttin' together a new staff, for the Miami Piranhas."

Staff. He wasn't calling because he wanted Davis to be a quarterback on his roster, he was calling him because he wanted to . . . *hire* him?

A little more of his heart died, at yet another coach, yet another team, that didn't trust him to take the field. But he didn't hang up, because he reasoned, how many more phone calls was he going to be getting?

Asa Dawson didn't need any introductions.

Previously, Asa had coached at Tennessee, and once a year, they'd played each other. Davis and his team, the South Carolina Gamecocks, had been one of the few stumbling blocks Asa had ever experienced at Tennessee. When Davis had played, he'd been proud every year they gave the Volunteers hell. They'd even beaten them a few times.

"Come to Miami," Asa said, "and help me mentor this new quarterback. Well, not *new*, he's played for a year, but last year was a fuckin' disaster, so it almost doesn't count. But his confidence, well, it's in the shitter, Davis. Don't expect that I need to tell you 'bout that."

Davis couldn't argue with that.

He only had one question. "Why me?"

Coach hesitated, so briefly Davis had barely heard it, but he was listening for it, so acutely, his suddenly damp hand sliding on his phone case, that he couldn't have missed it. "You mean, why don't I agree with the rest of the fucking idiots who think you're washed up and a problem? That you're worse than some asshole who beats his wife and his mistress and his girlfriend?"

Davis swallowed hard. "Yes."

Asa's voice was so kind, it nearly broke what was left of his heart.

"Son, I watched you for years. You've got juice left in the tank, and if the rest of them are too stupid to use it, then I will. I got this quarterback who doesn't know which end is up, they messed him up so bad. You wanna come and fix him?"

When Davis hung up the phone, he wasn't sure who he was going to fix—Paxton Kelly or himself.

Maybe both.

The next day, impossibly, was even better.

He took a flight to Miami, and to his shock, Asa hadn't sent an assistant or his son, Beau, to meet him at the airport, but Paxton Kelly himself.

He knew of him, of course, because when the last year of Davis' NFL career was coming to an end, Paxton's had just been beginning.

He'd seen him play at USC; the whole *country* had seen him play at USC.

When he'd declared for the draft, even the most critical of sports commenters had unanimously agreed that he was the best quarterback to come out of the west in ages, since Sam Crawford.

There were some analysts who thought he might be even better than Crawford.

Pax had been drafted to replace Colin O'Connor, a Hall of Fame–bound legend. That was never going to be an easy path to walk. But then he'd struggled out of the gate, with a historically bad team surrounding him, and like the NFL often did, they wrote him off so quickly that Davis imagined he'd never even gotten a chance to catch his breath before they were declaring him overrated, a draft bust.

But watching Pax on TV was different than coming face to face with the man for the first time.

Up close, it was impossible to miss the uncertainty buried in his eyes. So many questions lingered in his gaze, the kind of questions you never got an answer to.

At least, ones he'd never been able to answer for himself.

But you're here to give him the answers, he reminded himself, *even if you haven't got a fucking clue what the right answers are.*

"Hi," he said, reaching out his hand. "I'm Pax."

Pax's hair was ash brown, lightened in places from the sun, and his face was undeniably tan, but even more, it was a *friendly* face. Even more, he didn't give Davis a look that said, *what the hell are you doing here, you're nobody, not anymore.* Maybe he still thought it, but at least, Davis thought, he made sure Davis didn't see the disbelief in his eyes.

"Davis Abernathy," he said, reaching out and shaking Pax's hand.

Pax had a surprisingly good grip. Confident, even though Davis had seen the shadows in his light hazel eyes, full of questions without answers.

That, he wasn't all that surprised about.

He'd done his research in the last twenty-four hours on Paxton Kelly. Watched several compilation videos. Some interviews. He had a good idea of what Pax's weak spots were.

But the sudden flare of attraction the moment their hands touched, despite the brisk professionalism of the handshake, *that* was entirely unexpected.

Davis froze.

He'd known he was bi since he was seventeen and he'd had a brief, but intense, affair with another guy on his team.

It had ended badly—and he'd vowed to never get involved with another player. Even if he wasn't a player himself.

Luckily it hadn't been a problem.

Until now.

Sure, Pax was a handsome guy, with his hazel eyes and his golden skin, with all that hair, even if it was a shade too messy, sticking up in wavy tufts, but Davis had met plenty of hot football players before. He'd even seen plenty of them naked, in the locker room and in the showers.

But he'd never taken any of their hands and wanted, more than anything, to shift the handshake to something else. He'd never wanted to slide his own hand higher, to trace his fingers over the muscles on Pax's forearm, and then tug him closer, tip their heads together. Feel just how soft the scruff on his jawline was on his lips.

It blew his mind apart that it was Paxton Kelly who was making him think these things.

He'd not even thought it, not once, watching him on TV before, or on YouTube last night.

But face to face, where he could see the way Pax's eyes lit up, see the hundred shades of blond in his beard, in his hair, the softness of his gaze . . . that was a whole other story.

You're not gonna think about it, and you're definitely not gonna do anything 'bout it, because you got one fucking chance left, and this is it. You told Coach you'd fix his QB, and that's what you're gonna do.

Davis saw Pax's expression change and realized that he'd been silent for too long. Held on to his hand too long.

Because he didn't want to let go.

In the last fourteen months he'd been buried in the house he'd built, back in the wilds of Carolina, not wanting to see anyone, definitely not wanting to touch anyone.

That's why you can't let go, Davis told himself, forcing himself to do it anyway, *because you've been denying yourself for a whole fuckin' year.*

But he knew, deep down, that wasn't the only reason why.

"Uh, sorry," Davis said, and forced his fingers to loosen.

Pax's lips quirked up. "You're not what I expected." His gaze swept over Davis, and he felt it nearly like a physical touch. From the top of his hair, even more overdue for a cut than Pax's own, down to his freshly shaved chin, stuttering just long enough at his lips that Davis knew that the attraction he'd felt wasn't one-sided. Then lower, skimming across his shoulders, his torso, and then even lower still, lingering at his hips, his calves.

Pax's gaze lit him up inside, and made him feel more alive than he had in months.

Fourteen months, specifically.

"What did you expect?" Davis knew all the stories that had circulated about him over the last year. He was selfish, he was a bad teammate, he was mean and judgmental, he ruined teams just by being on them—even though he'd only ever been on one team for his entire professional career, and as far as Davis was concerned, they'd ruined themselves by pursuing Taylor.

None of that was him, it never had been, but during the worst of it, he'd stopped looking in the mirror, afraid he'd see evidence in his eyes that the rumors contained even a grain of truth.

Paxton shrugged. "That you'd look older, I guess. More worn out."

"What are you never supposed to do? Tell a woman she looks tired?" Davis teased.

"Coach said you were still hungry, and you *look* hungry."

He was. Hungry to prove that everyone was fucking wrong about him.

But to do that, he'd need to prove that those ghosts in Pax's eyes were only that: ghosts.

"Hungry to get started," Davis said. They started walking towards the exit. "Coach said he was sending someone to pick me up, but I never imagined it'd be you."

"Coach thinks . . ." Pax hesitated as they passed the baggage claim. "No bags?"

Davis already had his duffel on his shoulder. He knew a diversionary tactic when he saw it.

"Nope," he said, then dragged both of their attention back to the real subject. "So what *does* Coach think?" He knew enough about Asa to know one thing he had in spades was opinions. And then there was Beau, his son and assistant, who was apparently a genius. Davis guessed he had plenty of opinions of his own.

Would that be too many people in Pax's ear? Davis also knew that Asa had hired Randy Foreman to be the passing coordinator. He didn't know Randy personally, but from what he'd read, he was solid. Efficient. No-nonsense. Much like Asa himself.

AKA none of them would hesitate to offer their opinions.

And no doubt Paxton, who'd been so damn good in college but struggled during his first year in the NFL, would want to listen to all of them, because deep down, he was like all of the quarterbacks that Davis knew: a winner, determined to keep winning.

In Pax's case, to *start* winning.

"Coach thinks I need to listen to you. Learn from you. Get close to you, I guess."

Davis ignored the part of him that was very excited at that last possibility.

There wouldn't be any of that kind of closeness.

Even if it wasn't against policy for a coach to get involved with a player—and it *was*—Davis wouldn't have done it anyway. It was foolish to think that you could keep the personal and professional separate. On top of that, Asa was right, because for Pax to trust him, to really learn from him, to buff up that dinged-up confidence, they'd need to get close.

"He's right," Davis said, thinking of the quarterbacks coaches he'd had during his NFL career. There had been three of them, and he'd known them better than his own family. Certainly he'd talked to them more.

It was going to be difficult to keep the line intact when the easiest thing in the world would be to blur it.

This is your last chance. Nobody else is callin' you. You know that.

If he fucked this up, he'd go back to Carolina and lose himself forever.

At least *this* part of him. The part that craved validation, that knew the feel of a ball in his hand better than anything else. The part that had worked so goddamned hard to make it *out* of Carolina.

"I thought so," Pax said, and he suddenly sounded dejected. "I barely ever saw the quarterbacks coach last year."

Davis had had a feeling, but this confirmed it. "Why the hell not?"

A hard emotion passed over Pax's face. He couldn't play poker, he'd lose all his money in minutes. "Too busy tryin' to save his job, I guess," Pax said.

"Fucker."

Pax's mouth quirked up into another quick grin. "My thoughts exactly."

They exited the airport, and the June sun was intense, the humidity of southern Florida hitting Davis like a hot fist to the face.

"My Jeep's just over in the short-term lot," Pax said, gesturing.

"Coach said there was a condo I could stay at . . ."

"Yeah." Pax didn't look in his direction, as they walked towards the open garage. "I'm staying there, too, til I find a place."

"Oh. Great." Inside, Davis was cringing. It was going to be hard enough to not make a move, especially when Pax kept giving him these speculative, secret looks that he thought Davis didn't notice. But Davis noticed. Felt each and every one.

And when they were stuck together in an eight-hundred-square-foot condo with two small bedrooms and only one bathroom?

Yeah, Davis had a feeling he was gonna become real familiar with his right hand again.

"Is it?" Pax looked concerned, all of a sudden. Even stopped, halfway down one of the rows of parked cars. "Is that gonna be a problem?"

"Course it's not gonna be a problem." Davis forced himself to reach out and touch him again, because he was gonna need to get used to it, touching Pax without feeling that inevitable flare of want. He made sure it was a real friendly touch, a quick pat on the shoulder. "Should be just fine. Easier, even."

"Oh good." Pax looked relieved.

He'd faced his first real question, Davis realized as they reached Pax's Jeep, painted bright green and tricked out with big, shiny wheels, with the black leather soft top down, and at least this time, he'd given the right answer.

Maybe he didn't know how to do this, but at least they'd started out on the right foot.

The drive from the airport to the condo was short, and Pax didn't say much, as it was too hard with the wind blowing through the Jeep. Davis took the opportunity to enjoy the feel of it, through his hair and on his face. It was the second thing that had made him feel really alive again, and by the time Pax pulled up to the condo, he was more determined than ever to make this work. Not just because Pax needed the help—and he definitely did—or because this was maybe his own last chance, but because of what had made him such a great quarterback.

Whenever he was faced with a situation where the odds were stacked against him, he was ready and prepared to do anything to win.

Of course, that was when he made his first mistake.

Pax showed him into the condo, taught him the door lock code, so he could get in, and they'd just settled down on the couch in the tiny living room—the entire condo was even smaller than Davis had anticipated, and he'd tried not to freak out too much about how the bedrooms were practically stacked on top of each other, or how they were right next to the bathroom, or how the living space seemed determined to squeeze the two of them together as tightly as possible—and he'd glanced over at the coffee table and seen a tablet sitting there.

The front case had a Piranhas logo on it, and Davis said, "Oh, is that your playbook?"

He'd get one tomorrow, when OTAs—optional team activities—started, but for today, they might as well study Pax's together.

Pax's blond eyebrows drew together, and he looked . . . not upset, but not necessarily *okay* either. "Yeah," he said shortly.

"We could go over some of them, I know we will tomorrow . . ." Davis trailed off, only partially aware that he was stepping into a minefield—and not sure at all how to step out of it.

He'd enjoyed opening each year's playbook and studying it. Had taken pride in having it memorized by the time camp had rolled around.

"There's not just plays on there," Pax said. His voice was curiously neutral and he'd tilted his head away, so Davis couldn't really see his face.

Clearly he wasn't going to talk about it out of choice, but it was Davis' job to figure out what was bothering him—figure it out and *fix it*—so instead of continuing to pull the truth out of him one word at a time, he reached out and picked it up.

It was easy to guess the password. It was *piranhas*, and he swiped through the various apps until he found the one that must be bothering Pax so much. The one he didn't want to talk about.

Pax stood and started pacing around the tiny living room. There wasn't much room, but that didn't seem to matter. "They want me to go through videos from last year and identify on each play what I should've done instead. Figure out my mistakes and fix them."

It was not a surprising tactic. Davis had done it enough times. It never felt *good* but it was necessary to learn, to retrain your brain to consider other options. In the moment, when the ball was in your hands and the defense was rushing towards you, there was only a split second to make a decision and execute it.

From Davis' experience, it was easier to do this on your own. To lick your wounds in private, instead of having them exposed and analyzed in front of an audience.

Pax might not see it this way, but Asa had taken it easy on him.

"It's not easy, sure, but . . ." Davis started to say, but Pax turned and the betrayal on his face made it clear that he'd made his first wrong move.

"Sure, it's not easy. Do you know how many fucking plays are in those videos?" Pax demanded.

"No, I don't. But does it matter?"

"It matters." Pax's voice was full of bitterness. He flopped down on the couch. "I was supposed to be the next phenom, the next superstar, and instead I'm analyzing every game I played in, even *college* games, for everything I did wrong."

"Nobody's perfect," Davis offered. He'd learned *that* the hard way, too.

"Didn't you hear everyone? I *was*," Pax muttered.

"And I was supposed to win the Condors a Super Bowl, someday," Davis said. Ignoring the way the words stung him, deep inside. Maybe if Pax knew some of *his* pain, the acidic wretchedness he held close, that poisoned him every second of every day, he'd understand that he wasn't alone.

Pax glanced up, and Davis forged ahead, because he'd started, he'd loosened the leash, and he couldn't stop now. "We all have things we wanted, expectations that we made, or were made for us, but the truth is, they're what's holding us back. You're not perfect. You were never gonna be perfect. And the . . ." Davis swallowed hard, not used to talking about this. "And the Condors? They were never gonna give me that chance. There was never a ring for me there."

Pax didn't say anything for a long time.

This was the tough love that the previous quarterback coach should have given Pax. Should have taken him aside, from the very beginning, and made sure he knew that the praise everyone was spoutin' was mostly bullshit and speculation—that it was up to *him*, to work hard and make it real.

But nobody had done that. They'd used him and then spit him out when he wasn't the total package they'd been promised.

"Is that why you're here?" Pax asked, finally.

They weren't going to get anywhere without honesty, so Davis gave it to him.

"I'm here because nobody else wanted me. Nobody except Asa Dawson, who saw I still had something to prove, something to give. And he thought . . . hell, I guess he thought I might have something to teach you."

"Do you?"

Davis shrugged. He wasn't going to lie to him. Not after he saw how bad this situation was. No wonder Asa had called him, out of everyone. Nobody else would understand, not like him, the way it felt to be chewed up and spit out by this particular system. "I guess we'll see, won't we?"

"You don't know how to do this," Pax said. His gaze hardened. "You're not a coach, you're a quarterback who isn't even a quarterback anymore."

It was harsh, but also happened to be true. "I *don't* know how to do this, but nobody else is coming to help you, Pax. Just me. So we can either watch these videos together, and you go in tomorrow prepared, or you ignore Coach's request, and then you get to see how it feels to have a team move on before you're ready."

"The backup . . ."

One of the first things Davis had done after Asa's call was look up who the backup was in Miami. It was Blake Jones, who'd been around the league forever, almost exclusively as a backup. All *his* dreams had probably died, and now he was just collecting paychecks, hedging against the day when no team wanted him to ride the bench anymore, and he was done holding clipboards.

"Yeah, I know about Jones. But there's a few guys floatin' around still, haven't signed with anyone, who can play. If you don't think this is a test . . ." Davis knew it was a test. A learning tool, but also a test.

Could Pax pull himself out of his insecurity spiral and find the confidence needed to be a good quarterback? Asa wasn't the only one he needed to prove it to—first and foremost, he needed to prove it to himself.

"I tried," Pax admitted. "I couldn't even get through the first video without . . . *ugh*."

"Come on," Davis said. "You got beer in the fridge?"

Pax nodded.

It was probably that bullshit light stuff, but then if Davis was going to do this, he couldn't keep letting himself go drinking whatever he wanted, either. "Well, get two beers, and we'll sit here and do this together."

It wasn't what he'd intended to do the first day—honestly, he hadn't even really gotten far enough to figure out what they were gonna do on this first day—but he decided that the best way to really learn what made Paxton Kelly tick, to identify his strengths and his weaknesses, and to form a bond of trust so that he'd listen when he coached him, was to dig right down to where he hurt the most.

Pax dutifully stood and got the beers, popping the tops open and setting one in front of Davis. He propped the tablet up on the coffee table in front of them, and found the app. It was the same one they'd used in Charleston, where someone created an initial video of a play, or a series of plays, and whoever they shared it with could add commentary.

Coach had shared twenty-four videos, but none of them, Davis could see, from a quick glance, had any comments.

That was up to Pax.

"Okay, first one," Davis said, clicking the top video on the list.

They watched it once, in silence, as Pax's small figure dropped back, but the offensive line didn't hold back the defensive end, and he had only had a moment, a split second of indecision, to hold the ball longer. He had three options: hope that the defensive end wouldn't end up sacking him for a loss; get rid of it, essentially giving up on the play; or lastly, throw early, and hope that Johnson, his receiver, would be ready for it.

They watched the play once, then twice, and then a third time.

Each time, of course, the play ended the same way. Pax had taken door number three, pitching the ball down the field, not seeing that the safety was crossing over the zone. All he'd had to do was jump up in the air and the ball was his, tucked under his arm. The Jets had scored seven points off that particular mistake.

Davis wanted Pax to be the first to speak, but after the third time, it grew harder to watch it, knowing what was going to happen, so he paused the video before it could start again.

Pax took a long drink of his beer, eyes never leaving the screen.

"I guess you think I should've thrown the ball away," he finally said.

"What I think doesn't matter," Davis said honestly. "Coach wanted to know what *you* thought your mistake was, and what you could've done differently."

"Okay, fine, I should've thrown the ball away," Pax said, and the edge of his tone was defensive.

The hardest thing that Davis had learned as a young quarterback was when to give up on a play and just throw the ball away.

It hurt, each and every time. But sometimes . . . it was better than the alternative.

"Yes and no," Davis said.

Pax looked up in surprise.

"It wouldn't have been the wrong choice," Davis continued. "You'd have saved the interception and had another down to get your ten yards."

"There's a *but* there," Pax muttered darkly.

"Yep." Davis pointed to the screen. "See there? You've got two other options, besides tossing the ball into the sideline or gettin' sacked. Your tight end, out there alone. *And* there's the other way.

You're a young guy. Pretty mobile. You could've run the other way, extended the play, made something else happen. But instead . . ."

"Instead I took the first option and threw it where I was supposed to, but early."

"Leading to the interception," Davis finished for him. "Probably that first option was available a lot, at USC."

Pax nodded.

"You had a killer offensive line. They kept you upright, kept your plays intact. You've got to learn to pivot. In a split second."

Not everyone could do that. Not everyone got good enough to make that transition. It was what separated the boys from the men.

Davis took a sip of his beer, watching Pax's expression morph into thoughtfulness. "I guess I do," he said.

Davis did not think it would be this easy. After all, there were some bad habits here, some from college, some from that disastrous first year, that were going to have to be forcibly trained out of him. But the guy was smart. He gave a shit. He didn't already think he was the greatest thing since sliced bread. *Mostly.*

Davis could work with that.

Now, would it have been a whole lot fucking easier if he didn't feel a lick of heat up his spine every time their eyes met? Oh yeah. So much easier. But he could ignore the heat.

It was just sex. He could just pretend it wasn't there. He had plenty of self-control.

That, he decided, was going to be the easy part of dealing with Paxton Kelly.

They watched the remaining videos, plowing through another pair of beers, and by the time they were done, the sun had fallen,

Davis had a headache and he didn't want to admit it to himself, but he felt . . . twitchy.

"I think," he said, glancing outside as Pax stretched on the couch and Davis did his best to ignore the way his t-shirt rode up, exposing a sliver of entirely lickable skin, "that I'm gonna take a run."

"I did my workout this morning," Pax said. "I think . . . I think I'll review these again, if that's okay."

Davis didn't want to admit he hadn't worked out this morning, or the last . . . well, so many mornings that he didn't want to contemplate. But there was no time like the present to start again.

"Sure," Davis said.

He changed in the tiny box that was his bedroom, throwing on a pair of athletic shorts and an old t-shirt and slipping into the running shoes he'd thrown into his duffel at the last minute, thinking that it would probably be terrible to end up on the field and *not* be able to run worth a damn.

When he came back out into the living room, Pax was absorbed in the play on the tablet, and he gave a quick wave as he pushed open the door and let it close behind him.

The air was still hot and muggy, but he stretched, and then pushed off anyway, tracking the miles on his phone, but not putting his headphones in. *Silence,* he decided, *that's what you need.*

He might not have set out on the run to punish himself, but it felt like a punishment as he pushed himself further and further, sweat beading on his face, and trickling down his neck.

It had been too long since he'd done this. Too long since he'd worked his muscles. They were still there, they hadn't atrophied completely, and they responded when he called on them, but it was hard work, hard enough that by the time he got back to the condo, pulling his shirt off to wipe his face, his mind was blissfully blank.

Until he opened the door and Pax was standing there, frozen in the hallway, staring at his bare chest.

Chapter Two

Paxton had spent almost no time at all thinking about the quarterback coach who was replacing the waste of space and energy who'd left at the end of last season.

Frankly, pretty much the entire coaching staff had left. And anyone who hadn't, Asa Dawson had fired.

When he'd first met Coach Dawson, he hadn't been sure yet who was going to be the new quarterback coach. "I've got my eye on a few options," he'd said nebulously, which was something he'd learn, very quickly, was a hallmark of Asa Dawson's coaching style.

He told you what you needed to hear, when you needed to hear it, but anything else? Good fucking luck.

He *had*, at least, reassured Pax that he was the quarterback that he wanted playing for him. "I know last year was . . . well, it was a cluster," Coach had said, "but we're gonna turn that around."

Frankly, Pax didn't know how—but he had faith. At least he *wanted* to have faith.

Then he'd surprised him even more by calling him up this morning—it had been *six* in the fucking morning, no joke—to tell him that he needed to go to the airport to pick up his new coach, who was, also no fucking joke, *Davis Abernathy*.

Everyone knew Davis' story. Everyone knew he'd basically been fucked over. And he'd been . . . well, God knew, in the last year, doing nothing. Certainly not playing ball.

But, Coach had reminded him, he'd been excellent in Charleston, before they'd thrown him under the bus. Abernathy knew how to be a good quarterback, and, Coach added, he would teach Pax to be a better one.

The one thing he'd learned was you didn't argue with Coach, because then he'd pause, a long, nearly eternal pause that had you sweating bullets, and then he'd say in that long Southern drawl of his, *well, guess you're gonna have to find out the hard way.*

Pax did not want to find anything out the hard way.

He'd already done that, for an entire fucking season, and he was done with that.

So he'd agreed to pick Davis Abernathy up from the airport.

Otherwise, he hadn't known what to expect.

He hadn't expected that they'd shake hands and he'd feel a thrill in a place he had absolutely no business feeling a thrill, especially where one of his coaches was concerned.

He might be gay, but he'd never dated a player. He'd learned from witnessing a few catastrophes that was always a recipe for disaster. And a coach? Not only was it forbidden, but Pax could only imagine how bad that could be.

He had not expected the thrill.

He hadn't expected to see a flare of interest in Davis' eyes when he'd indulged a little and let himself look his fill.

Davis might be older and a year out of football, but his shoulders were just as broad, his chest in that tight polo shirt still undeniably ripped. His dark hair was shaggy and maybe in need of a haircut even more than his own, but those eyes . . . deep and dark and blue . . . they pulled him in and didn't seem to want to let go. Pax hadn't missed the sadness in them, but there'd been hope too, and it was the intoxicating combination of the two that grabbed him. Attracted him. Caught him.

So that had been the first surprise. Unexpected, for sure. Unwelcome, definitely.

But then Davis had proven to be a straight shooter. He hadn't coddled Pax or told him what he wanted to hear. He'd told him what he *needed* to hear. He'd helped him pull his head out of his ass, or at least started the process.

Maybe this wouldn't be such a disaster after all.

He'd announced he was going for a run, and now he was back, and well . . . it was undeniable now. This was going to be an absolute fucking disaster.

Pax had gone into the kitchen to grab some water, and instead of empty hallway, there was Davis, fresh from his run, sweaty and somehow even more appealing now that he was wet all over.

He was naked from the waist up, his shorts loose and hanging from his hip bones, his chest bare and sprinkled with dark hair, just a trail of it leading down through his abs and then lower still, towards . . .

Pax swallowed hard.

How many naked chests had he seen in his time as a football player?

So fucking many.

Hundreds, probably. Maybe even thousands. And he'd always compartmentalized like a champ, never letting himself become aroused or tempted into wanting something he couldn't have.

But he wanted Davis.

He wanted, more than was sane or logical, to reach out and touch.

Alarm bells sounded in the back of his head.

"Oh, hey," Davis said.

"Water," Pax croaked. Feeling stupid. Feeling aroused. Feeling somehow sixteen again and erratic and totally out of control.

"Yeah, yeah, I should grab some." Davis slid by him, and he even still fucking smelled good, which as far as Pax was concerned, was just plain torture. Why was this happening? Why, after all the shit that had gone down last year, was fate not playing nice with him? He deserved this, a good coach who'd guide him the right way, who he didn't want to have bend him over the kitchen counter and fuck him ten ways til Sunday.

Pax couldn't help himself, his eyes glued to the muscular line of his back as he opened the fridge and pulled out a bottle of water, twisting off the cap and chugging half of it, his Adam's apple working as he swallowed.

Awkward silence fell between them.

"Good run?" Pax asked, trying to break it. Hoping that Davis wouldn't notice how high and squeaky his voice was.

Davis turned, pushing his hair back, and *why* did his new coach have to have a profile carved by the Gods?

He might not have cared really, one way or the other, except for that undefinable spark of attraction between them.

The spark that made him want to get close and then closer still.

"Yeah, but I need to get off my ass more often," Davis said, sighing. But there was a light in his eyes that Pax hadn't seen before. A light he recognized.

Pax understood. After last season, he'd gone home to his parents' house in San Diego, and licked his wounds—until one day his mom had announced that she was tired of him lying on the couch, watching *Grey's Anatomy* reruns, and that he needed to do something productive with his life.

I'm trying, he'd wanted to tell her, *but there's nothing I can do about it.*

Except, he'd already known that was a lie. There was plenty he could do to be a better quarterback. After another full week of sulking on the couch, he'd called up one of his old coaches from USC, and he'd ended up staying with him up near Huntington Beach for almost six weeks, working daily on his footwork, his delivery, his mechanics.

And now he had Davis, who was here to help him get his brain straight and to teach him better instincts than his own.

"Maybe tomorrow we can head over to the practice facility early, get some reps in together," Pax suggested, even though he knew how hard it was going to be to watch Davis work out. But to keep seeing that light in his eyes? He was willing to suffer.

Maybe he'd learn something that disgusted him, and he'd get over this annoying and sudden crush, sooner rather than later.

"Sure," Davis said, and he was grinning, suddenly. He patted his pretty flat stomach, the faint muscle outlines that Pax already wanted to trace with his tongue. "Could use some work, for sure."

He was perfect the way he was.

But Pax wasn't going to say that, because it was already terrible enough that he was attracted. He certainly didn't need to say anything to make it worse.

"Great," Pax said.

"I'm gonna shower. Then you wanna grab some food, and we can go over some of those plays on your tablet?"

"There's a great pizza place down the street," Pax said. "I could order?"

Davis shot him a smile, full of white teeth, and it had a nearly visceral impact on Pax's insides. God, he *hated* this. "Anything but olives."

"Olives, the devil's fruit," Pax agreed. "Especially on a pizza."

Davis tossed his empty water bottle in the recycling bin with impressive accuracy. "See," he said as he exited the kitchen, walking right by him again, this time putting a hand on Pax's shoulder as he passed, Pax feeling the touch of it down to his toes, "we're gonna get along just fine."

Pax woke up the next morning and gave himself a very firm pep talk: *you're going to get over this.*

He'd spent eight hours with the guy. He wasn't in love with him. He'd move past this, because he needed to.

It was easy enough to continue the pep talk while he was drying off in the bathroom, getting ready for their first trip to the practice facility. "Your last coach didn't give a crap about you, he fucked around and then fucked off before the end of the season. Davis is here to help you. He gives a shit about you, he's already done more than the last guy."

His expression in the mirror was serious; he *felt* serious, the necessity of this self-lecture clear as day to him.

And then he opened the door and Davis was standing there, hand hovering, like he'd just been about to knock.

His hair was rumpled, his eyes were sleepy, and running down one side of his face was the crease of a pillow.

Pax tried to tamp down the inevitable flare of attraction, but it was undeniably there.

The last thing he wanted was for Davis to be an asshole—he clearly wasn't, that much was obvious, even though they'd only spent half a day together—but he kinda wanted him to be, if only at least because it might kill this stupid crush dead.

"Hey." Davis' morning voice was sleepy and a little rough around the edges, appealing without even trying to be. It was annoying, because every single bit of him was appealing. Even the sadness lurking in his eyes.

"Hey. Bathroom's yours," Pax said.

It was a small hallway. Very small. The whole condo was pretty dang small, honestly. Pax wouldn't be disappointed when he found his own place, and he got some space.

Except, as they squeezed by each other, their bodies brushing in half a dozen places, he'd miss *this*, and that, Pax decided as he practically ran back to his room, might actually be disappointing.

But easier, he reminded himself.

He ignored the way that Davis looked just out of the shower. He ignored the way he smelled. He ignored the lopsided smile he shot him when Pax made him his own protein smoothie.

In his Jeep on the way to the practice facility, Pax asked, "Should I be calling you Coach?"

Davis laughed. "God, no. Please don't."

"Are you sure?"

"Listen, think of me like that old geezer in your QB room, the one who takes you aside and tells you that you're complete shit, but that he's gonna help you get better."

"You're not old," Pax said.

"Then why do I feel old?" Davis asked.

Pax had a feeling he didn't want an answer, even though he thought he might know—or at least have some kind of an idea. What he'd been through would make anyone doubt themselves. Make any quarterback think that maybe they weren't as good as they tried to be.

Make them feel a little old.

"So no Coach, then. Coach Davis?" Pax said, trying to change the subject. He'd thought that maybe if he used Davis' actual title, then maybe the air between them wouldn't feel so . . . charged. Maybe each look they shared wouldn't feel intimate.

He'd remind himself every time he addressed the other man that he was off-limits.

"If you call me Coach Davis, I'm gonna exact painful revenge," Davis said dryly.

"But what about Coach . . ."

"Coach," Davis said firmly, "is gonna let me do things my way. He made that clear. And this is my way."

"I thought you didn't know what you were doing," Pax said.

Davis laughed again. "I don't. But this much I do know: you aren't callin' me Coach." He paused, changing the subject. "I've met Blake a few times. We're friendly. He might not have played much, but he's got plenty of experience in the QB room. So between the two of us . . ." Davis grinned. "We're gonna pull you aside, tell you that you're complete shit, and promise to help you get better."

It stung, hearing that from Davis' mouth. Stung more than it might've, if it had come from Blake Jones. He, on the other hand, didn't know Blake at all, even though they'd exchanged a handful of texts when he'd been added to the roster in the off-season.

"Complete shit, huh?" Pax asked as he pulled into the parking lot.

"Listen," Davis said, catching his arm as he went to get out of the Jeep, "we're all complete shit when we get started. Anything you did before, in college . . . it doesn't count. We all have to start over."

"Did someone say you were complete shit?" Pax found himself asking, even though he hadn't meant to.

Davis chuckled. "Yes. Yes, they did. And they meant it, and they were *right*. But they helped me get better. Refine my instincts. Learn how to be an NFL quarterback. In college, you get by on hopes and dreams and prayers and a hell of a lot of talent and a little luck. The NFL is different." He hesitated. "You learned that, last year."

Pax realized Davis was worried about bringing up what happened last year, maybe he was even worried about eroding his confidence, even though he'd made him sit down yesterday and face the worst of his mistakes.

He wasn't going to be that sensitive; he *couldn't* be that sensitive.

After all, he didn't need Davis to tell him that he needed to get better; the stat line from last season proved that.

And then there was Blake. He might not be a marquee starter, but he was always there, lingering in the background. Coach might decide that he was better off with someone solid like Jones, instead of risking the outcome of the season on Pax, who was still pretty raw.

"Yeah, it really is different," Pax said, even though it cost a little of his ego to say it out loud. "I'm . . . well, I need to get better."

"And you will." Davis patted him on the shoulder reassuringly. "We'll get you there."

When they got into the practice facility, Beau Dawson was standing there.

Beau was Coach's son, and he'd met him, along with Coach, when Rudy Gonzalez, the owner of the Piranhas, had brought them on board.

He liked them both, but Coach scared him a little bit. Beau, on the other hand, was his age, and had a friendly, entirely non-intimidating smile.

"Hey, Davis, Pax. Glad you're here." Beau shook their hands, and gestured towards the offices. "Coach wants to see you, Davis, and I'm gonna be taking you around, Pax, getting you set up for this year."

"Set up?" Pax, who hadn't been nervous before now, discovered that he was suddenly unsure. "I played here last year, you know, I know it wasn't very . . ."

But Beau cut him off with a friendly smile. "Yeah, but we're gonna do things differently. Better, I hope."

It was a little bit easier, away from Davis. He'd nearly convinced himself, as he spent the morning with Beau, walking through the facility, discovering that *yes*, Coach Dawson intended to do a lot of things differently, that he'd imagined his attraction. Had imagined that it might possibly be mutual.

But then when Davis dropped down opposite him in the cafeteria for lunch, a surprising twinkle in those dark blue eyes, Pax realized that he hadn't imagined anything.

"So, you and Beau are tight now?" Davis asked, as he dug into his salad.

"He's nice," Pax said.

"He's brilliant," Davis corrected, "and a not-very-surprising chip off the old man's block."

"How do you know? Do you know him?" Pax hadn't really gotten the impression before that Beau and Davis had been friendly.

You are not jealous, Pax told himself firmly, *even if you know Beau's out, and he's attractive, and also not nearly as off-limits as you are.*

"Oh, spent some time this morning looking over some of the new plays, some of the new ideas that Randy and Beau put their heads together and came up with," Davis said. "It's a good plan. Doable, especially for you."

"Why, 'cause I'm total shit and can't be expected to do any better?" Pax grumbled into his pulled pork sandwich.

But Davis only grinned. Wider than Pax had seen him smile before.

He really wished he could dislike the guy, or at least feel ambivalent about him, but that ship had sailed.

"You're not *total* shit," Davis teased. "So, what's the plan, week to week?"

"The plan?"

"Yeah, the *plan*," Davis repeated.

Pax shot him a blank look. It was bad enough being caught out being unprepared by the other coaches, or by Coach Dawson, even, but it was extra bad being caught by Davis, because . . . well, that was a path he wasn't going to go down right now.

"Nobody helped you develop a weekly plan last year, did they?" Davis sighed.

Pax took a bite of his sandwich, chewed and swallowed, even though it tasted like sawdust in his mouth. "No."

"That should've been your QB coach's job, and the veterans in the room. Who was the backup last year? Not Blake Jones."

"No, he's new this year. It was Mick Reynolds. He . . . well, he thought he should've been the starter. Told me weekly that I sucked and that they only started me to sell jerseys."

It had not felt much better when Pax had both sucked on the field, just as predicted, *and* had sold twice as many jerseys as the next guy.

Even worse than hearing Mick's weekly pronouncements had been the fact that they'd all come true.

Davis raised an eyebrow. "He told you you were shitty and then didn't teach you how to be any better?"

"No."

"Huh." Davis set down his fork and leaned back, crossing his arms over his chest. His broad, muscled chest, looking undeniably broad and undeniably muscled in his Piranhas polo shirt. That was new. He hadn't been wearing that this morning. But it fit him well.

Too well, Pax's traitorous brain chimed in. *Maybe he should size up.*

"And I'm assuming the QB coach didn't step in to intervene, to tell you what the veteran in the room didn't."

Pax shot him a look. "What do you think? The guy was too busy going to the gym and trying to fuck women who weren't his wife to give me any advice."

"Sounds like a real winner," Davis said dryly. "Okay, so here's the thing. We're gonna have to start from scratch."

"Not from *scratch*," Pax protested. "I know how to throw a fucking football."

Davis rolled his eyes. "We're gonna repeat your first year. You've got talent. You've got skills. They're just raw. Unformed. And we're gonna form them."

"Okay," Pax said. He could work with that.

"First thing is you need a schedule."

"You mean like Tom Brady?"

Davis shot him a look. "How many rings does he have? And how many do *you* have? Yes, a schedule like Tom Brady. But he's not the only one. You look around the NFL, and every successful franchise quarterback, they all rely on a schedule. Day to day, what are you doing in the weight room? The film room? We havin' a meeting? What about the backup? Are you meeting with your center? Your offensive line? You takin' them to dinner each week? On a specific day?"

"I . . . uh . . ." Pax found himself floundering, and he *hated* that. He'd floundered all last year—so maybe Davis was right, maybe he was onto something. Maybe he'd floundered because he hadn't had any of this structure. Nobody had given it to him, and he hadn't known how to implement it himself.

"It's okay." Davis' voice softened. He leaned in, and Pax found himself mesmerized, without even wanting to be. There was something magnetizing about that dark blue gaze, how it saw him, saw *all* of him, that made it so he couldn't quite look away. "We're gonna fix you up."

"I don't know if Jones is showing up for OTAs," Pax said uncertainly. "Maybe we should wait to plan the schedule til he gets here."

"Is Jones the head of your QB room?" Davis asked, raising an eyebrow. "Or is it you?"

"I'm the starter, Coach said I was," Pax said.

"Then, you make the plan. If he has other ideas, then we'll listen, but we don't have to incorporate them. The idea is the plan should work for everyone, but you're the starter. It needs to work best for you."

Pax didn't like to admit it but when he'd come out of USC, he'd been cocky and full of ego. He'd listened to everyone who told him how great he was, and everyone who believed he couldn't do any wrong.

It hadn't taken very many NFL games to show him that he was wrong. Ego? That was a thing of the past. But even Pax knew he hadn't quite recovered his confidence. At least not enough to stand up to Blake Jones, with his ten years of experience, and tell him that this was the way they were doing things.

Who was he to know?

"*That*, that's the look," Davis said.

"What look?"

"That look of uncertainty. Get rid of it. You gotta be confident," he said.

Pax knew he was right, but his confidence was currently MIA, and he'd thought maybe stepping back into the Piranhas facility, with a new coaching staff, determined to see him succeed, would've brought it back.

But it hadn't.

Instead, it felt more lost than ever.

"You'll get there," Davis added, with a wave of his fork, like it was so easy to find. So easy to fix.

Pax knew he knew better; after all, his own was probably just as damaged.

He might have said something, but he'd learned, even though he and Davis barely knew each other, that he hated the look on his face—a lost look full of regret and pain—whenever the subject of the Condors came up.

He didn't want to talk about it, clearly, and Pax, who might've pushed back with anyone else, didn't want it for him, either.

That look, it felt too familiar.

Hit too close to home.

"We'll figure out the schedule this afternoon," Pax said, trying to pretend he *was* confident. *Fake it til you make it*, he told himself.

"Tonight," Davis said. "We're having a meeting this afternoon with Randy, to start learning the new offensive system. And then there's a meeting with Coach, about last year's plays, you know those ones you worked on last night. But tonight, we'll settle in with a beer, and outline a schedule, okay?" Davis' face was sympathetic, but it didn't feel galling. It just felt . . . *good* . . . to have someone on his side, for once.

Nobody's on his side, and yet he's here, trying to be on yours. That's gotta mean something.

Pax swallowed the last of his sandwich—and his pride.

"Thanks. I'm real glad you're here," he said quietly.

Davis' smile was soft and kind, and yet it filled Pax with a longing for things that weren't soft and weren't precisely kind, either. "Me too," he said. "Me too."

Pax had learned last year that OTAs lived up to their name. They were optional, not everyone came, and they were more team building than skill building.

Most of the veterans, and usually all the rookies, showed up at the practice facility, and spent a few days hanging out, talking to the coaches, getting to know everyone, and sometimes, they'd go on the field and do very light run-throughs of new plays.

More players showed up this year than last, probably because there was a new head coach and a whole new staff. Nobody knew what to expect, so both out of a sense of curiosity and also a sense of self-preservation, the building was a lot fuller than it had been last year.

Even Blake Jones showed up, even though Pax had gotten the impression he wasn't going to.

"When I heard you were here, *coaching*, I had to come check it out," Blake had said to Davis after they'd greeted each other.

Pax wasn't going to discount that Blake's motivation might be entirely curiosity. Davis Abernathy coaching for the Piranhas was big news. He tried to avoid most of the sports media, but he'd seen flashes of it—they'd been unavoidable—and most of the sports media seemed torn between thinking Asa Dawson was crazy or believing that he might be brilliant.

Pax didn't care which it was. He only wanted to win games. Something they'd only managed twice last year. Truthfully, he wasn't used to losing, and he'd had his fill of it now.

Davis was seemingly everywhere, a quiet force in meetings, rarely saying anything, but when he did, it was usually relevant. He didn't lead *for* Pax, but tried to show him, tried to stand back, and let him figure his shit out, while offering just enough pointers.

By the end of the three days, Pax was beginning to understand exactly why Asa Dawson had picked him to be the new QB coach.

He could be tough on Pax, but he seemed to instinctively know the line where *just tough enough* crossed over into *too tough*, and he walked it carefully.

As much as he tried not to, because it wasn't relevant, and wasn't really important in the scheme of things, Pax just plain *liked* Davis.

He was quiet, but every word he said was worth listening to. And Pax, who hadn't felt particularly comfortable since being drafted by Miami, hadn't found a place he could just *be*, discovered that the place wasn't a place at all—but a person.

Their friendship—because that was undeniably what it was, even though it had just begun—was of course complicated by the attraction that Pax couldn't quite forget.

Sometimes Pax thought that maybe he'd imagined that look of Davis'. That maybe he wasn't attracted to him back, that he'd dreamt up the whole thing, that the strength of his own attraction had colored his impression of the other man.

But then Sebastian Howard had made an offhand comment to Davis, one late afternoon in the locker room, about how small the closet was, and Pax realized that Davis had to be queer, too, and Sebastian knew.

Pax didn't say anything. He didn't know how to say, *me too*, even though they were only two words, because the *me too* was tied up with too many other things, like how he lay awake in bed at night and Davis' face was the last one he saw.

At the end of the three days, they went their separate ways. Pax had considered going back to California, to his parents' house, but he decided against it. He needed to get out more, see more people, maybe even find a few hookups, because if he spent any more time on his parents' couch, he might become part of it—and also because if he didn't, he might never get over this annoying attraction to Davis.

And he was determined that he'd do it, too, before training camp started in late July. Besides, he needed to buy a place here, anyway. He was tired of renting. He'd use the next few months to find a permanent place to live.

Davis seemed uninterested in buying in Miami—of course, he probably thought he wouldn't be here long—and he'd said that he was going back to South Carolina, to the house he'd built on the coast.

"We'll keep in touch," Davis said on the last morning, as they got in Pax's Jeep, so he could take him to the airport. "I want you to keep studying the playbook, okay?"

Pax rolled his eyes. Like he was going to do anything else.

"Of course I will."

"Coach, Randy, and I are gonna have weekly meetings," Davis said. "I'll let you know what comes out of them."

"Weekly?" Pax raised an eyebrow as he turned off the freeway, towards the airport. "You're gonna be lucky if they're just weekly."

Davis chuckled. "I don't mind," he said. "I like . . . I like this, actually. Wasn't sure I would."

"That's all me," Pax boasted.

Even though his eyes were on the road, he couldn't miss the way Davis' gaze skimmed over him, the way it heated his skin.

Every time he had himself convinced that it was only him suffering this way, Davis would tease like this, and then suddenly, Pax wasn't quite sure.

"Maybe it is," Davis said quietly. *I think I can help you.* Pax heard the second half of it, as clear as day, even though Davis hadn't said it.

They pulled up to the Departures curb at the airport.

"Well, you get bored in Carolina, you can always stay with me," Pax said, turning towards him.

Even though that hadn't been the thing he'd intended to say at all.

"You're staying in a hotel," Davis said, quietly amused.

"When I buy something, that's what I meant," Pax said. He hadn't even thought about it, he just knew he didn't want Davis to go just yet.

He wasn't a lifeline, not exactly, because Pax didn't like to think he'd been drowning, but whatever Davis was, he made life easier. He made Pax smile. He made Pax want to be better. He also made Pax want to be not good at all.

Davis reached over and he was roughly tugging him into a hug before Pax could acclimate himself to the idea that it was going to happen.

They touched, because football players were all a touchy-feely bunch, but they'd never embraced like this.

Pax expected it to be quick and fleeting, not quite enough to get more than a vague impression of Davis' body pressed against his. But then Davis, unexpectedly, lingered.

Maybe he didn't want to let go either.

Whichever it was, Pax's fingers dug into Davis' shoulders, and for a single forbidden second, he breathed in the smell of him, trying to memorize everything about him.

This was the very opposite of what he should be doing—trying to forget, trying to move past this ill-advised crush—but Pax also hadn't expected it to feel this good, either.

"You need me," Davis said, his voice quiet but gruff, "I'm here for you, okay?"

Pax's fingers tightened, but Davis didn't seem in any particular hurry to move either. His palm was big and warm on his back, and it hadn't moved, but Pax could imagine, so fucking easily, how it might feel to have it stroke him, in long, comforting sweeps.

How it might turn into something else, just as easy as breathing.

He pulled back, letting go even as his body protested.

Davis' eyes were so deep and blue, and Pax couldn't look away.

It was funny, how Pax had never looked at Davis Abernathy before the last few days and thought, *oh, he's hot, he's really fucking hot*, but now he couldn't think anything else.

Before they'd met, he'd just been another guy, another quarterback, and he'd barely thought twice about him, except, Pax supposed, to feel sorry for him.

If he'd thought about attractive quarterbacks, there was always Sam Crawford, who probably could've been a model in a different timeline. Or even Heath Harris, his boyfriend, if you liked that stern tough type.

Davis wasn't a model and he wasn't a hot asshole either.

He was just himself, and seemingly by being just that, he was irresistible.

"If you need *me*," Pax said quietly, "I'm here for you, too."

Meant it. And would do it, even if it killed him, which it might.

Davis nodded silently. Opened his door, and was turning to get out, but then hesitated. Looked back at Pax. The moment drew out even further, and Pax's breath caught in his chest. Was this it? What was he going to say? *I can't do this, I can't coach you, because I want you?*

Pax didn't know how he'd feel about that. Ecstatic, he'd imagine, and disappointed, all in the same breath.

But he didn't say anything, just reached out and put his hand on Pax's shoulder, gripping him one last time, and then he was gone, slipping out of the passenger seat, his duffel on his shoulder, and as he walked away, he didn't turn back, even though Pax expected—*wanted*—him to, and lingered, with the hope that he might.

Chapter Three

July

Davis had just come in from the pole barn he'd had added to his property a few years back, for off-season workouts, wiping the sweat off his face, when his phone dinged.

He didn't have to look at the screen to know that it was Paxton.

It shouldn't have been so easy to fall into this texting thing with him. He'd said he was there for him, that they'd stay in touch, and they had, but at first, it had been football-related texts.

Davis wasn't stupid. He knew why and how it had started to bleed into more, but he didn't quite have the willpower to stop it—and he had *plenty* of self-control, thank you very much. He'd stopped himself from kissing Pax at the airport, hadn't he? Even though he'd wanted to, so badly it had hurt.

But he'd known the consequences of doing it, and the consequences of calling up Asa and saying he couldn't coach Pax after all. Because while it had only been three days, it had been three days of seeing what Pax could be, if he had the right coach, and the right support system, and someone who truly believed in him, who could help him learn to believe in himself again.

That was what had stopped him in June, after OTAs.

But he couldn't quite find it in himself to either stop texting Pax or to try to turn their messages back to more professional, football-related topics.

Part of him thought, what could it hurt, to text Pax, to be his friend.

The other part of him thought, *this is all you're ever gonna get, so you might as well enjoy it.*

I wanna know why they got rid of McSteamy, this particular text read when Davis skirted around his kitchen island to find his phone, charging on the counter.

Pulling off his damp shirt, he wiped down his face and arms, and tossed it into the laundry room, thinking before he replied.

When he'd been young and stupid—naive, his father would say—he'd spoken a lot before thinking. It had gotten him into trouble, and he'd always believed that maybe some of the shit he'd thoughtlessly said had been the root of why the Condors had ultimately gone in a different direction.

Had any of it really been that bad? Of course not. But it was the secret fear he held close—probably too close—that kept him up nights when he should've been sleeping.

Staring at the screen, he thought about what he might say.

What he *should* say to Pax.

And because he really didn't have the kind of self-control he should, he texted something else entirely.

Like an older man, do you?

As soon as he'd pressed send, Davis was pretty sure it was a mistake. He knew Pax was not straight. He had no poker face, no ability to dissemble. He'd checked out Davis so many times, too many times, when he'd wanted to pull the guy aside and say, *you keep lookin' at me like that, I'm gonna have to do something about it.*

He hadn't, of course, because he wasn't stupid.

But he knew, at least he suspected, about Pax's sexuality, and he had a feeling that Pax suspected the same about him. Though they'd never explicitly talked about it.

Maybe now was the time. It wasn't a secret he was trying to keep from Pax, he had just believed that it wasn't relevant—though truly the reason was he worried that if they started talking about it, they wouldn't stop at just talking.

Pax's reply came through almost immediately. **Maybe I just like him as a character.**

No fair, Davis texted back, **that was always my excuse. You can't have it.**

This was probably not the conversation they should have over text, but somehow it made it . . . easier. Allowable.

Your excuse for why you liked McSteamy? Pax tacked on about four side-eye emojis. Then he sent another text almost immediately after. **There something you need to tell me, Davis?**

Yep, he replied back, **my deepest, darkest secret. Mc-Dreamy was totally overrated, McSteamy's where it's at.**

And then under that he added one more additional text, because he couldn't leave well enough alone. **And yeah, I'm queer. You got a problem with that?**

He'd barely set the phone down when Pax replied. **Not unless I've got a problem with myself.**

Davis leaned back against the kitchen counter and told himself that this was the right thing. Maybe he could mentor Pax here too.

Yeah, his brain unhelpfully supplied, *you can mentor him on how to be deep in the closet, and alone, and unhappy. Sounds like a great plan.*

Also, I think I'm more of a Karev guy, myself. I like the snotty sarcastic ones, apparently.

Davis told himself that this text was 100% not about him. Nope.

Okay, maybe he had a dry sense of humor. Very dry, at times. But he wasn't like Alex Karev. No way. And while he might be older than Pax, the whole damn world felt like it was older than Pax.

I think you're watching too much *Grey's Anatomy*, Davis texted back. **I thought you were supposed to be looking for a house.**

I am, but everything's wrong. Too big, too small, too impersonal, wrong neighborhood. Maybe I'll end up renting after all. You're renting, right?

He was. He'd found a condo in the same building that Beau lived in. It was only a few blocks from the stadium complex and practice facility.

Yeah, he texted back. **A condo. Close to the stadium.** He'd rented it sight unseen, but it was just a place he'd sleep, because he knew during the season how much time he'd be spending working.

Maybe I should do that instead, Pax said.

But Davis knew how much he wanted to settle. Pax hadn't had to say so, it was obvious. It had been impossible to miss the yearning he felt in between the words when Pax had talked about the house he'd grown up in, the house his parents still owned.

You will not offer to come to Miami and help him find a house, Davis told himself.

You'd hate living in a condo, is what he texted back instead.

He didn't particularly like it himself, but at the end of the day—the end of the season, really—he got to come back to a place he did like. Ironically, it was the place he'd kept trying to escape from, but he'd made his peace with it, at least.

He got why Pax wanted that kind of place. He wasn't sure it was in Miami, but Pax was still young. He had his whole life ahead of him, a whole life full of choices, where he could figure out what he *did* want.

Yeah, but I'd hate living in a house I hate more, Pax replied. **What's the building you're renting in?**

Davis didn't want to tell him. Except it was a big building, and he knew several players were already living in it. What was one more, even if it happened to be Paxton, the one player he couldn't seem to resist?

So he sent Pax the info, and wasn't surprised when two days later, Pax texted him back, telling him that he'd rented one of the condos in the same building.

Just for the season, he wrote, **and because my realtor might kill me and you'll never find the body if she has to show me another house.**

Not ideal, but at least I'd know who to track down, Davis texted back, as he reclined on the back screened-in porch, a light beer set on a coaster next to him.

Aw, you'd avenge my death, how sweet is that, Pax teased.

Davis stared at the screen, at the words Pax had written back to him. They'd been texting back and forth for weeks now—about important stuff, of course, *football* stuff, but also about stupid stuff, like Pax binge-watching *Grey's Anatomy*, and the dominoes Davis had played with his pops during the long holiday weekend, and even the brand-new tires Pax had just gotten for his Jeep.

He was also decorating his rented condo, and he kept sending Davis pics of the most random shit he could find at IKEA.

Davis had a feeling that when he finally returned to Miami and to the condo *he* was renting, Pax would have a box full of every single oddly shaped candlestick and bizarre kitchen utensil ready for him.

But first, before he moved to Miami, the whole team was going to central Florida for training camp, which was held at a small Division Three school. They took it over—the facilities, the field, and several dorms, where all the staff and players slept.

In five days, he'd drive down, his truck loaded down with everything he'd need for the next six months of his life.

In five days, he'd see Pax again.

He'd convinced himself, mostly, that his reaction to the guy was because he'd spent so much of the last fifteen months of his life alone. Yeah, sometimes he got a little charge when he saw a notification from Pax on his phone, and occasionally their messages got a little . . . well, flirty, but Davis believed that when he saw Pax again, all he'd feel was the solid foundation of a friendship. The comfortable familiarity of a mentor and mentee.

But this text of Pax's . . . it made him hesitate.

Would he avenge Pax's death at the hands of his realtor?

It had just been a joke, initially, but it had struck a chord in him.

A chord he didn't want struck.

He wrote out and then deleted a handful of messages—every single one reflecting a truth that Davis wasn't ready to face.

Finally, he sent, **Me and my golf club would hunt that bitch down, for sure.**

Pax sent a picture then, a selfie actually, of his unimpressed face.

Just opening it and looking at it brought that momentary heart-skipping, stomach-clenching feeling back again.

He was wearing a turquoise-blue tank top, his tanned arms exposed, looking more chiseled than ever—he'd clearly been putting in the kind of work in the weight room he promised he was, and his scruff was becoming almost beard-like, a mix of gold and brown that seemed to gild him even more, especially with the sunshine streaming across his face.

That's just because you think he's hot, the unimpressed part of Davis' brain supplied.

No, the very impressed part retorted, *it's 'cause he is hot.*

You're terrible at golf, Pax added.

He was, but Pax only knew it because the last time he'd played, with some old college friends who'd come to visit, he'd drunkenly texted a hole-by-hole analysis of his dumpster fire of a game.

Maybe I'd have better luck with your realtor as the ball, Davis answered.

Pax sent a gif of a nodding Ariel, her chin sitting on her hand, and Davis smiled, despite himself.

How was he going to put the kind of necessary space between them when all he wanted was to tug Pax close and hold him there?

He didn't know, but he'd need to spend the next five days figuring it out.

Davis had just reclined on his twin XL bed, remembering exactly why he'd hated the dorm in college, when there was a knock on his door.

Two days ago, rookies had been asked to report early, but Pax had texted that he wouldn't be able to make it til tomorrow, real early in the morning, so he knew it couldn't be Pax.

It might be Beau, wanting to discuss one of the plays they'd run in practice today, or it might be Wade or Tristan, wanting to go over a formation in the playbook. Or it could even be Coach himself, with another question.

With a groan, Davis levered himself out of bed, and decided that it was late enough, and this was *his* room, that he didn't need to throw on the shirt he'd pulled off and tossed on the back of the chair when he'd come in a few minutes ago.

Walking to the door, he yanked it open, and even though he'd told himself for years, for his entire fucking life, that was something romance authors made up to sell books, he felt his heart stutter.

He'd believed that with the space and time, his insane and inconvenient attraction to Pax would fade. They'd been texting nonstop, but the tone of that had been friendly—*just* friendly. Sure he'd felt a pulse of . . . *something* . . . whenever Pax sent him a text, but he'd identified it as residual attraction and hoped it would eventually disappear.

Spoiler alert: it had not disappeared.

In fact, face to face with Paxton again, his tired eyes, his bright smile, his tan brightening his hair and somehow impossibly darkening his eyes, Davis realized he'd totally fucked this up.

He didn't feel *less* attracted to Pax now, because they were friends. He felt *more* attracted to him.

Pax stared at him, not saying a word, and then Davis remembered that he hadn't thrown his shirt back on.

It was not a big deal for anyone else.

But Pax's gaze . . . wherever it fell, his skin burned, and he was looking everywhere, heating him up until he was surprised he didn't crackle with heat.

"Hey," Davis said, after a very long moment where neither of them said anything.

If he was smart, he would march down to Coach's room and say, *I can't do this.*

But he'd already lost everything. This was the one chance he had left.

If he told Asa that fucking Pax's brains out was more important than football . . . well, that would be *him* giving up, and it wouldn't be like before, when everyone had given up on him.

But Davis? He'd never given in before, never bowed to the inevitable.

"You've been working out," Pax said as he walked in and let the door shut behind him. His voice was soft, deep. Gravelly, almost. And he was still looking at Davis' chest.

He felt a pulse of what had to be embarrassment. The last time Pax had seen him without a shirt on, it had been after a year of sulking in Carolina.

He hadn't been in game shape; he hadn't been in any kind of shape, to be honest. But in the last six weeks, he'd worked hard, seeing the transformation in the mirror as he turned his body back into the machine it'd been for years.

Even if he hadn't seen the results in the mirror, he would've seen them in Pax's eyes now. They were full of admiration and pride and *God*, Davis didn't even want to see it—or acknowledge it—but passion, too.

He did not want to turn Pax on. He didn't want Pax to turn *him* on.

But that ship had absolutely fucking sailed.

"I thought you were getting in tomorrow." He'd been preparing himself for that.

He was not prepared for Pax showing up at his room at eleven at night, with the only light the dim one over the bed.

He could go put his shirt back on, but that would look like he thought neither of them could handle a little bare chest.

You can't. He can't. That's pretty fucking obvious.

Davis ignored the voice.

"Thought I'd get in early, surprise you," Pax said. "Surprise," he added weakly. Uncertainly. Like suddenly he was unsure of his welcome.

There was a small part of Davis—tiny, really, and insignificant—that had wanted that extra night, to build his walls a little bit higher, so he could maybe keep Pax out. But there was another much larger—much *louder*—part of him that was fucking thrilled to see Pax again.

You're never gonna be able to keep him out, no matter how many nights you have, or how high you try to build your walls.

He's already in.

"I'm glad you're here," Davis said, and meant it, and ignoring that voice, screaming now in his head that he was making a tactical error, he reached out and pulled Pax in for a hug.

Anything, even testing his own control, was better than seeing that self-doubt in Pax's eyes.

Pax fit into his arms like he'd been made for him. He was nearly his height, and only a tiny bit slighter, but they slotted in together like puzzle pieces. Pax let out a sigh—happy, relieved, or contented? Davis wasn't sure, but he knew he felt all three—and dipped his head just enough that his chin connected with Davis' shoulder.

He should have let go immediately. All he'd intended was a quick, friendly hug. But what he'd ended up with was something entirely different.

Something he'd fantasized about too many times, during too many long, sleepless nights during the last month.

It would be so easy to slide his hands down, press Pax's body closer to his own, tilt his head and when they kissed, it would be so good. Davis already knew it. Could see it way too fucking clearly in his mind's eye. Could *feel* it way too clearly.

Instead he let go, like he'd just been burned.

"Uh, well, like I said," Davis stammered, "real glad you're here."

Pax's expression was shocked, like he hadn't quite expected what happened.

Maybe he'd been depending, too, on the friendly nature of their texts to kill any attraction between them.

Davis was going to have to figure out how to walk a very fine line between being there for Pax, being his coach and his friend, and not crossing a boundary into something more.

Into making them both long for something more.

Too late for that.

"How was practice today?" Pax eyed the available surfaces in the room and picked the chair.

Smart boy, Davis thought, and didn't take the bed either. Stayed standing, arms crossed over his bare chest, like he could stupidly *hide it* or something, and said, "Real good. Though it'd have gone better if Blake Jones and I weren't the only QBs taking the snaps."

Pax smiled. "You're a great quarterback, Davis, you know that. The guys would be lucky to catch some of your passes."

"Nicholson's coming along, though his routes still need work. You're gonna have to lead him, just like we thought you would. But I think he can learn."

"What about Lewis? He looked good at OTAs."

"Looks even better. He's been puttin' the work in. Hard, if I had to say."

Pax nodded.

"And Kenyon's here, he's eager to go. I don't think he much liked losing last year either."

"Does anyone like losing?" Pax pointed out with a sigh.

"Logan, he's fucking awesome though. A really great franchise center. I have to give the Piranhas credit, they didn't have to blow up the team and give you a whole new, *better*, team. They could've just told you, *get better*, and you'd have had to deal with what you had."

Pax looked apprehensive. Not what Davis had intended. He should be excited, thrilled, ready to get started on the work. And he was, all of those things, Davis knew it. Because he knew Pax.

But there was something else too.

"Doesn't that just add . . . I don't know . . . *more* pressure?" Pax wondered out loud.

Davis was pretty sure that was more a rhetorical question than an actual question, but he answered it anyway. "Maybe," he admitted, "but you know what it does give you?"

"What?"

Pax looked so young in the dim light of the room. He might be twenty-six, but there was still an innocent openness in his face. He hadn't learned to hide his fear yet. To bury it deep, until nobody could see it.

Davis hadn't managed to hide all of his, until he'd had no other choice.

"A way higher chance of succeeding," Davis said firmly.

"You think so?"

"I know so," Davis said. "Coach has been putting some real good pieces around you, pieces that will make you better."

"Then . . ." Pax shot him a lopsided smile. Davis' heart clenched, even though he told it, firmly, to cut it out. "Then, I guess we better figure out how to make *me* better."

"You're already on your way there," Davis said, though he thought Pax's confidence could still use some work. If he didn't know he was already better than he had been last season . . . well, at some point he'd *have* to see it. There'd be no other choice.

Quarterbacks were made in that split second, with their backs to the wall, when there was no option but to just push forward, damn everything in their way.

Pax was going to have to find that drive.

But that, Davis thought, watching Pax try to stifle a yawn, was a problem for a different day.

"Come on," Davis said gruffly, "time for bed. It's an early call tomorrow."

"Yeah," Pax said and stood, heading towards the door. "I know, I just . . ." He turned, and there was a yearning in his expression that Davis didn't want to recognize but did, anyway. "I wanted to see you."

He should shut him down.

He should tell him that it could've waited.

He should be a *coach*, but Davis had known when Asa hired him that he wasn't really looking for the traditional kind of coach for Pax; he was looking for a mentor. And a friend.

"I wanted to see you too," Davis said quietly as Pax's hand hesitated on the door handle.

Pax flashed him the brightest smile he owned. "I thought so," he said, and then he was gone, slipping through the door, leaving Davis with too many thoughts that wouldn't stay in their little boxes.

August

Pax could tell from the unimpressed look on Davis' face that he wasn't exactly thrilled with the condo.

He'd warned him, hadn't he?

They were impersonal boxes.

Everything was either off-white or gray. Even the pictures on the walls . . . Davis peered closer at one, and Pax almost laughed at his bewildered expression.

"Is that . . . is that an amoeba?"

"I think so," Pax said. "And speaking of unidentified objects . . ." He lifted the box he'd been saving. "I brought you some."

Davis rolled his eyes but looked pleased as he carted the box into the kitchen. "Did you go shopping for me, Pax? At IKEA?"

Pax grinned. "I couldn't help it. They have so much great stuff there."

"Because I don't have enough stuff with me, already," Davis said, gesturing to the suitcases, duffel bag, and multiple boxes that were stacked in his foyer. "Pops insisted I bring so much shit."

"Pops?"

"My grandfather," Davis said, pulling out a bright blue plastic something out of the box. Pax didn't know what it was. He hadn't known what it was when he'd bought it for forty-nine cents, but the actual purpose of the tool didn't matter, he'd known Davis needed to have it. "He came to see me off, help me pack up for the season." Davis shook his head. "He's incorrigible, but I think you might actually put him to shame."

"Yes!" Pax said with an enthusiastic first pump. "A compliment! I feel like I'm finally getting somewhere."

Davis shot him a look as he pulled a long metal rod with wires sticking out the end out of the box. "You realize what this is, right? Why did you buy me a whisk?"

"It's a whisk?"

Davis laughed, and the sound warmed Pax all the way through.

"What on earth do you think I need a whisk for?" Davis continued.

"I don't know, to whisk things? Do you even whisk things?"

Davis was still chuckling. "Actually, more than you realize, and I'm not sure I actually brought one so . . . kudos. You redeemed yourself."

"You'll have to whisk something for me sometime," Pax said, hearing the teasing note in his voice. The flirty note. That was still reasonable, right? Maybe he'd barely seen his coach last year, but it was already clear that wasn't the norm.

But was it the norm to want to spend *all* your time with your coach? Making him laugh? Hoping that he came a little closer? Praying that he took his shirt off again?

Okay, that was probably not normal. But Pax couldn't stuff all those thoughts back into the box. They existed. They had life.

Why shouldn't he hope that they happened, even if technically he knew they were off-limits?

"You seem pretty sure that I'm capable," Davis teased right back.

"I mean look at you . . ." Pax said, trailing off. Letting his gaze go from top to bottom. "I think if you *do* cook, we might be talking about perfection here."

Davis rolled his eyes. "Hardly," he said. But he still looked pleased as he unloaded a lamp shaped like a dildo out of the box, giving it a hilarious side-eye, then a pencil-shaped box of colored markers, and finally a small red, heart-shaped pillow with plush arms extending out of either side of it.

"I can see you made good use of your time," Davis said dryly. "And your money." He picked up the pillow. "What is the point of this?"

"When you need a hug, *plus*," Pax said, tugging it from his hands, "it's an excellent designer piece. Makes that couch look like a million bucks."

"I was right, you're more incorrigible than Pops."

"He didn't come with you to Miami?" Pax asked casually as Davis actually detoured into the living room to toss the pillow onto the couch.

"Oh, he's fine where he's at in Hilton Head," Davis said. "I wouldn't ask him to come."

But of course Pax realized that didn't mean he hadn't wanted to.

Only that Davis hadn't asked.

The more time he spent with Davis—and the more texts they exchanged, which was this point, a *lot*—the more Pax realized that when the horrible situation with the Condors had gone down, he'd retreated.

Physically.

And mentally.

The good news about that, Pax thought, as he watched Davis give the lamp a second scathing side-eye, was that there was nothing he enjoyed more than bringing Davis out of his shell. Getting him to laugh, to smile, maybe even to randomly take his shirt off?

Those little things, they made his whole fucking day.

Which . . . maybe that was a problem.

But it was going to be a problem for a different day.

Chapter Four

Week Two

Pax felt fucking awful.

Sebastian had picked off the Texans, giving him the ball in just the right spot, and he'd failed, completely utterly fucking failed, to drive down the field and get the Piranhas their first win.

That felt bad enough.

And then he'd gone in front of the sports media for the press conference, and had to defend his choices. Why had he made this throw and that one? Why were they even in that position, down two points late in the fourth quarter?

It was his fault, Pax thought. It was always his fault, because he was the leader of the team, and the blame had to begin and end with him.

In this particular case, it was definitely his fault, because Sebastian had gotten him the ball with two minutes to go.

Perfect two-minute-drill scenario.

And he'd bungled it.

After the nightmare of a press conference, he'd come back to his impersonal condo that he was renting for the year, and not for the first time, he wished that he'd bought one of those houses, even the ones that hadn't really suited him.

It would be better than sitting on a couch that wasn't his, better than staring at a TV that wasn't his, better knowing he was settled. Instead, he felt a creeping sensation that he was more unsettled than ever, that his position, with the first two losses of the season, was more precarious than he wanted to acknowledge.

He'd flipped the TV on after collapsing onto the couch, because the noise was better than the sound of his own thoughts—and then turned it up twice because it seemed even the latest *Grey's* episode couldn't drown out the worst of the criticism circling around his brain.

When he finally heard the knocking on the door, he had a feeling it had been happening for awhile. Probably one of his neighbors, annoyed that he'd had the TV volume up so high. With a sigh, Pax pulled himself off the couch, glancing down at his slacks and the white tank he'd worn under his shirt for the press conference, and decided that, along with his bare feet, was perfectly acceptable to answer the door.

But when he pulled it open, he wasn't confronted with an annoyed neighbor.

It was Davis.

He was still wearing what he'd had on during the game—black slacks that clung to his long legs, and a white Piranhas polo that he filled out a little too well for Pax's peace of mind.

Pax had hoped that as time passed, he might become less attracted to his coach and mentor. Instead, it felt like Davis got hotter, as he returned to the gym, and then there was that look in his eyes—the one that told Pax he knew where he was, and that he'd been there, too.

Yeah, becoming friends with Davis hadn't done a damn thing to cool all that white-hot wanting.

"You aren't answering your phone," Davis said impatiently as Pax silently stepped aside, letting him into the condo.

"Done plenty of talking tonight, already," Pax said.

"You wanna do no talking at all?" Davis asked.

Oh, God.

Pax imagined what it might feel like if Davis returned even half of what he felt, if he let the rules go, if he ignored all the good advice in the world and pulled him in, and kissed him.

If they didn't talk at all, but spent the next few hours in Pax's bed, hands everywhere, saying everything that they couldn't.

It would be so fucking good, and such a fucking disaster.

Everything's already a disaster, Pax thought, *what's one more?*

But then Davis lifted a bottle, and gestured towards the couch.

"No talking, and more forgetting," Davis said.

Pax knew the right thing to do would be to detour to the kitchen, grab two glasses, and make the whole thing formal-ish, just two friends enjoying a late-night drink after a bad day.

But instead he joined Davis on the couch, and watched with an intent gaze as Davis opened the bottle and took a swig of whiskey.

Pax watched as he swallowed, his throat contracting. He wanted to press his fingers there, feel the tendon there, as he sucked his cock deep.

Davis tipped the bottle towards Pax, and he took it. He didn't particularly like whiskey, but the burn as it went down his throat felt good.

At least it didn't feel *bad*.

The episode of *Grey's* played on, but Pax had a feeling, as they traded the bottle back and forth, that even though their eyes were on the screen, neither of them was watching.

It was almost over, some long, slow, inspirational song playing over the final montage, when Davis spoke up. His voice was rough, from the whiskey, and maybe even from something else.

"Sometimes," he said, "I wish that if you were gonna fail, it happened quick, like all at once, yank the Band-Aid off, no time to prepare, no time to dread, no time to wonder where the hell you'd gone wrong. But no. Instead, it's like a slow, fucking inevitable march to failure. You see it coming, but sure as shit, you can't stop it. You can only feel it."

"And it feels like shit?" Pax wondered.

"Yeah, it feels like shit."

Pax knew that Davis' career wasn't the only one hanging in the balance here. This was still his first contract, only his second year. If he bombed in Miami, someone else, some team somewhere, might take a chance on him. He'd been too good in college to not have some coach wonder if he just hadn't been transitioned to the NFL right. They'd think he could still be fixed.

But Davis? He wouldn't get another shot. They'd believe, all of them, that he was broken. This was it, for him.

Maybe he had plenty of money in his bank accounts, maybe he had more than one person could spend in a lifetime, and a few good years to look back on, but Pax knew Davis had more gas in the tank. He still burned to win. He still wanted to take the field, and be QB1.

And if they failed here, in Miami, he'd never get that shot.

You shouldn't give more of a shit about Davis than you do your own career, he thought, but the truth was undeniable.

He didn't want Davis to slink back to Carolina, with his tail between his legs, and try to ignore all the talk that he'd been the final nail in the coffin of Pax's time in Miami.

"I'm sorry," he said to Davis.

Not the first apology he'd made tonight. He'd apologized to Sebastian too, outside the press room—because he'd done what they'd needed to win, and Pax hadn't delivered the way he should have. And he'd apologized to Coach, who hadn't accepted it, only told him in that gruff way of his that they were gonna right this ship.

The whiskey was lighting him up inside, one sip at a time, and he thought, stupidly, *if the ship's going down anyway, we might as well enjoy it.* What would Davis do if he leaned over—it would only take a little movement, because even though they'd started out a good foot apart on the couch, somehow they'd ended up much closer than that, a physical manifestation of how much they fucking gravitated towards each other—and kissed him?

He was just contemplating it, the booze making him think that it might not be such a disaster after all, or at least only a disaster on top of another, much larger disaster, so less disaster-like, when Davis said, "Don't apologize to me."

"Why not?" He might not be drunk, but he certainly wasn't sober either.

Davis shot him a look. He definitely wasn't sober either. "'Cause I fucking hate it."

"Join the club," Pax said. "You didn't have to sit in front of all the vultures and listen to them pick you apart, and agree with everything they said."

"You got it, you got that thing . . ." Davis sighed. Then he reached over and pressed his palm against Pax's chest, right where his heart beat. "You're true. You're gonna get it done. I know it, because I believe in you, more than anything. Hell, more than I ever believed in me."

"No," Pax said, shaking his head. But Davis' hand didn't move. He wasn't stupid; he knew why Davis didn't touch him much anymore.

It hurt too much.

But this felt good too, and the sharp razor edge of the pain that only made the pleasure brighter, better.

"You're a great quarterback," Pax continued. "So fucking great. I . . . you shouldn't be here with me, letting me drag you the rest of the way down . . ."

Davis withdrew his hand, and was silent for a long time. Wouldn't look at Pax. He took a drink out of the bottle, and then another.

"You know why nobody called?" he asked.

"Because they're fucking stupid?" That much Pax knew. Anyone who actually spent the time to *know* Davis Abernathy would know that he was nothing like the Condors claimed he was.

"Because I had a panic attack," Davis said bluntly. His voice was cold, remote. Like it was someone else entirely talking.

"What?" Pax couldn't believe it.

"Right after . . . right after they traded for Taylor. And people found out, I don't know how but they did, and then nobody would touch me. Can't trust me. I don't even . . ." Davis swallowed hard. "I don't even trust myself."

"*I* trust you," Pax said.

"You shouldn't," Davis said, his face full of disgust. "I'm no good. Broken."

Pax didn't know much about panic attacks or anxiety, but he had a feeling none of that was true. He refused to believe it. "No," he said with confidence, certainty. "No, you're not broken. You're the most . . . intact person I know."

Davis sighed. Met Pax's eyes for the first time since he'd confessed the truth. "Maybe I just wanted you to feel that way."

"Doesn't matter," Pax said, "I'd feel that way . . ." He hesitated. He'd known his feelings were big. That they were growing, no matter how he tried to push them down. "I'd feel that way no matter what. Nothing you say or do would make me feel differently."

Davis' gaze softened. "You're a good kid."

"I'm not a kid," Pax retorted.

"No, but it's easier if I try to remind myself of that."

They'd never talked about it.

Even when Davis had come out to him, over text, they'd never talked about their attraction. How it was mutual. How it felt like a string tied between them, yanking them together, no matter how they fought it.

"Not easier for me," Pax admitted.

Davis stood.

No, stay, Pax's brain screamed. *Make him stay.*

"Where are you going?" Pax asked, following Davis to the door.

Davis turned. Expression wry. "Away. So I don't do something we'd both regret in the morning."

"I wouldn't," Pax vowed quietly.

"Yeah, me either, which means it would be very, very bad," Davis said.

It was only when the door closed behind him that Pax realized what he'd meant. That it wouldn't just be a hookup, that it wouldn't just be scratching a persistent itch. It would mean more. It would *be* more.

Pax got ready for bed in a daze, feeling like he was just going through the motions.

He finally climbed into his huge bed, never feeling more like it was just too big for only him, but instead of falling asleep, he thought about everything Davis had said. Everything he'd admitted.

Because I had a panic attack.

Pax grabbed his phone off the nightstand next to him and googled them. Googled why they happened, treatment options, and most importantly, what you were supposed to do when confronted with someone else's panic attack.

Maybe they couldn't make a huge mistake, maybe they couldn't be together in that way, not when it would kill Davis' career, but he could be a friend. He would be there in the only way he could.

Week Six

"Is all we gonna do is kick field goals?" Pax asked more than a little despondently as he collapsed onto the bench after the last drive had sputtered out only twenty-four yards away from the end zone. Leading to yet another field goal.

"Hey." Davis smacked Pax on the shoulder pad. "Dylan's out there winnin' the game for you. Five field goals and counting. Don't knock that. And don't knock what you're doing to get him the chance."

"Let's look at the last set of plays," Pax said, changing the subject, and reaching for the tablet in Davis' hands.

Davis batted his hands away, and sat down next to him, holding the screen out so they could both watch. He pointed out a few things Pax could've improved on—Pax rolled his eyes, but he accepted them.

When Davis had come to Miami, one of the first things he'd discovered about Pax was that he hated to get corrections during a game, it was something they were working on, and Pax was dealing better with it, but Davis didn't *like* to do it, because instead of focusing on how to get better, Pax was focusing on how to not let it get to him.

When he'd gone to Asa, wondering how he should handle it, Asa had surprised him. "Why does he need to learn how to take criticism during a game?" he'd asked.

"Well, obviously, because sometimes there's gonna be adjustments and he needs to see the things he missed . . ."

"What I mean," Asa had interrupted, "is, why are we going to change *him*? Why don't we change *our* approach?"

Davis hadn't retorted that was because the coach's word was law, and everyone had to follow it, no matter what. That was professional football. The coach didn't bend, gracefully or otherwise.

But Asa clearly didn't give a shit about that.

Instead, together they'd developed a technique where he gave Pax some suggestions, and then he followed it up with a segment where he showed Pax everything he'd done right.

Positive reinforcement, Asa called it.

He did it today, offering a handful of mild suggestions on several plays—though, honestly, and he told Pax this, he'd played well on this drive. The defense was just really talented.

"You're movin' the ball," Davis reminded him. "You're getting Dylan into the right position. You're scoring points. That's what matters. Just keep doing what you're doing."

Pax shot him a look.

"Maybe we'll try one of those long buttonhooks that Tristan likes so much, next drive," Davis suggested, after pulling down his headset so that Randy, up in the booth, could hear them. "What do you think about that?"

"These corners are aggressive," Pax said. "They could jump the route, if they see it coming."

"Then, you know not to throw it."

Pax nodded.

A crackle came through his headset. It was Randy, the passing coordinator. "I want to try more moving plays. Where Pax leaves the pocket. Give him some more mobility."

"Then Pax has gotta keep his hips loose," Davis teased.

Pax did not like that. "My hips are plenty loose."

"Actually . . ." Coach Randy said hesitantly.

"Ugh, fine, I'll make sure to keep my hips loose," Pax retorted.

Except when Pax grabbed his helmet and jogged out to the field, he didn't look particularly loose.

That was the problem. He *was* loose, and then he got so goddamn focused on his footwork, on diagnosing the defensive formation, on directing the play, that he tensed up, all that intensity internalizing, and then he wasn't loose at all.

"We're gonna have to do something about this," Randy observed through Davis' headset as they watched Pax try to scramble to his left.

"The hips? Yeah." Davis had some ideas.

He didn't think Pax was gonna like them much, but it was clear from his frustrated expression that he didn't like what was happening whenever he tried to go mobile, either.

Something was going to have to give.

Davis gave him credit, watching him after the game, because he put on a good face. The kind of face that a leader would wear when one of his players had an extraordinary game, and Dylan undeniably had. He'd tied the record for the most field goals made in a single game.

Davis thought he might be the only one who saw the frustration lingering in Pax's face. The only one who looked close enough to see it.

After he finished with the press conference, Davis went to find him.

And found him, just as he'd expected, back to the wall in a tiny empty hallway a few doors down from the media room.

This was always where he went to decompress after a game, and after the media had finished tearing him apart.

Davis knew it wasn't goddamn easy, and he didn't begrudge Pax the quiet time he needed. Whatever was required to rebuild the confidence, to shore up the walls that everyone constantly kept trying to tear down.

When he appeared in the mouth of the hallway, Pax glanced up. "I just need another minute," he said.

"It's cool," Davis said. He took the spot right next to Pax, leaning against the wall, too. Didn't say anything else. Just watched.

It wasn't really allowed to watch him this way.

But he did it anyway.

Pax's head was tipped back, eyes closed, as the stress of the day slowly slipped off his face. He had a good week's worth of scruff, golden brown and glinting even in the darkened light of the hallway. He'd unbuttoned his suit jacket, and Davis could see the shadow of his torso under the white shirt he wore underneath it.

Davis' fingers flexed. He wanted so bad to reach out and touch, even though he knew he couldn't.

But for one minute, for sixty seconds, he let himself really want it; for once, didn't try to bury the desire, just *felt* it. It didn't make this any easier, but there was something freeing about letting himself have this. Even if it was only for a brief moment.

He was on second sixty-seven when finally, Pax spoke.

"My hips weren't loose," he said ruefully.

"What? I'm shocked," Davis teased.

"No, you're not." Pax sighed. "What are we gonna do about it?"

"How do you know there's something we're going to do about it?"

Pax shot him a look. Hot, singeing him around the edges. The desire flared, but this time, Davis stuffed it right back down, right back into its box, straining at the corners and joints. But it held. Barely.

They'd won the game today. They were four and two, and they'd won their last four games. Pax had come so far. The last thing Davis needed to do was lose himself.

"Okay, fine, yeah, I'm gonna do something about it. But you're not going to like it."

"Oh, I didn't think I was going to *like* it." Pax's voice was very dry. He still hadn't opened his eyes, but Davis knew that if he did, he'd see amusement in them.

And trust. So much trust.

Was it any wonder he couldn't betray that?

"If it's any consolation, I'm not sure I'll like it either." He already knew he wouldn't. But it would make Paxton a better football player, and that was the only thing that mattered. Not all of his sleepless nights, not all of his pointless yearning, not any of the feelings that he kept trying to push away.

When he left here—and he had a feeling there wouldn't be a second year, Asa would find a much more conventional quarterback coach after this—he'd go back to Carolina and that would be the thing that kept him warm at night: the knowledge that he'd transformed this kid into a man. A raw rookie into the once-in-a-generation talent that he really was.

"Why wouldn't *you* like it?" Pax wondered.

Davis realized then that he'd made a misstep, and he wasn't even fucking drunk. *No excuse*, he told himself forcefully, *there's no fucking excuse.*

Because the solution to Pax's tight hips was going to be difficult for him for one reason and one reason only: watching was gonna burn him up from the inside out.

Not because he was Pax's coach, but because he was a man.

He laughed, and it sounded fake, even to Davis' own ears. It would to Pax, too, because the problem was that they *knew* each other now, deeply and intimately—though not nearly as intimately as he *wanted*—and Pax was going to figure out that he was lying.

"Probably 'cause I'm gonna have to do it too. Gotta keep my hips limber, too, right?"

Pax chuckled. He didn't look convinced. "What do you need more limber hips for?"

It was a valid point. He wasn't going to end up playing for another team. Deep down, he knew it. Pax knew it too, ever since the secret of his panic attacks had come out. No team was going to want a QB who couldn't control himself.

But Davis couldn't say that he needed limber hips so he could fuck him into next year, either, because that definitely wasn't happening.

He shrugged.

"Okay, fine, be secretive, but I better see you suffering right along with me," Pax said.

Don't worry; there's gonna be suffering in spades. Plenty of plain fucking torture.

"You want me to learn to *dance*," Pax stated, shock rippling across his features as they approached the front door of this dance studio, tucked away in one of the endless strip malls in Miami. No wonder Davis hadn't told him what they were going to do to fix his hip problem.

He absolutely would have said no. No way, not under any circumstances.

He did tell you that you weren't going to like it.

"I do," Davis said calmly. "But not ballet, that's not going to help you."

"Oh, that's reassuring," Pax said dryly.

"You're gonna learn to salsa. That's all hips," Davis said. "Besides, we're in Miami, aren't we? It just makes sense."

"Sense," Pax said, hearing the disbelief in his voice.

Davis shrugged. "Maybe you'll like it." He pushed the door open.

There were several studios, connected by a single sparse waiting room, populated with several chairs and a sad, droopy-looking ficus.

At least the rooms all appeared to be empty.

"I'm not going to like it. I'm a fucking terrible dancer. Even that swaying shit, I really can't do it."

Davis smiled. Amused, but not dissuaded in the least.

God, sometimes Pax hated him.

Most of the time he was crazy about him—way too crazy, he knew that, it was a distraction at best, and impossible at worst—but sometimes, he was so tempted to strangle the man.

"That's why Senora Floria is going to teach you," Davis said.

"She's gonna teach you too, right?"

Davis shot him a look.

"Hey, you said it, not me."

"I'll watch, okay?"

Pax rolled his eyes. It was annoying how Davis could wiggle out of things so easily. Even more annoying how Pax always *let* him.

"What is this about watching?" The door to one of the studios opened, and it turned out it wasn't empty at all, because there was a steely-eyed woman there, her dark hair liberally sprinkled with gray slicked back into a tight bun at the base of her neck, and a short wrap skirt with a flounce showcasing a pair of truly exceptional legs.

"Senora Floria?" Davis said, offering his hand.

"Floria to you, young man," she said.

Pax rolled his eyes again.

"And this," she said, turning that extraordinarily focused gaze onto Pax, "must be Paxton. I am Senora, to you."

"Hello, ma'am," he said.

She eyed him, up and down. Pax had been through a Pro Day, the NFL combine, and then the NFL draft, and he didn't think he'd ever been sized up quite so thoroughly.

"He'll do," she finally said briskly. And then she turned to Davis. "And so will you."

"Me?" Davis' eyebrows nearly reached his hairline, and Pax could barely muffle the amused chuckle that snuck out of him.

"He needs a partner, doesn't he?" she asked tartly.

"I . . . *does he?*" Davis asked.

"He needs a partner," she said with absolute certainty. Then she paused. That gaze narrowed. It was like an arrow, seeking out all your soft, vulnerable places, hoping to skewer you. Pax hoped that Davis was regretting this a lot. At least as much as he was. "Are you telling me," she continued softly, but with each word framed in steel, "that you will not partner him, because you are both men?"

"That's not going to be a problem for me," Pax spoke up. Maybe Davis had dragged him here, and didn't really deserve to be saved, but it was instinctive.

"Not a problem?" she questioned.

"Uh, well, I . . . prefer that, to be honest," Pax said.

It was Davis' turn to roll his eyes.

He could almost imagine what he was thinking. *You want to stay in the closet, you don't go around telling people you prefer to dance with men.*

That was probably true, but there was something about Senora that reminded Pax of a bear trap.

Besides, he was sure that she'd had to sign an NDA anyway, in order for him to come take these lessons.

Davis looked like he was having an intense argument with himself. Pax knew which side he'd end up on, because he was smart like that. He hadn't gotten to where he was by taking unnecessary risks.

But then Davis shocked him by saying, "Yeah, definitely not an issue, as I prefer that as well."

Pax knew he was staring at him in utter surprise, but Davis would barely meet his gaze, and he'd started shifting his feet uncomfortably, like he was dropping back in the pocket and a linebacker was coming for him.

"Good," Senora said, and then clapped her hands. "Let's get started. We will start with warmups."

"The hips . . ." Davis started to say weakly.

She turned, skewering him again. "We will get to that. The body must be warm. You understand that, you warm up before you throw balls, right?"

"It's a little more than that." Pax was secretly, incredibly amused. Maybe this wouldn't last, but while it did, he was gonna enjoy it.

"Here, you are two dancers, not two football players," she said.

She showed them to the studio, gestured for them to take the center of the room. Glancing down at their athletic shoes, she pursed her lips. "Those will . . . suffice, I suppose."

She clicked on some music with a small remote and then her back, impossibly, straightened even more and she didn't walk to the center of the room, straight in front of them, but *glided*.

"That's what I need to do," Pax murmured to Davis under his breath.

Senora didn't turn, but he felt the edge of her voice like a whip. "We will *focus* now, yes?"

"Yes," Pax said. Clearly, talking in dance class was not allowed.

The music had a tropical beat, and even though Pax was convinced he didn't have any rhythm to save his life, he found he was able to follow it pretty easily, mirroring Senora's simple movements. One foot forward, and then the other back. Shifting his weight between the two. Rinse and repeat.

"Like so, *all* the weight on the front and then *all* the weight on the back," she instructed, slowing her movements down so that they could see exactly what she was doing. "Yes, that is the way. You have got it."

Pax discovered his hips *were* tight, and that fact actually made it hard to do this.

"You were not exaggerating about the hip problem," she said to Davis.

Davis might be doing marginally better, but Pax thought *only marginally.* Senora didn't need to talk about him *in front of him*, like he wasn't even here.

"I tend not to do that," Davis said dryly.

She clapped her hands again as the song came to a close. "Now," she said, "we will try this together."

"Together?" Pax said apprehensively.

"This is a simple movement," she said firmly. "Now, face each other. Davis, you will be leading."

"What?" Pax squawked embarrassingly.

"He is taller. Not much, but he is taller," Senora said, her tone broking zero arguments. "Now, Pax, put your hand on his left shoulder, and, Davis, yours will go underneath, and then take each other's hands."

Pax inched forward. Surely they'd done something like this before, been this close before. But it didn't feel like it.

It felt brand new, like the first time they'd ever touched, even though Pax knew that wasn't true.

There'd been casual touches, dozens of them over the last few months—a reassuring pat on the shoulder, an outstretched hand, helping each other up, a smack on the knee. A palm on a back. A few hugs. Some of them even lingering.

One time Pax had fallen asleep in front of the TV and he'd woken up with his head on Davis' shoulder.

They hadn't talked about it that morning or since, but Pax thought about it all the time.

Now he was going to think about *this* all the time.

He set his hand as lightly as he could on Davis' broad shoulder. Watched as Davis slid his hand around the outside curve of his own.

Was that trepidation in his eyes as they reached for each other?

Davis might not be actively playing but he still had the callouses and Pax's own slid against his.

You will not shudder. You will not enjoy this.

Except it was kinda impossible not to, considering how long he'd wanted this.

"Closer," Floria barked. "You must be closer! Are you afraid of each other?"

Desperately, Pax thought.

"Of course not," Davis blustered, taking a big step closer, but it was so easy to see through the lie because even as he pretended like it was no big deal, Pax could feel his hand trembling in his own.

"Better," Floria said. "Now you will move together. Paxton, you move forward, yes, while you, Davis, move back." She rolled her eyes. "To the music! To the music! You are dancing, not merely moving. Dancing . . . it feels the music!"

Floria made it sound easy. Simple and easy and straightforward. But it was hard as hell, and Pax's legs caught Davis'. For a brief second, he felt his thigh brush Davis' and now it was he who was trembling.

"Sorry," Pax said, his neck flushed. With embarrassment and with a lot of other things.

"Again. Let the music speak to you!" She clapped again, and slowly, painfully they began again.

"The music isn't telling me anything I want to hear," Davis said under his breath as they tangled limbs and then had to untangle for the third time.

But after she'd started the music again, Paxton thought they had it down pretty well. He hadn't looked in the mirror, so he didn't know how good they looked—if he had to guess, it wouldn't be all that great, considering Floria's pursed lips—but they weren't falling over each other anymore.

"Your hips, Paxton, they are so tight!" she exclaimed, as she walked behind him.

"That's what everyone keeps saying," Pax grumbled.

Davis laughed.

"Free them. Let them move. Do not worry about being a big manly football player. Let the music take you! Own you!"

"Apparently you're not supposed to just listen, you're supposed to let it take over," Davis murmured.

Pax burst out laughing. He didn't even care that Floria's glare was deadly.

To Pax's surprise, even though they'd only been stepping forward and backward, tangled up together, by the end of another round of music, his forehead was dotted with sweat.

Finally, Floria gestured that they were supposed to break apart. "Next week," she said, "we will attempt turns. Paxton, you must feel your hips between now and then."

"Sure, yeah." Pax narrowly did not roll his eyes.

He had a feeling no matter how he felt them, it wasn't going to magically loosen him up. But then, Davis was convinced this would do it.

"Next week?" Davis asked.

"I told you, he will need months of classes, to make progress. You will come every week."

"But . . ." Davis looked like he was about to argue, but Floria's glare shut that possibility down immediately.

"You said you wanted him to improve. He does not improve in *one lesson*," Floria insisted.

"Alright," Davis said, giving in. "But every week?"

"How else is he supposed to improve? And you must come too, as his partner."

"Oh don't worry," Pax said, dryly, reaching out and patting Davis on the shoulder, "he'll be here."

When they walked out of the studio, the sun was setting over the Miami skyline.

"Well, that was sure interesting," Pax said, because he didn't like the awkward silence that had fallen between them. "Big points for surprising me."

"That wasn't the idea," Davis said dryly.

"Course not, but probably an extra bonus, right? Plus, you'll get to rub it in that you turned me into a salsa dancer."

"Oh . . . uh . . . I was sort of thinking this would be our thing. Coach knows, of course, but the other guys . . ."

Pax was surprised. He stopped and Davis turned back. "You don't want to tell them?"

Davis shrugged awkwardly. "Just think of how funny it'll be when one day we take the dance floor at Hibiscus and show them how it's really done."

For a second, Pax let himself think about it. Think about the shock in everyone's faces, the possession he'd feel as he put his arm around Davis' shoulders, and felt his own hand grip his in return, how freeing it would feel to finally acknowledge just how much they liked touching each other. Touching each other and *dancing* with each other. Because after they'd gotten the hang of the very simple movements today, Pax *had* enjoyed it. And for one reason and one reason only: because it was just him and Davis.

Then he pushed the dreamy fantasy away because he wasn't stupid enough to believe that it could ever happen. Not in real life.

It would be a massive conflict of interest, and he already knew he wouldn't be able to pretend like it didn't mean anything.

Everyone would look at his face and know just how he felt.

"Sure," Pax said, because it was easier to just agree now, rather than point out all the reasons it could never happen.

Starting and ending with . . . *I'd enjoy it way too fucking much.*

"That's settled, then," Davis said. He pulled his keys out of his pocket as they approached Davis' big truck.

Pax wished then that he hadn't agreed to carpool—even though they were going from the practice facility back to the building they both lived in. It was . . . too much . . . and he needed a moment to screw his head back on straight.

To get the feelings off his face.

But instead, he was going to be stuck in the same truck cabin as Davis, at least for the next fifteen minutes.

Remember, Pax thought as he climbed in and Davis turned the engine over, *when you thought you'd get over this, that it would pass, that it would get weaker and less painful in time?*

Yeah. He remembered.

Maybe it had been stupid, because when did that ever happen?

Davis pulled onto the freeway, and merged with a sudden burst of acceleration. "So I guess that worked out okay," he said.

"If you want me to tell you that you were right, that remains to be seen," Pax said primly. "I don't know if she's going to loosen my hips or not."

Davis did a pretty decent impression of Floria's pursed lips then. "It won't work if you don't commit, Pax. You know that."

"Listen, I'm salsa-ing with you. If you don't think that's committed . . ."

"It's committed," Davis said in a hurry. Like he didn't want to dwell too long on the fact that Pax had said *with you.*

Pax couldn't blame him.

He didn't want to dwell too long on that either, but instead, he couldn't stop thinking about it.

Even after they went their separate ways, Davis getting off the elevator at the seventh floor of their building, Pax riding to the tenth.

Not for the first time, he wished there was someone he could talk to about these feelings.

But all the guys on the team were off-limits because these weren't feelings that were supposed to exist.

Beau was definitely a no-go, even though Pax had imagined he could tell him just about anything before the season started.

His best friend was Davis—and he could hardly go to him and say, "there's this guy that I'm crazy about, who's crazy about me, too, but it could never happen. How do I spend all day, every single day, with him and not go out of my mind? How do I resign myself to the inevitable?"

But obviously he couldn't do that. Besides, even if he was stupid enough to bring it up, it was clear that Davis hadn't found a solution either, so there wasn't much he could do to help.

Someday, Pax thought, as he climbed into bed, their situation was going to come to a head. Someday, the tension would break.

He just didn't know when. As he lay in bed, he thought about all the ways it could go down.

But he still never imagined that it would happen like it did.

Chapter Five

Week Nine

At first, Pax didn't understand what the headline flashing on his phone meant.

Sure, he knew the definition of all the words.

But the enormity of their meaning eluded him for that half-second. At least until he heard the gasping breath rattling in Davis' chest.

"Davis," he said, cautiously. Carefully. Not sure how Davis would take the news.

They'd discussed it only once, in the last few weeks, after Davis' agent had told him that the arraignment was coming up.

"I'm not allowed to say a damn thing," he'd said, the injustice burning in his eyes telling Pax everything he needed to know about what he *wanted* to say.

But there hadn't been much to discuss really, or else Davis hadn't wanted to talk about it—and Pax hadn't pressed.

You should have. You should have asked him how he was doing, if he'd had any attacks with this bullshit coming up, you should have been there for him, been a friend.

But Pax had a feeling that Davis wouldn't have let him. Not about this.

During Tom Taylor arraignment, the headline read, **charges dropped.**

Pax didn't need to read any more. He hadn't needed to open the article to know why—though he had his suspicions—he only needed to do one thing: make sure that Davis was okay.

But clearly, Davis was not okay.

He was sitting in his favorite recliner that he'd confiscated from some other random room in the Piranhas facility. He always gravitated towards it, after practices, and he'd sit there and review plays and film on his tablet, while Pax got showered and changed.

But he wasn't just sitting, he was hunched over now, where only a moment ago, he hadn't been.

"Davis," Pax said more sharply, hearing the rattling of his breath in his chest, painfully loud in the suddenly silent room.

His phone fell out of his hand and hit the concrete of the locker room floor.

Pax didn't need an invitation.

After Davis had told him he'd had panic attacks, he'd done the reading. He'd learned what you could do to help someone through one. God knew, Davis would never *ask* because that wasn't like him, he wanted to hide it, to pretend they didn't exist.

But the panic attacks were part of him now, as much as his blue eyes, as much as his broad shoulders, as much as his quiet, unassuming smile that brought so much comfort to Pax when *he* was hurting. And Pax, as much as he wasn't supposed to, as much as he tried to deny it to himself, loved every part of Davis. Even this one.

He didn't even think it through, he just moved, instinctively, crouching down near Davis' feet, hoping that maybe Davis seeing him, recognizing him, knowing he was there would help the attack pass faster.

"He was supposed . . ." Davis' voice cracked. "He was supposed to pay."

It just about broke Pax's heart.

"I know, I know," Pax said. "Believe me. I know." He felt like he was *this goddamn close* to his own voice breaking. But he couldn't break down now, not when Davis needed him.

"He needs to *pay*," Davis repeated helplessly. He was still shaking, and there were tears in his eyes, spilling onto his cheeks.

Pax knew he meant that Taylor needed to pay, not just for what he'd done to those women, but what he'd done to Davis' career.

Davis might be collateral damage, and the Condors might not have cared what happened to him, but damn it, *Pax* cared.

He laid a land on Davis' back. Without even thinking about it. Without even considering the consequences. The only thought in his head was that he needed to make sure that Davis knew he was here.

He knelt closer, until his forehead was nearly touching Davis'. "It's okay," he murmured, quiet enough that he hoped nobody would hear. But they probably all could. "Look at me, Davis. Just at me. That's right." Davis' gaze flickered and then latched onto him like he was a lifeline. "It's just you and me."

It wasn't supposed to be.

But somehow, impossibly, it was.

Davis' chest heaved harder, and the tears were falling freely now, his choked sobs so loud in the quiet. "That's right, just keep breathing for me. In and out. It's just us. Just me and you," Pax continued talking. Not even thinking about what he was saying. Not looking too hard at it.

Frankly, not giving a shit if anyone took what was happening and extrapolated the truth from it.

He kept talking, because that was all there was. His hand on Davis' back. His words in the air between them. And gradually, so fucking gradually, he started to breathe more normally.

Then he was just resting on Pax's shoulder, taking a shuddering breath every once in awhile, but it was essentially, finally, over.

And that was when a voice spoke up from the doorway.

"That's enough, let's finish gettin' dressed," Coach said, and Pax knew the words weren't for the two of them, but for the rest of the players, who were all watching like this was the most fascinating gossip in the world.

And no doubt, for them, it was.

But for Davis—and for Pax—it was his fucking *life*.

Coach walked over to them. "You okay?" he asked.

For a second, Pax was afraid that Davis hadn't heard. That he'd been so focused on Pax and Pax alone that he hadn't heard Coach speak. But then, slowly, he nodded his head.

"Let's go, take a moment for yourselves," Coach said in a quiet voice.

"Okay." Pax helped Davis up. He was still unsteady. But there was humiliation burning in his eyes now.

Everyone had seen.

It wasn't a secret anymore.

Coach led them out of the locker room and down the hallway.

"Take the time you need," Coach said, turning to Davis. "Then let's talk, okay? Pax, time to go to the QB room. I'm sure you've got some studyin' to do."

He did, because there was always something to watch, to see, to analyze. But he didn't want to go to the QB room, because what he needed was to be there for Davis.

What if Coach fired him?

Surely, he knew about the panic attacks in the past, but what if him having an attack now made Coach rethink things?

He hesitated. "Pax, go," Davis said. His voice warmed a little. "I'll be okay."

Pax was not convinced of that.

What if he wasn't around to intercede?

But there was nothing else to do but look at the dismissal in both Davis' and Coach's gazes, and turn and walk, albeit reluctantly, towards the QB room.

Coach wouldn't fire him. He wouldn't do that to Davis. Not when he was the only one who'd called him, the only one who'd thought he had something to give.

Except the thought wouldn't stick, wouldn't lock in, and Pax spent forty minutes in the QB room, staring at the screen and not seeing anything, before he decided that he couldn't let it go.

He was going to have to speak up, make sure that Coach knew just how much Davis meant to him, how instrumental he'd been in turning him into the quarterback that he was today.

He stood. Blake looked at him, confusion on his face. "Where you goin'?" he asked.

Blake was nothing particularly special.

He was basically a career backup, someone to hold the clipboard on the sidelines, and to come in if Pax got the wind knocked out of him.

He generally didn't have much to contribute to the conversation, and, Pax decided, it wasn't really his place to contribute now.

This was between Davis and him.

"Out," Pax said, and turned and walked out of the room.

Davis still couldn't quite catch his breath. It felt clogged in his throat, even though he knew he was breathing just fine, getting plenty of air.

It was the feeling of it, like he was being slowly choked to death.

During Tom Taylor arraignment, charges dropped.

His agent had called him two weeks ago, reminding him that if he was asked by any of the media, he didn't have any comment or opinion on the case.

Except that wasn't true at all.

He had so much to fucking say, the words felt like they were choking him.

Tom Taylor didn't ruin my career, but it's ruined anyway, and if someone is gonna pay for that, it should be him.

Tom Taylor is a fucking garbage dump of a person, who doesn't give a shit who he hurts, and he should be the one sitting at home, waiting for a call.

Instead, he's making two hundred and seventy million dollars, guaranteed.

Davis was mad for himself.

He was mad for the women that Taylor had hurt.

He was mad for all those impressionable kids out there, who'd seen Taylor fuck up, and then get paid for it, just because he could throw a ball real well.

It was completely, totally unfair, and not just to him.

Davis leaned against the wall outside of Coach's office, shifting his weight from one foot to the other, and tried to keep breathing.

He wasn't going to get fired for having a panic attack.

He wasn't going to get fired for having Pax talk him through the panic attack.

That was what he kept telling himself, but even he didn't quite believe it.

He knew what that scene had looked like. Him completely freaking the fuck out, and Pax at his feet, talking him through it.

I need you to look at me, and I need you to breathe.

He'd done it, not just for himself, but for Pax, and they'd all seen it. The whole fucking team. Even Asa.

Look at me, Davis. Just at me. That's right. It's just you and me.

He couldn't have been the only one to hear the intimacy in his voice. The way he hadn't been able to help himself from latching onto Pax. Not wanting to let him go.

Sometimes, he felt like the only sane thing in an insane life.

Not just sometimes, his brain added.

That was the problem, wasn't it? The problem, and the reason why he was currently standing outside of Coach's office, waiting for the ax to fall.

Nobody wants a quarterback who can't keep it together.

He already knew that. He'd learned that lesson the hard way.

But his job with the Piranhas had brought stability and peace of mind and *purpose*, and with all those things, and with *Pax*, he'd gotten better, hadn't had an attack in months, but he supposed he should have been bracing for all this shit to crop up again.

He didn't know where Pax was, but an hour ago, when Coach had told them both to come with him, he'd told Davis he had some time to get himself together, and then he wanted to see him.

Pax, he'd dismissed to go to the QB room, to watch film with Jones.

It wasn't exactly a surprise, because Pax was a promising young quarterback. He wouldn't get fired for forming too close of an attachment. It would be Davis answering for that, because he was older, he knew better, and he was Pax's *coach*.

The painful irony was that with everything they had—their close friendship, the camaraderie, the fact that Pax was the first person he wanted to see every morning, and the last person at the end of every night—he'd gotten to a place where he believed it was *almost* enough.

And here he was, about to be told that even this much, even what felt like *not-quite-enough* was going to be too much.

You should just quit. Pack your bags. Turn your playbook in and say you can't do this.

But that wouldn't be the right move for Pax. He was becoming a better quarterback, he was finding his feet, and his confidence, and to abandon him now? Davis couldn't do it.

Which meant that now, whenever Asa called him into his office, he was going to have to convince him not to fire him.

Not for him. But for Pax.

Pax, who deserved better.

Pax, who deserved the whole fucking world.

Speaking of Pax . . .

Yep, that was definitely him walking down the hallway, a determined expression plastered across his face.

He was not sitting in the QB room with Blake after all.

"What are you doing?" Davis asked in a low voice when he got close enough to hear.

"I'm here for you, you idiot." Pax said it fondly, and the glow in his eyes said it all.

Things were even worse than Davis had imagined.

Pax had *feelings*.

Yeah, so do you, even though you keep trying to pretend they don't exist. It's easier if you just want to get into his pants.

But deep down, he knew that while, *yeah*, it was totally like that, it was more than that, too.

"There's nothing you can do," Davis said gruffly. How was he gonna convince Asa not to fire him if Pax was *right there*, clear and obvious evidence that while they hadn't crossed a line, the desire was there. "Go back to the QB room, like Coach said."

"No," Pax said firmly.

Of all the fucking times for Pax to find his confidence. Davis inwardly groaned.

"Listen, this isn't about you," Davis said, but Pax interrupted.

"That is absolute bullshit," he said, "I was right there, with you, and you're *my* coach. And not just my coach, but my *person*."

Oh, God, he was totally going to obliterate any argument that Davis could make.

"I am not your person," Davis hissed under his breath, except that he was.

They were each other's person.

If you wanted to fuck your person ten ways from Sunday and also cuddle with them and marry them and play football with them for the rest of their lives.

Pax's expression hardened. "You are too, and you know it, and I don't know why you're lying."

Davis didn't waste any time. He took Pax's arm and dragged him down the hall, to a small offshoot corridor that held the executive bathrooms. Praying the whole time that nobody would come along and see this conversation.

"I'm not your person, I'm your coach," Davis said.

Pax frowned, his golden-brown brows drawing together. "It's not just me, I know it isn't, I know you . . ."

Davis didn't let him get any more out. "It doesn't matter," he said with steel-edged finality, "it doesn't fucking matter, okay? I'm your *coach*, that's all I am. That's all I'm ever gonna be."

"You don't even want me to go in there? I can tell Coach that I need you."

I need you, too.

But needing and wanting and all those other impossible things were gonna get him dismissed from Pax's side, and he couldn't risk that.

"You don't need *me*. You need a coach."

"Yes, I do," Pax said stubbornly.

Then to Davis' shock, he was crowding him closer against the hallway wall. Pax was strong, he knew that, but he was strong too. Still, he couldn't budge from Pax's grip, from the way his thighs trapped him in.

"I know you feel this way about me, too," Pax said in a low voice. "I see the way you look at me, when you think I don't notice."

This was going to be the worst conversation of Davis' life. The worst five minutes.

And he'd been humiliated and shamed and fired from a job that he loved, that he'd worked for his entire fucking life.

"I don't know what you're talking about," he said.

It was the shittiest lie he'd ever told.

"What?" Pax croaked. Davis had been afraid that he wouldn't believe it, that he'd still march into Asa's office and demand to keep Davis because he was his person, because he needed him and wanted him, and all kinds of things that would give their feelings away instantly.

But it was even worse than that, watching as Pax believed it.

"I think you're imagining things," Davis said. Hating himself every second. Hating the shut-down look creeping into Pax's gaze.

The betrayal.

He'll get over it, and you'll go back to being just a quarterback and his coach.

But had they ever been just a quarterback and his coach?

Suddenly, Davis wasn't sure.

"You're lying," Pax said abruptly. "I don't know why, but you're lying to me."

Because it's forbidden and you know it, even if we haven't crossed the line.

We've wanted to, enough times.

"It doesn't matter what I'm doing," Davis said, "as long as I'm being your *coach*."

Pax took a step back. "I see," he said, and that shuttered look in his eyes told the whole story.

Maybe he'd broken a little corner of Pax's heart, but he'd saved this relationship.

He'd saved Pax's future, and his own.

The crazy thing, Davis realized as he watched Pax turn on his heels and stomp out of the hallway, was that he was no longer entirely sure which was more important.

Breathing, even though it shouldn't have been, seemed harder with Pax gone. But he took one deep breath, and then another, and then when he felt he could face Asa, walked down the hallway towards his office.

"Ah, I'm glad you came by," Asa said, standing as Davis paused in the doorway. "Come in, and shut the door, alright?"

Asa had a famous "open door" policy. He rarely shut it.

Davis felt his lungs squeeze, but he did as Coach asked and shut the door behind him, coming to sit in one of the chairs opposite Asa's own.

"You doin' okay now?" Asa asked kindly, taking a seat again.

"Fine," Davis said shortly.

"I just want to say it's a fuckin' crime that they're not punishing him, either to the full extent of the law, or at least suspending him indefinitely." Asa shook his head. "Someone like that shouldn't be taking the field, no matter how much they've paid for him."

Davis swallowed hard. Gripped the edge of one of the chairs. Saw his knuckles turn white with the force of it.

"But," Asa continued, "I suppose I don't have to tell you how unfair the rules can be."

"No, sir," Davis said.

Asa leaned back in his chair, crossing his arms over his chest. "You were upfront about the panic attacks, and you know I appreciate that."

"You were very understanding," Davis admitted. He felt raw. It wasn't just the panic attack, though those always left him feeling weak and vulnerable, but the step he'd had to take to make sure Pax hadn't crashed this meeting.

What would Coach have done if he'd barged in and started making impassioned, emotional declarations, like *Davis is my person* and *I need him*?

Davis didn't want to think about it.

Coach, who was a fairly even-keeled and understanding person, wouldn't be willing to go that far. Not even him.

"Course I was," Asa said quietly. "You said they were gettin' better."

"They are." He didn't say *why*, because that was another thing that he couldn't be honest about.

But Coach was so fucking shrewd. He wouldn't be as brilliant as he was without it. "You know why?"

"I think . . ." Davis wet his lips. "I think having a purpose, that helps. Helping Pax. Helping him get better."

"About that . . ." Coach hesitated. "Are we gonna have a problem there?"

He'd said it nicely. Vaguely, at least.

He hadn't laid down the hammer, and told Davis something that he already knew, which was that it wasn't allowed, that it was explicitly and implicitly against the rules, and that breaking them would lead them into a situation that neither of them wanted to face. Asa being kind should have helped the bitter pill go down easier. And it did, Davis supposed, but it was never going to go down *easy*.

He cared too much about Pax for that to happen.

"No, Coach." Davis made sure his voice was steady. Made sure he emptied the pain of it out of his eyes.

He'd known, of course, that it was impossible. That they'd grown too close. It was a fucking miracle he hadn't been called in here before because of it.

"Good, 'cause, Davis? You're doin' great stuff with Pax. I want you to keep doin' it."

"I want to keep doing it. He's got . . ." Davis hesitated. Searched for words that wouldn't sound like overpraise. Searched for phrases that didn't feel like too much, like his feelings hadn't crossed over from the professional to the personal. "He's got real potential. His confidence is better. His decision-making is improving. His arm, well, you know how good that is. What kind of throws he can make, in the clutch."

"He's movin' around better in the pocket too. Taking that chance to extend the play without gettin' burned," Coach said, nodding along, clearly agreeing with Davis' assessment. "I'm not stupid. Never was. I know that's you, and your influence. You were always one of the better-thinkin' QBs out there, Davis. It's why I wanted you."

"Well, we're getting there."

Normally, Davis enjoyed talking to Asa. He wasn't like any other coach he'd ever played under. He wondered if some of his players, especially the ones new to the league, knew just how unusual he was.

Logan did. Sebastian did. Surely, even Beau did.

He wondered, sometimes, if Pax had let them slide so far into this difficult situation not because of a lack of self-control but because he'd assumed that Asa's leniency would extend to this.

If they kept winning games, that he wouldn't give a shit what his QB and his QB coach got up to.

But Davis wasn't naive enough to believe that.

There always had to be limits, a line you couldn't ever cross, and he'd always known this would be it.

"Well, I just wanted to check on you. Make sure you're okay. I . . ." Asa took a deep breath. "I care about you, Davis. Give a real shit about you. That's why I brought you here. Not just 'cause I like to thumb my nose at all the other crap that everyone says."

Davis smiled. It wasn't a big smile. Wasn't a full smile. It didn't warm him all the way through; he was too cold, in too much pain for that. But it helped, at least a little. "And you enjoy that, too," he added.

Asa shrugged, not even looking ashamed to be caught. "Sure. But you need anything, you come see me. My door's always open, sure, but for you? It's propped wide open."

Davis stood, extended his hand, and Asa shook it briskly, with his normal force. "Thank you, sir. And again, for the chance. I said I wouldn't phone it in and I haven't."

"Course you wouldn't," Asa said. "Wouldn't have hired you if I thought you'd even be tempted."

It should have made Davis feel better, as he left Coach's office, but it didn't.

The lie he'd told to Pax still lingered, a nauseating knot of pain that he wasn't sure how to dissolve.

Maybe he'd give it a day. Give Pax a day.

He'd get over it, maybe they'd *both* get over it.

But even though he hoped it would be true, Davis didn't really believe it.

Chapter Six

Davis would've liked to give Pax a few days to calm down. Would've liked to keep his distance, let their relationship sort of re-settle into something more like a quarterback and his coach, but with the game coming up that Sunday, there was no way to do that. There was practice to prep for and tape to be analyzed.

Instead, he passed yet another sleepless night, tossing and turning in his bed in his bland, impersonal condo. He nearly got up half a dozen times and took the elevator three floors up, to Pax's place.

But he didn't.

What would he say?

I'm sorry? I didn't mean it?

Of course he hadn't meant it, and at least, Pax had realized that. But Davis didn't think that was going to win him any points—because Pax was going to want to know why he'd lied, and what was he supposed to tell him?

You were going to go into Coach's office and make that conversation a hundred times worse.

It had already been shitty enough.

You were gonna push for something that couldn't ever happen?

He would have, Davis knew it. Knew Pax well enough to know when he wasn't going to just let something go.

So he didn't get up and try to smooth things over. He definitely wasn't going to apologize for what he'd said, not when he'd *meant it.*

At dawn, he got up, took a shower, trying to clear his head, falling back on his regular morning routine, trying to let it calm and relax him. Made himself a protein smoothie. Had two cups of coffee, and some eggs. Packed his duffel for the day, and then at 7:01, he let himself out of his condo, and headed towards the elevator bay.

Since they were living in the same building now, they'd started carpooling into the Piranhas complex. At seven on the dot, Pax would take the elevator down, and he usually ended up stopping and picking up Davis.

Without a text from Paxton, he had to assume that their regular routine was still happening.

But as Davis pushed the button and then waited for the elevator to arrive, it was almost impossible to ignore the apprehension and uncertainty surging through him. What if Pax wasn't there? What if he'd ditched him, without a word?

If he had to drive in by himself today, it would serve him right.

He'd let them get too close.

He could have pushed Pax away. But he hadn't.

You couldn't. You couldn't have done it, even if you knew what was coming.

The elevator dinged, the doors opened, and there was Pax standing there, his expression wiped totally clean.

There wasn't hurt or anger or frustration in his gaze.

There was . . . nothing.

"Hi," Davis said uncertainly, stepping into the elevator, the doors closing behind him.

"Hi," Pax said back. No inflection in his voice whatsoever.

Usually, even though it was way too fucking early in the morning, Pax would bubble out something funny or cute or interesting. He'd ask about a play he'd watched on the tape, or repeat a joke he'd seen on TV the night before. It was usually only seven hours since they'd seen each other—and typically they texted off and on during them—but today, there was nothing.

You deserve this, Davis told himself, refusing to acknowledge the surge of hurt. *You did this.*

"Ready for practice today?" Davis asked as the elevator descended towards the parking garage.

"Aren't I always?" Pax said neutrally.

He was. Of course he was. But Davis had been trying to fill the ugly, uncomfortable silence with *something*.

"Yeah, you are, I just thought . . ."

He didn't know what he thought, so he trailed off, acutely aware of the sudden gulf between them.

Just because he'd created it didn't make it hurt any less.

"You thought what?" Pax didn't even sound annoyed. He sounded . . . like nothing. Definitely nothing like the Paxton Kelly he'd come to know. Or the Paxton Kelly he cared about.

"Nothing," Davis muttered.

They drove to the practice facility in silence.

When they got to the lower level of the complex and the weight room, they went their separate ways—Pax to get his morning workout in, and Davis to his first meeting of the day.

How he was going to sit there as Randy went over the plays for the week, he didn't know, but there wasn't any other choice.

Football didn't stop for life. The opposite, in fact. It ran right through it, pushing it aside like it was meaningless.

They'd both chosen this sport, and this lifestyle.

But again, as Davis took his seat in the conference room, that didn't make dealing with the consequences any fucking easier.

"Hey," Beau said, taking the chair next to him, "how you doin' today?"

Like absolute rotten shit, Davis thought.

"Fine," he said instead. "I'm fine."

"Coach said so, but I wanted to make sure," Beau said. It was just like Beau to come and check on him. He was a good guy, and truthfully, a good friend.

More than once, Davis had considered confiding in the guy.

But there was one reason he hadn't—and that reason was walking into the room, Randy next to him as they discussed a play from last week.

Asa was primarily a defensive coach. He'd played linebacker in college, and before he'd become the head coach at Tennessee, he'd been a linebackers coach, and then a defensive coordinator.

Beau had told him that when he'd coached in Tennessee, he hadn't normally come to the offensive meetings, but Davis knew why he was doing it now.

The defense was playing well, but the offense hadn't been playing to its potential.

"Also," Beau had said wryly, "he's a micromanager. If he can find an excuse to be there, he will."

It was a lot for any coach to handle, but Davis got the impression that Asa didn't care if his entire life was football.

He probably even liked it that way.

Randy started the meeting, Asa taking a seat at the table with the rest of the coaching staff and assistants. He outlined the offensive plan for the week. Davis made notes, which he didn't always do, because it kept him focused.

That meeting segued into a smaller meeting, with just him and Randy and Beau, as they went over, in detail, all the plays that they were going to run in practice today, in preparation for the week's game. Beau broke down some of the tape of their upcoming opponent, the Cowboys, and Davis made more notes, things he wanted to pass on to Pax and Blake, at *their* meeting.

Then it was lunchtime, and he headed towards the cafeteria.

There was a QB meeting directly after, followed by practice, followed by an informal meeting that Pax had set to review both game and practice footage.

He'd implemented a plan, which he'd stuck to over the last nine weeks, even when it was tough, even when he was tired, even when Davis could tell that he was frustrated and sick of it. He'd still done, and he continued to do it.

That, Davis had always told him, was the mark of a great quarterback. They did the work, even when they didn't want to. Even when they thought they didn't need to.

Usually they met up for lunch in the cafeteria. Sometimes they sat with Dylan and Logan or Beau and Sebastian or even Tristan and Wade, or occasionally a combination of all of them, but usually, they sat alone, and Pax went over with him what he'd learned.

But today, Davis wasn't sure where he stood. He grabbed his favorite Asian chicken salad, and a can of Coke Zero, and made his way over to their usual spot.

To his surprise, Pax was already there, and when he sat down, he glanced up from the tablet next to his tray.

"Hey," Davis said.

Wondering if the coldness and the awkwardness of the morning was still around, or if maybe, God willing, it had faded a little.

He really wouldn't blame Pax if it hadn't, he'd been unnecessarily cruel to him, even if he'd done it for a reason, and if that meant he had to endure Pax's cold shoulder, then he would.

"Hey," Pax said. He had thawed perhaps a fraction, but there was still a distance in his eyes that Davis hated. He might've deserved it, but that didn't make him hate it any less.

"You have a good morning?" Davis asked hesitantly.

"Lots of tape," Pax said. "Blake's joining us in a minute."

Blake never joined them for lunch. He'd tried, at the very beginning, but after the second week he'd stopped because he said it felt like the two of them were in their own little world and he was third-wheeling.

Frankly, that should've been an indication right then that they'd gotten too close.

But what had Davis done?

Allowed them to grow even closer in the last two months.

"Ah," Davis said. He knew why Blake was joining them now, even if Pax didn't say so.

Pax didn't want to be alone with him.

If only either of them had had a fraction of that kind of sense ages ago.

Blake showed up five minutes into the silence that had fallen between them.

Only then did Pax speak up, talking about the film they'd watched.

Today, which was Thursday, was designated for third-down plays and figuring out ways to make them more efficient.

They talked through several more options, all of which Davis noted that they'd try at practice this afternoon, finished their lunches, and headed to the QB room.

They had an hour before practice started, and for the next thirty minutes, Davis pushed the difficulties of their friendship to the side and did everything he could to professionally prepare Pax for the upcoming game.

He went over every defensive package wrinkle and all the analysis Beau had passed onto him, and then it was time to get ready for practice.

Usually coaches didn't play alongside the players, but when the season had started, Davis had still fundamentally considered himself a player, and he spent time, too, demonstrating plays, so from the beginning, he'd dressed for practice right along with the players.

It might be a normal Thursday, and they were doing their normal schedule, but none of it felt particularly normal.

Still, appearances were important.

If anyone noticed that things had cooled between him and Pax, nobody said anything. And, Davis realized as he was heading towards the coach's locker room, to shower after practice, it was entirely possible that nobody *had* noticed.

At practice, they were usually focused, and today that wasn't any different.

But whenever Davis tried to find his footing again, tried to return their relationship to its normal easy camaraderie, Pax froze up again.

Froze him out.

It would've been weird if he'd skipped their usual post-practice breakdown, so he didn't, even though he wanted to.

But once they'd gone over everything from today, analyzing the tape from the plays Davis recorded, he stood.

"I'm gonna get a quick workout in."

Pax frowned, for the first time expressing what felt like a human emotion connected to something Davis had done or said. "But . . . you don't usually work out now."

Davis stared at him. Willing him to understand.

If he didn't go work off some of his excess frustration, he was going to end up pounding his head against the nearest wall, and that wasn't going to help anything.

"Fine, yeah, if you want to," Pax said, glancing away. "We'll leave at the usual time."

Davis took a deep breath. "We should talk . . ." he said, his expression full of regret.

"Talk about what?" Pax said flatly. "There's nothing to talk about. We've gone over the game film. We've broken practice down. I have a few things I want to do to prep for tomorrow, but you never needed to hold my hand for that before."

"I don't need . . . *fuck,*" Davis broke off, swearing.

Blake eyed the two of them. "I'm gonna get some water while you do . . . well, whatever this is." He left, the door shutting behind him.

"We need to talk," Davis repeated. He knew it was a mistake, but he couldn't take another moment of this.

"About what?" Pax said neutrally.

Davis wanted him to raise his voice, to echo his own rising temper. He wanted Pax to yell at him. Let some of the frustration that had to be bubbling away inside of him rise to the surface.

But it seemed that Pax wasn't going to give him the satisfaction.

"You know what about," Davis said, grinding his teeth together. "About the stuff we talked about . . ."

"About you being my coach?" Pax raised an eyebrow. God, he could be such a little shit.

Davis was torn between wanting to kick his ass and kiss the hell out of him.

"I believe," he continued, his voice frigid, "we've already established that. I'm the QB, and you're the coach."

Davis just stared at him. He thought he'd known the man so well. Had believed . . . well, it didn't matter what he'd believed about his feelings now.

"I'm staying late," Davis finally said, "don't bother to wait around for me. I'll catch a ride with Beau. Or walk."

He couldn't spend another five minutes alone in the car with Pax, that awkward silence filling every inch of space. Not tonight. Not when it used to be so much different.

"Fine," Pax said. Like he couldn't care less.

But Davis didn't miss the emotion that flickered across his face. He cared.

He just didn't want to.

Well, Davis thought as he headed towards the weight room, *that makes two of us.*

Pax wasn't happy.

Understatement, he mentally corrected, *you're fucking furious.*

Not just because Davis had lied to him and tried to push him away.

But because in the last three days, whenever he'd frozen Davis out, or tried to do exactly what he'd wanted which was to *only* treat him as his coach, it had epically sucked. But while it went against every single instinct he had screaming at him, they'd accomplished a lot not only in the QB room, but on the field.

During the game against the Cowboys, despite the coldness he'd raised between them, they'd never been more efficient.

It was as if stripped of every other thing, with only football to focus on, they reached a new level of symbiosis.

Drives went better. Pax felt machine-like, precise, devastating, in the pocket.

But even when they won the game, Dylan kicking a last-minute field goal to seal the win, it felt fucking joyless.

He couldn't even celebrate properly with his teammates, because it felt like the wall of ice he'd erected around himself, to try to keep all the boiling anger he felt at Davis inside, also kept him removed from everyone around him.

Even from the people he *wanted* to be close to.

"You sure you're okay?" Beau asked him as he gathered his stuff together in the locker room, getting ready to take off for home.

"Fine," Pax said in a clipped voice.

"You don't seem fine, and you and Davis . . ."

"Are fine," Pax repeated.

It was a lie, and Beau was too smart not to realize it, but he couldn't talk about this.

Not now.

Not ever.

Anger and frustration warred with stomach-curdling frustration.

How had he ever believed that things could be different?

"You keep sayin' that enough times," Beau said leaning against the locker next to Pax's—Blake had cleared out only a few minutes earlier, "maybe you'll actually start to believe it."

"Hey, we won today, didn't we?" He was careful to keep his voice totally neutral, but he wasn't quite sure he fooled Beau.

"Yeah," Beau said quietly, "we sure did."

The last thing Pax wanted was to talk about how fucking miserable he was, so he closed down. Tried as hard as he could to not let a single bit of it show on his face, or come out of his mouth. If it showed, he might have to talk about it, and he wasn't going to get through this if he had to talk about it.

This was so fucking miserable. Could he get through another two or three months like this? And what about next year?

Would it ever end?

Eventually, he told himself, the sting of it would fade.

But Pax knew he'd never felt about someone the way he'd felt about Davis. Would it fade? Maybe it would always feel this horrible. Maybe he'd never really get over it.

That felt too depressing for words. So, he pushed the thought away, finished gathering up his stuff, and headed to the player parking lot.

Davis' truck was still there.

They'd barely spoken after the game.

If you didn't count football, they'd barely spoken in days.

Pax drove home.

When he dumped his duffel bag on the couch, he checked his phone, and sure enough, Davis had texted him twice.

First: **Hey, you left.**

Second: **I just wanted to say, awesome game. You played great.**

Pax didn't answer. What was he going to say? *Yeah, it was a terrific win, but it was also fucking miserable, and I'm fucking miserable and I hate doing this with you. Why did you have to say all that shit when I know you didn't really mean it?*

That was the kicker, honestly.

He hadn't even meant it.

He'd said it just to hurt Pax. Just to push him away.

He watched an hour of TV, even though he sat there, not really seeing the screen, then he gave up and went to bed.

Of course, even then he didn't exactly fall asleep. He tossed and turned, the frustrating thoughts churning through his head.

He regretted not even acknowledging Davis' text.

He was trying to be . . . well, maybe not a friend. Definitely not a lover. But what he was supposed to be. A coach.

The problem was, even though he *knew* it was impossible, Pax wanted Davis to be all three.

A friend. A lover. And his coach.

Pax woke up to someone pounding on his front door. Loudly. Insistently.

He groaned and rolled over in bed.

He never slept in, but on a Monday morning after a win, he hadn't bothered to set an alarm.

Glancing at his watch, he swore.

It was after ten.

He never slept this late, even accidentally.

But then he usually slept easily and well, too, and he hadn't been. Especially last night.

Dragging himself upright, he didn't bother to throw anything on, just went to the door in his boxer briefs. Whoever it was, Pax decided he wasn't awake enough to care who got an eyeful.

But when he opened the door and it was Davis standing there, he regretted it. Davis wore a sheepish expression on his face that quickly morphed into . . . something else.

Frustration?

Or was that actually lust, hiding in his dark blue eyes?

You know better than to open the door like this. Who's the only person who'd come see you here? It's Davis. It's only Davis.

It was true, deep down he'd known that the person at the door had to be Davis.

Why hadn't he thrown on shorts, at least?

Maybe part of him wanted to punish Davis for what he'd said.

Remind him of what he could never have.

What you're never gonna have either, that uncooperative part of his brain added. *It's a freaking double-edged sword.*

"Hey," Davis said, clearing his throat, "I thought I'd stop by with a peace offering." He held up a bag with the McDonald's logo emblazoned across the front. "Your favorite breakfast sandwich."

"You brought me a sausage egg McMuffin?" It *was* his favorite breakfast sandwich. The problem was, just when Pax wanted to hate him, he couldn't.

Davis was too thoughtful for that, constantly showing just how well he knew him. Better than anyone else, because nobody else wanted to know Pax the man, they only ever wanted to know Paxton Kelly, the Miami Piranhas' quarterback. Even his own goddamned parents seemed to have forgotten who he was. It was only Davis who consistently reminded him that he was still a guy who liked McDonald's in the morning, and could quote most of *Grey's.*

"I did. Thought maybe we could eat and go over the game tape."

They often did this on Mondays.

Especially after a win, Mondays were supposed to be a day off, but even reviewing tape with Davis, on his couch, with whatever junk food they'd craved that week, felt like playing hooky.

Pax considered leaving him on the doorstep. He could. This was his day off. They didn't have to review the film together; he could always do it by himself.

Begrudgingly, he opened the door wider.

"Since you're already here," he said.

He detoured into the bedroom, threw a t-shirt and shorts on, and then into the bathroom, brushing his teeth and throwing water on his face. He was already regretting saying yes, letting Davis into his condo, when he didn't really want him here—while at the same time, he didn't want him to be anywhere else.

That was the whole fucking problem, wasn't it?

"Let me get the tape up," Pax said, pulling out his phone and navigating to his email. Like clockwork, the video guys always sent it over after the game was over, and they'd had time to edit it down, removing the commercials, the extra time between plays, and the plays where the defense or special teams were on the field.

He clicked on the attached video and clicked on the button that they'd set up, so he could play stuff from his phone on his TV. Before the video could start, he clicked pause.

Normally, he and Davis sat side by side on the couch.

It was cozy. Very cozy.

But now, Pax hesitated. Davis had set out his sandwiches on the coffee table like he'd be taking his normal spot, but could he really just go back to the way things were, that easy? Like what he'd said didn't matter? He'd just brushed it aside, like it didn't exist. Like it hadn't wrenched Pax's heart out of his chest.

Like he wasn't struggling to contain all the hurt and the anger, and hating every moment of it.

He'd tried so goddamn hard not to show how bothered he was.

"Is that how it is?" he asked. "You bring me some of my favorite breakfast sandwiches and show up like nothing's wrong? Like you weren't . . . like you didn't . . ."

Davis looked up in surprise. Probably at the vehemence in Pax's voice. The anger that he'd been hiding away all week.

"Like I didn't what?" Davis asked calmly.

It was the calm that did it.

The wall holding all his anger back cracked and then broke.

"Like you weren't a fucking *asshole*, when all I was trying to do was help you."

"Oh, help me. Like you mean, charge into Coach's office and tell him that I'm your person." Davis met his glare with one equally as strong. "Yeah, that would've really helped. If you wanted to get me fired."

"I wouldn't have said it that way!" Pax exclaimed. He wasn't *stupid*.

"Yeah, you would've. I know you, Pax. You'd have marched in there and made it . . ." Davis swallowed and licked his lips. Looked away. "Made it obvious."

Pax stared at him. He didn't have to ask what would've been obvious.

His feelings.

All these fucking feelings.

"I'm not an idiot," he said in a low voice. Hearing the hurt in it. "I know it's . . . I know you're just supposed to be my coach. But I thought we were friends, too."

"That's what I'm trying to be, Pax. Your coach, and your friend."

But there was a distance between them now. A distance that Davis had put there.

"Not the same way," Pax said, and regretted it immediately.

He sounded like a whiny, petulant child.

Davis stood then. He looked calm. Calm and dreadful. Pax recognized it, because he felt the exact same way.

"I let things go too far, and that's my fault," Davis said coldly. "Coach reminded me what my job is here, Pax. It's to be your coach. I want to be your friend, but being your coach comes first."

"Don't I get a say?"

"I came here, didn't I? We probably shouldn't have been doing this tape review here, but we were, and I thought, maybe we should keep doing it."

"And what . . . you *let* that continue?" Pax stared at him. It was like staring at a stranger. Still Davis' familiar face and the same eyes—but they were empty of everything he recognized. Every emotion that he'd become as familiar with as his own.

Like he was pushing it all away.

"We were real effective out there yesterday, you know that. We can't throw all that away because . . ."

Pax wanted to demand he finish that sentence.

But at the last second, his courage failed him.

What if he wouldn't say it?

What if it wasn't what he'd always believed?

What if he hadn't been about to say, *because we really, really like each other?*

A voice inside him that sounded suspiciously like Coach's added, *And y'all are gonna have to work together for the next few months. Don't fuck this up.*

"Fine," Pax said stiffly. "We won't." He glanced over at the television screen on the wall. "No reason for us to do this together. We'll review it tomorrow, with Blake."

"You're kicking me out," Davis said. And there it was, a flash of emotion in his eyes, a flash of hurt, he couldn't have hidden it, even if he'd wanted to.

But Pax didn't let it move him. "Yes," he said in a clipped voice. "You want professional, you're gonna get professional."

He turned and didn't watch as Davis walked out.

He wasn't sure how long it was after he heard the door slam shut that he turned back. A long time.

His sandwiches had long gone cold.

He stuck one in the microwave, more to do something than because he was actually hungry and wanted to eat.

Why hadn't he just let Davis have his distanced and professional friendship? Why hadn't he just accepted it and moved on?

Because you never wanted just that. You always wanted more.

He pulled the sandwich out of the microwave and stared at it. Suddenly the thought of eating it made him sick to his stomach.

Davis had come here, with a peace offering, like he could just change everything as easy as blinking, but it wasn't that easy, was it?

It wasn't easy at all.

Chapter Seven

Davis didn't realize just how much time he'd spent with Paxton until he cut him loose.

He didn't kick you out, he got justifiably angry because you were being a distant asshole.

That voice, reminding him of exactly why Pax might not want to spend as much time with him, was not only annoying as hell, it had been ever-present in the last day since their argument Monday morning.

He'd gone home to his own condo. Had sulked plenty. Had finally watched the tape.

And he'd seen exactly what he'd expected: the best playing from Pax that he'd seen since the preseason. He'd been efficient and confident, playing in the perfect rhythm that he and Randy had been trying all season to find.

It shouldn't have annoyed him, but it did.

The painful truth of it, lodged right under his breastbone, chased him out of his apartment, once the sun went down. He wandered the downtown streets a little aimlessly, finally ending up in front of the building he knew Sebastian lived in.

Beau had mentioned that there was a great restaurant on the bottom level.

He could get some dinner.

Beau had also mentioned that they made a great drink.

That's something you could definitely use.

He didn't want to get drunk. He just wanted to quiet his fucking brain, that was all.

That was how Beau found him an hour later, nursing a gin and tonic, a mostly untouched plate of guacamole and plantain chips in front of him.

"Imagine finding you here," Beau said dryly, taking a seat on the barstool next to him.

"Can't a man sulk in peace?" The words were out of his mouth before he could snatch them back. Maybe shouldn't have had two gin and tonics on . . . Davis realized he hadn't eaten anything all day. He'd left his breakfast on Pax's coffee table, and then the very idea of eating had seemed unappealing, until now . . . when he realized he should be eating something to soak up all this booze.

He scooped up some guacamole with a plantain chip. Not just because he was suddenly starving, but also to avoid the sympathy in Beau's eyes.

Of course Beau had realized what happened. Beau was a freaking genius, and it didn't take a genius to put the pieces together.

"Well, you're doing a credible job of it," Beau said, helping himself to the food.

"What are you even doing here?"

"I practically live in this building," Beau said, with a glimmer of a smile. In case everyone didn't know how much time he was spending at Sebastian's place. "I came to pick up some dinner."

"What, not cooking for your boyfriend?" Davis tried to drag himself out of the sulk and tease Beau a little. If he couldn't even do that . . .

Well, he didn't want to think about what *that* might mean.

"If you'd ever had me cook for you, you'd know the answer to that question. But the good news is that Sebastian really likes the Peruvian chicken here, and I'm real good at ordering takeout." Beau paused. "So why are you sulking? Pax throw you out?"

It was too close to the truth; Davis wanted to shy away from it.

"Of course not," he blustered.

"You know, nobody blames you for what happened last week, and nobody blames Pax for helpin' you through it."

"I know that," Davis said. But he couldn't help but remember the conversation he'd had with Beau's father.

Are we gonna have a problem?

"But do you, really? 'Cause you wouldn't be here, sulking, without Pax, if you did. Or . . ." Beau paused. "Is it something else?"

"I was trying to establish some boundaries. Boundaries are good, yeah? They always seem like a good idea," Davis rambled. The two gin and tonics plus the lack of food today was really loosening his tongue more than he'd expected. Or maybe he'd been sitting here, really wanting to talk about this more than he'd realized. "Everyone always thinks they're a good idea, til they don't. And then they get pissed off at you."

"Ah, so that's the weird tension between you and Pax this week," Beau said knowingly.

"You could tell?" Humiliation speared through him, right to the heart. God, everyone knew what a fool he was over Pax.

"Only because I was paying attention."

That didn't help anything either. Davis threw back the rest of his drink and held up his hand, ordering another.

"Not because my dad wanted me to," Beau continued. "But because . . . well, because I was worried. About this."

"Congratulations, you were right," Davis said glumly.

"Listen, I didn't want to be right, I know this sucks, I know it *really* sucks, and it probably doesn't help to hear that you're doing the right thing, 'cause it sucks so much."

Even though he knew Beau was just trying to help, Davis shot him a glare. "Ya think?"

"It'll even out between you two. He's mad now, but he'll get over it. He's young."

As if Davis needed another reminder that Pax was off-limits.

He was young. He was a player. Davis was his *coach*.

The power dynamic was all wrong, but when they were together . . . it still felt all kinds of right.

It just wasn't fair, but what was Davis going to do about that? Nothing.

He was going to do nothing.

"I hope so," Davis said, not feeling particularly optimistic that Beau's prediction would come true. He wasn't even sure he wanted it to. If Pax got over it so fast . . . that would mean that he hadn't really cared after all. He'd only lusted, but for Davis, it had been so much more than that.

"Eat something, and stop drinking like the world's about to end," Beau said, patting him on the back.

It was easy for him to say, Davis thought resentfully, as he watched Beau flag the bartender down and order food for him *and* for his boyfriend. He had someone waiting for him just upstairs. Someone who loved him, who respected the hell out of him, someone who he could keep.

And Davis didn't have any of that.

Beau was right. It was a cold fucking comfort that he'd done the right thing.

Even though they'd been coming to Senora Floria's studio for weeks now, every Wednesday night like clockwork, Davis wasn't sure if Pax would actually show up.

Yesterday and today, for their regular meetings and practice, he'd been there, because of course he was, Pax was a freaking professional.

But that was all he'd been: clipped, terse, *professional.*

So much for smoothing things over.

He'd failed at that utterly; all he'd managed to do was piss Pax off more.

He's gonna get over it, he's young, Beau's voice echoed in his head as he waited outside the dance studio for Pax.

Would he show?

This was not technically a required activity. It was optional.

It was also something they did together, a secret both of them kept.

And while he knew Pax still wanted to throttle Senora Floria sometimes, it was something they both *enjoyed.*

Maybe because it was the one time a week when they were not only allowed to touch each other, to enjoy each other, but *encouraged* to do it.

Of course, that meant that Pax was definitely not going to come. The last thing he was gonna want now was a reason to touch Davis.

Except, that was his Jeep, pulling into the lot.

Davis watched as he parked and got out, walking over to the entrance.

He stopped in front of him, his eyes still cold.

Too cold.

But he's here, isn't he?

He might be here, but it was clear from the expression on Pax's face that he didn't want to be.

"Hey, I'm glad you came," Davis said, trying to make up for the warmth that he *wasn't* getting from Pax's general direction.

Pax raised an eyebrow. "Did you think I wouldn't?"

Yes.

"No, of course not, I know how you feel about Senora."

"Right." Pax didn't sound convinced.

But again. *He was here.* He hadn't bailed, he'd actually shown up, even though he clearly didn't want to. Out of a sense of responsibility—Davis knew it existed inside him, it was one of the reasons he was going to be a great quarterback—or maybe because he also hated this horrible awkwardness and resentment growing between them.

Davis knew which answer he wanted it to be.

"Well, let's go get our salsa on," Davis said jokingly. Pax didn't smile, but that was okay, Davis decided, he could wear him down. He wasn't the funniest, most charming person on the planet—he wasn't Tristan or Sebastian—but he did okay for himself, if he put the effort in.

And the only one who'd ever made him want to try was Paxton.

Not helping. Really not helping.

Senora Floria greeted them inside as she usually did, brusquely, with a brief hello, and instructions that they were to get warmed up. By now they both knew the routine, and as soon as the stereo started playing, they both launched into the warmup she'd begun with during their first class.

For the last month, salsa class had been both the highlight of Davis' week, and also, a complete fucking curse.

Coaching Pax was tough enough, but holding him in his arms, watching as he bit his lip in frustration at Senora's barked instructions, seeing the joy in his eyes as he got a step exactly right . . . it was torture. The kind of torture he never wanted to end.

Today's class, however, was the first class they'd had since their big fight.

Since Davis had drawn the line between them and said, *we can't cross this; we won't cross this.*

"Enough warmup," Senora said, clapping her hands. "Now, we merengue."

Unlike the first class, usually they reached for each other with zero hesitation, understanding the way they fit together like two puzzle pieces. But today, Pax sidled over a lot more slowly, and when he put his hand on Davis' shoulder, it felt like he was going through the motions, but the light brush of his fingers was just that—*light.* Like he could barely stand to touch him.

"Yes, like two stalks of wheat weaving in the wind," Senora barked. "You will *feel* the wind. *Feel* the music."

As far as Davis was concerned, Floria was an absolute fucking delight, and adding more evidence to that was the fact that even in whatever horrible mood he kept trying to hang onto, she never failed to make Pax smile.

She did it now, the smile creeping out and quirking up the side of his mouth. Almost like he didn't want her to win, but she always did.

Maybe it wasn't quite as good as *Davis* making him smile, but at this point, he'd take it.

"I am wheat," Davis muttered under his breath, trying to find the beat with his uncooperative legs.

"More like a baguette," Pax teased back.

Davis' fingers tightened on Pax's. For a second, his face was open. Open and hopeful and yearning, but then before Davis could catch it and hold onto it, it disappeared.

"You mean," he said in a hushed voice, because Floria would go berserk if she caught them talking and not dancing, "'cause I've got great posture? And I'm nice and tall, with big, strong muscles?"

Pax grinned, like he couldn't even help it. "No, like you're big and tall and freaking stiff. Not waving in the air like a stalk of wheat. More like a stick in the mud."

If teasing him relentlessly was what it took for Pax to be okay with him, then Davis would take it. Gladly.

"I don't think waving stalks of wheat have stiff hips, though," Davis pondered.

"They're getting better," Pax protested, except on cue, they totally stiffened right up, ruining their rhythm and their legs, moving in pretty good unison before this, tangled, and Davis had to grab onto Pax's hand much tighter to prevent them from falling right over.

"Well," Floria said with pursed lips, "that *was* better. But more dancing, less talking! Merengue again, and then we will start the Cumbia. I thought you were ready but if you are not . . ."

"We're ready," Pax said hastily.

Floria raised a single dark eyebrow. "You will keep your hips loose? Let me see. Show me how you *feel* the music, feel the rhythm in the air as you move together as one body."

Davis nearly opened his mouth and offered a suggestion that they avoid promises they couldn't deliver on, but then the music was staring again, and he kept quiet.

Tried to focus. Not only on the music, and the rhythm, but on Pax.

Didn't look over his shoulder, at the crack in the far side wall, but looked right into his eyes. They were honey brown, wide and questioning, and once he allowed himself, he was pulled right in, like Pax was the magnet and he was exactly the right composition to be irresistibly attracted.

The studio fell away—the fluorescent lights, the cracked walls that needed to be painted, the smell of old sweat and wax, even Floria's voice as she cried out suggestions and corrections.

Pax's fingers gripped his tighter, and they moved together, just like she's said—like one body. Like the way he'd been wanting to move with Pax since the very first moment they'd met.

It felt more than good, it felt *right*, to see those brown eyes soften, for the joy to fill Pax's face, mirroring his own.

It felt right to touch him, and be touched in return.

Then the dream ended.

Pax jerked away, and turned his head.

It was too much, Davis couldn't even argue with that, even though it was only a pale copy of what they both really wanted—but the pull had been so undeniable that he felt lost in it still.

"What is wrong?" Floria demanded to know. "One moment you are dancing, really truly dancing, and now you are . . ."

Davis didn't blame her for not finishing the sentence. He didn't know what they were doing either.

"We need to take a break." The frigid edge was back in Pax's voice, and when he shot Davis a brief look, it was full of ice, missing all of the warm honey it had contained only moments before.

"Why?" Floria asked tartly.

"Because I don't want to do this, and I need to take a minute," Pax said tightly, and turned and marched out.

Floria turned on him. Because of course she did. He was the only one here, and naturally, he was also the person she'd decided had caused this problem.

You did. You did cause this problem. Because you can't stop, even when you know what's good for you.

"Go talk to him," she said, leaving no room for argument.

"Trust me," he said, shrugging, "that is not going to help the situation."

"No?"

"It hasn't helped any time so far," Davis muttered. In fact, he was pretty sure that, despite all his good intentions, every single time he opened his mouth around Pax, he somehow made everything worse.

"Then keep trying," Floria said, like this was the most natural conclusion in the world. "You are hardly one to give up, Davis Abernathy."

For a long time, he'd thought he was exactly that kind of guy. For all those months. But maybe Floria wasn't wrong. He'd just been waiting, in a holding pattern for the right chance to prove that he wasn't washed up, that he still had juice left in the tank, that he wasn't a destructive force in the locker room.

You're a destructive force now, look at what you've done to Pax.

Except, he hadn't really done it *to* Pax. They'd done it to each other. And nobody, certainly not the Charleston fucking Condors, could've predicted this turn of events. They hadn't even known Davis liked men, because he'd never trusted them enough to tell them.

"No," Davis agreed.

He followed Pax outside, despite all the voices in his head yelling at him that he was going to fuck this all up worse.

Pax was leaning against the side of the worn stucco building, head down, fists clenched on either side of him. He glanced up and did not look particularly happy to see Davis.

"What are you doing here?" he demanded to know.

"I'm here, because we've got to cut this crap out," Davis said plainly.

Not your best opening line.

Great, now his inner voice sounded exactly like Floria. Judgement and all.

"Oh, do we? I thought we were getting along okay."

Davis shot him a look of pure disbelief.

"Fine. Not *okay*, but . . . we were figuring it out."

"No, you were freezing me out, trying to out-professional everyone else in the room," Davis countered.

"I'm surprised you know what that even looks like," Pax said with a sneer that wasn't like him.

How did they even get to this point, taking potshots at each other?

Oh, that was how. *You started it,* Davis reminded himself.

He sighed. "Are we really going to do this?"

"Have another argument?" Pax paused. "Seems likely, since you can't seem to stop pushing me."

"You're the one who freaked out back there."

Davis told himself that he shouldn't feel guilty about it. Yes, he'd probably brought it on by all the soulful staring he'd been doing into Pax's eyes. The way they'd moved as one body, not two.

You were only following Floria's instructions, he told himself. But he didn't quite believe it. He did keep pushing. Pax kept doing what he'd asked, and he still kept pushing.

"Exactly. You freaking pushed me again. All this, *I'm only your coach* shit, and then you look at me like . . ." Pax stopped abruptly. Looked nauseated.

Just about how Davis felt.

"Look at you like *what*," he demanded.

Except he knew. Of course he knew.

He looked at him like the best thing that happened to him all week was Pax being in his arms. Because it was. Hands down. Absolutely no contest.

"Never mind," Pax said, clearing his throat. "You know, it doesn't matter. Not anymore. Let's just get this done."

"Fine."

If he'd thought Pax was cold before, it was nothing like the next half an hour. He acted like it was an inconvenience to even touch him, and not once did his eyes leave the spot right above Davis' shoulder.

They danced, but it wasn't as one body. Nope, it was two very separate ones. Two bodies who very much did not want to be sharing the same space.

Finally, Floria gave up, and said, in a disgruntled voice, "We will try the Cumbia again next week. Hopefully . . ." She paused, meaningfully, shooting a frank glare in Davis' direction. ". . . the two of you are more willing to work together."

But Davis wasn't going to hold his breath.

After the disaster of the salsa class, Pax wanted to crawl into a hole.

A hole that was precisely sized to just his body, so Davis couldn't decide to crawl in too.

Because knowing Davis these days, he'd proclaim that it was much too small, much more suited for just Pax, and then he'd crawl in anyway, wedging himself in before Pax could even protest.

Because that was what he kept doing, wasn't it? Insisting on distance, then getting pissed off when Pax gave him what he wanted, and then pushing his way in anyway, like he freaking belonged in Pax's personal bubble, like giving him his space was too much to ask.

It wasn't like Pax liked it either. He *hated it,* in fact, but he was willing to do it because that was what Davis kept insisting on.

By the time the offensive line dinner rolled around on Thursday night, he was in a hellish fucking mood. Pissed off at Davis. Pissed off at himself.

Pissed off at fate, who'd given him all these feelings he couldn't do fuck all with.

"If you keep glowering at that steak, you might accidentally resuscitate it and bring it back to life. Have to catch it again, if it tries to crawl off the table."

Logan was trying to be funny and distract him from his wretched-ass mood, and there was part of Pax that really appreciated that. That always appreciated Logan having his back, on *and* off the field.

There was another part of him that didn't give a fuck how funny Logan thought he was, he just didn't want to hear it. Period.

"Sorry," Pax said, because the second voice was kind of a bitch, and he was trying, though he wasn't sure how well he was succeeding, to keep his shitty mood away from his teammates. First, they didn't deserve it, and second, the Piranhas were six and three. They were second in the division. They were contending for a potential playoff spot. The last thing he wanted—the last thing he *needed*—was for his anger and frustration to boil over and infect the rest of the team.

What the Piranhas needed was to keep winning games. There was nothing Pax wanted more than that. He wanted it enough he'd swallow all his own pain and hope it faded, rather than trying to talk about what a bare fucking wasteland his heart currently was.

"Here's the thing," Logan said quietly, turning towards Pax, "I'm not sure you *are* sorry."

"Sorry," Pax said automatically.

Logan rolled his eyes. "I think we established that you'd *like* to be sorry. But again, not buying it, dude."

Pax sighed. "Did you and Dylan ever fight about anything?"

He didn't know why he asked—*though, yes, he did, he absolutely fucking did*—because Dylan was Logan's boyfriend, not his coach.

"No, not really. Never had a reason to. I keep waiting for us to have one of those big blowouts, you know, where you fight tooth and nail and hurt each other in all those extra special ways because you *know how*, and then you make up so hard you never want to let the other person out of your sight. But no. Not yet."

Davis knew him well. Maybe not in all those extra special ways, like Logan said, but well enough. Well enough to hurt him, maybe even if he wasn't meaning to.

Not for the first time, Pax wondered if Davis felt the same way he did, pulled and stretched between two diametric opposites that couldn't possibly be reconciled: Davis was his coach and his mentor and Davis was also the man he wanted to fall in love with.

But no, he wasn't going to be sympathetic.

Not when he'd gone all gooey and heart-eyed at salsa class, and Pax had felt like his heart would just explode with the desire to pull him close, to tell him all the things that Davis had already insisted he didn't want to hear. Not when he'd done that, while at the same time, continuing to insist that he was just Pax's coach, that was all he was and that was all he was ever gonna be.

It had hurt too much, to get so close to that fire and then have to turn away.

Just for that pain alone, Pax was angry.

"Why?" Logan asked, curiosity obvious in his voice. "This about the cold shoulder you and Davis keep givin' each other and the way you keep staring at your dinner like you'd like to incinerate it with your gaze a la Superman?"

"No, of course not, I don't know what you're talking about. Cold shoulder, ha," Pax said. But even he could hear that he wasn't particularly convincing. Logan was smart. Too smart.

"Things have been strained between you two since . . . well," Logan continued apologetically, "since he bawled all over you in the locker room."

"That's not why," Pax said stiffly. Defensively. "I don't judge him for that, he's been through hell, and those women, they deserved to sue the hell out of Taylor."

"They did," Logan said with a nod.

"And I knew. About the panic attacks. I'm not mad at him for those, either."

"Never thought you were," Logan said.

The question hung between them, unspoken.

Then why are you and Davis fighting? Why aren't you the greatest twosome on turf anymore?

"Is it about . . ." Logan continued, and then hesitated, like he really wasn't sure he should say what he was thinking. "Is it about something other than football?"

"What would we have *other* than football?" Pax asked, pushing a bite of mashed potatoes around his plate.

Logan's gaze turned painfully sympathetic. Pax wanted to hate that Logan felt sorry for him, but he didn't because it was so damn nice for *someone* to give a shit.

"You know y'all have more than just football," Logan said.

"Yeah, but apparently we're not supposed to." The words spilled out before he could stop them.

"Not usually, yeah," Logan admitted. "Did Coach . . ." He cleared his throat. "Did Coach give you the speech?"

"What speech?"

"*The* speech," Logan repeated. "You know the one. Wade and Tristan got it. Then Beau and Sea Bass. And then Dylan and I . . . though at the time I guess we weren't officially dating, so I'm not sure it really counts, and Tristan thought we should've gotten it again, when we *did* become official . . ."

Logan trailed off, almost certainly because of the confusion blooming across Pax's face.

"You mean the *you can do whatever you want to off the field but don't let it cross onto the field* speech?" Pax asked in disbelief.

Logan nodded.

"We're not . . . we're not involved like that. Not like that." Pax shrugged awkwardly, hating answering a question that Logan hadn't even asked. "We were just tight, you know. Close friends."

Logan shot him a knowing look. "Yeah, you don't have to bullshit me, Pax. We all see the way you look at each other."

"You mean the way I look at Davis?"

"No," Logan corrected gently, "the way you look at each other. I know it's not really . . . *allowed*, but maybe Coach could make an exception, like he's made exceptions before."

"First off, no, Coach didn't say a damn thing, and second off, why would he make an exception? Y'all are just players. Well, Beau's his son, and his assistant, but Davis is my coach, you know?"

As soon as the words came out of his mouth, Pax was painfully, horribly aware of a growing realization. *What if Davis was right? What if he'd been right to pull away?*

Because he and Davis *were* different. They weren't two players like Tristan and Wade or even Sebastian and Beau, a player and the coach's special assistant, who existed mostly outside of the hierarchy of the coaching system.

Davis had said, on that horrible day, *I'm your coach. Just your coach.*

It had never occurred to him that Davis had said that and meant it, but that he hadn't *wanted* to say it.

Did that make him any less angry?

Not really.

Maybe less angry at Davis. More angry at the universe, who'd plopped the one man in front of him that he really wanted, but had made sure he was plastered with *do not touch* signs.

"I do know he's your coach, but he's also . . .well, is he really a coach? In the traditional sense?"

Pax could tell Logan was trying really hard to justify it.

The way he'd been justifying it this whole time. Like how Pax had been holding onto his anger and his resentment.

Had those words hurt? Absofuckinglutely.

But they were also true.

Davis *was* just his coach.

Those looks that he intercepted occasionally, the taut, thick air between them during salsa class, when he just wanted nothing more than to fold himself into Davis, until they were one person, and not two, it might all be real, but it was also hopeless.

"Does it matter?" Pax asked bitterly.

"It matters," Logan said seriously, "especially if you're fighting about it."

"I wanted . . ." Pax swallowed hard. "I wanted something that was impossible. He just made that clear. That's all."

"You're not even going to fight for it?"

Pax shrugged. "What is there to fight for? I don't even know if he feels . . . well, if he feels the same way I do."

"Right." Logan didn't sound convinced.

Pax couldn't even think about it. It made it even worse, if they were both suffering like this.

Even though they tasted like dust in his mouth, he put the bite of mashed potatoes in his mouth. He needed to eat, keep his energy up, keep his mind sharp. The game was in two days, and it was an important one. If they won, they'd be in first place in the division, and their opponent, the Vikings, always played tough.

CHAPTER EIGHT

It was second down, ten yards to go.

Pax leaned over, in the huddle, consulting the list of plays written on his wristband, as Coach Randy, the passing coordinator, called in what he wanted them to run.

At the beginning of the season, Pax hadn't had a lot of flexibility in the huddle. He ran the play that he was told to run.

But now, with his growing confidence and abilities, occasionally Coach Randy would call in two plays, and it would be up to Pax to either run the initial play, or if they got to the line and Pax saw a defensive scheme that might thwart them, he could change to the alternate.

After calling the play, he clapped, splitting up the huddle.

Immediately, he took in the defensive formation, gaze flicking from one player to the next. If they ran the running play that Randy had called in, Kenyon would get stuffed at the line—or maybe even worse, tackled behind it, and they'd lose yards, not gain them.

"Blue, blue, LSU," Pax shouted, standing up, letting his voice carry. He'd learned, the hard way, not to let his eyes meet the receiver who was getting the change in play—in this case, it was Tristan—and his gaze slid over him, just long enough for him to make sure that Tristan had gotten the play call.

He repeated it twice more, then bent down behind Logan, and a moment later, the ref's whistle blew, Logan snapped the ball, and he dropped back, counting in his head. *One Mississippi, two Mississippi, three Mississippi.* Kept a wary eye on Tristan streaking down the field, his hands hesitating on the ball for just one brief second longer, letting the offensive line be pushed to their breaking point.

He felt more than saw the line curling around him, and he knew if he didn't throw the ball now, it wasn't going to leave his hands.

He curled his palm around the ball, willed Tristan to turn, and he did, right on time, and he threw it, a perfect arching spiral. Tristan plucked it out of the air, tucked it away and turned up field.

He'd gained ten yards before the Vikings' safety crossed over, and tackled him.

But it was a twenty-five-yard play and enough for a first down, moving them past midfield, and into Viking territory.

Fifteen more yards and Dylan could line up for a field goal try. Forty more yards and they'd be in the end zone.

The Piranhas had scored once, already, in this half, but the Vikings were pressing the defense hard, and as always, Pax felt the pressure to not only deliver points, to keep them in the game, but to keep the defense off the field so they could return fully rested and energized, ready to stop the Vikings' offense.

What they really needed was another touchdown.

Not to turn the ball over. Not to settle for a field goal.

Pax moved the huddle down field, and pulled everyone together briefly. Coach Randy called in the play and the alternate.

They'd talked before this game about how the plan was to get Kenyon more involved—Coach Dawson never wanted Pax to carry the whole game on his shoulders, he *always* wanted to get the running game going, and while Pax got why, it also frustrated him.

Did it mean that Coach didn't trust him? Didn't think he was competent enough to move the ball on his own?

Davis assured him that wasn't why, that it was actually *easier* for Pax to run the offense if there was a balance between run and pass plays.

But even he hadn't managed to make that questioning voice die entirely.

Lack of confidence, the NFL scouts would've said. *He'll never make it in the big leagues, if he doesn't find some.*

Except that when he'd come out of USC, lack of confidence hadn't been his problem at all. The opposite actually.

Then his first year had happened and he'd learned, the hard way, that he wasn't God's greatest gift to football after all.

That everything he knew was now completely, totally, fucking obsolete, and he had to learn it all again, just differently.

He gave the play to the huddle, and then settled behind Logan, catching the ball in his hands on cue, and then he turned, handing it off to Kenyon in the motion that they'd practiced hundreds of times.

Coach had a mania for ball security, and he never wanted a play to fail because of a bad handoff.

He jogged back, separating himself from the play, and watched as Kenyon dodged and darted through the offensive line's blocks, zigzagging six yards ahead.

It was a good run, solid work from Kenyon, but then Pax never expected any less.

Nobody on the field worked as many long hours as he did—it was just an inevitability since he was the leader of the offense, and essentially the leader of the whole team—but Kenyon put in solid work, too. Never shirked practice. Hadn't ever hesitated to put the handoff work in when Pax had suggested it.

They moved down the field slowly but surely. There was a little buttonhook route to Wade, who pushed forward, getting the first down.

Then another great run from Kenyon, putting them squarely into what the coaching staff called "the red zone."

Randy called in the play, and also an alternate.

Occasionally in the last few games, the offense had gotten stymied right at the edge of the red zone. In one game, Dylan had even kicked eight field goals, tying the current record holder for the most successful field goals in an NFL game.

But that wasn't going to happen today.

They were going to score touchdowns.

Pax felt the certainty of his purpose harden inside him, and push him forward. He checked the defense, and hesitated, because this was a new wrinkle that they hadn't shown him before. He wasn't entirely sure if they'd stay this way or switch back . . . but glancing up at the play clock, he realized he didn't have time to wait. He needed to make a decision now.

He changed it, calling out the verbal cues for the change, letting everyone on the line know what the new play was going to be.

They'd run the opposite of this earlier in the drive, and Tristan had broken away from his coverage, getting a solid twenty-five-yard gain. If he could do the same thing, that would be a guaranteed touchdown.

Pax knelt down, called for the ball, and it landed squarely in his hands. He had a second to check the coverage, and then another half a second, but he could already feel the left side of the pocket collapsing in on itself, the left guard being pushed around by the Vikings' big defensive end, and he didn't have quite as long to hold the ball as he wanted.

He was going to have to throw it, if he was going to throw it at all.

Reaching back, Pax tossed the ball in Tristan's direction, the spiral spinning through the air and then landing not in his receiver's hands, but in the hands of the safety, who'd read the play, and had crossed over just in time to catch it.

"Fuck," Pax swore, and dug his cleats into the turf, launching himself in the direction of the safety, who had turned and was now trying to make a move downfield.

The offensive linemen were arrayed out in front of him, pulling off their blocks, and Tristan had turned too—and he was undoubtedly fast—but Pax could already see that the player with the best chance of stopping him was going to be him.

He was going to have to make the move on the safety to try to tackle him before he could get by him and score a touchdown.

Occasionally they practiced this, but right now, in the middle of this situation, Pax felt clueless. Obviously he knew how to tackle, but the safety crisscrossed the field, taking a really strong angle, right into the empty flat. Pax pushed himself harder, sprinting down the field, knowing that if he didn't catch him, nobody was going to.

Quickly, he figured out that if he didn't cross over, taking a hard right angle, there was no way he could stop him. He was *fast*, and while Pax was athletic, he knew he wasn't the fastest runner on the team. Not even close.

Once he committed, he pushed his legs harder, churning through the burn until he was only an arm's length away, then he was only a fingertip away, and breath clogging in his throat, he flung his whole body at the safety. He hit the ground, with a jarring thud, and maybe it wasn't a picture-perfect tackle—frankly it wasn't even close—but it was enough.

The safety went to the ground, right at the ten-yard line.

He'd prevented the touchdown—for now, at least, but the Vikings' offense was going to get the ball deep in the red zone. A touchdown might not be inevitable, but it was a strong possibility. To say nothing of a field goal. It'd be an easy three points.

You gave that away. You tried to save it, but you didn't. You couldn't.

Jogging over to the sideline, he was panting hard.

The other players cleared a path for him to the bench with its oxygen apparatus.

Nobody said a word, but their eyes said it all.

Another interception when we needed to fucking move the ball and score.

They might not be saying it out loud to Pax, but he *felt* the sting of it. The failure of it.

He'd just flopped down onto the bench, and was reaching for the oxygen mask when suddenly his vision was filled with Davis' big broad shoulders and a furious expression.

"What the fuck were you thinking?" he demanded.

Since he'd become his coach, Davis hadn't ever talked to him like that.

Sometimes, he'd told him truths he didn't want to hear. But never *during* a game. He was always honest after, and sometimes those conversations were uncomfortable and painful, but somehow, they'd never felt as bad as they could've, because this was Davis, and maybe someday . . .

But now Pax knew that the someday, that faraway idea that maybe they might be more than friends eventually, was never gonna happen.

Davis had told him it wouldn't, and even though Pax had fought hard against it, he'd been forced to finally give in and acknowledge that as much as it sucked, as much as it hurt, Davis wasn't wrong.

"What the fuck was I thinking?" Pax retorted back tiredly. He took one long pull on the oxygen and then another, feeling the burning in his muscles begin to recede. "Which time?"

"You fucking threw that pass even though it was early, even though if you'd actually *looked*, the safety was right there, eyeing you like he couldn't fucking wait to eat you alive."

Pax shrugged. Maybe when he looked back at the tape—because that was *also* inevitable—he'd realize that Davis was telling the truth. It would be yet another learning opportunity. But how many of those was he gonna get before people started running their mouths again, questioning if Paxton Kelly was a quarterback who could hack it in the NFL?

"And don't even get me started on your fucking tackle. I can't believe you went after him. Let someone *else* go after him. You want to get injured? Leave us in Jones' capable hands?"

"No," Pax said in a low voice.

He'd never seen Davis like this. He was furious, the anger rolling off him in waves, his face incredibly flushed.

"Tackle him, sure," Davis said, "but you flung your entire body, laid yourself out, anything could have happened. *Anything*. You fucking realize that, right?"

"I realize I stopped him from scoring," Pax retorted.

Davis ran a hand across his face. "How am I supposed to coach you when you keep making stupid-ass decisions?"

"I don't know," Pax said, his temper rising. "You're the one who's so determined to be my coach. Just quit, if it's so fucking painful." *And then maybe we can finally do something about all this stupid sexual tension.*

Davis stared at him.

"I'm not leaving, I'm gonna fucking coach you, if it's the hardest thing I ever fucking do. And you're sure making it that way. Throwing into double coverage, pushing for a touchdown when we could've gotten a field goal, and then turning around and tackling a safety bigger and stronger than you are. And for what? To stop him at the *ten-fucking-yard-line*? Who the fuck cares? If I'd known you'd be so difficult, I'd never have come here."

Pax was vaguely aware of Logan sliding onto the bench next to him. He made some kind of noise, and later Pax would realize he'd been trying to ask if everything was okay.

But everything was not okay, and Pax didn't *want* it to be okay, and clearly Davis didn't either.

Too much tension, too much left unsaid bubbled up between them.

"I bet you wish that all the time." Pax stood, and realized he was yelling, if only because Davis' eyes grew wider with shock. "'Cause I sure as fuck do."

It wasn't true.

Davis had taught him to be a more responsible, more organized quarterback. He'd taken some of the unbearable pressure pushing down on his shoulders and helped Pax learn to exist with the rest of it.

And that was nothing compared to how much he just plain fucking *liked* him.

Davis had made him feel not alone for the first time in forever, the first time someone had actually liked him for him, not just because he was Paxton Kelly, potential superstar quarterback.

Until now.

Beau appeared next to Davis, concern creasing his face. "Everything okay?"

"No," Pax said. "He's . . . *fucking impossible.*"

"Me? *Me?* I'm not the one throwing into double coverage!" Davis exclaimed.

"No, the only place you're throwing is on the sidelines and on the practice field," Pax said. And then immediately regretted it.

Not just because it was mean—cruel in a way he'd never been, in a way he'd never wanted to be—but because of anyone, he knew just how much Davis had been hurt by the situation with the Condors. He'd internalized so much of it, and while he could pretend to the world that he didn't give a shit, Pax knew better.

Pax knew better, but he'd said it anyway.

Davis' face went dark. Cold. Numb.

"Right," he said, his anger fading to an absolute calm, "how could I have forgotten that?"

"You didn't, I'm . . ." Pax stuttered.

Even Beau looked shocked, like he hadn't expected Pax to go there.

Well, that made two of them. Pax definitely hadn't expected himself to go there. Or for Davis to look so fucking defeated.

"No," Davis said shortly. "No, you're right. What the fuck am I trying to do? I don't even know. Go learn your own shit, Pax. You know better, anyway, right?"

"But I . . ."

Davis was already turning and walking away though, and Pax felt his heart sink.

Why had he said that?

He didn't even mean it. Davis had been invaluable to him, didn't he know that? Was it so easy to convince him otherwise?

God, you really suck. Not only do you throw interceptions and jeopardize your career by trying to tackle a tough-ass safety to prevent a pick six, you have to insult the one person who's always believed in you.

"What's the deal?" Beau asked flatly. "Do I need to get Coach over here?"

Even he seemed pissed off.

In the last five minutes, the defense had clearly been playing lights-out, trying to prevent a touchdown, and from Pax's vantage point, Coach was clearly wrapped up in that, pacing back and forth, his eyes glued to the action on the other side of the field.

"No," Pax said. "No. I'm . . . I'm fine." He wasn't. He wanted to go chasing after Davis, but he had a feeling that was only going to make everything worse.

"I wasn't talking about you, though Davis wasn't wrong. Don't put yourself in danger, again, okay? You're our quarterback. We don't want to lose you, especially for a dumb-ass reason, okay?"

"Okay." He knew better. He'd *known* better. But he'd done it anyway.

You need to stop trying to carry the whole team on your goddamn shoulders. The voice in his head sounded just like Davis' because he'd said that to him enough times.

He'd listened, of course, because he tried to always listen to what Davis had to say, but had he really believed? Pax didn't know.

He *wanted* to be as sure as Davis was, but he just wasn't.

Maybe he wouldn't ever be.

Maybe it should be Davis out there, quarterbacking for the Piranhas, instead of Paxton.

He'd definitely done a hell of a lot more to earn it.

"Let's go over the plays," Beau said, pushing him down by a shoulder pad to the bench. It was usually Davis' job to do that, though occasionally Beau did assist. But Davis was nowhere to be found, and Pax had a feeling that Beau wasn't going to call him over here anytime soon. "You good to do that?"

Pax tried to clear his head. Tried to refocus. It wasn't as successful as he'd have liked, but they were in the middle of a game. He didn't have the luxury of additional time.

"Yeah, I'm good."

Beau shot him a look. "I'm really not sure that's true, but full points for the attempt."

Pax shot him a look. "Okay, I'm pissed off. Is that what you want to hear? At myself, mostly."

"And Davis," Beau said, as he pulled up the last drive's plays on his tablet.

Pax didn't trust himself, so he didn't answer. Even though it didn't really seem like Beau *wanted* an answer.

For the next five minutes, they went over the plays. And sure enough, when they got to the last one, to the interception that Pax had thrown, there the safety was, hovering right in the zone, ripe to cross over and pluck the ball right out of the air, just like he'd done.

He'd missed it. In his eagerness to make the play and get the touchdown, he'd just fucking missed it.

"Hey, it's all good, okay?" Beau asked, as the defense held, and the Vikings' kicker came out to nail a field goal right between the uprights.

"It's all good," Pax echoed. Did he feel it? He didn't know. But it wasn't going to matter if he felt it or not, because in a minute or so, the Vikings would kick off, and he'd get the ball back, and the only thing that *did* matter was what he did with it next.

Davis had never been a quitter in his entire life, but he'd never wanted to quit more than he did right now.

But even then, despite the overwhelming desire, he lingered on the sidelines. Watching as Pax led the Piranhas' offense down the field.

Even though Randy was in the upper box and shouldn't have heard about the argument they'd had, he'd clearly heard about it—he could probably thank Beau for that one—because the first three plays he called were running plays.

Kenyon, Davis assumed, trying to think logically through the thick fog of hurt and frustration swirling in his head, was going to get a lot of touches today. It made sense, Pax was going to be jumpy. Inconsistent. You didn't want to count on him, only for him to not be able to bear that burden. And yet, he was the team's quarterback; that was his whole fucking job.

Still, Davis was impressed that between Kenyon's running plays and a handful of quick, unpressured throws by Pax to Wade and Carter, the other starting wide receiver, they moved the ball just enough to get Dylan out there to kick a field goal.

The same play calls continued after the defense made a stand, and Sebastian in particular made a killer play.

Usually Davis would've come over to the bench while the defense took the field, and gone over the plays with Pax, but even if he wanted to, he decided it was better to keep his distance.

Pax didn't look particularly happy about the way the game was going, even though the Piranhas were ahead.

He knew Pax. Pax would want them to win the game because of him, not despite him.

But in the end, that was exactly what happened.

He could see from the way Pax's head bowed, the frustration in every line of his body, that even the win wasn't enough.

Davis didn't want to feel sorry for him, didn't want to understand how he felt, because he should be angry, he should be fucking furious, and he *was*, but that didn't really change anything.

Didn't change how he felt, deep down.

Because even as pissed off as he was, even as shitty as the thing Pax said was . . . God, he still cared way too much about him.

And that was the goddamn kicker, wasn't it?

After the game, Davis should have found Pax, cleared the air, but he didn't. He avoided him instead, showering in the staff locker room and changing, staying in the front of the bus on the way to the airport.

Sometimes he and Pax sat together on the plane, though technically he should've kept to the staff section, and Pax should have kept to the player section, but Asa never seemed to mind if there was co-mingling.

But tonight, he kept to the front for the flight back to Miami.

Everyone, seeming to sense his terrible fucking mood, avoided him, though Beau had stopped by briefly, putting a hand on his shoulder, making sure he was okay.

"Sure, yeah," Davis had said.

But was he really?

Eh.

Then, he hadn't been okay for a while now, and he'd dealt with it fine, hadn't he?

Of course, meeting Pax had changed things. For a little bit, everything had been more than okay.

He just remembered what it had been like to watch Pax go after that huge fucking safety today. How terrified he'd been. The fear coalescing coldly inside him when he'd laid himself out, his body more vulnerable than Davis ever wanted it to be.

The anger he'd felt had come from fear. He realized that now.

But where had Pax's anger come from?

Probably from all this goddamned tension you can't seem to shake.

It wasn't like Davis hadn't tried. He *had* tried. He'd tried to reason with himself, and with Pax, and ultimately done everything he knew to get them back on track. He'd tried to re-establish a friendship completely removed from the terrible yearning that had defined it from the beginning, but that was the problem, wasn't it?

They'd never had just a plain, simple friendship. It had never been that. Maybe it couldn't ever be that.

Maybe what he wanted was impossible.

Just like everything else you want. As far as the fucking moon.

Maybe you really should just quit, leave Pax to the wolves. Go back to Carolina and try to forget all of this.

He considered it. Seriously, shockingly considered when they got back to the Piranhas facility from the airport, that he'd walk into Coach's office and tell him that it had been a good experiment, a good theory, but that in practice, it hadn't worked.

But it did work. You and Pax were gettin' somewhere. It just wasn't a place solely about football.

Davis knew that he couldn't walk away now. Because maybe Pax shared his feelings—in fact, it seemed more and more likely, the deeper they got into this mess—but he couldn't abandon Pax now, not when he needed him, just because he couldn't keep *his* feelings under control. That just didn't seem fair, and considering how much the unfairness of the NFL had punished him, Davis wasn't going to be party to more.

He got off the bus, and after dropping off his notes and his tablet in his office, he headed to the parking lot. He'd drive home, get some sleep, and come back the next morning, even though the next week was their bye, and there was no real rush to analyze the offense.

Work, he decided, would keep him occupied and his mind busy.

Except when he walked back into the parking lot, almost entirely empty now, everyone in a hurry to get home or wherever they were going for the week off, Pax was leaning against his front bumper.

Davis sighed.

Maybe after whatever went down now, he was going to end up marching into Coach's office and giving his resignation anyway. Because if they couldn't fix this thing between them, there was no point in continuing. As much as Davis hated the thought of that, he knew, deep down, that was the truth.

"Hey," Pax said as he walked closer. "I was hoping you weren't going to do something crazy like sleep in your office." He looked sorry; it was radiating off him in waves. Accompanied by a heavy dose of disgust, clearly directed at himself.

"I'm not Coach," Davis said carefully. "And if I was dumb enough to sleep in my office, I'd at least find a couch that fit me." The one in his office currently was at least two inches too short for him to stretch out entirely, and was crazy uncomfortable as a result.

"Right." Pax had that puppy dog look on his face. Expectant. And sorry.

"Listen, I'm sorry I yelled, I shouldn't have done that." He'd always hated it when coaches yelled at him on the sideline, especially when he *knew* how he'd fucked up and usually how he needed to fix it. He didn't need someone to make him feel additionally shitty, not when he was decent enough at that himself. And he never needed anyone to do it in full view of the rest of the team, and on top of that, all the cameras that were likely to capture any potential sideline drama.

He'd promised himself, when he'd begun coaching Pax, that he wouldn't even if Pax gave him a hundred reasons to do it. And mostly, Pax hadn't. Even today hadn't really been enough. There'd been no reason to yell and snipe at him, except that the fear had pushed him. Fear that he didn't want to question the origin of, because he was afraid he knew where it had come from.

"You . . ." Pax gawked at him. Davis knew he should keep his distance, but he was so fucking tired of keeping his distance, and he joined Pax, leaning against the truck bumper, right next to him, their shoulders nearly touching. "You don't have to apologize. In fact, it should be *me* apologizing, I fucked up, I threw the interception—and you were right, by the way, he was right there, hiding in the zone, just like you always warn me about—and then instead of taking responsibility . . ." Pax hesitated, swallowed hard, hard enough that Davis could see his Adam's apple bobbing, and he wished, more than anything else, that he didn't know how he felt right now. But he did. "I lashed out at you. I was shitty to you, so incredibly, unacceptably shitty. I shouldn't have said that."

"Yeah, but it was true." Now that the apology was actually here, it was funny, because Davis couldn't find the anger anymore that it was supposed to appease.

"Doesn't mean I should've said it," Pax said quietly. "I knew it was wrong, I knew I shouldn't have said it the moment it came out. I'm sorry."

"And I shouldn't have been yellin' at you, either." Davis heard the regret in his voice, loud and clear.

Pax nudged his shoulder, leaning a bit closer, until they were nearly touching from shoulder to hip. In the week since their horrible fight, they'd barely touched—except for dance class, and that hadn't exactly been a success either—but Davis had forgotten how it felt. How he had to steel himself against all those casual touches, because inevitably he always wanted more.

"No, but I probably deserved it," Pax said wryly. "The safety *was* hangin' back in the zone. I should've seen him."

"Beau show you that?"

"Yeah, but I didn't need him to do it. I saw it with my own two eyes." Pax hesitated. "Just too late."

He sounded so young and so defeated, how was Davis supposed to stay pissed off?

He couldn't.

You will regret this, he told himself, as he reached out and tugged Pax into a quick hug.

They didn't hug almost ever, even though football players were generally a touchy-feely bunch—because they weren't stupid, and since his life had blown up, Davis tried not to play with fire—but now felt like the perfect time to give in. Frankly, they could both use a little comfort of the physical variety.

He felt the impact of Pax's body against his own, the curve of his hips, the firmness of his stomach, the perfection of his arms as they closed around his shoulders.

This is home. This is where you're meant to be.

The thought crossed his mind before he could muffle it.

Davis just closed his eyes and, instead of overthinking this, just *felt* for the half a second they remained tangled together.

But instead of letting go, Pax held on.

"I hate this," he murmured so quietly that for a moment, Davis thought that maybe he hadn't heard him. But he must've, because the same thought was clanging in his own stupid, uncooperative brain.

"Me too," Davis echoed.

He hated that instead of hanging on, instead of pulling Paxton even closer, holding him like his life depended on it, he should let go.

It was Pax who was strong enough to pull away, but he didn't let go entirely. His hand lingered on Davis' shoulder, like they were going to salsa across the asphalt. "Then we gotta stop doing it to ourselves," he said seriously.

Like Davis hadn't fucking tried.

For a second, he seriously considered admitting that he'd nearly quit tonight. Nearly marched into Coach's office and told him, *yes, this is a problem*, and resigned.

He wouldn't have to go back to Carolina.

He could stay, here in Miami. And every night, Pax could come home to him, to his bed. To the circle of his arms, and he'd never have to feel guilty about it.

But already he knew that wasn't going to be true, because while Asa would undoubtedly find someone else to coach Pax, and Beau would certainly help, he understood now that he was uniquely suited to helping Pax develop into the quarterback he could be, with time and patience and confidence.

He knew why Asa had brought him here. He'd come to Miami because finally, someone had thought there was something he could give, but that wasn't why he'd stayed.

He'd stayed for Paxton.

The last thing he'd do now was abandon him.

Even if it meant he'd be able to warm his bed at night.

Even if it meant that all this horrible, painful yearning might finally end.

You're stronger than that, you've always been stronger than that. You can do this; you need to do this.

"Agreed," Davis said.

It felt like hope dying, even though he'd known the entire fucking time that there was nothing to do about the way he felt. But now, he let himself believe that it was never going to happen.

He was going to be Paxton Kelly's coach.

Just Paxton Kelly's coach.

Pax didn't look any happier about it either, but there *was* relief in his face, like he'd finally understood that they'd been edging right up to the line—that the line existed at all.

It felt . . . well, not *good*, but there was at least a cold comfort that it was over.

Once and for all.

"So, tomorrow, tape?" Paxton asked.

Davis nodded. "We'll do it here."

There would be no more intimate hangouts on Pax's couch. He was always so dangerously tempted in those moments, and there could be no more temptations. No more slippery slopes of *oh, but this is okay for now* situations.

Pax took a deep breath. "Okay. I'll see you tomorrow, then."

"Yeah, tomorrow."

Pax turned and left then, and when Davis drove the handful of blocks to the garage of his building, he told himself the clog in his throat was stupid, pointless, unnecessary.

But he still felt like crying the whole way home.

Chapter Nine

"So what are y'all doing for the bye week?" Wade asked, tipping the bottle of beer back and taking a long sip after he directed the question toward Logan.

They were at Hibiscus for their weekly celebration of winning another game that nobody had thought they could win.

"We're going to Seattle, hang out with Levi for the week, catch his game, and"—Logan exchanged glances with Dylan, the intimacy between them as clear as day—"sleep in. Go to the waterfront. Watch them throw those fish at the market. Drink too much coffee."

Pax had come tonight, even though he hadn't really felt like celebrating, because he felt even less like explaining to anyone his complete lack of festive mood.

But the rest of them were making up for it. Tristan and Sea Bass had done shots, Beau laughing as Sebastian had pulled him into a tequila-wet kiss afterwards.

Dylan and Logan were there. Kenyon was even there.

And Davis—though Paxton had been really surprised when he'd walked up the stairs, wearing a bright blue button-up shirt, and a pair of khaki shorts, shadows under his eyes.

They'd met earlier and gone over the plays of the game.

It hadn't felt good.

In fact, Pax had felt like crying the whole time. But he told himself it would get better now. It *had* to get better, because he couldn't keep feeling like this.

Hope was dead, and the anger had finally burned out of him.

There was nothing left to do but go through the routine, and put one foot in front of the other, and believe that maybe in time he wouldn't feel so absolutely fucking wretched. That maybe someday he and Davis might truly be able to be *just* friends, without all that other crappy baggage dragging behind them.

"What about you, Pax?" Tristan asked, sliding into the loose circle of Wade's arms. The softness of Wade's gaze as he did hurt.

You're not going to have that. Not with who you really want. But maybe someday . . . you'll meet someone else who makes you feel like Davis does.

It was weak. Didn't make him feel all that much better, but what else was he supposed to do? Curl up in a ball and *die* from how shitty it felt?

"Uh, I guess, stay here." He didn't have plans. "Work on some new plays."

"You're gonna work, aren't you?" Logan asked.

"Yes," Pax admitted. Though truly, he hadn't thought about it. He hadn't been able to see more than a day or two at a time—up til the next game—and then it started all over again.

But now he had two weeks til the Piranhas played again.

No official practices for the next eight days.

What was he going to do? Go stir crazy?

He didn't want to, but maybe he'd come to Hibiscus and try to pick someone up. Get drunk enough that he wouldn't feel wretched it wasn't Davis.

"You work too hard," Logan said. The irony, considering how hard *he* worked.

He swallowed a long sip of beer. "That's a matter of opinion."

Normally, Davis would back him up here, whenever Logan got worked up about the long hours he put in in the QB room.

But Davis had been even quieter than he normally was—even quieter than Pax himself, tonight.

He was pretending he didn't know why, but he knew why.

"No," Logan said. "And about that . . ."

Beau and Sebastian had been laughing over by the bar, but they circled closer, and suddenly, Paxton looked up and realized that the group had essentially closed ranks, and he'd ended up in the middle.

"About what?" he asked suspiciously.

He had a very bad feeling about this.

"Yeah, you work too hard," Sebastian said casually. But too casually. Like Pax was a horse he didn't want to spook.

Except that he already felt spooked.

What the fuck was going on?

"Not just that," Tristan piped up. "You're making yourself fucking miserable."

"I'm . . ." Pax started to argue, to try to defend himself, because why did it *matter* if he was fucking miserable? It wasn't like there were any alternatives.

"No," Logan said, and he held up a hand. Sometimes it was easy to forget the sheer size and force of Logan Banks, but there was a hardness in his eyes now that Pax couldn't remember ever seeing.

"No *what?*" Davis asked.

Pax knew, because he *knew* Davis, that he'd been hanging back, waiting to see what happened, how this was going to develop—but truthfully, his first and second and last instinct was going to be to have Pax's back.

That was just the way he was.

It was why Pax loved him.

"We wanna have a little chat," Sebastian said. "What did you call it, babe?" He directed his question towards Beau.

"An intervention," Beau said.

"Oh, shit, I almost forgot the sign," Tristan swore under his breath, and suddenly, he was reaching underneath his chair and whipping out a homemade paper sign he'd created by unevenly taping several pages together. On it was written, in bright pink Sharpie, the words, *Welcome to your intervention.*

"What the fuck is this?" Davis asked. He sounded edgy. Nervous. Right on the cusp of his temper flaring.

"Listen," Logan said, "we get it, okay? Players and coaches aren't supposed to date. It's bad."

"Super bad," Wade added.

"We're . . ." That was all Pax got out before Logan interrupted him again.

"Yeah, we know, you're not dating, we get it. That's why we're having this intervention. It's a *dating* intervention." Tristan pointed excitedly to the sign he was holding.

This is an intervention.

It wasn't an intervention so they'd drink less or work less or spend less time together.

It was an intervention so they'd spend *more* time together.

Paxton wanted to die.

Just sink through the floor and die.

"You're not supposed to, and you've been trying hard not to, we give you guys full points for keepin' your hands to yourself,"

Sebastian said. "But what we're trying to say is that maybe you shouldn't."

"Not *maybe*," Tristan said, tossing Sebastian a glare. "What we're saying is that you *should* put your hands in plenty of places you shouldn't. Lots of times. Rinse and repeat."

Pax stared at his friends with incredulous disbelief. Couldn't bring himself to look at Davis.

"You're . . . having an intervention so we . . ." He couldn't bring himself to say the words. *You're having an intervention so we finally fuck?*

"You were dealing with it, and again, props for doing it for so long," Logan said. "God knows I barely managed to control myself with Dylan."

"That's for sure," Wade said. "And everyone gives *us* shit!"

"What we're saying is that it's getting . . . that's what Coach always says, right? It doesn't matter what you do off the field, as long as it's not intruding onto the field." Logan paused. "It intruded yesterday."

Pax felt guilt swamp him. He'd lost it. Davis had lost it. It hadn't been pretty, there was no way around that, and no way around the fact that they'd all seen it.

"So, we were thinking, we'd have this little chat instead of Coach," Sebastian said. "It's intruding. It's gettin' in the way, and seriously, no judgment about that, like we said, you guys tried real hard, and maybe it's time to just . . . *not* try anymore."

Pax tried to unstick his words. "You're saying you want us to . . ." He swallowed hard. He couldn't even say it.

"You don't know what you're talking about," Davis said in a clipped voice. "This is completely ridiculous."

"But is it?" Sebastian demanded. "And yeah, if it was just an itch to scratch, sure, we'd tell you to go find someone else to fuck, and maybe you'd get over it. But that's . . . that's not your deal, guys. You know that."

Pax knew it. He knew his feelings ran deep. He loved Davis, more than he'd ever thought he could love anyone.

He'd resigned himself to never knowing what it felt like to just *be* with the man he loved, never knowing how it would feel to have his love reflected back when Davis reciprocated.

If Davis reciprocated. But he did, didn't he? He had to. There was no way so much misery only went one way.

"We're tellin' you," Wade said gently, "that we get it, and that you have our okay and our permission."

"No offense," Davis said sarcastically, "but it wasn't really *your* permission we were waiting for."

Everyone's gaze, Pax's included, swung to where Beau was standing, next to Sebastian.

He looked resigned more than surprised. "I'm not here in an official capacity," Beau said carefully, "but I'm not *not* either."

"What the hell is that supposed to mean?" Pax demanded.

"It means he doesn't even fucking know," Davis muttered. "I've heard enough, I'm leaving."

But Sebastian's hand shot out and gripped Davis' forearm. Tightly. Davis didn't fight it, but his jaw tightened. "It's bad form to leave an intervention in the middle," Sebastian said, "especially when it's *your* intervention."

Tristan waved the sign again, like being told again *this is your intervention* was going to somehow convince Davis to stay.

"What I mean," Beau said, "is that no, my dad doesn't know about this. But when Logan told me what y'all wanted to do, I didn't disagree. He did give us all that same speech, didn't he? *What happens off the field stays off the field?* But it's not with you two. Not anymore. So it makes perfectly logical sense to me, to do what you need to do to change the status quo. In your case, that's not keeping your hands off each other, it's . . . well, it's putting them *on* each other." Beau almost looked apologetic.

"You're not gonna get official permission," Sebastian said, "but this is as official as it's gonna get."

"And what, we take your *permission*," Davis said, his voice going hard and unrelenting when he hit the last word, "but when we get found out, how much water does that hold? I don't want to get fired. And I don't want Pax to pay for this."

Pax was surprised. So surprised that for the first time he looked at Davis—really *looked* at him, since Tristan had held up that stupid-ass sign. He looked torn.

You knew it wasn't just you.

But he didn't look nearly convinced enough.

Pax was ready to take Davis' hand and leave and start the putting-their-hands-on-each-other part of the program *immediately* but he still looked agonized. Conflicted.

Pax wanted to shake him and say, *isn't this what you wanted, more than anything, because it's here and somehow you're still fighting it, that's crazy.*

"Then make sure nobody else finds out," Beau said.

Maybe if he hadn't spent the last four months trying to pretend he wasn't feeling the way he was, Pax might've balked more at starting a relationship with Davis and hiding it from everyone.

But his mind kept tripping over the one thing—*starting a relationship with Davis.*

"It's your call, we just thought we'd give you . . ." Logan said, and Dylan finished with, "A much needed push."

"Yeah, a little push. Encouragement, even," Sebastian added.

"But it's up to you two, of course," Tristan said in a rush, even though he hadn't let go of that stupid sign yet.

"And we brought you something that might help, if you *do* decide to give it a go," Logan added. He made a gesture towards the bartender, who was suddenly setting a big cardboard box on the bar.

Logan grabbed it and put it down in front of Pax. He peered inside.

"My stupid brother got me these when I started dating Dylan," Logan explained. "They're date boxes. Like . . . ideas of things to do, questions to help you get to know each other, activities, music, just stuff that's . . . *nice* to do. That's all. And we've got so goddamn many we've run out of room in the hall closet, so we thought we'd gift you a few."

Disbelief was written across Davis' face. "You think we need to do *activities* together?"

Personally, Pax could only think of one activity that he desperately wanted to do.

A whole fucking lot.

"We think you should do *something*," Dylan retorted.

"A-fucking-men," Sebastian echoed.

"Y'all are crazy," Paxton said. *Crazy and amazing, and I love you. Even if it never goes anywhere, even if Davis never gives in . . . this'll always mean everything.*

"Maybe, a little," Logan conceded with a grin.

"Not just a little," Davis said in a hard voice. "There could be consequences for this. You could get into trouble. Big trouble." He shot a look right at Beau. "Especially you."

Beau didn't look nervous though. He looked the opposite. "If I pay for this, then I pay for it," he said. "I still think it's the right thing to do. Sometimes the best path forward means breaking the rules."

"Well, enjoy the date boxes," Logan said. "Dylan and I have a flight to catch and . . ." He hesitated, a sly amused expression lighting up his face. "And I'm sure y'all have a lot of other *important* things to get to."

"Yeah." Tristan grinned impudently and took Wade's hand as they faded into the crowd on the dance floor.

"Definitely," Sebastian said, and he was looking right at Beau, who was gazing back like he never wanted to look anywhere else.

And suddenly, with their bomb dropped, everyone left, and it was just him and Davis and a whole cardboard box full of date boxes sitting at his feet.

"They're insane," Davis muttered.

Pax had thought all his anger had burned itself out, but he felt a spark of it now, again.

"Not that insane," he said.

Davis shot him an incredulous look. "Less than two weeks ago, Coach pulled me into his office and asked me if this was going to be a problem. If it *was* a problem. I had to tell him no. You understand that, right?"

Paxton nodded. He'd wondered, late at night, when he couldn't sleep, and he went over that day, that fight they'd had, the lies that Davis had tried to tell him, and only one explanation ever made sense: Davis had done it for him. To prevent him from showing up at Coach's office and giving away his way-too-obvious feelings.

From telling Coach that Davis was his person. In every single way that mattered.

"I do get it," Pax said slowly, "but I also get what Beau said."

"I don't," Davis said. "I'm done having this conversation."

He turned to go, and Pax felt a surge of something—it wasn't just anger, but frustration and this undeniable sense of stubbornness, that he wasn't going to let this go. Not again. Not ever.

"No," he said. Pax picked up the box—he wasn't going to leave it, not when the possibility existed, even as miniscule as it seemed that they could work this shit out—and followed him. "No, you don't get to do this again."

Exasperation crossed Davis' face. "I'm doing this for you," he argued as he headed down the stairs towards the ground level.

"Yeah, except you don't get to say what's best for me, that's not your call." Pax juggled the box from one hand to the other, pushing the downstairs door open with force so it wouldn't swing closed.

Davis turned. Frustration was etched on every single one of his handsome features.

There was nothing that Pax liked to see more than Davis' face. Even like this, even when he was trying to push him away.

Because that was what he'd done before, when they'd fought. In some completely and utterly selfless move, he'd been trying to do the noble thing.

But Pax had a stake in this, too, and he wasn't going to let Davis sacrifice both of their happiness, not without saying what was in his heart.

His resolve hardened inside of him.

"This is just the way it needs to be," Davis said.

He didn't sound happy about it, but he also sounded unbearably certain.

"Listen," Pax said, but Davis was already turning away again. "Goddamnit, stop walking away from me and just *listen*."

He didn't think Davis would, but he actually did. He stopped, right in the middle of the sidewalk down the block from Hibiscus.

"If you want me to listen, then talk," Davis said, turning around.

They were already halfway to their building, and part of Pax wanted to say *no, can't we just do this when we're in private and there's no one potentially listening in, and I'm not on the spot like this?*

But he had a feeling that if he told him they needed to wait, like they'd been waiting for months, the window would pass, and he'd never have an opportunity to say what was in his heart.

Pax put the box down. This stupid box. Why hadn't he left it upstairs? Made Logan take it back? Hope. That was why he was dragging it around with him. He still had hope that they could fix this thing between them, maybe even make it better.

"Here's the thing," Pax said, shoving his hands in his pockets. "I . . . I love you. I care a hell of a lot about you. I know we had a . . . well, a thing, almost, from the very beginning. I shook your hand, and I never wanted to let go. But then you sat down next to me, and you said everything I needed to hear. Not what I wanted to hear, but what I *needed* to hear. It felt like you were the only one who saw me, who really saw Paxton Kelly, and wanted to see *him*, and talk to *him*. You wanted me to be better, but it was because you gave a shit about *me*, not because you wanted the Piranhas to win football games. And I love you for that. And I love you because I want to start touching you and never stop. And I love you because you listen to me bitch about *Grey's Anatomy* and about how Blake always steals the last of the pretzels in the quarterback room. But mostly I love you because you're my person, goddamnit, even if you don't want to be, and that's not going to change. Doesn't matter if we never do anything about it, doesn't matter if a year down the road we don't even talk. Doesn't matter if you're my coach, or not my coach. It doesn't matter if you want to hear it or you don't. I love you anyway, and I always will."

Mic drop, Pax thought, an exhilarating combination of freedom and terror whirling through him as he stared at Davis, who hadn't said a word. Who'd barely even blinked.

Probably because he'd said all of that to him on the sidewalk of a busy Miami street.

What had he been thinking?

You were thinking you should've said it ages ago. You knew it ages ago.

But Davis just stood there. Staring, his gaze almost unbearably intense. Like he couldn't bear to look away.

"Come on," he finally said, his voice low and rough. He turned and Pax couldn't do anything but follow, picking up the box of dates and chasing after him as he ate up the city blocks with his long stride.

It took less than five minutes to get to their building.

Paxton didn't know where he was going in such a goddamn hurry, but how could he do anything else but chase after him?

He reached the lobby, and crossed it, picking up speed as he went, barely giving Arnold, the concierge on duty at the desk, a glance.

Arnold was used to rich, eccentric people, but Pax still hoped that he wouldn't think Davis was being rude—usually he stopped and chatted. At least had a nice word to say.

But not today.

Today, Davis pressed the elevator button with determination.

He didn't glance over at Pax once.

Even if he did, Pax wasn't sure he could figure out what the fuck was happening. All he was doing was following, helplessly.

The elevator dinged, and they walked in.

Davis reached out and immediately pushed the button to close the doors. He clearly did not want to be bothered with anyone else.

The floors ticked away. Davis still hadn't looked at him, but Pax couldn't look anywhere else.

He stared at his profile, the words he'd repeated clanging in his head over and over.

Here's the thing. I love you.

I love you anyway. And I always will.

With anyone else, in any other scenario, Pax might've worried that he was being dragged to a quiet place, just the two of them, so Davis could let him down easy—and maybe he was imagining it, or wishing for it so hard he believed it might be true—but there was an anticipatory edge to the silence.

The floors ticked by, and finally, the elevator opened on Davis' floor.

Pax didn't know if he was supposed to follow him, but before he could ask, his hand whipped out and closed around Pax's wrist, the calloused fingers sliding roughly over the skin there, making him shiver.

He tugged him out of the elevator and down the few dozen yards towards Davis' door.

He tapped in his code, pushed the door open and Pax followed him in, still carrying that stupid box like it was a lifeline.

The door closed behind him, and Davis let go of his wrist, gently pulling the box out of his other hand. Setting it down.

Pax didn't know what was going to happen—he knew what he *wanted*, but that seemed almost too good to be true, an impossibility he kept trying to will to life with all the fierce desire bubbling inside of him—but truly, the last thing he expected was for Davis to move closer to him.

To push right into his personal space, until they were as close as they were when they danced in Floria's studio. Then Davis reached up and cupped his cheek with his palm.

Pax gasped at the sudden feel of it, skin pressing to skin. Every time they touched, he knew why they didn't. Because it felt so goddamned good. But this time, Davis didn't flinch, didn't move away. Instead he took another half a step closer, until *yes*, those were his hips against Pax's, his shoulder against Davis' collarbone, his shoe bumping Davis' own.

Davis stared at him, deep in the eyes, for one last moment, and then he closed the final inch between them.

For a heart-stopping moment, Pax couldn't move, couldn't breathe, couldn't do anything but just *feel*: Davis' lips against his own, surprisingly soft and shockingly gentle, the hand cupping his cheek trembling with the sweetness of it.

Pax had always imagined if they broke down, if they crossed the line into mistake territory, that it would be hot and wild and undeniable. But this was so sweet, a slide into the inevitable, the rightness of it overpowering him.

Davis pulled back a fraction, and Pax nearly chased his lips with his own. Surely he would get more than that, surely this wasn't a sweet goodbye kiss. Or was it? Was he doing it once, because he couldn't bear to do anything less, only to tell him that was the last time?

But then Pax really looked, and there were lines in Davis' face, tension-filled and pained, smoothing out. A soft, fulfilled happiness in his eyes he'd never seen there before.

"I wanted to do this a thousand times," he finally murmured into the miniscule space between them, "so many fucking times. But I never did it, I always stopped myself, but it was never as hard as it was when you told me . . . when you told me you loved me. You love me, when I love you so . . ." Davis hesitated, and Pax felt joy surge through him. He'd *known,* of course that he wasn't alone but to hear it . . . "I just *knew* I had to do this, and I thought, the whole time, when we were walking back here, that if I hesitated for even a moment, that I wouldn't, that it wasn't right, that I was making a mistake. But I never thought it. Not even for a moment. I wanted it even more the second the door closed."

Pax had nothing he could possibly add. Happiness—and *freedom*—swelled through him in a dizzying rush, the realization dawning on him that he could do anything he wanted now. Nothing was off-limits.

He reached up and tugged Davis' mouth down towards his, and this time there was no hesitancy, and though it *was* sweet, it was so much hotter too, their mouths working together in perfect unison, like they'd been made for each other.

Pax's hands dug into Davis' hair, and he stumbled backwards, his back hitting the door.

It was *almost* enough just to do this, kiss and kiss and kiss, his tongue stroking Davis'—'cause goddamn the man could kiss, and it wasn't like Pax hadn't had secret hopes and expectations of this moment and he was still blowing them right out of the water—but then Davis' thigh pushed against his, pressing him firmly back against the door, and oh *God*, that was the hard line of his cock. Pax could feel it, after so long of only imagining it. Almost brushing up against his own, throbbing and ready in his own jeans.

Davis froze, and Pax realized that he must've stopped moving too. Must've stopped kissing back. The sudden and insane rush of desire paralyzing him. He'd never wanted anything more in his entire life than to strip Davis naked and touch him everywhere.

Pax's hand curled around Davis' waist, and tugged him back in, pulling up his t-shirt at the same time that Davis' hands, hot and rough, pushed up under his own shirt.

It was one thing to look at his broad shoulders, at the ridges of muscle that always drew his eye, it was another entirely to touch. To trace his fingertips across them.

To swallow Davis' moan with his own mouth as he touched him everywhere he could reach.

They only broke apart for a second so Davis could yank Pax's shirt off, and then they were back on each other, even more ravenous than before, Davis' mouth moving eagerly against his own.

Then Davis' thigh nudged him again, this time right where he wanted it, big and firm and right against his hard cock, and Pax's head fell against the door as he groaned with the pleasure of it.

His dark blue eyes gleamed with determination and delight, and the curl of his lips, red and wet and swollen from Pax's own, was sexy enough that arousal shot through him, making him even impossibly harder.

Trailing his hand down his chest, Davis stopped right where he wanted him more than he wanted to take his next breath.

He was one hungry moment away from just plain begging for it, when Davis trailed his fingertips across the hot ridge of his cock in his jeans.

Then with a twist of his wrist, he popped the button, and pulled the zipper down.

With trembling fingers, Pax mirrored his actions. The button. The zipper. But Davis was half a step ahead of him, and everything he wanted to do fell away, lost and forgotten, when he felt Davis press a palm against his aching cock.

It shouldn't have felt any different than any hand in the world, even his own, but just *knowing* it belonged to this man, to this man he adored and loved and worshipped, made him tremble with the force of the pleasure surging through him.

Davis pushed down his boxer briefs, following his jeans, and then it wasn't just the impression of heat and pressure, but he could feel every ridge and callous on his palm as he began to stroke him.

Not carefully, not hesitantly, but with purpose, like what he wanted more than anything was to overwhelm him with pleasure.

Like he'd never wanted anything else.

Pax gasped.

He fumbled with Davis' shorts, pushing them down, and realized, at the last second, that he wasn't wearing underwear. And that he was big, barely fitting into Pax's hand as he touched him, thumb circling the head, gathering the precome welling there.

Davis didn't look away, didn't blink, his heated gaze boring holes into Pax's own. Like he'd done too much looking away, like he couldn't do it a second longer, now that they were finally allowing themselves this.

Pax understood.

How many times had he forced himself to glance away? Because it was too much? Because it wasn't just one or the other, pain or pleasure, but it was both, mingled together? Too much yearning, not enough hope that anything might actually come of it?

Too many.

But he wasn't looking away now.

Pax let go for a second to bring his palm to his mouth to lick, and felt Davis' shudder as he returned, pumping him hard and fast, feeling every inch of him.

How would it feel to have all of that fill him up? There'd be no place left that he hadn't touched, inside and out, and suddenly, Pax wanted it so badly he could barely gasp out one breath after another, as it felt like Davis wrung his orgasm out of him.

"Yeah, *God*, sweetheart, give it to me," Davis crooned, speaking for the first time since they'd started kissing, the edge of his voice rough and desperate.

Pax's orgasm was right there, so close he could nearly taste it, but when Davis was calling him sweetheart, it was all over, and he shouted, the pleasure was so intense. Davis leaned in and kissed him then, kissed away his moans and Pax felt him stiffen too, and then he was groaning along with him.

Their kisses didn't stop as they worked through every last drop of the pleasure.

There'd been so much pain, it felt good to revel in this.

When Davis finally pulled away, he barely moved, his forehead tipping against Pax's, resting there.

For a long moment, neither of them spoke.

I don't even know what to say; maybe we both said too much.

Except it hadn't felt like too much at the time. It had felt perfect, like just enough.

"I love you," Davis said.

And oh, *that* was perfect. How had he known that Pax wanted those words? Wanted to swallow them up, and hoard them and never forget them?

"I love you, too," Pax said. "For a long time. Maybe since you went jogging and came back and weren't wearing a shirt."

Davis laughed, and for so long, his laugh had always felt hushed and small, like he was afraid to feel it, like he was terrified to let happiness in. But this was totally different, like he wasn't trying to hide it anymore.

"Me not wearing a shirt does it for you, huh?" Davis teased quietly.

Pax glanced down. His shorts were around his ankles, his cock was still resting in his messy hand, he wasn't sure he'd even caught all his come in it, and yet none of that had mattered. It had splattered up towards his abs, on the trail of hair that led downwards.

"Yes," he said. "You're so fucking perfect."

Davis groaned a little, and leaned in, clearly not caring about any of the mess either, tucking his head into the crook of Pax's neck. "That's you, sweetheart. How I kept my hands off'a you . . . I still don't know."

"Me either," Pax teased. "I'm the hottest new quarterback in the NFL."

Davis leaned back and the look in his eyes grew dark and intense again. "Don't need to remind *me*," he said.

Pax had never really believed anything people said. He looked in the mirror and saw . . . well, he saw *him*. Nothing particularly special. But when Davis looked at him . . . the yearning in his gaze, the incredulity and disbelief that he was *his* . . . he believed it now.

"Come on," Davis said. "Let's go clean up."

It was a mess. Undeniably a mess.

Literally. Metaphorically. But Pax found he didn't really care.

Still, he didn't exactly complain when Davis shed the rest of his clothes and headed deeper into his condo, towards the master bedroom—and its attached bathroom.

Or when Davis flipped the shower on and glanced back, the worship in his gaze lighting him up inside like he hadn't just come his brains out. "You gettin' in with me?" he asked softly.

And all Pax could do was nod.

They were in this, in the shower, and in *this*, no matter what. The die was cast. They both knew it.

There was no going back now.

Chapter Ten

How many times had Davis stood in this shower, under the hot spray of the nozzle, and imagined that Pax would follow him in here?

So many goddamned times.

And now it was happening, and yet Davis still felt a whisper of disbelief as Pax reached up and curled his palm around his shoulder, tucking himself in close until the spray was hitting both of them.

Pax was always beautiful, but he was fucking gorgeous wet. Then there was the look in his eyes, the quiet joy, the way he no longer held back the love in his gaze.

You don't have to, either, not now, Davis realized with a start.

"I just want you to know," Pax said, as Davis reached for the soap, "that none of this is happening because of the intervention. I should've just . . . *said* how I felt, ages ago."

Davis shot him a wry look. "You mean, when you told me in that hallway that I was your person."

"It was Coach I was going to say it to," Pax reminded him, groaning a little as Davis put his hands—and the soap—all over him, his chest, his thighs, and in between them, washing him carefully. Shit, when they were clean, and maybe even a little dry, he was going to put his mouth on him.

See how loud he could make his man scream. He had a feeling that Paxton could be plenty loud if properly motivated.

The truth was, Pax had always been his, long before he'd ever touched him.

"And you know why that would've been crazy and stupid, right?" Davis said. Trying real hard to follow the thread of the conversation, because he didn't just love touching Pax and hearing those incredible sounds fall out of his mouth as he fell apart, but he loved talking to him to. Always had, from the very first. It was why he'd known this wasn't just insane, off-the-fucking-charts lust. It was so much more than that. It had always been more than that, though the lust certainly hadn't made the situation any easier.

He'd reached out to shake his hand, and that single touch, only one hand clasped in another, had lit a fire inside of him that he'd never been able to quench.

"I do," Pax said seriously. "I still wanted to say it."

"Course you did," Davis said with a low chuckle. "Come on, sweetheart. Rinse off."

Pax's eyes fluttered open, golden brown and full of a quiet, satisfied happiness that Davis had never been prouder to put there. "You like callin' me that."

Oh, he did. He fucking loved it.

"Yeah," he admitted.

"Kinda think . . . kinda *hope* . . . you're a romantic," Pax teased as he turned around, rinsing off.

Davis got a long look at the pale muscular line of Pax's back, the way it curved into the irresistible swell of his ass. God, he was so gorgeous. And he could touch now, that was allowed. Well, not *allowed*. If Coach found out, he would be pissed off. There would be consequences. But here, in the privacy of his own place, he could. That was the line he was allowing himself to cross. Allowing both of them to cross.

"For you, anything," Davis said. And yeah, that was really fucking romantic, wasn't it? God, he was a sap. Not for anyone. Definitely not with any of the other guys he'd been with. But for Pax? *Anything.*

Pax's smile made everything—every risk, every potential pitfall—worth it. Then he reached for the soap and began to clean *him*. Honestly, feeling his hands sliding across his body, after so long never being touched, of avoiding people, Davis couldn't even put it into words. It felt indescribable.

How had they ever avoided this?

"Do we . . ." Pax hesitated, even as he slid the soap downward, carefully cleaning Davis off, in every nook and cranny, like he too had plans for later. "Do we need to talk about this?"

"About me being your person?"

Pax grinned.

"I'm your person too, you know."

"I kinda assumed," Davis said.

"Come on, rinse," Pax said, and Davis dutifully turned around, letting the water cascade down him. It didn't feel nearly as good as Pax's hands.

But then nothing did.

"But no," Pax continued after Davis flipped off the water and reached for towels. "I don't mean exactly that, though I suppose it's a way of looking at it. I mean . . . this isn't a one-off kind of thing, is it?"

Davis was sure that Pax believed he had a decent enough poker face.

Davis was here to inform him that he did not. Not even remotely. It was obvious from the uncertainty in his eyes that he was worried Davis would take all of this back.

Well, it wasn't entirely Pax's fault for thinking that. After all, they'd fought against this long enough. And just an hour earlier, during that god-awful intervention, Davis had still been determined not to let anything happen.

But then Pax had given him that crazy speech, had told him he loved him, and what was he supposed to do? He'd been so lonely and so completely, utterly miserable for so long, all those months, hiding out in his house out in the country, and now there was a chance he could be happy. Really fucking happy. Was he supposed to continue denying that? When it was clear that Pax felt the exact same way he did?

Davis didn't know if it was because he wasn't strong enough to resist it—or maybe that he was strong enough to accept it, risks and all, but whichever way it was, he knew that something had to change.

In the end, the decision had been so clear it wasn't really a decision at all.

He'd kissed Pax, and *everything* had changed.

"Trust me, this is not a one-off thing," Davis said. "Did you think it could be?"

Pax laughed, that uncertainty disappearing from his golden-brown eyes completely—replaced by a fierce mischievousness. "No," he admitted. "No, but maybe I still wanted you to say it."

Finishing drying off, Davis tossed the towel in the hamper, and turned back to Pax. He was naked as the day he was born, and maybe, right after Coach had called him, when he'd been living like a recluse and not exercising as much as he should've, he might have been nervous about that.

But then Pax had never judged. In fact, Pax had taken one look at him without a shirt on, in the hallway of that tiny little condo, and the expression on his face had been unmistakable: he'd wanted to eat him alive, even back then.

"Then I'll say it," Davis said softly. "I'm yours. No matter what happens. No matter what the fallout is. I'm yours, for as long as you want me, and probably a hell of a lot longer than that."

Pax's smile was soft. Sweet. Irresistible. He reached out and pulled Davis closer, and the frisson of awareness that rocketed through him, of his naked skin pressed against Pax's, was like electricity. "I think," he said, "we pretty much established that I'm yours, too."

"Yeah, who knew you had some kind of epic speech in you?" Davis teased. "Maybe you should start giving the pregame speech, instead of Coach."

"No way." Pax shuddered lightly. "I'm not normally good at that, but . . . it was easy with you 'cause I've known what I wanted to say to you forever."

The truth of his words, the honesty in his eyes, those things shouldn't have made Davis' throat grow tight or make it hard to even *breathe*, but they did.

He hadn't even known he was looking for this; it certainly hadn't even been on his radar when he'd arrived in Miami, but now he was sure of one thing—Pax was his miracle.

He'd brought him back to life, even when he hadn't wanted to.

But he didn't have the finesse with language that Pax apparently did, so instead of trying to say everything he couldn't put into words, he leaned down and pressed his mouth against Pax's.

He'd intended for it to be a sweet kiss, soft and tender, and reassuring of all the things he hadn't been able to say. But almost immediately it turned so much hotter than he'd anticipated.

Those were his hands, weren't they, sliding down Pax's back, and digging into his ass, yanking him closer as the kiss turned ravenous.

You spent too long wanting him and not having him, Davis' mind supplied, *it's fine, it's good, you can go with this.*

Pax certainly seemed down with going with it. He was panting into Davis' mouth, and his hand had already found Davis' cock, and between his kisses and the way Pax was pressed against him, and the exploratory touches of his fingertips, he was definitely getting hard again.

Then Pax dropped his towel to the marble floor and followed it, glancing up with a hot, mischievous look that pushed Davis from *I'm kinda turned on, what are we gonna do about it?* to *we need to fuck, right now.*

Before he could ask, it was clear what Pax intended to do about it.

The first touch of Pax's tongue, flicking out to touch just the tip of his dick, sent pleasure rushing through him in a dizzying wave.

Then his fingers and his tongue were everywhere, the pressure still light, as he explored his length, like they had all the time in the world. Like there was no rush, even though Davis was pretty sure he wasn't going to last nearly that long. Pax's touch felt that good.

"I . . . uh . . ." Davis stammered.

Pax's glance was knowing. "What, you don't like having your dick sucked?"

"Course I do," he said, rolling his eyes. "I just . . ."

"Then stop protesting," Pax teased, "and enjoy it."

He knew he was bigger than most guys. He didn't really think about it most of the time, but for a moment, he almost considered apologizing, because he knew it made blowjobs harder, but there was zero hesitation on Pax's part as he slid his mouth around him and began to suck.

And then Davis didn't think—or worry—about anything at all, because the suction was fucking perfect, Pax's mouth around him the most glorious thing he'd ever felt.

He squeezed his eyes shut and his hands drifted down, tangling in Pax's hair, and he groaned around Davis' cock, and impossibly, that was even better.

Pax's fingers curled around the base of his dick, working him as he sucked, and he already knew he wasn't going to be able to last much longer. It felt too damned good, Pax dedicating himself to sucking his cock like he dedicated himself to being the best possible quarterback he could be.

If he looked down . . . if he saw Pax with his mouth full of cock, with his mouth full of *his* cock, the way he'd fantasized about way too many times, it was going to be game over.

But the temptation to not just feel him, but to see him, to see the irrefutable evidence that Pax wanted him as much as he wanted Pax . . . it was irresistible.

He opened his eyes and let them drift downwards, down to the fucking sexiest sight he'd ever seen in his life.

It wasn't just the wet dream–inducing material of Pax sucking his cock, it was the downright bliss on his face, like this was all he'd ever wanted.

Like he could stay here forever, kneeling on Davis' cold bathroom floor, if he got to keep touching him.

How had he gotten so incredibly fucking lucky? He didn't know, but he was going to work hard to earn it.

He was just settling into the mind-numbing pleasure of it, the push and pull of Pax's movements, trying to prolong the sweet, dirty joy of it, when Pax slid a moistened finger back, behind his balls, and pressed right against his hole, and that was all it took.

He lost it.

His orgasm rushed through him so quickly he barely had time to give an extra hard yank of warning to Pax's hair, but he must've been okay with it, because he swallowed convulsively around Davis' cock as he came so hard his vision whited out.

It went on and on, the drugging pleasure spiraling out as Pax sucked him dry.

When it finally ended, his soft cock slipping from Pax's mouth, he looked down, and if he hadn't just come as hard as he ever had, he'd have been hard again in an instant.

Pax was touching himself, his hand working his cock up and down, the head flushed red and shiny with come as it peeked through his fist.

"Oh, God," Davis said unsteadily.

Pax gazed up at him with love and lust mingled in his eyes, and it felt like a complete no-brainer to reach down, tug him up, and pull him through the doorway into his bedroom.

He pushed him down onto the bed, and the whole time—the whole fucking time—Pax hadn't let go of himself, like without the pressure he'd die.

Well, if Davis didn't make him scream, *he* was gonna be the one suffering. He could already tell.

Pax's gaze was glazed over, a string of saliva dripping off his swollen bottom lip, and it was the sexiest thing Davis had ever witnessed.

He pushed Pax back even further onto the bed, and climbed over him, leaning down to kiss him. He tasted himself, the salty-sweet tang of it, and his cock throbbed, wanting another go at him immediately.

"Do you like that?" Davis asked roughly, lifting his head, even though it was *very* obvious that he did. The look on his face, and the hard cock in his hand made it clear.

Pax nodded wordlessly.

"I bet you'd like this even more," Davis said, and slid a hand down, tangling his fingers with Pax's own. And then slowly, he began to move with Pax's own rhythm.

Pax groaned then, head tipping back, and Davis gripped him harder, worked him faster. Oh, yeah, he liked that a lot. It was clear from how much louder he got. He liked it rough. And Davis was gonna figure out just how rough, and how well he could take it. He'd stretch him out, one finger, pumping slow, at a time, until he was begging for his cock. Then he'd give it to him as wild and rough as he wanted it.

"Yeah, sweetheart." Davis was surprised at how deep and guttural his voice sounded. How primal. "Come for me."

Pax would've screamed—Davis was sure of it—except that he'd seemingly lost his voice, and as his come pumped out of him, wetting their fingers, droplets spraying onto his chest, his mouth opened in a silent yell.

The sex had been all-consuming and so intense that Davis wasn't surprised when he came back with a wet cloth to help Pax clean up, his eyes were soft and drowsy as he lay there.

Just where he'd always belonged: in Davis' bed.

Davis finished cleaning him off, and tossed that into the hamper, and then settled back into bed, pulling Pax close with one arm.

For a long moment—for minutes, maybe—neither of them said anything.

Maybe words aren't necessary. Maybe you said everything you needed to say, except you didn't say it at all.

"I've only dreamt about doing that for months," Pax finally said in a quiet, contemplative voice.

"Maybe you should've just dropped to your knees and done it back then," Davis said with a chuckle.

"It's looking like I should've," Pax said seriously.

"But I'm glad we did it now," Davis said. "And not just because I've just had two of the best orgasms of my whole fucking life today."

"Yeah, I mean . . . that was all amazing. So fucking amazing. But this?" Pax paused, squirming a little closer into the circle of Davis' arms. "This is really great, too."

That tight-throat emotion was back, squeezing him so firmly that he couldn't reply. Not right away. Not the way he wanted.

"Me too," he finally said.

Pax was quiet for a few moments longer. "You have any big plans for the bye week?"

"Study more game film. Work out. Maybe go to the beach. You?" He hadn't really made plans, because before the last two weeks, he'd assumed that whatever he did, it would be with Pax. And then Pax had gotten pissed off, and he'd been stuck in this rut of trying to get Pax out of it, without actually changing anything about their relationship.

Well, he wasn't pissed now, and it had *definitely* changed.

"I hadn't really thought about it," Pax said slowly. "Guess I was too busy being angry with you. You know what I'm thinking, though?"

Davis hummed under his breath.

"I'm thinking we don't have anyone we have to see, anywhere we have to be. At least for a few days. Can't we just . . . be here?"

Yeah, that emotion was definitely constricting his throat something fierce. Davis had only experienced that feeling once before, and it hadn't been because someone wanted to be with him, just with him. It had been because someone—a whole team of someones—hadn't wanted him at all.

"Yeah," Davis said.

He could feel Pax's smile against his pectoral muscle.

Could feel his own, as the tension inside him kept slowly unspooling. Just when he thought he'd reached peace, it unraveled a little bit more. Davis realized he hadn't even known just how much shit he was carrying around, because right now, he felt so unbelievably light.

"I like the sound of the beach though. And getting takeout. And watching *Grey's* together. And . . ." Pax hesitated. "And maybe even doing one of those date boxes that Logan gave us."

Davis never thought he'd want to be that guy.

But now, he was beginning to see that was all he'd ever wanted with Pax. To be *that* guy. The one who was crazy about *his* guy, and wasn't ashamed of it. Not for a second. Maybe they couldn't give away their relationship outside of these four walls, but while they were inside of them? He didn't want to hold anything back. Not any longer.

"That sounds amazing, actually," Davis said softly, forcing the words out. "You want to do it now?"

You're not gonna cry, you're really not gonna do it, it's not like Pax would judge, because he'd never, but it's so . . . you don't want to be the kind of guy who cries because your man says he wants to keep you close.

"Really?" Pax sounded surprised. Surely he knew that this wasn't just sex. Surely, it felt just as good to him as it did to Davis to just lie here, touching.

"Well, we might've done that a bit out of order, 'cause aren't you supposed to have the date, and *then* have sex?" Davis wondered sheepishly. Had he already fucked this up? *God, don't fuck this up.*

"You'd want to have a date with me?" Pax asked in a quiet voice, full of wonder.

And Davis pulled him even closer, wrapping his arms around him and holding him against him as tightly as he could. "Yeah," he said. "Yeah. A lot of dates, okay?"

Pax pulled back, and grinned. "I love the sound of that." He was a little disappointed when Pax pulled away, though he was *less* disappointed when Pax pulled a t-shirt from his closet, and boxer briefs from his chest of drawers.

Watching Pax smile while wearing his clothes wasn't going to get old anytime soon.

He followed Pax into the kitchen, where he was bent over the box Logan had given him. It turned out it was full of a bunch of other boxes.

"Well," Davis said, "what are we doing?"

"I don't know," Pax said. "None of these are labeled. I guess we'll have to open a few and find out."

Davis helped, and it turned out that at the top of the box, there was a card that listed what additional supplies you'd need for each date.

"We can't do this one," Pax said, holding up the box he'd opened, "unless you have fresh mozzarella cheese in your fridge and a can of tomatoes hiding in your pantry."

"Unlikely," Davis admitted with a chuckle.

"I thought so," Pax said.

"But we *could* do this one." Davis extended the box towards Pax. "We just need water and milk, it says, which I've got plenty of, and it has everything else."

"Let's do it," Pax said.

They opened up the box on the kitchen counter.

"Oh, fun, we're tie-dyeing socks, and making homemade hot cocoa," Pax said, unpacking the box with more excitement than he'd expected. "And oh, look at this! They have a romantic playlist, too."

"I suppose we're gonna have to thank Logan for his donation," Davis said wryly as he pulled out the hot chocolate stuff separately. It *was* November, but it was November in Miami, which meant it wasn't really hot chocolate season. But that was okay, he could always push the thermostat down a few degrees. Might even convince Pax to cuddle with him some more, to conserve body heat.

Pax shot him a look. "If you're not interested in doing this . . ."

But that was the last thing Davis wanted him to think, so he pulled Pax in for a long, hot kiss. "No," he said firmly. "I've wanted to take you on a date for ages. It doesn't matter that we're probably going to permanently stain the sink and that it's way too warm for hot chocolate. The things themselves don't matter, just that I'm with you."

Pax's eyes lit happily. "Okay," he said. He got the playlist going, romantic music playing softly out his sound system, as Davis examined the instructions for the socks.

"I think I've got this," he said, setting out the different packets in order of usage.

"Do you think Logan and Dylan dyed socks?"

"I think Logan said they did a face scrub and a foot soak, and answered some questions," Pax said uncertainly.

"Questions? Oh, that must be these conversation starters," Pax said, waving a small, square card with writing on one side. "We're supposed to do these while the socks are dyeing."

"Well, let's get the socks going." Davis pulling out two sets of tube socks from the packaging.

They soaked the fabric with a solution of soda ash and water, and then wringing out the excess water, tied them off with rubber bands, and set about dyeing them.

"If I have to remodel this kitchen 'cause we destroyed it," Davis said, sticking out his tongue in concentration as he tried not to overturn the bowl of dye, "it'll be worth it."

Pax blushed. "One date with me and it would be worth it?"

Davis nudged him. "Yep, absolutely. But let's not destroy it, unless we have to, okay?"

They managed to avoid getting the dye anywhere, which Davis considered a minor miracle, and then after they left the socks to dry on a piece of plastic sheeting, turned their attention to the hot cocoa.

This wasn't so hard, because he was decent enough in the kitchen to be able to heat up hot milk and then stir in chocolate, topping each mug with too many fluffy marshmallows.

"This is actually really good," Pax said, sipping the hot liquid as they settled into the living room to have their "conversation starters."

"Like we need *help* starting a conversation," Davis grumbled as he set his mug down on the coffee table in front of them.

"I don't know, I'm pretty interested to hear your answers," Pax said. "First question. What do you think is the single most important thing for a relationship to be successful?"

That was easy.

"Love and communication," Davis said promptly. Not only because those were probably the "right" answers, but because they were also true.

Not that he knew much about successful relationships.

Pax rolled his eyes, and shoved an elbow into his side. "This isn't a test you're trying to pass, Davis."

"What! I thought those were good answers," he yelped, trying to avoid Pax's elbows, which were surprisingly sharp. "Not that I know jack shit about how to do a relationship right, but I always thought . . . you gotta remember that you love the other person. Even when you don't like them very much."

"I'd agree with that. And the communication. Though I'd add, *honesty*," Pax said teasingly. "Like I was very honest today."

"Are you gonna take credit for the start of our relationship forever?"

Forever, Davis thought, *that sounds really fucking nice.*

Pax didn't bat an eye. "Absofuckinglutely."

"Alright. Well, next question?"

"If you could wake up tomorrow morning with any new skill or ability, what would you choose?" Pax asked seriously.

"No fair that I always have to go first," Davis said, scrambling to think of something that wasn't the first thing he thought of—which was, of course, football. Being good enough at football that nobody ever wanted to get rid of him. There was no reason he had to be a Debbie Downer on his first real date with Pax. "What would *you* choose?"

"That's easy," Pax said with a grin. "The ability to keep my hips *real* loose."

Davis laughed. "Okay, you got that one." He hesitated, then decided that if he was going to say this, he could only say it to one person, and that was who he was *about* to say it to. "I guess I'd want to wake up and not . . . care anymore. To, like, permanently not give a shit about people who say crappy things about me."

Pax's gaze turned solemn and he reached out, grasping Davis' arm, tugged him into a tight hug. "Any time you need one of these," he said softly, "I can't promise it's gonna erase all that shit, because I know it can't, but I know whenever you touch me, it always helps me feel better . . ."

"Thanks, sweetheart," Davis murmured. "It does help. And I'll probably take you up on that."

"You do that," Pax said.

It was an inherently silly date—tie-dyed socks and hot chocolate confessions—but it was also the best date of Davis' whole life.

Pax woke up early.

His very first thought was the *feel* of the darkened room he was in felt both familiar and strange, and then his second was that a very warm arm was draped across him.

As his eyes finally adjusted to the dim light, flashes of the night before came back to him.

He'd said all those things to Davis. He'd stood there, his heart in Davis' hands, and then he'd *finally,* gloriously kissed him.

Pax had a pretty damn good imagination, but even he never could've imagined how unbelievably wonderful each moment of coming together felt like.

Like he was coming home.

They'd slipped in and out of consciousness while cuddling after their date ended. They'd talked when they wanted to, and didn't when they had nothing to say. Pax didn't think he'd ever felt more comfortable with a person in his whole damn life.

After they'd finished their date box, Davis had ordered pizza—pepperoni mushroom, *no olives*—and they'd curled up on the couch to eat it, while an episode of *Grey's* had played.

There hadn't even been a discussion of Pax going back to his own condo.

He'd assumed that he'd stay, and Davis had acted like the place he belonged was right there, in bed next to him.

They'd fallen asleep that way, and Pax would've sworn that you couldn't sleep with a smile on your face, but the way his cheeks were aching this morning made him think that you actually could, and he totally had.

Turning over, he saw Davis, still sleeping. His arm had shifted when Pax had rolled over, but it returned, seeking him out like it was instinctual and natural. Like he didn't want to let him go, even for a moment.

Pax felt . . . treasured. Wanted. Desired. *Loved.*

Sweetheart, Davis had called him.

And that had felt right, too.

The future might be full of unknowns but he knew one thing, unquestionably: that he was Davis' and Davis was his.

Whatever happened, they had each other.

For a while, he just watched as Davis slept. His face was peaceful, and from his angle, Pax could swear he was smiling, too. Happiness wasn't something he'd automatically recognized on Davis' face, but he saw it now, and it magnified his own, knowing that he'd brought that kind of joy to him, when he'd needed it most.

Sure, they couldn't tell anyone. But Pax didn't give a fuck who knew, as long as when the door to this haven closed, they could still have each other.

He'd been so absorbed in the way the sunlight played across Davis' features, the way he was allowed to look now, as long as he liked, with no fear that he'd be caught, that he didn't even realize that he'd woken up.

"I wanna think," Davis said, his eyes flickering open slowly, "that you staring at me and watchin' me sleep is creepy, but . . ."

"But?"

Davis' arm tightened across him.

"But I'm so goddamned glad you're here, you can be creepy all day long and I don't give a shit."

Pax chuckled. "Is that how it's gonna be?"

"Yeah, yeah I think so." Davis' gaze was sweet. So goddamned sweet and open. It was almost like Pax was seeing him for the very first time. *He's never let himself look at you, not like this, not if you could see him looking,* Pax realized.

And so for a long moment, he just looked, and let Davis look back.

There was nobody to stop them here, no rules, no guidelines, nothing to tear them apart again.

Then his stomach grumbled, and Davis laughed. "Hold that thought," he said, and to Pax's disappointment, he pulled his arm back and slipped out of bed. "I'll be right back."

He'd been about to protest, say that hunger could wait, that this moment was forever, but before he could, Davis was gone.

Pax could hear noise coming from the general vicinity of the kitchen, and when Davis re-appeared in the doorway, about ten minutes later, balancing several plates on one arm and holding a pair of coffee mugs in the other, he couldn't say he was particularly surprised, but he was pleased.

"Breakfast in bed?" Nobody had ever cooked for Pax before. Not like this.

Davis handed over one of the mugs with a smug grin. "I can't say it's gourmet," he said, "but I can scramble up eggs and throw bread in the toaster."

"And brew some fine coffee," Pax said, taking a sip. It was just how he liked it, deep and black and sweet.

The food was simple, maybe, but it was the gesture that mattered. Pax might never have been in a relationship before—and he was fairly sure that Davis hadn't either, that was the price you paid for being closeted and in the NFL, relationships just didn't happen—but he believed that relationships were made up of moments like this. Insignificant in the greater scheme of things, but meaningful nonetheless.

"I didn't know you could cook," Pax said, between bites of eggs. They were good. Well seasoned. Well cooked. And the toast was perfectly browned, with lots of butter, melting right up to the edges.

"It's eggs," Davis said wryly.

Pax didn't want to admit that he wouldn't even know where to begin scrambling an egg. Give him a football and plop him on a field, and he knew *plenty*, but in a kitchen? He was fucking hopeless.

"Hey," Pax said, lighter than he could ever imagine. "I guess you did finally whisk me something."

Davis chuckled. "Guess I did."

Pax cleaned his plate. Finished his coffee.

Davis didn't bother taking anything back to the kitchen, just piled the plates up on the nightstand, and then he scooted back, leaning against the headboard.

"So, what are we doing today?" he asked, smiling slow and lazy.

The routine of the season was so regimented, so planned out ahead of time, that he barely ever had a day where he could just do . . . whatever, but Pax supposed that today was one of those rare days.

"I don't care as long as . . . well, we gotta be careful, you know," Davis trailed off.

"Yeah, I know, but really it doesn't matter. I just want to be with you," Pax said quietly. Maybe with someone else, he'd have struggled to admit the truth, but with Davis, it was surprisingly easy.

"I thought . . . maybe this weekend we could go to the beach. And Wednesday, we have dance class. But today, we could just hang out here. Watch that show you can't get enough of . . ."

"You like *Grey's* too, you just refuse to admit it," Pax interrupted with a laugh. "Which is very silly."

"And maybe a run later. And then . . . I know we can't go on a real date, not that way but since last night was such a success . . . I thought we could go to that sushi place Sea Bass likes. They're . . ." Davis trailed off, looking uncomfortable for the first time since Pax had opened his mouth yesterday and told him that he loved him.

Except Pax understood what Davis was trying to talk around. Akio, who owned the sushi place that Sebastian liked, he was discreet. He could put them in a dark corner. Make sure that nobody knew they were on a date.

On one hand, Pax was thrilled. How long had he wanted Davis to take him out? On the other . . .

"How many times have we grabbed dinner together?" he asked.

Davis' gaze narrowed. "What do you mean?"

"I mean, how many times have we gone out to dinner together?"

Pax could tell the moment the point he was trying to make dawned on Davis.

"You mean, we've done it so many times, and *weren't* dating, that how would anyone know anything different?"

Pax nodded.

"Well, there's one big flaw in that logic." Davis grinned. He was so smug, and so goddamned sexy, Pax wanted to pin him to the bed. Have his way with him. "When you're on a date with me, you're gonna know it."

There was nothing else to do about that look on Davis' face.

Pax tackled him to the bed and kissed him.

Chapter Eleven

After their run, Pax went back to his own condo to shower and change.

It was stupid to hate leaving Davis, even for the half an hour it would take to get cleaned up.

The way that Davis pulled him in for one last sweaty kiss before Pax left made it clear that he was feeling the same.

"Meet up in thirty?" Davis asked when he finally pulled away. Pax was fascinated by the damp skin on his chest, so fascinated he couldn't stop touching it, even though the last thing *that* was going to lead to was them actually showering. Separately, anyway.

"I'll see you on the elevator," Pax said, finally breaking away from Davis' embrace. Nobody should be that sexy when they were sweaty, but somehow Davis managed to do it.

Or maybe it was just Davis, period.

Still, his own condo was somehow colder and more impersonal than it had been twenty-four hours ago when he'd left it to go to Hibiscus.

Davis' condo was exactly the fucking same, but somehow it was warmer, just because of who was in it.

He showered, and then toweling off, went into his walk-in closet.

Davis had made it clear this was a date *date*, full capital letter D, *Date.*

But that didn't help him figure out what the hell he was going to wear.

The khakis and polo he pulled on looked so goddamned preppy, Pax faced himself in the mirror and made a face. No way, he wasn't going to go on his first date with Davis Abernathy looking like a caricature of a spoiled rich frat boy.

Akio's sushi place was totally casual, even though the food was freaking incredible, and then there was the added bonus of how sensitive he was to the concerns of the professional football players who came to his place. They wanted a nice place to eat, and not to be bothered. Especially the players who weren't out, like Sebastian hadn't been before he'd started dating Beau.

Pax reached for his favorite jeans, and then rifled through his shirts, finally picking one he really liked, a dark blue long-sleeved button-up that he'd always imagined matched Davis' eyes. He rolled up the sleeves, and swiped a hand through his hair, wishing he knew what to do with it, while also acknowledging that there was no way Davis wouldn't completely mess it up later.

It was thirty minutes on the nose when the elevator doors dinged open, and he walked in, hitting the button for the first floor.

He and Davis had this down to a freaking science, and he wasn't surprised at all when the elevator reached Davis' floor and stopped, the doors opening to reveal the man himself.

He was wearing jeans too, nice ones that fit his thighs like a glove, and a light blue shirt that meant his eyes weren't the dark, rich shade of Pax's shirt anymore, but lighter, warmer. Sweeter.

He'd shaved, scraping away the dark scruff that had left Pax's skin abraded and sensitive in the best possible way. But he was so goddamned handsome like this. Eyes bright, features sharp, a wedge of tanned skin and a sprinkling of dark hair emerging from the open vee of his shirt. Then he walked in, and *God*, he even smelled good too. Like a human wet dream, like *sex*, and Pax wanted to climb him like a fucking tree.

The doors dinged closed behind him.

"Hey." Davis' voice was deeper, rougher than normal. And there was no mistaking the hungry look in his gaze.

Pax cleared his throat. This was technically a public place. They'd already agreed to keep their newfound relationship under wraps when they could be seen, but maybe one kiss wouldn't be so bad . . .

Davis must've been on the exact same page because they reached for each other at the same time, and Pax staggered backwards, back hitting the metal wall of the elevator, and he groaned as Davis' hands ran all over him. Over his shirt and his jeans, sliding around back and cupping his ass as his mouth devoured his own.

When they broke apart, Pax couldn't help the breathless laugh. "I guess . . . I guess maybe we weren't ready to go out in public yet," he admitted.

"I was ready til I saw you," Davis murmured, reaching up with his other hand and cupping Pax's cheek. "So hot. So *mine*." He still hadn't moved, his body pinning Pax's to the wall. The floors were ticking by and any moment now the doors would open on the ground floor.

But Davis didn't move away until the very last second, until he didn't have any other choice. He moved, his reflexes still as honed as they'd been when he'd been playing, a split second before the doors opened and they were revealed to the large, spacious lobby.

Pax took a deep breath, trying to get himself under control, trying to look like he hadn't just enjoyed a mind-blowing kiss in an elevator, and followed Davis out.

It was a pain in the ass to drive in Miami, and so he wasn't surprised to see that Davis called an Uber to pick them up.

It also meant that they could enjoy a few drinks without worrying about how they were going to get home.

The Uber was already pulled over in the valet station, and they climbed in.

It was only a short drive to Akio's sushi place, unassuming in its strip mall locale and with its basic facade.

But Pax liked it that way. He liked how when they walked in, Davis hovering just behind him, the heat of his body bleeding through Pax's shirt, that Akio immediately greeted them, and showed them to a table in the back, where they wouldn't be bothered. Where nobody would see them unless they were looking for them.

And nobody, *nobody*, would ever go looking, because they'd never imagine that the quarterback and the quarterback coach would go on a date. Together.

Akio came over to take their order himself. They'd been here a few times with Sebastian and Beau, and some of the other guys on the team, so they already had a decent idea what they liked, but Akio made a few additional suggestions, took their drink order, too, and vanished, leaving them alone.

"Last time we came here," Davis said, "I thought, if I ever took you on a date, I could take you here."

The last few months had been hard. It had been hard *and* incredible, since the moment they'd met last June. So many moments where Pax had wanted more; balanced out by moments when what they shared had felt like *just* enough.

Slowly, the former had begun to outweigh the later, Pax realized. Even as they'd held onto what they'd had, it had begun to cut them, to hurt them more and more. That was why they'd fought, not because he was so angry that Davis had lied and said he had only ever been his coach.

They'd argued because the situation had become unbearable, the tension too thick to cut even with a knife.

Maybe it shouldn't have helped to know that Davis had been struggling with the impossibility of it too, for as long as he had, but it did.

"Or every time I took the offensive line out to dinner," Pax said. "There's a reason I started bringing you."

Davis raised an eyebrow. "Did you think that was subtle? 'Cause it wasn't."

"Hey, if Logan got to bring Dylan, I didn't see any issue with me bringing you."

"Yeah, except that was a hell of a lot different, wasn't it?"

"It really wasn't," Pax said wryly, and Davis chuckled.

"Okay, it wasn't," he finally conceded. "It just didn't feel that way at the time. Like they could do . . . well, anything, right? They could even let everyone believe they were together, but we . . ."

"We couldn't," Pax said gravely.

He'd felt the weight and the frustration of it, pushing on him.

What had actually changed?

Pax supposed that nothing really had, they were still nothing like Dylan and Logan, who'd actually pretended to be in a relationship when they'd only been friends. Of course, anyone with eyes could've predicted that wouldn't last very long—and it hadn't.

"Listen," Davis said, leaning forward.

God, how could one person smell so good? Pax felt lightheaded with it. *Let's just pretend this date thing is a non-starter and go home and get naked again.*

Davis' face broke into a wry smile. "You're not listening."

"I *tried*," Pax protested, "but well . . . you're there, and I'm here, and well . . ."

He *could* focus, of course. How many meetings had they sat in and Pax had been good? Or at least *relatively* good? But that was before he knew what Davis felt like and smelled like and tasted like.

The desire—and the temptation to get carried away—had always been strong. But now it had claws, and it was tearing into all of Pax's self-control.

They'd wasted so much time. Pax didn't want to waste a second longer.

"I guess it's good we've got what . . . six more days before we have to go back to work?" Davis teased. "Maybe you'll get me out of your system."

Pax rolled his eyes. "Unlikely. Besides, we're on a date, aren't we? Aren't I supposed to find you irresistible?"

"That's *after* the date," Davis said, his gaze smoldering with heat, burning Pax as it drifted over him.

Clearing his throat, Pax said, "I'll keep that in mind."

How had they managed to keep their hands off each other before this? Pax really didn't know. Because just making it through an hour-long dinner felt impossible.

Akio arrived then with their drinks, and the first few plates of sushi that they'd ordered.

Davis chuckled under his breath after he left. "I guess we should be grateful that he's got impeccable timing."

"Yeah, I think you were just about to drag me out of the restaurant," Pax teased.

He couldn't deny he was a little disappointed that Davis *hadn't.*

"Here's the thing," Davis said seriously, "we might have to be . . . careful . . . but that doesn't mean I can't treat you right. Treat you like you're the most important person to me." He hesitated. "Because you are. Maybe I came to Miami because this was my last chance, because Coach was the only one who was interested in giving me a chance but . . . I stayed for you. Because I want you to succeed. Because I love you."

Pax froze, a piece of sashimi halfway to his lips. He set the sushi down. "Damn it," he said, gesturing towards him with his chopsticks, "you don't have to be all of this, *and* a romantic, too."

Davis grinned. "Yeah, yeah, I kinda do. But just for you, okay?" His blue eyes glowed, and even though Pax was already head-over-heels crazy about the guy, there was something extra special about seeing him like this: happy and peaceful and not hiding how he felt any longer. No longer fighting it.

But fighting *for* Pax, instead.

Despite the dark corner of Akio's restaurant, Pax knew they should save the gesture part of the romance for later, but he reached out with a foot underneath the table and knocked it against Davis'.

"Maybe," Davis said, clearing his throat, "we should talk about something else."

"Something less likely to lead to the date ending early?" Pax teased.

Davis nodded. "What about the next game? We haven't gone over the tape yet, but I'm sure you've got thoughts on it. You always do."

Pax thought about the next team up for a second, and then felt his insides go hard and cold. Davis must have forgotten, or else he wouldn't be talking about it so casually.

He'd had the next game circled on his calendar for ages, but somehow, he'd lost track of it, with the fallout from his argument with Davis, and then this week's bye.

But he knew, without even looking at his phone, because he remembered looking at the schedule and thinking, *oh good, we'll have an extra week to prep for the Condors, so we can kick their ass.*

It wouldn't fix anything for Davis, but Pax figured it sure wouldn't hurt either.

"Uh . . ." Pax hesitated. He couldn't quite believe Davis had forgotten either but bringing up the Condors was something he was always hesitant to do, because the last thing he ever wanted to do was hurt him.

And the Condors always hurt him.

Sometimes he was better at hiding it, better at internalizing it, but then all that agony backed up inside him, and then things like that horrible panic attack happened.

There were no easy solutions.

Beating the Condors' ass on the field suddenly seemed both incredibly petty and also like the only thing he could actually *do.*

"The Condors game is next week, isn't it?" Davis said. He didn't sound particularly disturbed, but the man was really good at keeping things under wraps.

Pax nodded.

"Not exactly date conversation, then," Davis said with a sigh. "But maybe . . . maybe we should just figure out how to talk about this, without you looking like you're going to hide under the table. I can handle this. I wouldn't be here if I couldn't."

"I didn't look like I wanted to hide under the table," Pax protested.

Davis shot him a look. "Yes, you did. And really, it's okay. I'm not going to fall apart."

"That's not what . . ." Pax cleared his throat. Took a long sip of beer. "I'm mad for you, I'm fucking furious, I want to go kick all their asses. They hurt you, and I hate bringing them up, because then it reminds you of the bullshit they put you through."

"I know," Davis said with a smile. "I know you do. But it's gonna be unavoidable. So, let's talk about it."

"On our date?" Pax could hear the incredulity in his voice.

"Yeah," Davis said. "Because this is part of us, too, isn't it?"

Pax thought about it. Football, yes, of course, because they'd connected over the game from the very beginning, but the Condors were an inescapable part of their story too. Without their treatment, Davis wouldn't be here at all. He wouldn't be sitting here, in this little sushi restaurant in Miami, across from Pax. Instead, they'd be facing off on the fifty-yard line in a little under two weeks.

They'd be opponents, not lovers.

"Yeah, I guess it is," Pax conceded.

"Besides, we have to be able to talk about the game, without you worrying I'm gonna panic. I won't. I promise."

"You can, you know, if you need to."

Davis leaned back in his chair, picking up his beer and taking a long sip. "I know," he said. "But I'm good. Solid. I wouldn't tell you that I was, if I wasn't."

Pax knew that too. Davis wouldn't ever lie to him.

Okay, he'd done it once, but it hadn't even been a very good lie. And they'd both recognized it for what it was.

"I think . . ." Pax took a deep breath. "I think we need to completely annihilate them. Make them all wish they'd never left Charleston."

Davis grinned. "Why am I not surprised that's where you started?"

"Win, that's a given," Pax added, "but I don't want to just win. I want them demoralized. I want them rethinking them being football players. I want them to go back home crying."

That earned him a laugh. A deep, true, belly laugh. And *God*, he loved hearing Davis laugh like that. Maybe this really would be okay.

"I always say it, but we've got the pieces," Davis said. "You could easily lay forty points on them, with the right plays and the right execution."

"Balance the running game with the pass," Pax said, picking up his sashimi again. Chewing and swallowing it, he continued thoughtfully, "and no huddle."

Davis was nodding. Pax could see the gears in his brain whirling, as he thought through what he knew of the new version of his old team.

"Definitely no huddle," Davis agreed. "They've got an aggressive defense, but if you can ruin their rhythm, wear them down, I think you can put a lot of points on the board."

"That's the idea," Pax said.

He hadn't been quite sure how the transition between lovers and coach and player would go. Would it be awkward? But it hadn't been at all. They could just slip from one to the other, easy as blinking, and Pax realized that this was why Sebastian and Logan and the rest had confronted them at Hibiscus yesterday.

They'd seen this possibility, and had known if they could make it a reality, they'd be even stronger together than they were apart.

They finished up their meal, taking their time. Davis even pulled out his phone and doodled out a play that he liked the look of them running next week, Pax offering suggestions to refine it.

Akio brought the check as their meal wound to a close, and Davis snatched it up.

Money was something they'd never really discussed, probably because they both had a lot of it. They'd been casually trading buying meals since the summer, so nothing was different here.

Except the way that Davis' gaze never left his face, the look in his eyes as good as a caress against his cheek.

Pax cleared his throat. "Dinner was great," he said. He hadn't really been nervous—more excited than anything else, honestly—but now that the date was winding down, he was struck by the thought that he didn't really *go* on dates.

Was this where he metaphorically jingled his metaphorical keys and angled to get invited back to Davis' place?

Or was Davis just assuming that he'd be coming over?

Davis finished up his beer, setting the bottle on the table. He stood, and Pax followed, trailing after him as they left the restaurant.

Clearly Davis had already hailed the car, because it was pulling up just as they walked outside.

And of course, he couldn't ask once they slid into the backseat.

Pax jiggled his leg nervously as the car pulled out of the lot.

He loves you. You love him. This shouldn't be so freaking complicated.

But it was, and there was an extra layer of complicated because Pax could hardly ask Davis what they were doing after in front of the Uber driver. Especially one who clearly recognized them, from the excited gleam in his eyes, and the way he kept chattering on excitedly about the season.

They'd probably just made his whole year by riding in his car.

Pax made a face, annoyed with himself. Annoyed that he couldn't just enjoy meeting this fan.

Davis nudged Pax's thigh with his own.

"You okay?" he mouthed.

Pax nodded, because what else could he do?

Say, *oh God, I don't know what to do about you, and about this, and about what we're gonna do at the end of the night? Yesterday, it was so easy. And today . . . ack.*

By the time they pulled up in front of their building, Pax was aware of two things simultaneously: *one*, he was seriously overthinking this, and *two*, he was going to invite Davis to *his* place if Davis for some reason didn't offer his own.

They'd spent way too much goddamned time alone.

It wasn't til they were standing in front of the elevator, thankfully with nobody else waiting, that Davis spoke up. "You sure you're okay? You're . . . practically vibrating over there. And not in the good kind of way."

"Yes, yes, I'm fine, thanks." Except he wasn't. Not even remotely.

"Okay, just you being neurotic," Davis teased. "Got it. You want to come up?"

Pax rolled his eyes so hard then that it was a miracle he didn't sprain an eyeball. "Was that so hard to say?"

"Well," Davis said with a nonchalant shrug, "I sort of assumed it was a given. Considering we were about five seconds away from jumping each other in Akio's mostly clean bathroom."

It was true. There'd been a moment, when Pax had literally not given a shit that they might be having sex again in a strip mall sushi joint bathroom.

He'd only worried because Akio was nice, and a friend, and that wasn't really the right way to repay him.

And also because he'd absolutely, one hundred percent tell Sebastian that they'd defiled his bathroom.

"I did too, and then I . . ." Pax trailed off. It seemed stupid not to admit the truth, because Davis already knew it, didn't he? He *knew him.* Better than probably anyone else did.

"You overthought it?" The elevator dinged and they got in.

In case Pax had thought it was going to be a G-rated elevator trip, as soon as he hit the button, Davis had him crowded against the back wall, but he didn't kiss him, just looked at him, his thigh pressed hard and relentless against his own.

Davis' eyes were deep and bottomless blue. A *hot* blue.

Pax swallowed hard. "I guess I overthought it," he admitted.

"I want you with me, in my life, in my condo, in my house, in your place, in my bed, or yours, it doesn't matter. Just you with me. Us, together. That's all I care about," Davis said. A tiny smile snuck out, the corner of his mouth turning up. "Have I made myself clear enough to prevent confusion in the future?"

"You want this. You want me," Pax stated, but didn't ask.

"More than anything," Davis said, and then kissed him.

Pax had known it from the moment he declared his love, and that was all it had taken for Davis to throw away all his restrictions and to quit holding back. He'd known it from the moment Davis told him he loved him, too.

But feeling Davis kiss him, both sweet and hard, impossibly at the same time, he *knew it.*

Just when it was getting good though, Pax panting into Davis' mouth, Davis' hands gripping his waist like he never wanted to let him go, the elevator doors dinged open.

"Come on," Davis said, and his voice was suitably rough as he took Pax's hand and led him out of the elevator.

Maybe it was a risk to hold hands like this, but Davis only lived a few doors down from the elevator, and Pax knew he wasn't ready to let go.

It seemed he wasn't alone.

But the moment they were finally alone again, the door closing behind them, Davis didn't immediately lead him to the bed, like Pax had imagined—had dreamed—that he might.

"You know what?" Davis asked, as he drifted into the living room—not the bedroom.

"Why do I have a feeling you're going to tell me?"

Davis chuckled.

"We've got dance class tomorrow. We should work on those turns."

Pax raised an eyebrow. "You actually want to practice before dance class?"

"Yes, but no," Davis admitted. "I know I'm not even supposed to be taking the class . . ."

"Yeah, it was supposed to be for me and my hips," Pax said, wiggling them suggestively. Davis laughed.

"It turns out that just like anything else we do together, I like it when I dance with you," Davis said softly. He reached for his hand again, tugged Pax closer, until they were hip to hip.

"It's my favorite part of the week, and yet, also the worst," Pax agreed.

"You think she's gonna guess?"

"Senora? That woman knows that I broke a window throwing a baseball when I was in the third grade," Pax said. "She yells at me not to tense my hips before I even do it."

Davis laughed again. "We'll just have to hope she's discreet."

"I think she is," Pax said. "'Cause I'm pretty sure she already knew something was going on."

Davis tipped his forehead against Pax's. Didn't kiss him yet. But Pax could already feel the brush of his lips.

"How about it?" he asked into the quiet. "You wanna dance with me?"

"Always," Pax said.

Davis pulled his phone out of his pocket, and scrolling through his music app, found something and flipped on the speakers.

The sound of Santana's guitar flooded the room, and after setting the phone down, Davis reached for him, tugging him closer, and then closer still, so much closer than they'd ever allowed themselves to be in Senora's studio.

With only the dim light from outside Miami shining through the floor-to-ceiling windows, and their bodies moving to the beat, it felt like a completely different kind of dancing than they did each week during class.

That dancing had a purpose.

This dancing was just because they wanted to, because they enjoyed the way their bodies fit together, because touching Davis was never going to get old, not when the heat in his eyes flared each and every time he did it.

Davis turned him, the way they'd been practicing, and this time, without the pressure of Floria's gaze, his hips didn't tighten and it went smoother than anytime they'd ever done it in class.

"If only Senora could see you now," Davis murmured under his breath as somehow, they moved even closer together, and yet still didn't trip over their legs.

"Kinda glad she's not here, actually," Pax said in a low voice, and then the moment he leaned in, so did Davis, and they slid into a kiss like it was the easiest, most natural thing in the world.

Forty-eight hours ago, you hadn't even kissed him yet, and now it feels like you've been doing it forever.

He'd always known they'd fit together. Their personalities had meshed from the first day; he'd felt like Davis had looked at him and *seen* him, more than anyone else, so it wasn't a surprise that Davis touched him exactly how he wanted to be touched. His hand slipped down, curling around his hip, holding him steady, and his other reached up, cupping his cheek in his palm again and tipping Pax's head until it was at just the right angle. And then they just devoured each other.

It had been building like this all day—and even though they were used to the pressure of desire—this time it hadn't exploded between them, like yesterday, when they'd pushed the tension as far as it could possibly go. Instead, it felt like a blessing, that gradual slide into acceptance, that they could just *do* this now, without agonizing over it.

With the hand firm on his hip, Davis dragged Pax even closer, the hard line of his cock pressing into his thigh as their mouths devoured each other.

When they finally broke apart, Pax was panting and shaky, desperate for something more than the unrelieved pressure against his fly.

"Guess it isn't a shock we barely made it through one song," Davis teased quietly. His pupils were blown and dark, and the intent in his gaze had Pax's blood heating even more.

He'd dreamed it could be this way between them, but he'd never imagined it would be this good, this all-consuming. That tracing a path down Davis' chest would make him twitch with desire. That he'd feel like he was burning, but still push himself even closer to the flames. He tugged Davis' shirt out of his jeans and the moment his palm met bare skin, the slight rasp of Davis' chest hair, he felt lightheaded with it.

Pax licked his lips, and watched as Davis' eyes followed every move he made. "Not so much," he agreed. His hands drifted lower, and he was nearly at the button of his jeans when Davis stopped him.

"You touch me . . ." he said wryly, "and I'm gonna let you do whatever you want."

"That's the idea." Pax grinned.

"Just . . . let me, okay?" Davis said, and there was such need—not just want, but *need*—in his eyes, and in his voice, that Pax didn't stop him when he tugged him over to the couch, and pushed him down, crouching in front of him.

First his shoes, then his socks, and then Davis was pulling his pants down, leaning in and tracing over the hard line of his cock, aching in his briefs, with just a fingertip.

"You want me to suck your cock?" Davis asked.

Oh, God, the determination and the lust in his face. Pax was going to die. He knew it already. The only question was how fucking incredible was the death going to feel?

He nodded.

"Good, 'cause I've been thinking about it all day," Davis said casually, like it wasn't a big deal. Like it wasn't supposed to turn Pax's hunger up to eleven.

But it did, and when Davis leaned and flicked his tongue against his twitching cloth-covered dick, he squeezed his eyes shut, pushed his fingers through Davis' hair, and leaned back.

You're gonna feel this. You're gonna feel everything.

He felt when Davis finally removed the cloth barrier between his cock and the wonder and glory that was his mouth, and the way he enveloped him in all that wet, delicious warmth.

He'd barely ever let himself even fantasize about this, because it had hurt too much to think it might never happen. But now it was happening, and the heat and the suction, and the knowledge that this was *Davis* sucking him, felt so goddamned good that all he could do was hang on for the ride.

He felt Davis push his legs apart, settle in more fully between them. There was no stopping his groan as Davis let his tongue meander lower and then lower still, sucking one ball and then the other into his mouth.

It felt damn good, so good that Pax was just riding on the wave of it, hoping it would last, hoping he could *make* it last, but then he felt a wet finger moving and then it was pushing right up against his hole, right where he was actually dying to be touched. Only he hadn't realized that he'd wanted it, that he'd needed it. But Davis did. Davis knew, because he knew Pax better than he knew himself.

He probably knew all the dirty, nasty fantasies he'd barely been able to voice to himself. The desire to be bent over the counter and fucked within an inch of his life. The need to ride Davis' big cock like he was born to do it, damn the consequences or the inevitable discomfort the next day. He wanted to fucking feel it in his *throat*.

"Yeah, you like that, don't you?" Davis crooned as Pax squirmed, trying to get his finger in him, trying to get it even deeper, when it only broached him the tiniest fraction.

Pax sobbed with the desperate need of it, as Davis sucked his cock down again, the pressure building inside of him as Davis slid his finger home, rubbing him in every spot that felt good, felt right.

"This time," Davis said with a gasp as he pulled off, "you're gonna come on my finger, and next time you're gonna come on my cock."

That was all it took. Pax felt the orgasm rushing in, the inevitable pull of it too strong to resist, and he let go, everything going white and fuzzy around the edges as he pulsed with it.

When Pax finally pried his eyes open, the sight of Davis licking his red, swollen lips was just about enough to make him hard again, if that had been possible.

"Damn," Pax breathed out.

"I could make you come like that a million times and never get tired of it," Davis said in a gravelly rough voice as he rocked back on his heels.

He'd reached down and was palming himself, his cock tenting his jeans.

It was the best fucking view. But it could be better.

"Take off your clothes," Pax said. He felt lazy, emptied out because of his incredible orgasm, but he heard the steel in his voice.

The order. And Davis must've heard it too, because he obeyed, pulling off his shirt, and then unbuttoning and unzipping his jeans.

Davis naked was a glorious sight.

Even more glorious when he closed his big hand around his big cock and began to stroke.

"Yeah," Pax encouraged, "just like that. Make yourself feel good, sweetheart."

Davis shot him a hot look. Maybe it wasn't supposed to be sexy, but Pax felt the heat in it sear every inch of him.

"What, you think I'm the only one who can be a sweetheart?" Pax paused, licking his lips, really enjoying the sight of Davis working himself into a frenzy.

"No." Davis' voice was low. And even harsher now as he strained against the pleasure, his hand moving faster, rougher, until Pax could tell that he was nearing the edge.

"Stop." Pax hadn't intended to say it, but the word came out before he could jerk it back inside.

Davis' stare was incredulous, but he stopped.

Didn't move.

This man is mine. All mine. Every fucking gorgeous inch of him is mine. He'd known it, because how could he not? But the evidence of it was astonishing, and even though he'd just come his brains out, Pax felt his cock twitch with a desperate need to somehow get hard again.

"Please," Davis finally said. Begging. Oh, that was even better. Pax felt a thrill deep in his stomach. Felt it wrench even a little tighter as Davis repeated the single word. *Please.*

"Keep going, but *slow*," Pax ordered. "Make it real slow. Yeah," he said, watching as Davis strained against the request, "just like that. Make it last."

"I'm gonna . . ." Davis ground his teeth. It looked like it hurt, holding back, as he barely moved his fist.

"Not yet," Pax warned.

"Soon," Davis bit off. "I can't . . ."

Pax leaned forward, just enough that his gaze was nearly even with Davis' desperate one. "Now," he said, and he closed the distance the last little bit, kissing him hard and fierce, swallowing the bellow Davis made when he began to orgasm.

Pax felt him go slack as he finally finished coming, and leaned back, breaking the kiss.

There was a dreamy wonder in Davis' eyes that he'd never seen before, even yesterday, and he knew that what he'd done had been exactly what Davis wanted. What he needed.

Just the way Davis knew how to weasel his way inside of him, and learn all his secrets.

"You're gonna pay for that later," Davis said, but he was still smiling that lazy, satisfied smile.

"Oh, I hope so," Pax said.

Davis laughed then, throwing his head back and just plain cackling.

Pax had known he loved him long before he'd ever touched him. But there was knowing you loved someone, and then falling deeper and harder and sliding into an incredibly intense feeling that you knew would never fade.

"I love you," Pax said quietly, with intent.

Davis tipped his head against Pax's. His eyes fluttered shut. He was so beautiful like this. And he was all Pax's. "I love you, too."

Chapter Twelve

"Yes, yes, just like that, *exactly* like that," Floria bellowed as Davis led Pax into the merengue turn just like they'd practiced.

Was it like the night before? No—because nothing could be like that. It had been extraordinary: the hushed intimacy, the feeling of finally being able to hold Pax so tightly against him, the way they'd moved together like one person, not two.

In fact, Davis didn't even *want* it to be like last night.

Because if it was, *one,* he was definitely going to get hard, just thinking about it, and there was no way that wouldn't be awkward, and *two,* while he wasn't necessarily against Floria being aware of their deepening relationship, because he trusted her enough, he wasn't willing to go around publicizing it either.

This was their first test, since they'd started this thing between them, and Davis had taken it seriously—and he'd known Pax did too. They'd driven together, but that was normal. They'd done that all the time, before they'd ever gotten involved, but once they'd entered the studio, he'd felt the distance grow between them. It was the same distance they'd had before, at least before they'd started fighting, and so it shouldn't have felt wretched. But it did.

That's just because you're not used to it, Davis had told himself firmly. *You have to be able to pretend, and pretend better than this, or else you're never gonna fool a single person at work.*

But as soon as they'd touched, to start the merengue, it had all come rushing back. Davis ended up looking at that same spot over Pax's shoulder, the crack in the seafoam green wall, counting under his breath as they danced.

He didn't even need to listen to Floria, or to see the knowing look in her eyes, to acknowledge that whatever they were trying to do, it wasn't quite good enough.

"Yes, yes, you have got the loose hips of a gazelle tonight, Paxton. Where have these hips been for the last month?" she asked archly.

Pax flushed as Davis turned him. Was it crazy to assume it might be because having half a dozen orgasms in less than forty-eight hours was enough to permanently loosen him up?

"Uh, um, well, you know, I've been stretching a lot." Pax flushed even redder.

Nope, it was not crazy to assume that.

"Well, keep up the good work," Floria said brightly.

Pax was currently the dull brick red of the Hollywood Stars uniform, and Davis was absolutely, most definitely not trying to hide his shit-eating grin. Nope, not at all.

"Davis!" Floria barked. "You are spending too much time smiling at Paxton, and not enough time keeping rhythm. You are the man and the leader, so *lead.*"

"Sorry," Davis mumbled under his breath, but the more he tried to contain his expression, the more difficult it became.

Until his cheeks hurt, he was smiling so hard.

"What?" Pax hissed. "What's wrong with you?"

Except it wasn't what was wrong with him, it was what was right with him.

"I'm just . . . happy," Davis admitted.

"Talking!" Floria yelled.

"Really happy," Davis added, which was even more of a sacrifice because he knew just how pissed off Floria was going to get if he didn't shut his mouth and concentrate on the rhythm of the merengue.

Floria gave an exaggerated sigh full of frustration and raised the remote in her hand, pausing the music mid-beat.

"I am sure we're all pleased that you're so happy," she said, her voice full of steel, but her eyes full of knowing laughter, "but *I* would be so happy if you would concentrate on what you are trying to accomplish here. God knows, it's only a matter of time before Paxton's hips decide to stop cooperating."

"Hey," Paxton protested. "Maybe they're going to keep cooperating."

If it was the sex, then Davis had every intention of making sure they kept cooperating for the next hundred years, but he couldn't exactly tell Floria that.

"Last time you were here, you didn't even want to touch each other . . ." Floria said quietly, "and now you will not stop." She gestured to where Davis was just casually holding Pax, even though the music had stopped. He realized, abruptly, that normally when the music stopped, they pulled apart. But they hadn't today.

Well, damn.

"This studio," she continued, "is a place of honesty. A place where all the pretense falls away, and it is only you and the music. Today, you let yourselves just *feel* the beat and each other, and it was beautiful."

Davis tried not to panic.

How were they ever going to fool anyone?

But then again, maybe Floria was right, and this shabby little room, with its cracks on the walls, and its ugly, fading paint, was a place of honesty. Maybe they could truly be themselves not just in their condos, but here, too.

"Now," Floria said, clapping loudly, before Davis could acknowledge her words, "we will continue. You will feel each other and the music and, Paxton, you will think of one thing and one thing only."

"Keeping my hips loose," Pax said dutifully, but there was a happy light in his eyes. He'd felt her acceptance, too, just as surely as Davis had.

All the way home from Floria's studio, Davis told himself that he wasn't thinking about it.

He hadn't been telling himself this lie all day, but he'd certainly been thinking about it enough.

Next time you're gonna come on my cock.

He'd thought about it on their run this morning, until he'd had to stop because jogging with an erection wasn't much fun. He'd thought about it in the shower—and pretended that he wasn't disappointed that Pax hadn't joined him, going back to his own place to clean up. But then, after that, they'd sat down on the couch to go over hours of tape of the Condors' defense, prepping for next week's game.

It was usually easy to lose himself in the details of breaking down a defense, and planning how they could circumvent it, but Davis couldn't deny that it was harder this time. Seeing those familiar orange and blue jerseys, and remembering a time when he'd thought he'd wear the same for the entirety of his career, wasn't particularly easy.

He hadn't expected that it would be, but he'd promised himself—and promised Pax—that he could do this. He wasn't going to fall apart, just because the Condors were coming to Miami.

Coach had offered a few weeks back to give him some time off, if he needed it, but he'd vehemently denied the offer.

But pushing through the pain, even though Pax, without a word, had made sure that he didn't see a single glimpse of himself or Taylor, had taken a toll. For a few hours, he *hadn't* thought about Pax like a lover. He was Davis' quarterback, and it was ultimately his job and his job alone to make sure he was as prepared as he could possibly be. Randy would be coming in next week with lots more ideas, because he too didn't know what time off looked like, and there was no doubt that so would Beau and Coach, but it felt right to be prepping Pax like this.

Because he wanted to win this game, too.

It wasn't until dinner, and then the weekly torture session, AKA salsa class, when he realized that they hadn't had sex all day and somehow, impossibly, suddenly, that was all he could think about.

The promise he'd made.

How he wanted to deliver.

Especially because now, he didn't have to deny himself. He was *allowed* to touch Pax now. He wouldn't have to spend the whole hour loving the feel of being so close, only to have to go home to his lonely, empty bed.

"You look tense," Pax said casually as they stepped off the elevator on his floor. Pax had suggested they come back to his place tonight, as he had a better view from his balcony.

"Maybe we can share a beer and just hang out," Pax had said, but Davis wasn't stupid.

He knew they weren't going to be spending any time on Pax's balcony.

And if they had a beer, they'd be sharing one in post-coital bliss, in Pax's bed.

"Not tense . . ." Davis said, trailing off.

"I know it was hard on you this afternoon," Pax said, punching in his door code and pushing the door open to his condo. "I wish . . . I wish there was some way I could make it easier."

"You're already making it easier," Davis said gruffly, as he followed him into the kitchen. Okay, so Pax was really following through with this *share a beer on the balcony* game plan. But instead of grabbing a pair of beers from his fridge, Pax leaned against the far counter and gave him a hard stare.

"You were distracted during dinner, and even during dance class," Pax said.

Pax wasn't wrong; he definitely had been. But it hadn't been because of watching the Condors tape this afternoon. It was because once he started thinking about what he was going to do to his man when they were finally alone, he couldn't *stop* thinking about it.

"Uh, yeah, well, that's true," Davis admitted, rubbing his neck.

He was going to have to tell Pax the truth—though it could hardly be an issue. Surely he'd be glad that instead of angsting over the Charleston fucking Condors, he'd been fantasizing about how to make Pax come his brains out.

"So, what is it?" Pax asked.

Davis gave up the fight, and moved closer to where Pax leaned against the counter. From the way he melted against his body, it was clear he hadn't liked the distance either.

Sometimes it was necessary, like this afternoon, but somehow, it felt even better to come back together afterwards.

"Honestly," Davis said, murmuring roughly into Pax's neck, pressing his lips against the skin there, in one brief kiss, "I was thinking about how good it would feel to get you naked again."

Pax froze for a second and then chuckled. "And here I thought you didn't mean it."

"Oh, I meant it," Davis said, knowing exactly what Pax was referring to. "Hundred and ten percent."

"I decided you just dirty-talked a lot of nonsense when you were fucking."

Davis scoffed.

Pax soothed him with a palm to his cheek, leaning in until his mouth was so close to Davis' that he could nearly taste it. Couldn't *wait* to taste it. "Yeah, well, I kinda hoped you meant it," he continued. Davis couldn't miss the hopeful, heated look in his eyes. "Wanna prove that you did?"

Davis didn't need another invitation—Pax's gaze burning hot as caramel definitely would've been enough to do it, even without his request. But he couldn't deny him now, even if he'd wanted to.

He pressed his mouth against Pax's, kissing him hot and rough, and then reaching down to tangle his fingers with his, tugging him in the direction of the bedroom.

Pax landed on the bed, and was already pushing his shoes off, chuckling under his breath as Davis slipped his own off, and then pulled his t-shirt off.

"God, yes, get naked *please*," Pax chanted as he shoved his shorts off.

Davis could already see his cock hard and straining against his briefs, and he swallowed hard as Pax palmed himself, pushing into his own touch.

"Hands off," he said, even though he sure liked watching Pax touch himself.

"You gonna be bossy again?" Pax teased.

"You wanna get fucked?" Davis challenged.

Pax met his gaze, heat clashing against heat, and *God*, there was nothing he loved more than the challenge of this man.

For a moment, Davis wasn't sure he was going to give in. Though was it *really* giving in? They both knew he wanted it. And maybe someday, in another situation, Davis was going to want it equally as bad.

"Yes," Pax said, finally speaking up in a soft, quiet voice.

He moved his hands, and curled them into the comforter.

"I'm not . . . exactly small," Davis warned.

"Trust me, I know," Pax retorted, a little of that challenge back in his tone. "You say that like it's a bad thing. It's not. God, I want it."

"Well, we just gotta be careful." The last thing he ever wanted was for Pax to be hurt. And what he craved, more than anything, was to make Pax scream his name.

"Lube and condoms in the drawer," Pax said, gesturing to the bedside table, the subtext in his words clear: *get on with it already.*

But Davis had wanted this for a very long time—both of them had wanted this for so long—and he had every intention of savoring every moment and taking his sweet damn time with it.

So instead of *getting on with it already*, like Pax wanted him to do, he bypassed the drawer and leaned over Pax's body, caging him in with his arms, and kissed him thoroughly.

This was about sex, sure, but it had always been about more than just sex.

The kiss deepened, Davis stroking Pax's tongue with his own, feeling the deep rumbling groan as they kissed and kissed, unable to get enough.

When Davis finally pulled back, Pax already looked wrecked. Forehead damp, lips red and wet, eyes blown.

"So fucking gorgeous," he murmured, and then and only then did he reach for the drawer.

He wasn't really all that surprised to see that the lube was brand new, as was the box of condoms.

He knew Pax hadn't been sleeping with anyone since he'd come to Miami—he'd hardly have had time, even if he'd had the inclination—but the unopened lube and condoms told a whole story of hope and yearning.

Pax had *hoped* that this might happen.

Davis knew he hadn't been waiting for anyone else; just him.

The knowledge made his touch much more tender than he'd intended, as he cautiously wet his fingers and slipped them downward, circling around Pax's hole, making him squirm on the bed.

"God, please," Pax pleaded, "you're killin' me. I'm gonna come before you ever . . ." He swallowed hard. "Before you ever fuck me."

Truthfully, Davis was killing himself a little bit, too. His dick had never been harder in his whole life, and he was afraid the moment he actually slid inside Pax for the first time, he was gonna lose it.

Just from the single finger he'd pushed inside, Pax was so god-damned tight and hot, and he knew he'd fit so perfectly around him.

How did he know that?

Because Pax was perfect for him in every other way, and he didn't expect this to be any different.

But Pax wasn't wrong; he was probably going to make both of them lose it.

That doesn't matter, as long as it feels good. Feels the best.

Davis never doubted if it would be good for him, because this was *Pax*, and it couldn't be anything else.

"Okay, sweetheart, I got you," he murmured, leaning closer, setting one knee on the bed, and a second finger slid alongside the first, making Pax moan.

It was gratifying to know that he'd been right from the first: Pax was loud in bed, and he loved not only forcing these noises out of him, but knowing that it was *him* who was making him groan.

When he hit the right spot, Pax nearly vibrated off the bed, wailing out his pleasure, and Davis had to grit his teeth. He'd never come in his pants before, even as a young, inexperienced teenager, and he wasn't about to start now. Not when he had a Pax kind of feast laid out in front of him.

Feeling Pax really relax around him, he added a third finger, concentrating now on making sure that when it was his cock, and not his fingers, that was thrusting into Pax, all he'd feel was bone-melting, screaming-level kind of pleasure.

"Enough, enough, I'm gonna come, feels too good," Pax chanted, squirming on his fingers, until Davis finally pulled them out.

"I told you, you're gonna wait, and you're gonna come on my cock," Davis said, after he fumbled with the box of condoms, trying to grab just one, but he came away with three. He yanked one out of the wrapper and, taking a deep breath, shed his boxer briefs, palming himself briefly, the rush of sudden pleasure after so much denial making him lightheaded.

After he finished tugging on the condom, Pax hooked a foot around his knee and was pulling him towards the bed, and there was a pleading look in his eyes that Davis couldn't have denied, even if he'd wanted to.

He definitely didn't want to.

"Sweetheart," he breathed out as he leaned over, kissing Pax's mouth as he snubbed up against his hole.

He'd had sex before. Of course he had, but when Pax wound his arms around his neck, fingers digging into the back of his skull, and tugged him down, his cock slipping in the first little bit, he wasn't really sure he had.

Because it had never felt like this.

His heartbeat accelerated as he pushed further in. It felt glorious, like coming home, Pax's face open and vulnerable underneath his, his eyes blown, his mouth slack.

"God, you feel so good," Pax huffed out. "So fucking big, though."

Davis felt it. Pax was so tight, he worried, but then he slid in a bit further, and Pax groaned. It took everything he had, every single bit of self-control, not to go chasing after his own pleasure, but he had to make sure Pax was okay.

He hesitated, muscles straining, as Pax clenched his fingers in his hair. And then suddenly he was arching into him, forcing him the last little bit of the way, and Davis couldn't help it. He leaned in, kissing him then.

It didn't feel like just sex. It felt precious, a way to be even closer to the man he loved.

"I love you," he murmured as he finally began to thrust, the words echoing from his thoughts. "I love you so goddamn much."

Pax's mouth slipped open, even as his eyes squeezed shut, and his hand slid downward, grasping his own cock, pulling it in time with Davis' thrusts.

Make it last, make it good, his brain was screaming at him, but he was overwhelmed with the physical pleasure of it, and the emotional rightness of the moment, and the second Pax tipped over the edge, spasming around him, shouting his name, Davis followed.

He pulsed into the condom for what felt like an eternity. And then collapsed, jelly-kneed, on top of Pax.

Neither of them spoke for a long time. It had been a *moment*, and Davis—and it seemed Pax, too—was happy to just *feel* it, for right now.

Then finally, Pax said, "You're crushing me, you know."

"I know," Davis admitted. Not even feeling that bad about it. And definitely not moving, even though he knew he probably should. He was heavy, but then Pax wasn't exactly a small man himself. He could take it.

He sure took it good just now, his mind slyly supplied. If he hadn't just come his brains out, he'd probably have gotten hard again.

"It's a good thing I like it," Pax professed with a happy sigh.

"Me too," Davis said, his cheek plastered to Pax's sweaty right pectoral muscle. He could hear his heart beating away, firm and steady, under his touch, and he wanted to squeeze his eyes shut and remember this moment forever.

There was no telling how long this extraordinary euphoria would last.

After all, he *was* the poster child for fucking up a situation—or having a situation fucked up for him—and everything was so uncertain.

Would he have a job after this year?

Would Pax?

Would they end up on opposite ends of the country?

Whatever happened, Davis decided, they would have this. A week of completely uninterrupted, peaceful, loved-up bliss.

But finally, they had to move.

That was real life for you, always intruding at the most intimate moments. Davis leveraged himself off Pax, regretting it even as he headed towards the bathroom, cleaning up and grabbing a damp washcloth so Pax could do the same.

After that unpleasant bit of cold, hard reality was dealt with, they climbed into bed together, and even though his orgasm had happened at least fifteen minutes ago, Davis still felt like his heartbeat was still desperately trying to return to normal—sometimes it felt like it was still trying to return to baseline after the last few days.

And then, reality interrupting even more abruptly, his phone rang.

"Ugh, tell whoever it is to go away," Pax said, as Davis left the warm cocoon of his arms and rolled over, grabbing his phone from the nightstand.

Davis had every intention of doing just that, but then he checked the screen, and after groaning a little, picked it up.

"Yes?" he answered. There was nothing he'd wanted to do more than send the stupid caller to voicemail and go back to cuddling—the second greatest sport on earth—but the ID had identified them as calling from his security company. Not the kind of call you were supposed to send to voicemail.

"Mr. Abernathy," the voice on the other end of the line said, "I'm so glad we caught you."

"What's going on?"

Davis could feel Pax's interest growing, a shadow of concern in his eyes. That answered the question of whether Pax knew him well enough to identify his worried voice.

"Hi, this is Mackenzie Porter, your account manager, Mr. Abernathy. We just wanted to let you know that an hour ago, the alarms on your house were activated. We dispatched a team, who identified that a break-in occurred, but it doesn't look like anything was stolen or damaged. We also called the police out, who verified that your locks were broken, but nothing seemed to be taken."

"So who broke in, then?" Davis asked testily. He had a feeling he knew who was behind this. For awhile now, he'd had annoying visits from guys who lived around the same area who claimed to be fans. Dealing with them himself had become annoying. And his agent had pleaded with him not to beat the crap out of them when they'd flung shit his direction. Metaphorical shit, at least, but *still* shit.

The local police had proven useless, small-town and inexperienced, and he'd been additionally convinced they were the ones who'd leaked his address in the first place. He'd ended up hiring this expensive and high-end security company, and since he'd done that, there hadn't been any issues.

Until now.

"We're not sure," she said hesitantly. "It could've been animals, except the locks were clearly broken."

Davis felt himself tensing up. When would those assholes just leave him the fuck alone? Was it not bad enough that his reputation was in tatters? They had to harass him over it, too?

Fans could be so fucking entitled. He knew players who'd been sent death threats.

Neal Fisher, who'd missed a winning kick in the Super Bowl, had gotten thousands of them. He'd been fired and his reputation shot, and they still hadn't thought that was enough. They'd had to harass him, too.

"How do you know nothing was taken?" He absolutely had valuables in the house. The electronics alone would be worth thousands, but everything else, all his expensive watches and additional cash was kept in a well-hidden safe.

But was there stuff he gave a shit about that they could've taken and had no one be the wiser? Absolutely.

"That's why I'm calling, as well as to inform you of the break-in," Mackenzie said hesitantly. "We'd like you to come out, and verify that nothing was stolen."

Davis sighed. At least it was a bye week. He could easily visit his house, check things out, and get back in plenty of time for practice starting next Monday.

But he and Pax . . . they'd had plans. Plans he very much wanted to keep.

"I'll be there tomorrow," Davis said. "I'm assuming the house is now locked down again?"

"Like a fortress, sir," Mackenzie said apologetically.

"Good," Davis said.

When he hung up, Pax was looking at him expectantly.

"Someone fucking broke into my house again," Davis said with a frustrated sigh.

"What?" Pax sounded shocked. "*Again?*"

"The price you pay for not just being a quarterback, but a *notorious* quarterback. Also, pretty sure the cops gave out my address to all their annoying friends, who drink too much and then think it's fun to come harass me."

"Are you fucking kidding me?" Pax was clearly furious, his brown eyes flashing. "They get drunk and come make fun of you?"

"Well, not necessarily *make fun*, but yeah, give me a hard time, for sure," Davis said. Feeling the sting of embarrassment even with Pax—even though he shouldn't. Pax would never judge, and he knew the truth of everything that had happened.

"That's just bullshit," Pax said bluntly.

"Yeah, well, welcome to the bullshit timeline," Davis said with a shrug. "Anyway, they don't think they took anything, which is pretty much par for the course with these tools. Just assholery, not actual robbery. But they want me to head over to the house, to make sure."

"Your house in South Carolina?"

"Yeah, it's sorta midway between Charleston and Hilton Head. It's a long-ass drive, almost nine hours, but I can book a quick charter flight from here to Jacksonville, and that cuts the drive down to only a couple of hours."

Pax's expression was still serious. "Just to be clear . . . you're asking me to go with you, right?"

Of course Davis wanted him to. Now that they'd finally figured their shit out, Davis didn't even like it when Pax went to his apartment, because it felt like they'd already wasted too much time being miserable when they could really just be happy. But he also hadn't wanted to assume that Pax would want to spend part of his bye week going to Port Royal and making sure that he hadn't *actually* gotten robbed.

"Yeah," Davis said, before he could overthink. "Yeah, of course I want you to come with me, but I'd get it if you didn't . . ."

Pax reached over and pushed a finger against Davis' lips. "I want to," he said simply. "I really want to. I'd love to see your house."

Davis knew that they were serious. Pax had confessed his love before they'd ever even kissed, for God's sake, and they wouldn't be breaking the rules if this wasn't something they both wanted very badly.

But Pax saying he wanted to see his house . . . the house that he could be *sharing* with him someday, if this whole situation didn't go up in flames . . . well, it was a lot exciting and a little sobering.

"My pops lives in Hilton Head. We could always swing by and see him, too," Davis said, watching Pax's face carefully for any hesitation or trepidation that they were getting too serious, too fast.

After all, Pax had the poker face of an amateur.

"Really?" But all Pax looked was thrilled. "God, I'd love that. I know you talk about him a lot."

"That's 'cause he's the best," Davis said, and meant it.

"You're not worried . . ." Pax trailed off.

"That he'll know you're my boyfriend?" It was the very first time he'd said it—the first time he'd actually been *able* to say it—and to his pleasure, the words tripped off his tongue like he'd been born to say them.

Pax nodded, the happy glow in his eyes not dimmed even for a second.

"I sure hope he knows, 'cause I'm gonna tell him," Davis said. "He's known about me . . . well, forever, I guess. Probably before I even knew about me."

"You're close to him."

"Closer than my parents, yeah," Davis said. "They're both corporate lawyers. Super busy. I spent more time with Pops than I did them, hands down."

It didn't seem possible, but that glow in Pax's eyes was even brighter now. "That seems crazy to me," Pax said softly, "that anyone wouldn't want to spend as much time with you as they could."

That tight-throat emotion was surging inside him again. Davis tried to clear it, mostly unsuccessfully. "Well, my pops is great, and I think you're gonna love him."

"I know I will," Pax said firmly, and pressed his lips to Davis'.

It wasn't a big, passionate, *let's have sex again* kiss, but a sweet, reassuring, short-ish kiss.

And as Davis dialed the number of the charter company he liked to use, he realized just how lucky he was that he didn't just get *let's have sex again* kisses, but the other kinds, too.

He didn't know what he'd ever done to deserve being this blessed, but he wasn't going to fuck it up. Not now. Not ever.

Chapter Thirteen

Pax shifted uncomfortably in the seat of the rental truck that they'd just picked up, and hoped that Davis wouldn't notice.

He'd asked, of course, because Davis was Davis, and even when he was being sexy as hell, he was also unfailingly conscientious.

Just one of the reasons he loved the man.

But he didn't really *like* him when he'd asked, worry creasing his forehead, at breakfast this morning when Pax had just been about to sit down.

It wasn't like he hadn't been careful yesterday, prepping him. He had been. And it had hurt, a little, but it had been a good kind of hurt.

Still, it had been a long time since Pax had been fucked, and even though he'd wildly loved every second of it, he couldn't deny he was a little tender this morning.

Even if he didn't want to admit it to Davis.

Especially because he didn't want to admit it to Davis. Who, no doubt, would end up treating him like a piece of porcelain the next time they fucked.

Though, while cuddling afterwards, Davis had made it pretty clear that he wouldn't mind being on the receiving end next time, and now, Pax wanted *that*. Because seeing him like that, vulnerable and open, desperate and wanting, was suddenly all he could think about.

But before any of that happened, they needed to get to South Carolina.

Port Royal, specifically. That, according to Davis, was the closest town to where he lived.

Pax, who'd looked it up while they were on the quick charter from Miami to Jacksonville this morning, thought that calling Port Royal a "town" was being generous. It didn't even have five thousand people.

And Davis lived *outside* Port Royal.

"If you squirm one more time," Davis said conversationally, as he left the last skyscrapers of downtown Jacksonville behind, "we're going to stop and get you a pillow."

Pax made a face. "We absolutely will not. What would people say? How would we explain buying me an ass pillow?"

"Maybe you have hemorrhoids?" Davis said with a completely unrepentant grin.

"Yeah, because that's sexy as hell," Pax said wryly.

For a minute, Davis didn't say anything and Pax thought maybe he'd avoided the inevitable concern, but then he said, "I should've been more careful with you."

"Ugh, I knew you were gonna say that," Pax said with a glare. "I'm fine. I loved it. I wish you'd do it again . . ." He hesitated. "But maybe not today."

Davis chuckled. "Noted," he said. "As long as you're okay."

"Trust me, I'm fine," Pax said, rolling his eyes. "You don't have to treat me like I'm gonna break."

"No, I don't," Davis said, glancing over at him as they drove closer to the Florida border, "but I will treat you like you're precious, sweetheart, 'cause you are."

Pax's heart melted. Was it any wonder he adored this man? He was so goddamned sweet, but also gruff and sexy and then there was the way he fucked like a maniac.

The perfect combination.

Maybe not for anyone else, but he was just right for Pax.

"And that right there is why I can't ever stay mad at you. Even when you suggest we buy me an ass pillow."

Davis barely smothered his laugh. "I wasn't serious. But we *can* stop for lunch. 'Cause I know I'm starving."

"Yeah, I can't imagine why that would be," Pax teased. They'd foregone everything but coffee because they'd taken way too much time in the shower this morning—getting dirty, before they helped each other get clean again.

At the time, it had seemed like a worthy sacrifice, but now his stomach was grumbling too, even though it was barely eleven.

"There's a good sandwich place a few minutes away. Even if we weren't hungry, we should stop. There's not much between here and Port Royal."

Personally, Pax thought there wasn't really much *in* Port Royal, and it wasn't the kind of place he'd ever choose to live. But he'd grown up in Southern California, and gone to school there, and then he'd been drafted by the Piranhas, sending him to Miami.

He'd only ever lived in big towns, full of people. Maybe once he saw this house of Davis', isolated and private, he'd feel differently.

The future between them might be uncertain, because love wasn't always enough to keep two people together, but the one thing that Pax did know was that he was never going to try to change Davis from who he was. If he liked living in the middle of freaking nowhere, then they'd have to find a compromise to make that possible. At least some of the time.

The few minutes to the sandwich place flew by. They grabbed sandwiches to go, and as the miles ticked by, ate them.

Pax never would have dreamed there could be something sexy about watching Davis drive with one hand and eat a turkey sandwich with the other, but he was discovering that just about everything Davis did was sexy.

It was knowing someone and caring about them, and believing there was no way you could love them any more than you did—but you always could. There was no end to how deeply he could fall.

If you're lucky, Pax thought, stuffing the trash in the to-go bag, *you're gonna be discovering things you love about Davis five years from now. Ten years from now. A lifetime from now.*

He didn't know if that was possible, but it was still something he hoped for.

"We're 'bout an hour out," Davis announced as they passed another sign for another small-ass town.

Pax nodded and flipped on the radio. Clicked from channel to channel, only to discover that they had one thing in common: they all were playing country music.

Davis must've caught his grimace because he laughed. "Not a fan of country? Sorry, that's all they play out here."

"Apparently," Pax groused. "I guess you grew up listening to it."

"Yeah, I did. Doesn't mean . . ." Davis hesitated. "Doesn't mean I don't wish that country music wasn't full of homophobic assholes, either."

Pax hadn't thought about that. "Is that why you never came out?"

Davis shrugged. "Partly, I guess. 'Cause I just grew up with the understanding that if I was gonna get where I wanted to go, there were certain things I just couldn't get honest about. Like everyone knew Lisa, the realtor in town, she was a lesbian, but we never talked about it. Even Lisa didn't."

"It was my college coach," Pax said. He ached for Davis, who'd grown up believing that who he was wasn't something that people talked about, or even acknowledged. He was different. He'd grown up in a fairly liberal area. He'd had a semi-public boyfriend in high school. But then he'd gone to college, and everything had changed. "He told me that nobody wanted a gay quarterback, and they'd only accept me if I was a fucking great quarterback first. So I needed to focus on that first part, so that nobody would care about the gay part."

"That's bullshit," Davis said in a hard voice, his fingers tightening on the wheel til Pax could see his knuckles turning white. "Nobody told Sam Crawford he had to be good before he could be gay. Or, fuck, Colin O'Connor, either. They just *were.*"

"I know," Pax said, and then added, in a staunch tone, "And nobody said that the way your ass-backwards town had it was right either."

For awhile neither of them said anything.

Pax wondered but didn't ask if Davis would ever want to come out. He didn't know if Davis was even thinking about that right now; probably the only thing he was worried about was saving his career, and Paxton couldn't blame him for that.

But he also didn't ask because it seemed likely Davis would then ask *him* when he wanted to come out, and the truth was, he didn't know. He'd been out, at least sort of, before, and that hadn't been so bad. And it certainly hadn't been so bad for any of his teammates when they'd come out, except for maybe Logan, who'd been forcibly outed by an ex-hookup.

Honestly, he'd been so concentrated on this year *not* being a failure of epic proportions, not like last year, and then he'd been unavoidably distracted by his growing feelings for Davis.

He'd had his professional attention locked up, as well as his personal attention, and there hadn't been room for anything else, even as his teammates had slowly begun to trickle out of the closet.

First Wade, then Sebastian, then Logan and Dylan.

Maybe he should've been paying more attention.

"I have thought . . ." Davis said into the silence, and then hesitated. "I've thought, when . . . *if* . . . I retire in a year or two, I may just do it. Get it over with. If I'm gonna be retired, I want to do it on my own terms."

Pax thought he would have been surprised—but when he really looked at his reaction, he realized he wasn't at all.

Of course Davis wouldn't want to live a lie.

"Or," Davis said, shooting him a sideways glance, too quick for Pax to catch all the loaded emotion in it, but he knew it existed, because of his next words, "if I ended up dating someone that I didn't want to hide."

Pax considered this. "I'm sure that you didn't imagine that the next guy you dated would be someone you couldn't publicly date anyway." Because he wasn't stupid; despite the "dating intervention" and Beau's "permission," what they were doing was very much not allowed.

No matter how kindly and permissible and understanding Coach could be, none of his good-heartedness would go this far.

Pax knew that.

"No," Davis agreed. "Though . . ." He grinned, and that look he shot Pax now was like quicksilver in his veins. "Though, from the moment we met, I knew it was going to be you or nobody."

It shouldn't feel good, not when they were essentially condemning themselves to loving each other in private, but it did, anyway.

Because, damnit, Pax had felt the same fucking way.

From the moment he'd touched Davis, he'd never wanted to touch anybody else.

"As long as I have you, it doesn't matter," Pax declared.

Davis cleared his throat, and reached for his hand, squeezing it briefly, before he returned it to the wheel. Pax didn't need him to tell him how much he mattered, how much he loved him, because it was in every bit of his expression.

"It doesn't matter," Davis agreed.

It wasn't entirely true; of course it mattered.

But in the face of the other option—losing each other—coming out or living and loving publicly *didn't* matter.

They were quiet for the next ten or so minutes, and then Davis was pulling off the freeway, to a smaller country highway, and then an even narrower, less-inhabited side road, and then finally, slowing down to turn onto a gravel track, identified only by a plain mailbox and a discreet security company sign stuck in the ground next to it.

Apparently that hadn't been enough to deter the jerks who'd shown up to fuck with Davis' house.

The gravel driveway seemed to go on and on, cutting through the thick foliage on either side. Still, the truck handled the road well, and then finally, they came to a clearing, and there was the house.

It was painted white, with bright green shutters, and big, taking up a significant portion of the clearing, but it seemed like most of it was only a single floor. There was one section that was clearly a second floor, and when Pax got out of the truck, he realized that it faced the water.

Because yes, that was water. The trees leading up to the edge of the beach were cleared, and there was a wooden pathway leading out towards the ocean.

"You like it?" Davis' question was casual, non-committal, but Pax knew him well enough to hear the underlying eagerness.

He wanted Pax to like it; Pax's opinion mattered to him.

You want a lifetime with him, and maybe you could even get it someday, in this big white house, with its wraparound porch and its swing, where you and he could sit and hold hands.

Insert a brownstone in New York, or a condo in downtown Miami, and that sounds just about perfect, Pax added internally.

"I do," he said and didn't even have to lie. "I really love it, actually. I didn't realize you were this close to the ocean."

"You said you wanted to go to the beach," Davis said wryly. "So here's the beach. Surprise!"

"And nobody will bother us here," Pax said. They could hold hands here, too, not just in their own condos, or in Floria's studio. They could go to the beach and kiss. Hold each other. They wouldn't be bothered.

A few years of living like that didn't sound so terrible, not if he got to live those years with Davis.

"Hopefully," Davis said, as he grabbed their bags out of the back of the truck. Climbing up the steps onto the porch, he approached the front door, Pax trailing behind him.

"They changed the door code," he added, pulling a piece of paper from his pocket. "Because of those dickheads who apparently need a good ass-kicking."

"I hope they show up," Pax said. Meaning it. He'd happily bash a few skulls, despite the consequences, if that meant that Davis would be left alone.

If it meant *they* would be left alone.

Because, really, how long could they keep this secret if people from Davis' small town kept showing up here. Eventually they'd find it really telling that Davis wasn't coming here alone anymore, but instead, that he kept bringing Paxton.

How long would a secret like theirs last in such a small town?

It won't, Pax realized.

But that was a problem for a different day.

Davis typed in the code, and let them into the house.

It was light and airy, a ton of sunshine filtering in between the white wooden slatted blinds and through the skylights dotting the vaulted ceilings.

The floors were all wood, the walls were the color of coffee with too much cream, and one room blended almost effortlessly from one to the next.

Davis led him through the entry, through the living room, and into the kitchen. It had beautiful dark wooden cabinets, contrasted with the light granite countertops and the sea-green tile backsplash.

"I really, really like your house," Pax said, leaning against the large island.

Davis' eyes lit up. "I think you mean that." He went to the fridge, pulled open the massive stainless steel door, and grabbed two bottles of water.

He tossed one to Pax, and opened the other, taking a long drink.

"Of course I do," Pax said, fiddling with the cap.

"There's a friend in town who will come check on things for me, after storms and stuff, and make sure it's all locked down, if one's coming, and his wife will bring groceries if I ask. I had her stock some stuff, but not much, because we'll only be here a few days."

Pax realized with a start that meant they would be *cooking*. Or Davis would. Because he sure as fuck couldn't.

"There's some places in town," Davis said, "and we'll grab dinner out, but I wanted stuff for breakfast and lunch." He grinned. "You should've seen your face. Trust me, I'm not expecting you to cook for me, sweetheart."

Pax rolled his eyes. "You'd be waiting a long-ass time if you did," he retorted.

"Well," Davis said, and he sounded resigned. "I guess there's no time like the present to go through everything and make sure that nobody stole any of my shit."

Davis told himself that he wasn't going to give a shit if anyone stole anything.

It was all material, and it could all be replaced. Besides, he had good insurance, because this garbage kept happening, and he'd worried, more than once, that someone would eventually take something.

But no, as they walked from room to room, it was all intact. Even the liquor bottles hidden in the driftwood cabinet at the end of the living room were full.

They checked his office, at the far end of the house, with its dark paneled walls and big desk.

He'd had the interior designer add it, though he rarely used it.

But the TV on the opposite wall as the desk was still there, as was the expensive sound system that he'd installed last year.

He'd worried it would be boring for Pax to go through everything he fucking owned, but he didn't seem bored in the least. Instead, he was curious about everything, like he wanted to know every detail, and on top of that, it was kind of an illicit thrill to see each and every room of his house through Pax's eyes.

Someday, he could be sharing this with you. You never built it just for you, 'cause you never wanted to be alone, you just were.

His pops had been telling him forever that he'd meet someone who would make him want to settle down. But it had never happened, not til Pax.

He was both excited and apprehensive to introduce Pops to Pax, and see the dawn of realization on his face when he came to the same conclusion that Davis had. If he was very lucky, Pax was going to be by his side for the rest of his lifetime.

Pops was going to be so happy for him; and also, inevitably, he was going to be amused by the fact that he'd fallen for the very last person he should've.

"A glorious irony," Pops was gonna call it. He could already hear him cackling about it.

He'd already sent him a text, even though Pops was absolute shit with his phone, telling him that he'd be stopping by on his way home.

He hadn't told him that he wouldn't be alone, but it would be a good surprise.

Finally, they headed upstairs, up the long curved wooden staircase that was the centerpiece of the foyer. It led to his upstairs suite. The only rooms up here were his own.

"This is all mine," Davis said, shoving his hands in his pockets and watching as Pax took in the massive bedroom, with its private porch that faced the ocean, and the big bathroom, and the attached closet, big enough to fit clothes for a whole family.

"All yours?" Pax raised an eyebrow. "Were you planning on settling down with more than one person?"

It was a huge amount of space for even two people, but when the architect had mentioned it to him, it had seemed right.

"I like my privacy and it seemed nice to have the option to just retreat . . . when everyone got to be too much." Of course, it wasn't like other people visited him here. It was really too far for his pops to drive on his own, and his parents were always too busy to come here. Occasionally he hosted friends, from college and old teammates from Charleston, before the team had fucked him over, but it had never been the warm, welcoming home that Davis had intended it to be when he'd built it.

He'd never had a chance to give it that warmth.

It was still standing, empty and waiting for him to figure out the rest of his goddamn life.

Though, he had to admit, he was pretty damn sure that one of the most important pieces was standing at the glass sliding door to the porch, staring out at the bright, late afternoon sunshine hitting the water and making it sparkle.

"I know I keep saying it," Pax said, turning back towards Davis, dipping his head bashfully, "but I really fucking love your house."

He was so pleased, he couldn't hide it. "Good," he said, and it was a miracle that he could do this now, fold Pax into his arms, and just hold him close.

A month ago, he'd despaired because he didn't think he'd ever get over him, and he wasn't sure he could ever have him.

"I also really fucking love you," Pax said, his voice muffled by Davis' shoulder.

It was amazing, the peace and warmth those words brought to him.

"I love you, too." He hesitated. "I'm real glad you came here with me."

He'd known, of course, what his house was missing, but he hadn't known it was specifically a Pax-sized hole, not til Pax was standing in it.

A minute later, Pax pulled back, and he was grinning. "Why don't you show me your little stretch of beach?"

It was warm enough near the house, but it could be chilly with the wind, so they detoured to Davis' closet, grabbing two hoodies.

Pax glanced at a gray plastic garbage bag, bursting at the seams, that he'd shoved out of the way, that now lay forgotten in the corner. "What's that?" he asked.

It turned out that no, it didn't matter if Pax knew the worst of how the Condors had dumped him, unceremoniously, but it *did* matter to him.

He felt the embarrassment wash over him in a hot wave. "All my Condors stuff," he said. "Everything I could find."

Pax pulled the sweatshirt on as they headed down the big staircase. "Ah," he said, noncommittally.

"I had crazy wild plans to make a big bonfire one night and burn it all. Make a clean break. Maybe lay some of the . . ." Davis hesitated. He didn't want to just say pain, even though it had definitely hurt like fucking hell. "Ghosts, I guess, to rest. Move on."

"But you didn't," Pax pointed out as he pushed open the back door and they walked onto the wraparound porch, and then headed down towards the wooden bridge that would take them over the dunes, towards the sand.

Davis tossed the football he'd grabbed from the basket in the corner, from one hand to the other. It felt like it belonged in his hand. Like it was just an extension of his body. And maybe it was a little bit of a comfort, too.

"It felt real overdramatic, even for the shitty mood I was in last year."

Pax was quiet for a long moment as they walked over the bridge and hit the sand.

Davis was surprised to see him plop down on the sand and pull off his shoes and socks, digging his toes into the sand.

"You bring that just to toss to yourself?" Pax asked then, gesturing to the football in his hands.

"You wanna play a little catch?" Davis said, and when Pax nodded, he pushed his own shoes off, followed by his socks, and jogged backwards.

The sun was out, but the wind, he noticed as he lengthened the distance between them, was going to make throwing challenging. But then he'd grown up here, he knew how to take the breeze into account.

It felt natural, like the most natural thing in the world to send a picture-perfect spiral down the beach towards Pax. He grabbed it out of the air, flipping it a few times in a motion that was as familiar to Davis now as his own.

"You as good a receiver as you are a quarterback?" Pax's voice carried over the gusts, a clear challenge in it.

"I'm gonna have to be, with you throwing against the wind," Davis teased back.

And like he expected, Pax's first pass was buffeted by the breezes swirling around the beach, and he had to dive to catch it, his fingertips just scooping underneath it before it hit the sand.

But instead of looking frustrated, when he pushed himself back up, Pax was laughing, like this was the most fun he'd ever had.

He didn't give Pax a moment to breathe though, he pulled his arm back and, quickly calculating the strength he'd need to make the throw, sending the ball hurtling down the beach, and as a result, Pax had to run for it before he finally jumped up, snagging it out of the air.

And, Davis realized as his eyes tracked Pax's pass back, this *was* fun. When was the last time he'd thrown a football with no worries, no concerns, no ulterior motives? When was the last time he threw one just for the sheer joy of it? For the feel of it in his hands, the challenge of putting it exactly where he wanted it to go?

He certainly hadn't done it since leaving the Condors, and after he'd taken the job in Miami, every pass had been for a purpose. To teach Pax. Or to sub for him, to give the wideouts a workout.

They'd been tossing the ball back and forth for at least half an hour, sweaty and sandy, when Davis realized that while *yes,* he'd brought the ball to the beach, it had been Pax who had suggested this.

Pax, somehow, impossibly, had known that he needed this.

When he finally collapsed into a drift, tired and happy, a good hour later, Pax joined him, a bright smile on his own face.

"That was fun, wasn't it?" he said.

"I don't think you're gonna be giving Tristan a run for his money," Davis said wryly.

"God, I hope not. I don't know how he does it." Pax was in fucking fantastic shape—Davis was one of the coaches who made sure of it—and he was still panting, his chest rising and falling beneath his t-shirt, the sweatshirt long discarded next to them.

"He's insane, it's a pretty standard wide receiver trait." Davis hesitated. "I . . . I think I really needed this. Thanks."

Pax's smile softened. "You did. Sometimes, in college, I'd go to the beach and just throw the ball to whoever would catch it. I needed to remember that I just loved football. Not the bullshit or the politics or the adulation or the pressure. Just me and a ball in my hand and someone to catch it, you know?"

Davis knew.

"You, on the other hand," Pax continued, "would have made a *great* receiver. A tight end, maybe, 'cause you're so big. Strong, too."

"You totally looked that up," Davis said with a chuckle. "How else would you have known I played tight end in high school?"

"Til the QB got hurt, and you put your hand up and said, *Coach, I can throw*, and damn, you really could."

"Guess so," Davis said. "I liked playing tight end. But quarterback was better."

"Yeah, 'cause you like being in charge," Pax teased.

But was it teasing if it was really true? He did like it. Probably why he'd loved being a quarterback, and probably why, despite all his reservations about the situation and about his future career possibilities, he really enjoyed being a coach.

Of course, part of that was that he enjoyed being *Pax's* coach, but it was more than that, Davis realized. He just *liked* doing it.

"How do you know me so well?" Davis said with a little groan. "What if there's no sexy mystery left?"

Pax laughed, and pulled himself off the sand, reaching out with a helping hand so Davis could pull himself up, too.

"Trust me," he said, "I think there's plenty of sexy mystery. Let's go explore some right now."

They'd showered—spending a very long time in Davis' ridiculously large shower—and then changed, and had grabbed a whole bunch of peel-and-eat shrimp from a little seafood shop in Port Royal, popping them out of their shells and making a game out of tossing the discarded shells into the plastic bag on the porch, when Pax brought it up again.

It was full-on dark now, and Davis hadn't bothered to turn any lights on, hoping to avoid the worst of the mosquitos, who still annoyingly wouldn't quit, even in November, and they were cuddled up on the porch swing, just like he hoped they'd be doing years from now.

And he was just about to say it, to address that nebulous future that he kept building in his head, when Pax spoke up instead.

"I still think you should build a bonfire and burn it all," he said.

At first, Davis didn't understand what he meant. Then suddenly, it dawned on him.

"No, no, that's stupid, I don't need to do that. They've been sitting in my closet just fine this whole time, I really just need to throw them out. Donate them, maybe."

"No." Pax's gaze was steady. Sure. "No, I think you were right the first time. You've got to set those ghosts free, Davis."

He wanted to argue that they were, but he knew better, didn't he? He knew what it had cost him to watch the tape.

What it was going to cost him to watch the Condors swarm into the Piranhas stadium. What it would cost to watch Tom Taylor's smug face as he took the field, leading a team that was supposed to have been Davis'. That *had* been Davis'.

"Maybe it's not as easy as that," Davis said hesitantly.

"Maybe, maybe not," Pax said, and snuggled in a little closer under Davis' arm, "but it sure can't hurt."

"It's pretty fucking dramatic." Davis felt like apologizing for that. Who *burned* everything with their ex-team's logo on it?

"Does it matter if it is? Nobody's gonna know about it. Just you and me. And you know, you have to know, I don't judge you. Not for anything to do with those assholes."

Davis knew. It was one of the things he most cherished about Paxton.

He'd never even *seen* the version of him that the Condors had built.

More than once he'd said, "It was like they didn't even know you."

They had though, but when push had come to shove, they'd lied. Saved their reputation and staked it to Taylor's, while sacrificing Davis'.

Still, it meant a hell of a lot that Pax stood behind him. Stood next to him.

"I know you don't, but this is . . . I don't know, a step too far?"

"It's not." Pax sounded resolved. "I really think you should do it."

Davis heard the rest of that sentence, even though Pax didn't say it. *Because next week, the Condors are coming to town, and you're going to be swamped with ghosts if you don't exorcise at least some of them.*

"Okay," Davis said, giving in. It was horribly dramatic, but Pax was right. Nobody but he and Pax would ever know about it. And if it helped, who cared if it was dramatic?

He'd been trying, this whole damn time, to believe, in spite of his overwhelming certainty of the opposite, that the Condors hadn't ruined his life. Burning the clothes had felt like a further confirmation that was true, even if he didn't want it to be.

But, he realized, it wasn't that at all.

He was going to lay that worry to rest.

Let some of that burden go.

And finally, remove the pain—or at least a fraction of it—from where it was lodged, right under his breastbone, where sometimes it hurt so much it was hard to breathe.

"We'll do it tomorrow night, yeah?" Pax said. "Our last night here."

Davis nodded. "We'll do it tomorrow night," he agreed.

Chapter
Fourteen

Pax woke up slowly, brightness lighting up the room as it filtered in through the big windows.

He immediately knew where he was. First, there was Davis' arm, heavy and warm across his chest, and then all that clean, pure light streaming in.

They were in South Carolina, at Davis' house.

All he wanted was to stay wrapped up in Davis' warmth, but nature was calling, so he carefully slipped out, but not before glancing over at Davis' face and taking in how peaceful he looked.

He did his business in the bathroom, and he'd hoped that he'd been quiet enough to not disturb Davis, but when he returned to bed, Davis' eyes were open.

"Hey," he said, his voice sleep-rough. Gravelly, in all the best ways, at the edges.

"Sorry, didn't mean to wake you," Pax said, sliding back between the covers.

But Davis didn't exactly look bothered. "Come 'ere," he murmured, and when Pax moved even closer, he surprised him by tugging on his arm, pulling him until he was resting on him hip to hip, chest to chest, his chin resting on Davis' shoulder.

"That's better," he said, and Pax couldn't argue with that. "I was just thinkin' . . . how I was so fucking miserable in this house for so long, and waking up with you like this . . . it doesn't erase that, it couldn't, but it makes it . . . better, now. Like you've sucked all the sting out."

"Sucked it out, huh?" Pax teased, waggling his eyebrows in the silliest way he could imagine. Anything to make Davis smile. And he did now, so much brighter, and with way more regularity, than he had in the summer, when they'd first met.

He was right, Pax couldn't heal him backwards. Those were shitty things that had happened, and he couldn't change them, couldn't even make them better now. But he could bring as much joy and love to Davis as possible.

"I want you happy, however that happens," Pax said softly.

"Are you there?" Davis' accent was stronger here, in his house in the country, and it shouldn't have sent a shiver of awareness up his spine, but then there was also the hot molasses look in his blue eyes. The kind of look that promised he'd deliver everything Pax dreamt about in the dark, late at night in his bedroom.

"Yeah," Pax said.

"Then I'm happy," Davis said.

Pax wasn't sure who reached for who first, but one moment he was just lying on Davis' chest, enjoying the firmness underneath him, and the next, they were kissing, hot and wild and perfect.

He'd already been turned on plenty by being laid out like this, like Davis' favorite blanket, and seeing the sweetness and heat in Davis' eyes, but now he was kissing him, and that was all it took these days. He went from excited to burning up in a second.

Then Davis planted his feet and thrust against him, his hard cock rubbing insistently against Pax's own, and he lost himself.

In the feel of Davis' powerful body, wrapped around his, in the hot give-and-take of their kisses, the groans of pleasure as Davis lost *himself*, and in the pure, not-quite-innocent-but-still-lovely happiness that they were both here, and that it wasn't just him who was spectacularly, sickeningly in love.

He'd sworn off coming in his briefs like a teenager ages ago, but with Davis, it just felt natural to grind a little harder, and then Davis' fingers dug into his hip, holding him at just the right angle, at the same moment he nibbled on his bottom lip, just a hair harder than Pax had expected, and he came, pulsing in long, throbbing shudders.

Davis moaned, and followed right after him.

For a long moment, neither of them moved, even though the mess seemed inevitable.

"I could wake up like that every day," Pax said quietly.

Davis' grip on him tightened. "Yeah," he said.

He had to know, just as well as Pax did, that such a rosy and optimistic interpretation of their future was probably not realistic, but he also didn't correct him. Which Pax believed meant that he too wanted to pull this sweet, perfect bubble around them for as long as possible.

Someday, maybe even a day very soon, the bubble would pop, but even if it did, they'd still have each other.

He knew one thing and one thing only: Pax wasn't going to give Davis up, no matter how hard it was to keep him.

"I guess," Pax said, "we should get up. Run?"

Davis nodded, and they began the ugly process of unsticking each other.

It seemed a little silly to take a shower before working out, but Pax wryly admitted to himself they didn't have much of a choice.

After a quick shower, and an energy-boosting smoothie that Davis whipped up, they went for a run on the beach.

It was just as abandoned as it had been yesterday, nobody in sight.

"In the summer," Davis said as they jogged down the sandy stretch towards what looked like, in the very, very far distance, a very, very tiny town, "there's more people. But it's too cold for Carolinians to come to the beach."

It wasn't exactly chilly; Pax hadn't bothered with Davis' borrowed hoody, and the breeze seemed to just cool him off today. But he supposed if you were used to it being a heck of a lot hotter, this could be considered "cold."

After their run, they showered again, this time slower and sexier, trading blowjobs with the hot spray warming them through.

"I guess," Davis said as they got dressed, "that you should see the town."

"Is it a town? Can we really call it that? How about a village?" Pax teased, and Davis had made a face, but looked secretly pleased as they got into his truck, and he took them to Port Royal.

It *was* tiny.

But they had really good fish and chips at the single pier, and after, walked out onto it, enjoying the fresh sea air.

There were some little shops, clearly designated for the tourist trade, but they were all closed up tight. "Off-season," Davis said as they walked by their dark windows, "not a lot of tourists want to come right now."

"Kinda nice that it's just us," Pax said, meaning it. He didn't want to deal with a bunch of fans swarming them. Maybe Davis had gotten used to the fame and attention that accompanied being a starting quarterback in the NFL, but he hadn't, yet, and whenever he went back to California, he often found himself hiding out in his parents' house, not sure whether he wanted to deal with people.

In Miami, people mostly left them alone, which was nice, but in La Jolla, he was a local boy made good, and they couldn't help themselves: they felt like they *needed* to tell him how proud of him they were, even though it hardly mattered to him what every single person in the state of California thought of him.

"Yeah, it is," Davis agreed, shooting him a quick smile. "Nobody to tell me what a fuckup I am."

It should have occurred to Pax that they did that. Because they surely weren't holding back when it came to praise. Why would they when it came to criticism?

"I can't believe anyone would do that," he said, because he really wanted to believe that they wouldn't.

Was that what he was in for, if he crashed and burned in Miami? Everyone back home telling him forever that he'd fucked it up?

Davis just shrugged. "Worse 'cause it's their home team," he said. "Everyone's got skin in the game, you know? And the Condors . . . well, you know they did their fucking best to shift the blame."

They had, and apparently not only had the other NFL teams believed them, but the fans had too. Fans who should've been loyal to Davis.

There were days when Pax, seeing the toll their words had taken on Davis, seriously considered driving up to their headquarters and punching every single person responsible in the face.

But he didn't, because he was a grownup and a professional, and what Davis really needed was someone to be there for him, to be in his corner, one hundred and ten percent.

"Doesn't make it right," Pax said. "Or easier to deal with."

"No, but . . ." Davis trailed off wryly. "It is what it is, at this point. Just glad that you don't have to see any of it."

Pax was too, because if he was forced to stand by and listen to someone berate Davis for things he hadn't done, for ruining a team that had ruined themselves, for not possessing the exceptional leadership skills of *Tom freaking Taylor*, who liked to beat women as a hobby, the chances of him *not* punching someone were slim.

"Me too, 'cause I'd have done something Coach would hate me for," Pax said seriously.

Davis rolled his eyes, like he didn't quite believe him, but Pax meant it.

He had a temper—a slow-burning one, yes, but a temper nonetheless—and the way Davis had been treated was undeniably a match.

"Come on, let's head home," Davis said.

On the way home, they stopped and got brats and buns, and a load of wood from the little convenience store around the corner from Davis' house.

There was a big Condors flag hanging on the far wall, not that surprising, considering where they were, but Pax noticed that Davis made sure to pull his hat low and to avoid looking at the flag, even though there was no way they didn't know exactly who he was.

How many tall guys with dark hair and shoulders the width of a city block hung out around here?

By the time they got back to Davis' house, Pax believed he needed to exorcise those demons more than ever, and this time, it seemed like Davis finally agreed, because as soon as they put the food away in the fridge, Davis told him he was going out on the beach to dig a hole for their bonfire.

Pax nodded.

He considered suggesting he help, or offering his company, but there was a look in his eyes this afternoon—wild and a little desperate—that had him saying instead, "I think I'm gonna study up on some of these plays that Coach Randy just sent over."

Davis nodded, and a few minutes later, he was gone, the back door closing behind him.

Davis didn't know what had finally broken him, but something had.

Was it the fact that he was back home, in the spot where he'd wallowed in so much fucking misery? That he'd taken Pax into Port Royal and he hadn't realized how much he was bracing for someone to approach him with angry accusations until nobody had? Or maybe it was Pax, gently and kindly suggesting that maybe he try to do something about all this baggage he kept dragging around?

Or it's everything, Davis thought as he grabbed the shovel out of the detached shed that held all his tools. *It's everything, and maybe you could stand swallowing it all down before, but you can't, not anymore. It's time to do something about it.*

There were plenty of dunes and sheltered areas on the beach where they could start a fire. It wasn't that hard to find them.

But the moment his shovel hit the sand, he knew that somehow, digging this hole was the *doing something about it* that he needed right now.

He dug, and thought about how the Condors had leaked to the press that he was somehow less of a quarterback, less of a leader, less of a *man*, than Taylor was.

He dug, and thought about how teammates that he'd thought were friends suddenly turned on him, frustrated that he hadn't won them a Super Bowl ring yet. Willing, Davis supposed, to do anything and *accept* anything, just to hoist the Lombardi Trophy.

Was Tom Taylor really so much better a quarterback than he was? That was subjective, Davis knew, but the one thing he knew *wasn't* subjective was that he was a trash can of a human being, and while Davis had certainly done things he wasn't proud of, at least he'd never used another human being as a punching bag.

He'd tried his hardest to be the best quarterback he could be. The best teammate. The best person. And it felt like the world had repaid him for that effort with nothing but derision.

Davis' shovel hit the sand again, and using his heel to shove it deeper, he pulled out another chunk of it.

For awhile, he'd actually believed that yes, there must be some kind of truth to all of this, because why else would everyone believe it so easily.

That was when the panic attacks had started.

But, deep down, now that he was looking at everything more clearly, now that he'd managed to get out of this house, and out of his own misery, he could see that none of this was on him.

It had happened *to* him; he hadn't been the cause.

Sure, that still made him plenty pissed off. He was angry that he'd been dismissed without even a second chance. He was angry that his brain had betrayed him, just when he needed it to stay steady.

But there were lots of things these days that he wasn't angry about.

He sure as heck wasn't angry at Asa Dawson, who *had* given him a second chance, though it hadn't been what he'd wanted or expected.

He actually enjoyed coaching, far more than he'd ever anticipated.

And he adored Pax, who somehow had become the light in all his days.

Davis wiped his forehead with the hem of his t-shirt. It was growing darker, and it was getting colder out here on the beach, but he was warm from all the exertion he'd made digging . . . he glanced down . . . well, a massive fucking hole.

Too massive, it turned out, to make a fire in.

Whoops.

Davis stared at it for a moment longer, feeling the burn of all that work in his arms, and then filled it back in, leaving just enough room to set up the bonfire tonight.

He felt better. Cleaner, almost, because he'd let himself look all the injustices right in the eye, and he'd exorcised at least some of them.

Was it ever going to feel *good*?

Was he ever going to be able to walk into the shop around the corner and not feel a little flash of pain at their Condors flag, hung proudly on the wall?

Probably not.

But a little sting was a hell of a lot better than an all-consuming ache.

For too long, he'd believed he deserved to feel like that; wretched and lonely and sick with what had happened.

Responsible, almost, like it had been him, not Taylor, who'd taken his hands to those women.

But he wasn't. He hadn't had anything to do with that. And he'd done his level best to try to compensate for his successor's attitude and behavior, donating last year's salary to an organization that worked on the ground to protect people from abusive relationships.

It hadn't felt like enough.

Maybe it wouldn't *ever* feel like enough, but now, Davis could make his peace with it.

When he walked back into the house, shedding his sandy, muddy shoes at the doorway, and leaning the shovel against the outside wall of the house, Pax was in the living room, tablet open in front of him, watching a play unfold on the screen, little X's and O's moving in a flawless rhythm.

"That's a good play," he said. He was tempted to put his hip on the couch, but he was filthy. He needed to maybe burn *these* clothes too, but he'd settle for sticking them in the washer before he took a much-needed shower. "You're gonna have to . . ."

"Keep my hips loose? Yeah, I know," Pax finished for him, glancing up, so much love and light in his eyes, was it any wonder that these days Davis was finally seeing things more clearly?

With all that light, it was impossible to hide in dark corners anymore.

"Hey, you said it, not me," Davis said.

"Except, you were *about* to say it," Pax teased. He looked him up and down. "Is there any more sand on the beach or did you drag it all into the house with you?"

"There's some left," Davis said, not feeling even the slightest bit ashamed. He'd done good work. Then he'd undone it, sure, but how could he feel bad when he felt so goddamned much lighter?

"That's good to know. The beach might be sad without it." Pax leaned back on the couch. "This is good stuff, though, the plays Randy sent over."

"He's good, and so are you."

Pax rolled his eyes but he looked pleased. "Kinda can't wait to get to work on these, not just watching them on the screen, but doing them, you know?"

"You know, the bye week's supposed to be a break." Davis turned and started towards the combo mudroom/laundry room, and he wasn't surprised at all to see Pax get up and trail after him.

"Yeah, except . . . I don't really feel like a break."

"If you didn't have Logan and Rob and the other guys keepin' you upright, you would, guaranteed," Davis said as he shucked his clothes off, tossing them into the washing machine. "You'd need the time for your body to recover."

"But I'm young and hot, and have a great offensive line," Pax said with a fierce grin, his gaze heating up as he took in Davis' increasingly naked body.

And didn't that just give him another boost of self-confidence? Because Pax *was* young and hot, and he still looked at Davis like he couldn't wait to eat him alive.

"I'm gonna go shower," Davis said. "Get cleaned up, and then we can start our fire, yeah? Roast our brats."

"Oh, I'm definitely thinking about starting a fire," Pax teased, reaching out to brush a stray streak of sand off Davis' cheek. "Also thinkin' about sausage."

Davis laughed. "That really should've been cheesy as hell, but . . ."

"But it wasn't?" Pax retorted hopefully.

Davis leaned down and gave him a peck on the lips. "Go study your plays, sweetheart, I'll be back in a few."

He showered quickly, and in cold water, because even though Pax's lines had been cheesy, undeniably so, they'd still turned him on, because this was Pax they were talking about, and pretty much everything about Pax did it for him.

When he returned downstairs, clad in jeans and a t-shirt, with two sweatshirts thrown over one arm, and the garbage bag full of Condors gear in the other, Pax was back on the couch.

"Have a good shower?" Pax asked, innocence in his expression, but it was the knowing edge to his voice that told Davis everything he needed to know.

"No, it was way too cold, and somehow way too lonely," he admitted. "You've now ruined me for solo showers for the rest of my life."

Pax didn't look disappointed by this at all.

"Good," he said. "Come look at this play."

He hit the *watch again* button on the tablet, and Davis settled down next to him, his brain shifting into football gear almost immediately as he took in what Randy had sketched out.

"We've tried variations of this before," he pointed out as they watched it for a fourth time.

"Yeah, but never with Kenyon getting the ball," Pax said.

"You think he'd be down for this?"

Kenyon was an interesting guy; a lot of the time, Davis didn't quite know what to make of him. He showed up every day at the practice facility, he worked hard, but he kept himself apart.

Everyone knew he was trying to amass enough money to put towards his foundation, and the foundation was what took the majority of his time and energy.

He was a great running back, but he could have been a future Hall of Famer, Davis thought, if he'd cared more about football and less about the world he was trying to change.

But truthfully, giving more of a shit about what kind of person he was than what kind of stat line he produced only made Davis like him more.

"Yeah, I think so," Pax said. But he sounded a little uncertain. "We'll have to see what he says."

"Did he tell you where he was spending the bye week?" Davis wondered, even though he could probably already guess.

"In Cleveland," Pax said. "Doing ground work for his foundation."

"He's a good guy."

Pax nodded. "Sometimes I wonder if he'll just decide to retire. Like . . . who was that Steelers running back who decided to retire at the height of his career to become a writer? M . . . something."

"Mendenhall," Davis said. "It was Mendenhall."

"Sometimes, I think we're his side gig," Pax said, and there was no judgement there. Like Davis, he obviously believed that respect for the man was more important than respect for the player—though Kenyon was hardly a slouch on the field.

He put in his time, he worked hard, he moved them down the field.

But when the game was over, he was done, and he checked out.

Pax had invited him several times to offensive line dinners, and Davis knew Sebastian had also extended an invitation to their victory get-togethers at Hibiscus, but he was always busy.

Davis had asked Pax a few months back if last year had been the same, and Pax had hesitated before saying that he thought so. But at the time, he hadn't thought much of it, because he hadn't realized how unusual it was, being brand new himself.

He had to admit, he wished that he could get to know Kenyon, who seemed like such an unusual and chill guy, a little better. Maybe make another connection. Maybe he'd talk to him himself, persuade him to come to the offensive line dinner this week.

"Well, we'll see what he thinks about it," Davis said. "I'm sure that Randy sent these over to him, too."

"I'm sure he did."

"Come on, let's make dinner, and then get this fire going," Davis said.

Davis wasn't surprised when Pax took one look at the section of beach where he'd dug, and immediately noticed that he'd put at least half the sand back.

"Get a bit carried away?" Pax asked, raising an eyebrow.

Davis set the bundle of logs down on the beach, and after untying the cords holding them together, began to pile them into the hole he'd created.

"It felt good," Davis admitted. If he couldn't talk about the way he felt with Pax, then he couldn't talk about it with anyone.

And, he discovered, he *did* want to talk about it. For the first time.

"Felt like . . . I don't know . . . I was doin' something about it, finally," Davis said. "Maybe you were right about this 'exorcising ghosts' thing."

"Maybe," Pax said seriously, but there was a glint of satisfaction in his gaze as they put together the logs, then found some little bits of kindling.

Soon enough, the fire was burning, and they settled down next to it, Pax skewering the brats with the big long metal sticks that Davis had bought ages ago but had never used.

"I hope you brought mustard," Pax said as his brat roasted over the flames, fat dripping and sizzling into the fire.

"Of course, what else would we have?" Davis was mystified. Who ate brats without mustard?

"Ketchup," Pax said. "My family eats ketchup. Don't ask, 'cause it's weird."

"It's a good thing I like you," Davis said. "*Love* you."

Pax laughed.

They finished roasting their brats and ate them, drizzled with mustard, nestled in buns with only a slight sprinkling of sand, and Davis thought that while he'd had some five-star meals in his life, nothing tasted better than the half-burned brat he ate on the beach with Pax.

Then, after they'd cleared away the food, there was no avoiding the purpose of the bonfire anymore.

Davis opened the trash bag and set it in front of the fire.

One by one, he threw t-shirts and hats and sweatshirts and polos into the fire. A jersey, with his old number four glinting in the firelight. Maybe he should have donated them, but there was something inherently satisfying about watching as each and every piece caught fire and then slowly, inevitably began to curl up and blacken.

Pax had been right, it didn't fix it, it didn't change anything, but it was one more way for Davis to reclaim his life. To declare, once and for all, that he hadn't been the one who fucked it up.

And when it was finally done, the last piece of clothing turning into ash, Pax reached for him, and held him for a very long time, the heat of him leaching so deeply into his skin, his body, his heart, that Davis was sure that he wouldn't ever feel cold again.

Chapter Fifteen

Pax wouldn't say that he was nervous, exactly, but he wasn't *not* nervous either.

As Davis pulled into the retirement community where his pops lived, on Hilton Head Island, he felt the rather inevitable bubble of anxiety begin to grow exponentially.

What if Davis' grandfather, who'd practically raised him as a surrogate parent, didn't like him?

What if he thought they were making a mistake? Lots of people might.

"Don't look like I'm drivin' you to your own funeral, sweetheart," Davis said, breaking the silence.

"Ugh, I don't, I swear," Pax said, except that he was pretty sure he totally looked that way. It sucked, not being able to hide anything you felt from your face.

It sucked now, and it really sucked when he sat in front of the media room full of reporters, all hoping they could break him into saying something he'd regret later.

"He's gonna love you," Davis said firmly. Confidently.

"He's not gonna tell us that we're making a huge mistake, getting involved?"

That was the source of his anxiousness, Pax was certain of it. Was real life already going to intrude into their perfect, happy bubble? He knew it was inevitable that it would, but he wasn't ready for it yet. *We still have two days before practice starts up,* he thought, *I'm ready for it to suck then, not for it to suck now.*

"Pops . . ." Davis hesitated. "He's always just wanted me to be happy. And I'm happy. So I don't think he's gonna say a damn word." He reached out and took Pax's hand, squeezing it. "If I thought for even a second he'd be an ass about this, I wouldn't bring you."

"Okay," Pax said, squeezing back. He trusted Davis, and if he said it was going to be fine, then it was going to be fine.

Davis turned down a side street, lined with palm trees, and then into the driveway of an impeccable bungalow, painted a bright, sunshine yellow, with pristine white shutters. The grass was perfect, even for November, and Davis shook his head as he turned the truck off.

"Pops givin' the yard guys a hard time, that's not surprising," he muttered.

"Why?" Pax asked as he shut the truck door behind him.

"'Cause he's bored and micromanaging the yard guys is his one joy in life," Davis said dryly.

But Pax knew that was immediately wrong, because the moment the door opened, and a big man, almost as big as Davis, appeared, the smile on his worn face made it *very* clear what the real joy in his life was.

"Davis!" he exclaimed, pushing open the screen door.

He was dressed in khaki shorts and a light blue polo shirt with the Piranhas logo embroidered in the corner, and seeing it, Pax realized his one mistake: he'd believed that Davis' grandfather cared more about Davis' success than Davis himself.

But he only had to see his beaming face, and watch as he walked out, clearly fit and in great shape, with a head full of thick white hair brushed back from his face, the same blue eyes as Davis, still clear and sharp, to know that all Pops cared about was Davis, the man, not Davis the quarterback.

Pax watched as grandfather and grandson embraced, and knew what Davis had said was true. It *was* going to be fine. More than fine.

Finally, Davis turned to Pax with a flushed, happy face. "Pops," he said, "this is Paxton. Paxton, this is Hank Abernathy."

Pax knew then what it felt like to have that sharp blue gaze turned on him. It was so much the same as having Davis look at him, but different too. Older, quieter, but no less intense.

"Mr. Abernathy, it's really good to meet you, Davis has told me so much about you."

Pops shook his hand, as he tilted his head. "Paxton, huh? Pax, you're the quarterback, and Davis here is your coach, yes?"

Pax nodded.

"Pops," Davis said hesitantly, "Pax is more than just my quarterback. He's my . . ." He shot Paxton a quick look brimful of happiness and Pax realized in that moment what this meant to Davis, introducing someone he loved to the most important person in his life, the man who'd essentially raised him. "He's my person."

"Your partner," Hank said steadily. "Then, Pax, you should call me Pops, because I can't have Davis' man being so formal around me."

Davis' man.

He'd never thought of himself as that, but now that he did, he realized that Pops was right.

"I'm honored, sir," Pax said, meaning it.

"Pops, remember," he corrected with a twinkle in those familiar blue eyes. "Come on in, I have some lemonade and Mrs. Robb brought lunch over."

The inside of Hank Abernathy's house was as clean as the outside. Everything neat and tidy, and there was a feeling, as Pax walked in, that reminded him a little of the house that Davis had built. And he knew, without having to be told, that Davis had spent a lot of time here as a boy.

"I wish you'd told me that stupid security company called you," Pops said as he pulled glasses from the cupboard and a pitcher of lemonade from the fridge. Pax took a seat at the kitchen table, and Davis leaned against one of the countertops. "I'd have gone out to take care of it myself."

"You didn't need to. You know we're on our bye week, and well, it was nice to get out, and see the house." Davis took the glass of lemonade from his grandfather and handed it to Pax. "And to show Pax, of course."

"You like it?" Pops asked, that intense gaze suddenly pinning Pax in place.

"Yeah, yeah I did, actually. Not what I'm used to, but it's nice."

"Too remote, I told Davis he was crazy to settle all the way out there, when he could've built a really nice house here, on the island, but he wouldn't listen."

"Yeah, with all these damn people, always wantin' to pry into my business," Davis retorted. "Sounds like paradise."

"They'd have left you alone," Pops insisted.

But Pax knew better. Especially if Davis was a local boy.

"I hate going home," Pax said, and felt two sets of blue eyes swivel his direction. "Everyone feels like they own you, like you should stand there and listen to whatever they have to tell you, good or bad."

Davis nodded. "Honestly, I was relieved, when . . . well, when the stuff with the Condors went down. I could go hide."

"Not like people out there are any better," Pops said, shaking his head in disgust. "They still say shit to you."

"Yeah, but there's way less of them," Davis pointed out.

Pops was quiet for a moment. "Was it really like that for you here, son?"

Davis looked at Pax, the truth in his eyes. They understood each other, understood what it meant to be that local boy who made it. "Yeah, sometimes. But it's okay. I like comin' to see you, that's always the highlight."

Pax sipped his lemonade.

"Where are you from, Pax?" Pops asked archly. "Do I need to go over there and kick some butts, too?"

Pax laughed. "California. Southern California, just outside LA. Might be a bit far for you, sir."

"Might be," Pops said, cackling. "Must be real different here than it was there."

"Can be, sometimes, but . . ." Pax hesitated. Davis had made it clear what their relationship was and Hank had barely seemed to blink at the implications, but he still wasn't sure how much he was supposed to share. "But Davis has been a real good influence. The coaching staff last year was not very good, it turns out, and I didn't even realize how bad it was, until Coach Dawson and then when he brought Davis on board."

"I told him not to take that job," Pops said bluntly. "But I'm real glad he did. Real glad. 'Cause I think you're good for each other. Certainly obvious how much you like each other."

"Pops," Davis protested, even though he obviously believed it too. But it was cute seeing him like this, flushed and a little embarrassed. Teased about his love life.

Pops' expression turned more serious as he opened up the fridge again and pulled out a big bowl of what looked to be chicken salad. "But you're gonna have to be a lot more careful about it, you know, when you go back to Miami."

"We know," Davis said.

He shook his head, a half-smile tugging up the corner of his mouth. "You never gotta make things easy on yourself, Davis. Pick the toughest position on the field. Need to be the best at that, no matter what it costs. Now fall in love with the one guy you shouldn't."

"If he didn't, he wouldn't be who he is," Pax said, because he couldn't help but defend the man he loved. Sure, Davis made things tough on himself, but Pax did the same thing. That was one of the reasons they understood each other.

One of the many reasons they'd fallen in love with each other.

They understood, unlike almost anybody else, what a tough, hard, lonely road that was to walk.

"I do think I like you, Paxton Kelly," Hank said thoughtfully as he dished up chicken salad. Added in some fresh lettuce, and a handful of fresh vegetables on the side.

"That can't be a surprise," Davis said.

"Oh, it's not. I knew when you finally picked someone, you'd pick good, that was never a worry." Hank brought two plates to the table, and on his way back to fetch the last, he patted Davis on the head, like in his mind, he was still a nine-year-old boy. "You've got a good, strong heart. True."

"I couldn't agree more," Pax said, as they all sat down to eat.

Davis flushed again. "Y'all are being ridiculous," he said. But Pax could tell that he was actually really pleased.

"Which is why I never understood how anyone who met you could believe any of that bullshit the Condors spouted."

Pax watched as Davis' expression hardened. "I told you, I don't want to talk about it."

"Well, I do. I want to talk about how you never defended yourself. You just ran home and licked your wounds, all by yourself. Wouldn't let me come. Wouldn't let your parents come."

"Dad and Mom were too busy, anyway." *Like always*, Pax heard even though Davis didn't actually say the words.

"I'm just glad you aren't alone anymore, and you've got people. A *person*, actually," Pops said, like Davis hadn't even spoken. He turned to Pax. "You close with your family, son?"

"Uh, well, sort of," Pax said. He hadn't even talked about this with Davis, but it didn't really surprise him that Hank Abernathy would cut to the one subject that he felt awkward about. "They're busy too, like Davis' parents. And uh . . . well, real happy that I'm a pro football player. Makes them look good. They like that." Pax hesitated again. "Not that they're bad, they just . . . well, sometimes I think I'm more of a football player to them than a son these days."

Davis' gaze softened. "And a good man," he added.

"I concur," Pops said with a sharp nod. "Now let's eat, 'cause I know you two will need to get on your way back to Miami."

They were able to have a nice leisurely lunch—Mrs. Robb's delicious chicken salad, and even some of her incredible lemon squares—before they had to take off, and head to the tiny Hilton Head airport to catch their charter flight back to Miami.

"I'm glad you made time to stop by," Pops said to Davis as they were heading towards the front door. "Don't be a stranger, okay?"

Davis pulled his grandfather into a tight hug, and then Hank turned to Pax, and to Pax's surprise, he got the same treatment, a warm, firm hug. "And you too, Pax. You're part of this family now."

"Thank you, sir," Pax said, inevitably humbled. He didn't blame his parents for getting caught up in the whole "your son is an NFL player" mess, because it was so easy to do. Lots of parents ended up there, and lots of players, too. They let their egos run rampant and begin to control them, instead of the other way around.

He hoped, still, that with time, he'd go back to being, "our son, Paxton," instead of, "Paxton, the starting quarterback for the Miami Piranhas."

But until then, until they'd gotten used to the idea more, and it didn't overwhelm them, he could have Pops, if Davis would lend him.

"I'm here, if you ever need to get away for a day or two," Pops said. "Now have a safe flight home."

Players weren't officially due back at practice until Monday, but coaches were a different story. Davis had a meeting on Sunday. An optional meeting, is what Asa had called it, but he knew Asa well enough to know that even his optional meetings were important. And surprisingly, though he hated leaving Pax at home, he was actually kind of eager to get back to work.

Davis kissed Pax goodbye while he was still in bed, took a shower, and got his game face on.

He could absolutely go into the practice facility and pretend like he hadn't spent the last week fucking his quarterback's brains out and falling deeper, more irrevocably in love with him.

He totally had it together, was convinced he was acting normal, until he was sitting at the conference room table and Beau slid into the chair next to him, an irrepressible grin on his face.

"So," he said, "how was your week off?"

It was a totally normal question.

Beau didn't even have a particularly knowing look in his eye, which, the last time they'd seen each other, at that ridiculous intervention at Hibiscus, he definitely had.

And still, Davis froze, no doubt giving Beau the best "deer in the headlights" expression he'd ever seen.

You told yourself you were gonna be better than this.

Except, he wasn't. He'd always prided himself on his poker face, but apparently a whole week of bliss with Paxton was too freaking amazing not to give away immediately.

Beau chuckled. "I guess it was pretty dang good, then. Did you work?"

"Uh, I actually went home. Checked on a few things. Saw my pops. You know, just generally caught up on stuff."

"We could all use a little time to do that," Beau said with a serious nod.

"You and Sea Bass headed down south, yeah? To the Keys?"

"It was definitely a good time. We didn't take the whole week, 'cause God forbid we actually take a week off, but it was a long weekend at least. Sebastian's mom is so great. And it was nice to just . . ." Beau's voice grew wistful. "To just exist, you know? Lie on the beach and just talk about shit that wasn't football. To have a long leisurely brunch, no meetings to get to. You know how that is."

Davis knew.

Oh, he definitely knew.

And he was pretty sure that Beau knew too, but at least he was giving him some plausible deniability here.

"Oh yeah, that's the truth," Davis said enthusiastically.

"We . . . uh . . . I went to the beach, too. But it's a little colder up in Carolina. Not cold, really, but colder."

Beau smiled. He was too smart to have not caught Davis' slipup, but also too smart not to call attention to it.

"Your house is right on the beach, yeah? By Hilton Head?"

"About an hour-ish north, up the coast," Davis said.

"Well, you ready for this week?" Beau asked.

Normally, Davis knew he'd be angsting about the fact that the Condors were coming to town. That he'd have to face the team that rejected him. That he'd have to see Tom Taylor's obnoxious, punchable face grinning through his helmet, smugly pleased that he'd done whatever the fuck he wanted and paid zero consequences for it.

But truthfully, it was hard to get so upset, not when it felt like he was the happiest, the most at peace, he'd been in years. Even before everything had fallen apart.

Of course, then there was the inevitable focus-pulling distraction that he had to keep all that happiness and peace under wraps. At least most of it anyway.

'Cause if he came in today all blissed out, there was no way that wouldn't raise at least *some* questions.

"Yeah, actually I am. It was a good week. Peaceful. Helped me lay some of my shit to rest, you know?" That much he *could* admit to. Not who had been the instigator of it, but that it had happened.

Beau's face softened. "Good. You know we've got your back one hundred and ten percent."

"Yeah, I do." He did, and that didn't hurt either. "Pax is determined to kick their asses from here til next Sunday."

Davis was proud of himself for saying Pax's name and not stumbling over it, even the tiniest bit. Not even when the last time he'd said it, he'd been moaning it as Pax knelt between his legs and showed him exactly what paradise felt like.

"He played great against the Cowboys," Beau said with a nod. "So he's really gettin' the chops but . . . he just seemed, I don't know, a bit mechanical out there? Like he wasn't really enjoying it."

They hadn't talked about it, because their bubble of joy had felt too new, too perfect, to mar with some of the struggles they'd gone through after finally letting the fight go, but Davis wasn't stupid or blind. He knew how unhappy Pax had been. And yet, how beautifully he'd played. Like he'd focused every ounce of his brain and his body on the game, but even though nobody could argue with the results, he'd obviously been miserable.

It was a cold-blooded way to win, and while some quarterbacks might not have minded it, Davis knew that was never going to be Pax.

Because Pax wasn't just a quarterback with his head or his body; he was a quarterback with his heart, too.

"I don't think he was, but we're gonna fix that," Davis said. Hesitated. Unsure of how much to say, even though he was fairly sure of two things: *one*, that Beau had guessed what was really going on between them, at least since the "intervention," and *two*, that he wasn't going to tell his dad. *I'm not here in an official capacity,* he'd said, but he'd been there, anyway, and Davis had a feeling that if it came down to it, Beau would defend them and defend their choices. "I don't even think it really needs fixed anymore, honestly. I think he's . . . he's got his head on right, now."

"His head?" The corner of Beau's lips quirked up. "You mean his heart?"

"Uh yeah, that too," Davis said, uncomfortable at just how on the nose Beau was.

Because Pax's head and his body hadn't been the problem. It had absolutely been his heart. But now that was in the right place.

"Well, I'm real glad to hear it," Beau said, just as his dad walked into the room.

If anyone was worried that Coach wouldn't come to the meeting prepared to take on the Condors this week, they obviously didn't know Coach very well.

Clearly, while Beau had stolen a quick break down south with Sebastian, Asa had done nothing but work for the last week.

"If you've checked your email, we have a complete practice schedule and game plan for the week," Asa said.

He looked worn and tired, shadows under his eyes, and somehow much older than his late forties, but there was a smug satisfaction in his face, too, that Davis couldn't blame him for.

Nobody had expected the Piranhas to do anything but continue to lose this year—and they were doing a hell of a lot better than that.

Certainly, nobody had expected them to be eight and three and contending for the division title and a playoff berth.

It was undeniable that they were, but the Condors were a big test. They'd only lost one game so far this season, and they had a stranglehold on the lead in the division.

To beat them would establish them not only as a team to be reckoned with during the tail end of the season, but during the playoffs.

And it would feel damn good to be able to be part of that.

It shouldn't be personal, but it was.

"Didn't leave the rest of us any work, huh?" Brett Jackson, the defensive coordinator, said dryly.

"I was free, I had the time," Asa said.

Davis glanced over at Beau, and though he didn't roll his eyes, because he wouldn't, not in a coaches' meeting that his father was leading, Davis could *feel* the intense difficulty he had in holding it back.

Nobody said anything, but Davis knew they'd *all* taken time off.

Everyone except the head coach, apparently.

"Randy was around, he helped me put together some plays, and I know Davis and Pax had some excellent suggestions that we worked in," Asa continued briskly. "So let's pull up the practice schedule first, as I want to be completely prepared, absolutely no wiggle room, for the game this week. This is four quarters where we need to play as close to perfect football as we can. To win, we won't be able to make any mistakes. Offense, defense, special teams."

"We'll be ready," Randy said. "Pax is playing the best he's played all season."

Asa nodded.

"Davis has done a dynamite job of bringing him along. He's taking the field with a confidence we just didn't see before, but I want to get Kenyon more involved. Without," Asa said, pointedly glancing over at Davis, "Pax worrying that he's not carrying the team enough. He's doing plenty. He does too much, he makes mistakes."

Davis nodded in agreement. He could. He was still young and still learning. There'd be plenty of time for Pax to make the playoffs, to win playoff games, but there was something special about this year, about subverting everyone's expectations, about doing this *with* Pax, because truly Davis had no idea what he'd be doing next year.

Would he still be here, with Pax?

He hoped so, but there was still a part of him that hoped that maybe a team out there might give him one more chance to take the field.

Even with laying his ghosts to rest, he felt like he had one more try in his tank, an attempt to set the record straight.

This had gone a long way to doing that, but being a coach wasn't the same as being QB1.

"We're working on minimizing the mistakes," Davis said. "He's learning."

"He's comin' along just fine," Asa agreed. "Now, Beau, let's go over the practice schedule this week."

Asa had *definitely* overworked himself this week, because when Davis pulled up the schedule on his tablet, even the specific kinds of play packages were filled in. These were often details they worked in later in the week, during each day's standup meeting before practice started, but it seemed Asa knew exactly what they were going to need to beat the Condors.

A hell of a lot of skill and execution and then there's luck, too, Davis thought, but he felt really confident about it in a way he hadn't before this meeting. He, more than anyone else, knew how tough of a team the Condors could be.

Beau did as instructed, and they discussed each facet of the practice schedule. Davis had to admit it seemed really solid. Each facet of the offense that he'd been concerned about was covered. There was plenty of work between the running and passing squads, and extra work on blocking and quick handoffs, which the Piranhas would need to hold back the Condors' exceptional defensive unit.

And, Davis noticed, with surprise, they had a short day on Thursday.

"What's Thursday?" Randy asked gruffly, interrupting Beau.

"Thursday is Thanksgiving," Beau said. "Shockingly, my father decided you might actually want to spend it with your families."

There wasn't really time for him to go back to Carolina and see Pops, though Davis supposed he could, if he wanted to. And Pax hadn't mentioned his parents flying out, but he'd have to ask him tonight if he wanted to host a little get-together at his condo. Just the players who knew, or who had figured it out, anyway. That might be fun.

He hadn't ever cooked a turkey before, but he'd roasted a chicken and it couldn't be all that different, right? Besides, Davis was already thinking of the way Pax's eyes always lit up at the thought of him cooking. He'd really seemed to enjoy it before and

. . .

"Davis?"

Davis realized with a flush that Beau had been saying his name. "Uh, yeah?" he asked.

"Just checking in that there weren't any other packages or substitutions you wanted to work on specifically this week?" Beau asked, and there was no way Davis could miss the way he was definitely laughing at him, on the inside.

Well, Beau was still stuck in the honeymoon phase too, with Sebastian, so he could hardly judge, and as long as he didn't tell his father, Davis told himself it didn't matter if he'd guessed the truth.

'Cause he definitely knew.

"Actually, I'd like to get Jones more reps."

"Jones . . . you mean Blake Jones . . . the *backup*?" Randy sounded mystified. "Why? Is there something going on with Pax?"

"No, no, of course not, he's solid, you know that, we just finished talking about that, but I just worry . . . if we have to send Jones in, he's *not* ready."

"Okay, let's pencil in a segment of practice, putting Jones with the first team," Asa said, his tone brooking zero argument. "Now, onto the game plan." He motioned to Brett, closest to the door, to flick off the lights, and even though he could see Asa glance his direction, briefly, before he started playing Condors' film, he didn't say or do anything else.

Assumed, which Davis respected the hell out of, that he could handle it. And he could. He'd almost gotten used to it, from the number of times that he and Pax had watched it over the last week.

But this time, they weren't just watching the defense.

This time, they had the offense tape up on the screen, and there he was, at the tail end of two seasons ago, dropping back, his footwork pretty decent, finding Rhimes, his favorite receiver down the flat for an easy forty-yard touchdown.

He remembered that game, that play. Remembered the ease of it, how good it had felt, natural almost.

They'd won that game, won the division, and had lost in the first round of the playoffs.

At the time, Davis should have seen that it was the beginning of the end for him, but in the middle of it, he'd been too blinded by all the possibilities, by the chance they could just do it next year, to realize that the Condors had decided he wouldn't get the chance, and that he was a nice, easy scapegoat for all their problems.

Randy and Asa broke down some of the offensive formations, many of which the Condors still used.

Davis also had to give Asa credit, as much credit as he possibly could, because not once did he turn to Davis and ask a question about the Condors' offensive schemes.

It was all laid out on the tape, if you looked hard enough and long enough, but Davis knew plenty of coaches who wouldn't have bothered, not when the shortcut was sitting right there. Even when the shortcut was fucking traumatized by his ex-team's treatment.

The meeting finally broke up, and Davis exchanged a few words with some of the other staff, before heading down to the staff weight room, getting in his workout for the day, and after a quick shower, he headed back to his condo.

He'd texted Pax his door code a few days ago, so he wasn't all that surprised to see Pax sitting on his couch, laptop in front of him as he responded to emails, but he was still unbelievably pleased.

"Hey," he said, dropping down on the couch next to him.

Pax leaned into him. "Let me just finish this email, okay?" he said. "Then I want to hear all about how much torture we're in for this week."

Davis let him finish typing, just enjoying the warm weight of Pax against him. He'd missed him today, even though he'd been busy and focused on work. Even though he'd been trying hard not to think about him, because maybe his face might give away how absolutely fucking thrilled he was that he'd found the love of his life.

Because that was what Pax was, wasn't it?

He'd found him, and he wasn't going to let him go. No matter what.

"Okay, so tell me all about it," Pax said, finally shutting the lid of his laptop and turning to him, a soft smile on his face. "I missed you today, I don't know if I'm supposed to say that, but I'm gonna."

Davis leaned in and gave him a kiss. Meant for it to be short and sweet, but it lingered, 'cause it felt so damn good. "I missed you, too," he admitted. "And not necessarily torture, but it's real planned out. I think Asa barely slept, never mind took a break, during the last week."

Pax looked concerned—a concern that mirrored Davis' own, and one he knew Beau felt too. But you couldn't help someone who refused to help themselves, and on top of that, it wasn't exactly helpful that Asa's methods were proving to be very, very successful.

"Also," he added, "I had them pencil Blake in this week for some work with the first team. So don't freak out, okay?"

Pax shot him a look. "I'm not freaking out."

"But you're going to. You wouldn't ever say anything, but you'd be secretly angsting over whether you're being replaced. And I don't want you to worry 'cause you're not being replaced. I just want to get Blake some more reps in case anything happens to you. It's just a worse-case-scenario thing, prep for the future. That's all."

"Okay."

To Davis' surprise, Pax looked like he meant it.

"What," Pax continued, smiling now, "you really thought I was gonna freak out?"

"You *do* like to try to carry the whole team," Davis teased, nudging him. "It's one of your more endearing and yet most frustrating qualities."

"Yeah, yeah, I know," Pax said, still grinning. "I'm working on it."

"Speaking of that . . . there's gonna be more push to get Kenyon involved this week," Davis said. "And I also thought, he kinda keeps to himself, doesn't he?"

"Yeah, he does. I invited him to a couple of the offensive line dinners, 'cause it's not like he doesn't benefit from those guys killing it every week, but he said he was busy."

"I know he runs that foundation of his." But the more Davis thought, the less he realized he knew about their mysteriously quiet running back.

"Yeah, the one for disadvantaged kids. I sent a signed jersey over for them last year. I should really send another one, and some additional swag." Pax opened his laptop and began typing out another email.

"It's Thanksgiving this Thursday," Davis said, but Pax didn't even glance over.

"Oh yeah, I guess it is. You're not going home, and Pops didn't say anything about coming down, so I'm assuming he's not."

Davis had to smother his grin at Paxton calling his grandfather Pops. "Yeah, he'll go to Charleston. Spend it with my parents. But I'm at a loose end, and I'd guess you are too."

Pax nodded.

"Why don't we host the other strays here, at my place? I thought I'd invite Kenyon. Make it non-negotiable."

This finally got Pax's attention; he stopped typing and glanced over. "You really want to host a Thanksgiving dinner?"

"Sure. I can cook. Well enough, probably. Or I could get it catered."

Pax's expression was still dubious. "I guess we'd probably have to keep . . ." He gestured between them. "Us under wraps."

"I'm assuming that most if not all of the players that'll come were at that god-awful intervention, so they've already guessed," Davis pointed out dryly. "I know Dylan and Logan are with Logan's parents. I guess they rotate around all the Banks brothers for holidays, and they're here for Thanksgiving. But I know Wade and Tristan are at a loose end, and then there's us, and maybe Kenyon, if I can convince him to come."

"What about Sea Bass and Beau?"

"I'd assume they'd spend it with Coach . . . if he celebrates."

Pax didn't look convinced.

"Okay, I'll invite them, on the off chance they don't have plans," Davis said.

"You really think Kenyon is gonna come?"

Davis shrugged. "No idea. Guess we'll find out tomorrow."

Chapter Sixteen

Davis cornered Kenyon right after practice.

He'd already asked Wade and Tristan, who were enthusiastically on board. Beau had said that he was pretty sure Asa was going to be working—adding wryly that he'd had to remind him, even, that there was a fairly famous holiday this week, and that they'd need to cut practice shorter than usual—and if he was, then he and Sebastian would love to come.

The last person he needed to ask was Kenyon, who as usual, was already on his way out of the locker room right after showering and changing.

"Hey, Ellis," Davis called out, walking faster as Kenyon headed towards the door. "A second, if you have one."

Kenyon's expression when he turned around was friendly and open. That was the thing; he never seemed annoyed about stopping to chat or just generally shooting the shit. But he also definitely had places to be. What places, Davis wasn't quite sure.

Everyone *liked* him, but nobody really *knew* him.

"What's up?" Kenyon asked, shifting his bag from one shoulder to another. "Everythin' okay?"

Right there was the issue; he thought there needed to be something wrong for Davis to talk to him.

Davis resolved to make more of an effort. He'd tell Logan, too, who had never let anyone keep to themselves in his entire life.

"Thursday's Thanksgiving," Davis said, "and if you don't have any other pressing plans, I thought you might want to join me and Pax and a few other players at my place for dinner."

Kenyon looked surprised, and then hesitated. Davis was sure he was in for another rejection.

But Davis had already resolved he wasn't going to take no for an answer. Unless it was a really good, really firm no with an exceptional reason behind it.

"Listen, we really like you," Davis said. "And we'd really like you to come, unless you've already got plans with family or friends."

"I don't, actually," Kenyon said slowly. "But . . ."

"It's Thanksgiving," Davis said plainly. "Come hang out with us. We're your brothers, even if it's just for one day."

Kenyon raised a dark eyebrow. "It means something to you," he stated, rather than asked.

Davis nodded.

"Okay, I can come in the evening. When's your dinner?"

"Later, earlier, I hadn't really decided yet," Davis said with a wry chuckle. "So why don't you set the time that works for you?"

"Six would be good."

"Six it is," Davis said, and patted him on the shoulder. "I'm real glad you're coming."

Kenyon still looked faintly puzzled, but he said, "Me too." And it sounded like he meant it. "Can I bring anything?"

"Yourself."

"You're cookin' dinner?"

Davis shrugged. "My granny was a fucking amazing cook, and she taught me some stuff. I don't think we'll starve." Mentally he crossed his fingers. He could still call in some favors, maybe get it catered, but that felt a little like cheating. His granny would've been appalled at him inviting people over for Thanksgiving and not even attempting to cook some of the food.

"Sounds good," Kenyon said. "I'm actually lookin' forward to it."

"Me too," Davis said.

Now he was going to have to figure out how to cook a goddamned turkey. It couldn't be all that hard, right?

"You're going to actually roast that turkey?"

Tristan stared at the raw turkey sitting in Davis' sink, an incredulous expression on his face.

"No, silly, he's gonna use it as a football," Wade teased, nudging his boyfriend as he carried in the beer they'd brought. "Of course he's gonna roast it, and it's gonna be damn delicious."

Davis thought Wade was being pretty optimistic but he didn't say so.

He'd read up on turkey roasting, and of course, his granny had taught him how to roast a chicken. It couldn't be all that difficult, right? Except face to face with the raw bird, it was turning out to be a lot more difficult than he'd anticipated. He'd already had to send Pax out to find either a bigger roasting pan or a smaller turkey.

And right in the middle of that conundrum was when Wade and Tristan had shown up, early, ostensibly to see if they could "help."

Davis already knew there was nothing either of them could possibly do to make this dinner thing any easier. From the way Tristan and Wade were both eyeing the turkey, there was no way under the sun either of them had any more experience than Davis.

"There's always the Butterball helpline," Tristan added helpfully.

"We're not calling the Butterball helpline," Davis said, frowning at the raw turkey in his sink. "That's admitting defeat."

"And the great Davis Abernathy never admits defeat," Wade crowed.

Davis wasn't so sure about the great part of that statement, but he definitely wasn't going to let a turkey get the better of him.

The front door opened and closed, and to Davis' relief, it was Pax, carrying a big silver roaster.

"You don't want to know what I had to do to get this," Pax said, setting it down with a heavy thud on the counter. "It was the last one in the kitchen supply store, and it was *packed*."

"How many autographs did you sign?" Tristan asked with a smirk.

Pax flexed his hand. "Way too many," he admitted. "I even signed one woman's naked ass."

"In the kitchen supply store?" Davis asked, surprised.

"It was wild in there, okay? Don't ever ask me to go back there." Pax shuddered.

Davis picked up the roasting pan and, after peeling the stickers off, gave it a quick wash, then set it down on the counter. "Well, I guess I better make a damn good turkey, to repay your great sacrifice. A woman's ass, really?"

"Listen, according to her I'm the cutest thing since sliced bread."

Wade wrinkled his nose as Davis wadded up paper towels, drying the turkey's skin as advised in the tips and suggestions he'd read.

"Is sliced bread cute?" Tristan wondered.

"That sliced bread is *adorable*," Davis argued as he shoved the paper towels in the trash. What was the best way to get this behemoth into the pan?

Finally he just picked it up, plopping it down into the roasting pan. He got out his butter, as the Barefoot Contessa had told him to, and began to rub it down.

"Well, that answers the question I wanted to ask," Tristan said smugly.

Davis shot him a look over his bird. "Did you really think anything else was gonna happen? You made a *sign*."

"A damn good sign," Tristan said, popping a cube of cheese in his mouth from the tray on the kitchen island. "I didn't see anyone else committing that hard."

"Logan brought those date boxes," Wade said.

"Oh, yeah," Tristan said, "did you end up using those?"

Pax glanced down and Davis followed his gaze, nearly laughing out loud. He was wearing the horribly tie-dyed socks they'd made.

"Yeah, and it was fun," Pax said.

"We're gonna need to get our hands on some of those," Tristan said with determination.

"You know, you do them *out* of bed," Davis teased.

"Hey," Wade declared, "we do other things than have sex."

Pax patted him on the shoulder. "We know, Wade. We know."

"Not much else," Davis muttered.

There'd been a time when he'd actually been a little jealous of Tristan and Wade, when their obvious and open love and enjoyment of each other had seemed to fly in the face of everything that Davis wanted and wasn't allowed to have.

But now he could hardly be jealous when he'd woken up next to Pax this morning, and then proceeded to make him scream plenty, thank God for the excellent soundproofing in these condos.

He got the turkey in the oven as the rest of the group gravitated towards the living room and its huge TV, because the Thanksgiving games were just starting, and Logan's brother Landry was playing in one of them.

"He's one of us, by association," Wade declared. "So we gotta root for him."

A quarter went by before there was a knock on the door. Davis walked over, and when he pulled it open, it was to Sebastian, Beau, and the catering company he'd called, begging them to make all the sides.

Davis had decided, after doing his research, that roasting the turkey and also baking his granny's famous buttermilk biscuits was plenty of home-cooked for him.

"Aren't you forgetting something?" Sebastian asked, raising an eyebrow as he watched Davis unpack the containers with all the side dishes.

"Turkey's already in the oven, and I baked biscuits this morning."

"Biscuits?" Beau asked.

"Granny's secret recipe."

"And here I thought Pax just liked you for your big brawny muscles," Beau teased. "But you bake too!"

"On special occasions only," Davis warned.

"So who else is coming?" Sebastian asked. "I hear Tristan and Wade yelling at the TV."

"Landry's playing, and they've decided to adopt him," Davis offered. "And Kenyon is the only one who hasn't shown up early. Though I don't expect him to, because he set the time, for when he could make it."

"Huh, you actually got Kenyon to show up to a social event?" Beau sounded surprised.

"Hey, I like Kenyon," Sebastian said.

"I do too," Beau said.

"It's why I invited him," Davis pointed out. "But he wasn't gonna accept, just like he rarely accepts any invite. So I sorta bullied him into it. He's probably just going to show up just to make sure that I *actually* roast a turkey."

"Admittedly, the great Davis Abernathy roasting a turkey is an event I'm not sure anyone could miss," Beau said.

Sebastian laughed.

Davis decided this would be a good time to check the turkey in question because the last thing he needed was to completely bungle this. Beau was probably right; Kenyon was only coming to actually see if he could follow through on what he'd promised.

But the bird was coming along, beginning to deepen to a light, golden brown.

"Come on," he said, "let's go see what's going on with the game."

Beau and Sebastian followed him to the living room, and Davis thought, as they settled down, sharing one of his big club chairs, and he joined Pax in the other one, feeling no compunction about pulling Pax closer against him, despite all the catcalling, that this was actually *nice*.

He'd believed, when he'd played for Charleston, that those guys were his family, his brothers, but they'd never really been. Not like these guys.

And another little corner of his heart—of his soul—that he'd believed would never really heal, finally stopped aching.

Was it Pax's warm body pressed against his?

Or was it the friends who might tease but supported them all the way?

That nobody had ever judged him? That they'd never believed, like everyone else had, that he was poison? That he'd destroyed the vibe of the Condors' locker room?

They'd just accepted him, shitty history and all.

Davis decided it didn't matter which reason it was. It only mattered that it didn't hurt anymore.

Kenyon showed up when the turkey was done, Davis just having pulled it out of the oven and covered it with a huge swath of foil.

"Hey, can you grab that?" Davis asked, sounding a little more frantic than Pax had ever heard him before.

Tristan and Wade were arguing in front of the microwave as they figured out how to reheat the sides that Davis had bought from the catering company.

Pax opened the front door and Kenyon was standing there, hands shoved into the pockets of his jeans, looking apprehensive.

But Pax had trained himself not to hesitate in high-stress situations—and he thought hosting Thanksgiving for the first time with your brand-new boyfriend was undoubtedly a high-stress situation—and before he even blinked, he'd pulled Kenyon into a big hug. "So glad you came," he said, and meant it. "Come on, we're just about to sit down."

Kenyon raised a questioning eyebrow as soon as Pax led him into the kitchen, AKA chaos central.

"You sure about that?" he murmured as he took in the insanity currently occurring in every corner. Wade and Tristan had the microwave door open as they traded one hot dish for a cold one. Sebastian had to duck underneath it as he walked over to the oven to check on the biscuits, which were warming in a foil-wrapped packet. And then there was Davis, brandishing a huge, shiny knife, as he tried to watch an instructional video on his tablet and carve the turkey at the same time.

"Uh . . ." Taking it all in, suddenly Pax *wasn't* sure.

"Oh good, sweetheart, there's Kenyon." Davis turned towards Kenyon, looking a little frantic. "God, Ellis, you know how to carve a turkey?"

Pax wished he could save him, but he knew even less about carving a turkey. He turned to Kenyon, who was already shrugging out of his suit jacket and was heading over to where Davis stood.

"I got this," he said, taking the knife from Davis' hand.

Davis eyed him uncertainly. "Not that I don't trust you . . ."

"No, I've got this," Kenyon repeated. "Could carve a turkey in my sleep."

Davis gave him a relieved smile. "Great, we'll get everything else ready."

There was no room for all of them at the little dining room table that the condo had come with, so Pax helped Davis set all the dishes out, buffet-style, on the island, and finally, Kenyon arrived with a platter heaping with beautiful slices of turkey.

"Let's dig in," Davis said, and Tristan gave a little cheer.

It was not a traditional Thanksgiving by any means. They ate in front of the TV, scattered around the room, smooshed up together on couches and in chairs, Sebastian even taking the floor and stretching his long legs out.

But, Pax decided, as he looked around, it was the best Thanksgiving he could remember, and the one that felt most like a *real* holiday, where what mattered were the people around you, not Instagram-ready perfection or appearances.

Later, after they'd digested, watched Landry score the winning touchdown in his game, and the next one had kicked off, Pax found himself in the kitchen, rinsing dishes off in the sink, when to his surprise, Kenyon walked in with another handful, not Davis.

"Oh, thanks for that," Pax said, taking the stack from him and setting them in the sink, spraying them full-power with the hot water.

"No prob."

Pax could see him hesitating. Wanting to say something else. But hesitating, still. He wondered what it would take for Kenyon to trust him—to really trust any of them. Because it was clear he held himself apart.

"Hey, you know you're always welcome here, right?"

"In Davis' apartment?"

Pax realized how that sounded. Yeah, they'd not been exactly circumspect around anyone today, probably because they'd assumed everyone knew about them. Because everyone did. Everyone except Kenyon.

"Yeah, well . . . I spend a lot of time here," Pax said.

"Not really a shocker," Kenyon said, clearly amused.

Pax didn't know what else to say without implicating either of them even further.

"It's a sex thing, isn't it?" Kenyon asked, before Pax could figure out what else he could possibly answer that with.

"A sex thing?" His voice squeaked on the word, *sex*. Now he just sounded silly. Pax kicked himself, mentally, for not being able to handle this like an adult. Like a *leader*.

Maybe that was what Kenyon was waiting for, for Pax to be a real leader.

He certainly hadn't been much of one last year.

But Davis was showing him, one week, one game, at a time, and surely all the progress he'd made counted for something?

"Yeah, you and Davis. You're fucking." There was no judgement in Kenyon's tone. None whatsoever. This was completely opposite of the intervention that the other guys had held only a week and a half ago, but it felt like it might have the same purpose. Pax really wasn't sure.

"Uh, well, yeah, we are, but it's more than that."

It was only then that Kenyon's expression took on any form of astonishment. *Now he's surprised?* Pax wondered incredulously. *Only that we're not just fucking?*

"You have time for that?"

That was not the *last* thing that Pax had been expected him to ask, but it was very near the bottom of the list. His fingers slipped on the soapy sponge he was using to clean a dish. "We make time, 'cause it's important," Pax said slowly. "And no, we don't have a lot of free time or extra time or whatever, but . . . we matter to each other. So we make the time."

"Ah." Kenyon leaned against the counter. "And that works for you?"

"Well, it's new-ish, but yeah, I'm assuming it will."

"Huh." Kenyon still sounded surprised. "Fingers crossed."

"You're not upset about it?" Pax had to ask.

"You fucking your coach? Hardly," Kenyon scoffed. "I'm pretty open to anything. And I know Davis wouldn't fuck this up. He's a good guy. Got a bad rap."

"I think so," Pax agreed.

"I gotta run," Kenyon said. It was the most they'd ever said to each other that *wasn't* about football, so Pax supposed it only made sense that he was leaving now. Still, he felt like progress had been made. Kenyon had shown up. Been part of the group. Had given his approval, even if all Pax was doing was fucking his coach, and had even shared a miniscule bit about himself. That he was open to "anything," whatever that meant.

"We're glad you came," Pax said.

And to his surprise, Kenyon's face creased into a soft, pleased grin and this time it was him who hugged Pax. "Hey, me too," he said. "And thanks for sending over more stuff for the org, it's really appreciated."

"Of course," Pax said. "Any time you need more, just let me know."

"Will do," Kenyon said, and then he was out the door.

Davis came in a few minutes later. "Thought I heard the door close," he said. "Was that Kenyon taking off?"

"Yeah," Pax said. "He didn't care much about us, apparently, though he was convinced it was *just* a sex thing."

"Well," Davis said, waggling his eyebrows in a way that shouldn't have been sexy at all, but indisputably was, "it's *also* a sex thing. Should I kick everyone out so I can fuck you nice and slow against this kitchen counter?"

It sounded glorious. If only he wasn't so full of turkey. "Maybe in a bit," Pax said, patting his stomach, "if you want to fuck after dinner, don't go making such delicious food, okay?"

"Okay," Davis said, grinning, clearly very proud of himself for the turkey.

Chapter Seventeen

Pax would've been lying to himself if he said he wasn't nervous about this whole damn week.

First, could he and Davis go to practice, sit through all their meetings, and not give away everything they'd done over the bye week?

The first time they were faced with Coach, would it be written all over their faces—written all over *Pax's* face, because Davis had a decent poker face, unlike him—and he'd guess, immediately?

But he hadn't.

Each day had gotten easier, and by Thanksgiving, and the day after, the final full practice, Pax felt like they'd settled into a comfortable yet ambitious rhythm, Davis pushing him just the right amount, and Pax listening, and pushing himself the rest of the way.

He didn't want to say that it was easier now, once they'd settled the thing between them, but that was how it felt.

Like now, because a quarter of their brains weren't dwelling on what they couldn't have, when it came time to focus on football, they could *really* focus on football. And it wasn't that bloodless, painful, exclusionary focus he'd felt during the last two games, when they'd won and he'd played great, but totally different.

In fact, there was no other way to describe it other than joyful.

He was happy, every time Davis nudged him away and ran the play instead, letting him see exactly what he needed to see. Or when Davis jogged over from the sideline, that all-too-familiar crease between his eyebrows, frustration lighting up his dark blue eyes.

Just like now.

Pax lifted his hand, shielding his eyes, and watching, every step of the way, as Davis headed over to where the offense was huddled.

"You keep watchin' him like that, everyone's gonna know," Tristan hissed.

And yeah, okay, maybe he was watching him a little bit like a hero in a romance novel, striding across the moors with his perfectly tailored coat flapping in the breeze, but goddamn, this was Davis, and he was something else.

"I don't think so," Wade answered for him. "'Cause he's been watchin' him like that since day one."

"Truth," Kenyon said dryly. "It's amazin' that nobody's said anything yet."

Davis arrived.

"The handoff's not happening quick enough," he barked out, no greeting whatsoever. He was, Pax realized, beginning to take on Coach's habit of no wasted words. When he was focused, he was in a zone that didn't allow for any distractions, but Pax was okay with that. This game was really fucking important, both to the Piranhas and their playoff hopes, and personally, to Davis.

And that meant it was important to Pax.

"We gotta get the ball out faster," Logan said.

"They're gonna be coming for you like the apocalypse," Davis said, "and they're gonna try to get the ball. The Condors' defense is one of the top turnover units in the NFL. They're gonna go for the ball. Every single damn time."

Coach's phrase this week was, "no mistakes." He'd told them, unequivocally, that they had the tools to win, the skill and the talent, but mistakes would slow them down and hold them back, and prevent them from playing up to their best potential. "And," he'd added in a slow drawl, "why would we try to help *them* win? That's all mistakes do. Give the Condors the advantage."

The Condors were a great team, with a certain and confident identity, and it felt like the Piranhas were still trying to find theirs, but Pax still felt like they could win. Coach was right, they already had everything they needed to beat them.

"Let's practice it, then," Logan said. "Quick snap, on my count. Pax, you ready?"

"Born ready," Pax said.

He leaned over behind Logan, and listening intently to his snap count, focused on getting the ball in his hands, and then handing it off to Kenyon.

It hit him dead-on, because the one thing he and Logan had perfected early was a solid, accurate snap, and then he twisted, making sure to keep his goddamned hips loose, and Kenyon took the ball, jumping immediately to the left, making a cut designed to take advantage of the gap in the line, and hopefully, a gap in the Condors' defense.

It was a well-designed play, but it needed flawless execution—and they weren't quite there yet.

"Again," Randy barked into Pax's headpiece, and they ran it again, and again, and again, until their movements were precise and machinelike, the timing down to a science.

"Better," Davis said, appearing at his side as he wiped his face down with a towel, and squirted some Gatorade into his mouth as they finally took a break. "It's lookin' good."

When Pax glanced over, Davis' gaze was saying all the things that he hadn't earlier. "Hello," it said, "I think you're amazing. I love you."

And Pax knew he didn't have to say, "Thank you for making me amazing. I love you, too," for Davis to understand that was what he was thinking.

"Lookin' sharp," Coach's drawl interrupted their wordless conversation. "I like that play, I think we're gonna use it and all the variations a lot, especially when those Condors' defensive ends are on you like flies on shit."

"The line's gonna hold, they're working together better than ever," Pax said confidently. Logan and his group were undeniably stronger than they'd been at the beginning of the season, finally gelling into one cohesive unit. It wasn't a surprise that it had taken more than half a season, considering that most of them hadn't played together before.

"Speaking of workin' together," Asa said casually, re-adjusting his hat, and looking closer to his son's age than the forty or so years old he really was, "you two are really comin' along."

Don't freeze, don't freeze, he doesn't mean it like that.

"We had a bit of a rough patch, as expected," Davis said slowly, before Pax could even figure out *what* to say. "But yeah, it's goin' good now."

"An understatement," Coach said. "I love the wavelength y'all are on."

He wouldn't, if he knew what kind of wavelength it really was.

But Pax let himself relax into the knowledge that Asa didn't suspect anything, because if he did, he wouldn't be praising them, he'd be calling them into his office.

"We're enjoying it too," Pax said.

Another understatement.

How had it felt to curl up next to Davis on the couch, after all their Thanksgiving guests had left, and just bask in his warmth and in the knowledge that they loved each other and that wasn't ever going to change?

It was indescribable.

"Pax, you're bloomin' into exactly the quarterback you needed to be, the QB everyone thought you could be," Coach said, patting him on the back.

"Couldn't have done it without Davis," Pax said honestly.

"Course not," Coach said with an approving nod.

"Yeah, well, let's stop congratulating ourselves before we ever take the field," Davis said bluntly. "You ready to get back there, Pax?"

Pax set his Gatorade down, and gave his face one last wipe, clearing off the sweat. "What do you want us to run?"

"Let's practice those long timing patterns with Tristan. I want his timing to be dead perfect. You're only gonna get a second."

Personally, Pax didn't think Davis was giving Logan and the offensive line enough credit—they could hold off the Condors, surely?—but he was also willing to listen to Davis, because he'd not steered him wrong, yet.

"Okay," he said. "If you think we could use more work, then we'll do some more."

Asa smiled. "Y'all are really killin' it out there. All I wanted to say."

Davis nodded absently, already absorbed in the playbook on his tablet. He listed off the plays he wanted Pax to run, and then he jogged back onto the field.

After setting up, Pax took the snap from Logan, hesitating for only the second it took for Tristan to streak down the field, and adjust to the coverage, and then he pulled his arm back, making sure he calculated the distance to where Tristan would be and not where he was right now, and threw the ball—a perfect spiral arcing through the air.

Tristan plucked it out of the air.

They ran that play, and its variations, about a dozen more times, until Tristan was panting, and then they ran out patterns, using Carter and Wade, Tristan as bait, and finally, after another hour, Davis gave the signal that he was satisfied.

"I know," he said as they walked into the locker room together, "that you think I'm over-preparing."

"Did I say that?" Pax asked, stopping by his locker, pulling his sweaty t-shirt off and, making a face, tossed it into his bag, resting on the floor.

"You didn't have to," Davis said, crossing his arms and leaning against Jones' locker. Second team had wrapped up half an hour ago, they were probably already cleared out. "I could see it in your face. And before you freak out, probably just me could see it in your face. I know you, remember?" His voice dropped down during the last question.

Oh, he did.

"You know better than I do what we need to work on," Pax said slowly. And that right there, had been the biggest adjustment this season. Learning to trust that Davis knew better than he did. Working with him to understand why.

But sometimes, there was nothing else but blind trust.

If Davis said their handoff needed to be a half-second faster, and smoother, he wasn't going to argue.

Davis was a veteran quarterback in this league, and he had personally played against the Condors' defense more times than anyone else, in practice and in scrimmages.

Davis smiled. "Yeah, I do," he said. "But you guys got there."

"Thanks," Pax said. "I'm gonna hit the shower. Then tape and dinner?"

"I brought leftovers," Davis said. "I hope you like turkey. We have enough to eat it til the next century. And that was after Sebastian demolished about a quarter of it himself."

"Who could blame him?" Pax said with a grin. "It was a damn good turkey. Nobody would've ever guessed you didn't know what the hell you were doing."

"Get in the shower," Davis said, swatting at him with an open palm. Nobody else was paying attention to see his hand linger, but Pax felt it. Maybe they couldn't touch each other the way they wanted here, in the facility, but when they finally got home . . . it would be worth it. Each touch meant more, *felt* more, because they'd been storing it up all day.

Before they'd started dating like this, with almost nobody knowing, Pax had wondered if it could be okay. If he wouldn't feel like Davis' dirty little secret.

Well, he did, and it was the greatest thrill of his whole goddamn life.

He was Davis' dirty little secret *and* he was the man he loved, and it turned out there was nothing sweeter than that combination.

Davis was just finishing heating up their leftovers in the microwave in the staff break room when Asa cornered him.

"Hey, that smells good." Asa looked more closely at the container on the counter. "Looks suspiciously like the plate Beau brought me over last night. I'd guess he had dinner with you."

"Yeah, a couple of us strays hung together," Davis said.

He didn't like lying to Coach, but what was he going to do? Tell him the truth?

Pax and I hosted our first holiday and it was wonderful, not having to hide, letting everyone see just how much we love each other.

Yeah, no way that would go over at all, even with a guy as understanding as Asa Dawson. Everyone thought he was a ball-buster and he *could* be, but only when he thought you deserved it, not when the NFL or the media or the fans thought you did. He was unique that way.

"Glad to see you guys are all gettin' along," Asa said, shoving his hands into the pockets of his khakis. "And glad you invited Beau. It means a lot that y'all include him."

"Of course," Davis said and meant it. He liked Beau a hell of a lot—and not just because he'd been an "unofficial" participant at the intervention. He was a good guy, and absolutely fucking brilliant. The kind of analyst he'd *always* wanted on his team.

"Really though . . ." Asa hesitated, which was totally unlike him. "I wanted to check in. See if you were doin' okay."

Davis could pretend he didn't understand what Asa was talking about but of course he knew. "I'm hanging in there," he said slowly, really considering how he *was* doing. Was having the Condors, usually so detrimental to his emotional wellbeing, so present in his thoughts the last week easy? No, it wasn't. There were moments that Davis had to just close his eyes and go, as his therapist had suggested, when he'd first started getting the panic attacks, to a happy place.

Back then, the happy place had usually been at his house, with his pops, losing to him in an intense round of gin rummy or dominoes. But now, it was almost always Pax.

Pax smiling.

Pax sleeping.

Pax with his eyes rolling at something he'd said.

Pax laughing.

Pax telling him he loved him and meaning it.

"I know this isn't easy for you," Asa said. "But we're here for you, if you need us. You just let me know. Or Beau, I know he's talked to you before about it."

Davis nodded. "He has. And I appreciate it, but I think . . . I really do think I'm handling it okay."

Asa patted him on the shoulder. "Son, you've come a long way . . . brought Pax along just the way I thought you could. You given any more thought to signing a longer contract with the team? We'd love to have you."

Asa had made it clear from day one that he was interested in a longer-term quarterbacks coach. But Davis had never been able to see this as more than a single-season commitment. He wasn't really a coach. And even if he was, committing to the Piranhas meant that he was giving up on the possibility of ever taking the field again.

Could he do that?

He still wasn't sure.

"I can tell you're not ready," Asa said answering the question for him. "But you know, whenever you are, I meant it then, and I mean it now. I think this could be a real good thing for you. Look at what you've done with Pax. And how much you've enjoyed it. I've seen some real joy on your face."

There had been an immense amount of satisfaction involved, Davis could admit that. He loved coaching Pax, and not just because Pax was Pax and he was crazy in love with him. It was more than that.

But would coaching be enough? Even if there was a part of him that desperately wanted it to be?

He didn't know.

"It's been really good," Davis admitted. "But I'm thinking about it. I promise."

"I know. And you just keep thinkin'. No rush," Coach said, patting him again on the shoulder. "Now you better get that food to the QB room, before it gets cold."

Davis watched Asa walk off and realized he'd never said the other container of leftovers he was heating up was for Pax. But then he guessed he didn't need to.

Maybe there were some things that were just a given.

Davis, Pax realized as the first quarter of the game ticked by, had not been over-preparing them.

The Condors were everything they'd been promised, everything their record said they were: a really exceptional, totally complete football team. Aggressive on defense, skilled on offense, deadly and precise on special teams.

The Piranhas had had two offensive drives, and one had gone about thirty yards, only to end in a punt when Wade couldn't quite put his hands on a ball that would've guaranteed a first down. The second drive, they got almost all the way down the field, but they hadn't quite managed to get into the end zone, and Dylan had nailed a kick right between the uprights for three points.

Which meant, if their defense held strong on this drive, turning the ball over to Pax and his guys, they would still be ahead by the time the first quarter ended.

"No mistakes," Coach had repeated dozens of times during the last week, and they'd fulfilled that mandate, not making a single significant error.

Third down. Pax watched as Sebastian flew across the field, moving laterally, to tackle the outlet receiver before he could get the extra two yards he needed to get the first down.

Davis walked up next to him. "Just finished with Randy," he said, handing Pax his helmet. "This series, those handoff plays to Kenyon. I want to do a couple of them, and I want to try something deep, with Tristan."

He was feeling confident, then. And Davis' confidence bolstered Pax's own.

It was one thing believing he could do it; it was entirely another when Davis' faith was that strong. That unshakeable.

"Can do," Pax said.

"And watch that safety crossing over in the zone," Davis warned. "Look for him."

But Pax just nodded. He wouldn't make that mistake again. He wanted a touchdown, but he wasn't going to sacrifice this game to get it.

The Condors punted, and their returner downed it at the thirty-yard line.

Seventy yards to the end zone.

Pax's resolve hardened as he took the field.

They huddled, Pax called out the play, which was to Kenyon, and again their practice paid off.

Because the Condors' defense *was* pressing, pushing hard against the line, and even Logan, an exceptional center, was barely able to hold back and pull off the block, just in time for Kenyon to take the ball and cut over, squeezing through and gaining a solid seven yards on the play.

Randy called in the next play, and Kenyon got the ball again, this time doing a double feint move, Wade blocking as they moved together, and this play worked even better, moving the chains and gaining fifteen yards.

They were just about to midfield when Randy called in the long pass, the buttonhook play that he and Tristan had been working so hard on.

It was time. The defense was prepped for Kenyon continuing to run into their teeth, and the safeties had pulled back to help the linebackers stop the run.

Pax took a deep breath, called the play, met Tristan's eyes, and he nodded. Tristan nodded in return.

The huddle broke, Logan got set with the ball, and he crouched over, calling out the snap count.

Logan snapped the ball flawlessly, Pax catching it and dropping back. *Hips loose, hips loose,* he chanted to himself, eyeing the other side of the field, not even glancing once directly at where Tristan was streaking down the opposite sideline.

If he messed up and gave up even a single look in that direction, the deep safety might recognize the play, and cut him off.

But he didn't, and he held the ball for one second longer, feeling the pocket begin to close around him. Finally, at the last moment, he threw it, spiraling through the air, and Tristan jumped and caught it, tumbling into the end zone for a perfect touchdown.

Pax hesitated. He'd considered doing this. He'd considered telling Davis that he was going to do this.

But he hadn't, because he had a feeling Davis would stop him, if he knew.

He lifted his hands up to the sky, the way so many quarterbacks did, praising God, or whoever was up there, for their skill and the luck they'd needed to score.

But instead of praising God. Pax held up one hand, with four fingers.

Four, which had been Davis' number with the Condors.

And then he pointed directly at the sideline, at where Davis stood, his headset half-on, his face animated with excitement at the touchdown.

Pax saw flashes of confusion in the faces of the Condors around him. A sneer on one face, behind their helmet visor. Like they couldn't understand why he'd believe in Davis, why he'd support him. But the fact that he *knew* why made Pax feel goddamn smug. Maybe it shouldn't. But he was playing this game for two reasons: because this team was his family and he loved them and wanted to lead them to victory, and because *Davis* was not only his family, he was his everything.

He wanted nobody to be in *any* confusion as to who he was praising, who he was honoring, who this touchdown was for.

It was for Davis.

All for Davis.

At first, Davis was sure he'd not seen correctly.

Was . . . *Oh God, yes he was.*

Pax was definitely holding up four fingers, right up, and then he pointed, like anyone could possibly mistake what he was doing, right at Davis.

There was part of him that wanted to be angry, because what the hell was Pax thinking, possibly outing them like this, but there was a much bigger, much louder part of him that wanted to run out there and hold Pax and fucking *cry*. Thank him for believing in him, for trusting in him, when nobody else would.

When Pax returned to the sideline after the touchdown, Davis could only swallow his emotion and focus on the task at hand.

His gesture had meant everything, but they still had to win this game.

But then he did it again.

And again.

And a fourth time, scoring again on another long pass, this time to Wade, who shucked off three potential tacklers to sprint forty-five yards down field to the end zone.

The defense was holding strong, despite the strength of the Condors' offense, and Davis realized, with sudden blinding clarity in the middle of the fourth quarter, that they were currently winning this game 31 to 3, and other than there still being time on the clock, they'd wrapped up this game in the most decisive, confident way they could.

There'd been no mistakes, and Pax had played fucking lights-out, throwing for four touchdowns, and giving credit to Davis after each and every one of them.

After the fourth, Beau walked over, and just stood there next to him for a minute.

"He's a little outrageous, isn't he?" Beau said, but he said it so fondly, it was clear he wasn't exactly upset that Pax was practically declaring his allegiance right there on the football field.

"Yeah," Davis said, clearing his throat. "Yeah, he is. But the best quarterbacks usually are."

"You'd know," Beau said knowingly.

Davis suddenly wasn't sure if that was true, because Pax had just fought for him longer and harder than it felt like he'd ever been allowed to fight for himself.

But that was the key, wasn't it? *Allowed.*

His agent, who was a really freaking good agent, had given him advice—which happened to also be really freaking good advice—to keep his head down. Not generate any headlines. To not fight back, because the whole situation would only grow messier.

'Cause it hadn't already been messy enough, Davis thought wryly.

But maybe he should've pushed back a little more. Told his side of the story, even if it meant that he never got back on the field. Because following his agent's advice—while yes, undoubtedly it had been good advice—sure hadn't done anything to get him back to being QB1.

"Well, I'm damn proud of him," Beau continued, watching as the game clock ticked down. "And I know Coach . . . well, he's got a real funny way of showing it . . ." He glanced over to where his dad was currently pacing back and forth on the sideline, looking like the Piranhas were down by three, not up by twenty-eight. "But he's thrilled."

Davis chuckled. "I think we're all pretty damn thrilled."

Beau patted him on the shoulder. "Maybe Pax was the only one out there holding up four fingers, but we're all on your team now."

"Naw," Davis said, "but I'm on yours. Feels damn good, too."

Beau smiled. "I like the sound of that. Speaking of that . . . my dad said you might be signing another contract?"

Damn Asa and his enthusiasm.

It was both really freaking fantastic and also terrifying.

Because he knew what signing another contract would be saying—signaling not only to himself but to the whole NFL that he was done being a quarterback.

There'd be no chance to correct the shitty legacy that the Condors had stuck him with. *Just an opportunity to create a whole new one*, Davis thought, the voice in his head sounding suspiciously like Asa's.

"I'm considering it," Davis said.

Beau was still smiling, as Pax took a knee to finish out the clock. "Oh, I bet you are. No good reason why you wouldn't want to stay here."

"Really?" Davis questioned dryly.

"I'm just sayin'," Beau said, raising his hands in surrender, "better hanging out here than off in Carolina, by yourself."

It was.

Beau was definitely not wrong about that.

The clock was almost done ticking down to zero, with the Piranhas' defense on the field. Sebastian was flying around, like it wasn't deep into the fourth quarter, and he was tired. But he had to be, Davis reasoned. Still, it was hard to see it.

The whole team was electrified, brought to full power by Pax's gesture.

Then, out of nowhere, on a deep Tom Taylor pass, Sebastian leapt up, and connected with the ball, right in front of the receiver. The stadium roared as he ran it back twenty-four yards and knelt in the end zone as the clock expired, with one hand up.

One hand. Four fingers.

The rest of the defense joined him. Same hand. Same four fingers.

Emotion welled in Davis' throat.

The stadium, full of Piranhas fans, roared their approval of their team putting together the kind of win that not only had them sitting pretty on top of their division, but could mean home-field advantage in the playoffs.

Yep, the Piranhas, who had won two games and lost fifteen last year, were headed to the playoffs.

And he was going with them.

Coach dodged a full bucket of Gatorade, nimbly moving out of the way, only to have Beau greet him with another, even fuller bucket, dousing him in the trademark orange liquid.

Davis laughed, as the staff and players began to stream onto the field. He thanked everyone he could. It wasn't enough, but it had to be. Because he didn't have words for what they'd done here today. Not just played their hearts out, but done it for *him*.

He shook hands with lots of players, but the whole time, he was looking for Pax. He wanted—no, he *needed*—to talk to him. To yell at him, to thank him, to hold him.

To tell him that it was the exact same for him; Pax was the most precious thing in the world. That he'd cross burning hot lava and have his back, no matter what, *too*.

But he couldn't seem to find him. Every once in awhile he'd catch a flash of him, surrounded by other players and coaches, and then he was caught up with the media, giving post-game interviews on the field.

Finally, he gave up, and headed into the locker room. He showered and changed in the staff side, and then headed to the one place he knew he could find Pax, alone.

Sure enough, he was standing in his hallway, all the way down in the basement of the Piranhas stadium, in the corridor outside of the media room.

Pax glanced up as he approached. "Hey," he said.

Davis didn't hesitate.

He went to him, and cupped his precious, incredible face in his hands. "You are fucking crazy," he said, "and I should be mad as hell at you."

Pax grinned. "But you're not."

"But I'm not. You insane, wonderful, sweet man. I love you." Davis heard the gruff emotion in his tone. "I love you so fucking much."

"I don't care if everyone knows that I give a shit about you," Pax said lowly. "'Cause I love you, too. What they did was bullshit, and they should pay for it. Maybe all I could do was win this game, and score some touchdowns, and in the process, remind them that they screwed over one of the best quarterbacks, one of the best *men*, in football. I'm just not sure it feels like enough . . . but it was all I could do."

"Are you . . . are you seriously trying to *apologize*?" Davis asked incredulously.

Pax shrugged, and yeah, it was freaking incredible, but he clearly *was*.

Davis couldn't hold himself back any longer; he leaned and pressed a hard, quick kiss to Pax's mouth. "Stop it," he said. "Just stop it. It was amazing and wonderful and don't you dare second-guess it."

Pax grinned. "Okay."

"And damn it, I just love you." It was harder to resist a second kiss, now he had the feel of Pax's lips in the forefront of his mind. He took another one, longer and slower this time, even though there was a very large part of him that knew better. When he pulled away, Pax's eyes were so bright in the dim light of the hallway.

"You good to go now?"

Pax glanced down, a knowing smile on his face. "Give me a minute," he said, "I'm a little . . . uh . . . worked up."

"Post-game adrenaline surge?" Davis knew what those were like. He'd never really had an opportunity to fuck someone through one, and he wouldn't be averse to doing it now.

When they got home, of course.

"No, well, not really, anyway," Pax said, flushing. "Just you saying you love me . . . well, that alone is enough to get me going real good."

Chapter
Eighteen

"Goddamn, sweetheart," Davis ground out, and Pax reveled in the rough desperate edge to his voice, riding the most fucking insane high of his life.

It wasn't just that they'd won the game, in a landslide, and he'd played lights-out, and that he'd gotten to show everyone watching just how much Davis meant to him, but then there was all this . . . Davis spread out naked underneath him, his cock hard and wet against his own, as he pressed hot, damp kisses into his neck.

He'd woken up, even though they'd fucked hard last night, just as horny as he'd been after the game. At first, it had been just enough to make out, feeling Davis' naked body against moving desperately against his own. But then it hadn't been; he'd wanted it all again, even though he was still feeling the ghost of Davis' cock inside him.

But Davis had protested, and kept protesting, until Pax had decided more persuasion was needed.

He had a feeling Davis was just about to give in, though it was unclear if it was the way he kept nibbling at his neck, or the way he was rubbing against his cock, or the way he had three fingers buried deeply inside him, straining to reach the spot that never failed to make him scream.

"You ready to admit it?" Pax asked breathlessly.

"That I want you?" Davis' gaze was so hot, it seared him. "I don't think that was up for debate. Come 'ere, I'll make you feel real good, sweetheart. You know I can."

"Oh, I know you can." Pax lifted himself up by pushing a palm against Davis' chest and froze for a second as his fingers slipped in just a bit deeper. "But if you're real good, I'll let you just sit here while I make *you* feel good."

Davis groaned.

"I don't even wanna move to get a condom, just wanna slip it right inside me, just like this," Pax murmured, panting between each word. "You good? 'Cause I'm good. I was tested only a few weeks before we started this."

He pulled out his fingers and shifted his body. Wanting to be as close to the man he loved as he could, with nothing between them.

"I can't even fucking remember anyone else right now," Davis said, twitching against Pax's palm as he smoothed some more lube down his length. "Not when you're doing that."

"Well, you'd better tell me," Pax warned, even though he already had a feeling Davis hadn't exactly been going around fucking people.

He wasn't the kind of guy who freely let himself feel good. He worked for it. He pushed hard against it. He only let it swamp him when he surrendered to it.

And Pax knew he was real damn close to surrendering to it now.

"You already know it. There's been nobody else . . ." Davis' hand closed around his hip, and Pax exulted as instead of pushing him away, he pulled him closer. He felt his cock snub right up against his hole and then he pushed down, breathing through the stretch of it.

"Sweetheart," Davis said, and it was sweet and rough as he reached up with his other hand, cradling his cheek as he sank down on his cock.

It was a lot, even with the prep he'd done and the fucking he'd enthusiastically participated in the night before. And it was definitely a lot like this, and his hips stuttered, his fingers reaching for his own cock, which had begun to flag a bit.

"Shit," Davis said, and then suddenly, he was back against the sheets, as Davis used his sheer, brute strength to flip them over.

"That better?" Davis asked, giving him nice shallow strokes, all bone-melting pleasure as he got used to the length inside him again.

"God, *yes*," Pax cried out as Davis gave him exactly what he needed, nothing more and nothing less, thrusting gently but forcefully, working himself in deeper and deeper until Pax swore that he could feel him in his throat.

"You're so goddamned perfect," Davis groaned. "Yeah, sweetheart, come for me, come on my cock."

It wasn't going to be very difficult. Pax was already close, and then he slipped his hand between them, giving his hard, aching cock a few pulls, and he couldn't help falling over the edge then, spasming around Davis' cock as he felt Davis join him, groaning hard into his neck as they came together.

"Fuck," Davis said, collapsing on him. "I shouldn't have let you talk me into that."

"I don't think I *talked* you into anything," Pax teased, running a hand lightly down Davis' back. Enjoying the feeling of his muscles rippling as he absorbed the loving touch.

"Fair," Davis said. "Or *not* fair, actually, because you totally didn't play fair."

"I play to win," Pax retorted smugly.

It was the Monday after the big win, so there was no practice.

They could review film, but Pax decided there was no reason they couldn't do it from this bed.

In fact, he thought, as Davis finally groaned and stood, heading to the bathroom on gratifyingly shaky legs, there was no reason for them to leave the bed for *hours*.

A situation he very much approved of.

Except that on the way back from the bathroom, Davis' phone rang. "Hang on," he said, tossing Pax the wet washcloth, "I gotta take this. It's my agent."

"Probably congratulating you on nabbing such a stellar quarterback on your first coaching job," Pax teased as Davis grabbed his phone and headed out towards the kitchen. He was feeling so goddamned high that he wasn't sure he was ever gonna come down.

It wasn't just the spectacular sex, though that surely didn't hurt.

Pax cleaned up, tossed the washcloth into the laundry basket, giving himself a high five when he made the three-point shot, and then collapsed back into bed, propping himself up with a few pillows.

Anticipating that Davis would be back in a few.

But he wasn't. He was gone for five minutes. Then ten.

Then fifteen.

Pax was just about to reluctantly leave the warm enclave of the bed to see if he was okay when Davis' figure filled the doorway.

"What is it?" Pax said, his legs half-off the bed. "Everything okay?"

"You know Max Lang?"

Pax thought about this for a second, and then shook his head.

Davis came and sat down on the edge of the bed.

No, he didn't just *sit*, he plopped down with a sigh that might have meant half a dozen things. Normally, Pax knew he was really good at figuring out which one it was. But not today.

"He's the Riptide's backup quarterback," Davis said, his tone curiously emotionless. "He tore his ACL yesterday, in their game."

"Oh," Pax said. Not sure what this meant. Of course it was never good when someone got hurt.

"Yeah, he came in towards the end, guess they were up a bunch of points and, of course, they wanted to protect Crawford as much as possible."

"That sucks for him." Anything torn in the knee was rough. The best scenario was a whole off-season full of surgery and rehab and then physical therapy, hoping that the joint could return to normal. The worst was that Max Lang wouldn't ever play football again.

"That was my agent, the Riptide want me to fly out for a tryout."

Davis spoke so quietly that at first Pax was convinced he'd misheard.

"What? A tryout?"

"For the backup position, of course," Davis clarified. "And it's not a guarantee, either. But I think Heath spoke up for me—we're sort of friendly acquaintances—and suggested me. And then the game yesterday, you playing lights-out, proving that I guess I'm not such a shitty-ass coach, convinced the Riptide ownership that it'd be worth taking a chance on me."

Pax didn't know what to say.

What to think.

Davis was going to fly to Los Angeles, and if it went well, he'd end up playing for the Riptide.

As the backup, sure, because no way three-quarters through the season would anyone be challenging Sam Crawford for the starting spot.

But he'd be back on the field. Even as a backup.

You should be happy for him, this is what he wants and what he wants is what you want. You know that's true.

"You . . . you should do it."

Davis shot him a sideways look. "I don't know what I should do. I promised I'd stay here, and coach you."

"Not to your own detriment," Pax argued. "And don't tell me that Coach wouldn't let you go. I'd even guess that you have some kind of arrangement, that if you got an offer, you'd be free to take it."

Davis chuckled under his breath. "And they say you're just a pretty face. Yeah, we made an agreement like that."

"You should go," Pax repeated. Because if he didn't, he'd do something really stupid, like beg him to stay.

Or ask what this meant for them.

Even though he had a feeling he already knew; it would mean a long-distance thing. They'd be together in the off-season, but during the season, from July to January, they'd be possibly on opposite ends of the country, depending on if Davis signed a contract with the Riptide or potentially another team.

"I know I should," Davis said wryly. "Ever since the Condors dropped me, this is all I ever wanted: another chance. A final chance. But I never got one."

"You're gettin' one now," Pax said, swallowing his own terror down. What would it mean if they were separated? Would Davis decide this was a terrible idea? Would he decide that he didn't really love him after all?

Pax knew that wasn't true, wasn't even remotely possible, but the thing about fear was that it rejected logic.

"Yeah." Davis rubbed his face. "Now that I don't know if I want one or not."

"If you're hesitating for me, you know . . . you *have* to know that I want what's best for you. I think I made that pretty damn clear yesterday. You come first. And this is something you need to do."

"Even if it means we spend the next three months three thousand miles away from each other?" Davis didn't sound like he liked the possibility any more than Pax did.

"Even if it means that. Because I know it doesn't mean that we don't love each other. It doesn't mean that you aren't the most important person in the world to me. Do I want you to keep coaching me? Of course I fucking do. You . . . you pushed me to be the best I could, even when I didn't want to be. But I think Beau could continue to do your job adequately."

"Adequately," Davis said wryly. He hesitated then. "You really wouldn't be pissed off?"

Pax faced his fears square on. "Does it mean we're breaking up?"

"No," Davis said. "You've got me now. You're not gettin' rid of me anytime soon. If ever."

"Then . . . you should do it. You really *need* to do it. I know what this means to you." Pax told himself that this was the right thing. Davis had never gotten a chance to clear his name. To prove that he wasn't what all the rumors said he was.

Pax had gotten that chance. Davis had helped him, been absolutely fucking instrumental, in fact, in helping him make the most of it.

What kind of man would he be, what kind of *partner* would he be if he didn't do everything in his power to make sure that Davis got the same?

"Yeah, it's . . ." Davis stared ahead, like he wasn't even seeing Pax's bedroom wall. "It's not exactly the chance I wanted, because I know in my heart, I'm QB1, but those chances have probably passed me by. I'm gonna . . . if it's really okay with you, I'm gonna take it."

"It's okay. And I'm really fucking glad they called you."

Pax found he meant it.

Even while not meaning it at all.

He wanted to bury his head in the pillow and scream out all the contradictory emotions swirling through him.

But what he needed to do was remain firm and strong, confident, even, because if he wavered for even a second, he knew Davis would take that to mean he *wasn't* okay with it, and he'd never give himself the chance he deserved.

Davis felt lightheaded with . . . something.

Was it relief?

Was it terror?

Was it joy?

He didn't know.

Maybe it was all three, co-existing inside of him in a particularly uneasy soup.

He dialed Coach's number—there wasn't any time to waste, because the Riptide wanted him on a plane today, so he could participate in the tryout and in practice tomorrow—and listened to it ring. It rang four times, and then, to his surprise, it wasn't Asa who picked up, but Beau, sounding out of breath, his voice coming through muffled.

"Davis? What's up? Is everything okay?"

"I should be asking *you* that," Davis said. "Where's your dad?"

"Oh, finally sleeping. I convinced him to sleep late last night, or rather early this morning, and he's still sleeping, so I confiscated his phone, in case something urgent came up. And by the sound of your voice . . . it has."

There was nothing but to rip the Band-Aid right off and tell the truth. "Max Lang tore his ACL and the Riptide want me to try out for his spot on the team."

Beau didn't say anything for a long moment. "Holdin' a clipboard for Sam Crawford, huh? I can see why you'd be an appealing choice. All this starting experience, in case anything happens to him, and you know they're lookin' to plan a deep playoff run, so that's always something you gotta think about, plus you'd bring all this coaching knowledge you've been imparting to Pax. It's a win-win deal."

"That's what they think, apparently."

"And you?" Beau questioned.

"I think . . . I think I should at least go check it out. I wanted this for so damn long. I needed it. I don't know if I need it anymore, but I sure as heck think I won't forgive myself if I don't."

"And Pax?" Beau wondered.

"Oh, he's got it in hand. You can also help too, I know you can."

"I meant, what about *Pax*," Beau repeated knowingly.

Davis finally realized then what Beau was asking. Did this mean their affair was over? On hold? Or still going strong?

Davis decided that there was no time like the present to be one hundred percent, utterly transparent.

"Paxton Kelly is the love of my life, and as long as he wants me, I'm his."

"Good deal." Beau sounded briskly approving. Clearly, he was not worried at all about what kind of clusterfuck that kind of declaration could cause. "I had a feeling, but I wanted to be sure."

"Don't worry, you're not gonna have to pick up a broken-hearted QB off the floor," Davis said.

"I was more worried about him chasin' you out to LA, but as long as you two are solid, I won't worry about it."

"Good. I'm leaving tonight but I'll keep you both informed—you and your dad."

"Course you will," Beau said matter-of-factly. "Never expected anything less. When he wakes up, I'll tell him. But I know what he'll say."

"What's that?"

"Same as what I'm saying. Go kick some ass, Davis."

Davis grinned. "Thanks, Beau."

"You got this, don't let anyone tell you that you don't."

"That means a lot."

"It's just God's plain truth," Beau said, and hung up.

Pax was up, and came out of the bathroom when Davis hung up the phone. "You talk to Coach?" he asked casually.

Davis knew what it was costing Pax to encourage him to go to LA. He loved him even more for doing it, for being willing to make that sacrifice.

For believing he—and the love they shared—was worth it.

"Actually, to Beau. Coach's finally sleepin' and Beau didn't want to wake him."

"Ah." Pax was trying so hard to keep his expression neutral, keep the pain off his face, but Davis knew he was feeling it, because *he* was feeling it. "You leavin' tonight?"

"Late this afternoon. I've got to . . ." Davis gestured downwards, in the general vicinity of his own condo. "Get some stuff together." He swallowed hard. "Not sure how long I'll be in LA."

His agent had made it clear that if the Riptide liked him, he'd be in LA through the end of the season—and knowing how the team was playing, likely deep into the playoffs.

"You could come out of this with a ring, and then demand anything you wanted, afterwards," his agent had pointed out, excitement leaking into his voice. "You thought that part of your career was over, but it might not be."

It was true; he'd thought his opportunities to win a ring as a player were waning, if not outright over.

Did he really want to win a ring as Sam Crawford's backup?

He just didn't know anymore.

Maybe he wouldn't know until he got out to Los Angeles and saw the Riptides' setup.

"I guess you'd better do that, then," Pax said. And there it was, the misery surfacing in his eyes, just as clearly as Davis was feeling it.

"Come 'ere, sweetheart," Davis said roughly, and pulled him into his arms. Held him just as much for Pax's comfort as for his own.

They didn't move for several long minutes.

Davis wanted to remember what this felt like, when he was two months gone and he didn't know when he'd be able to hold Pax again.

There'd be no more byes, no more time off. And if the Riptide pulled it off, and made it to the Super Bowl, it'd be February before he could come back here. Come back home.

"It's not like I don't want you to do this," Pax said quietly, his voice partially muffled by Davis' shoulder. But he could still hear the emotion clogging it. "I do. I want it even more than you, maybe. But I'm just gonna . . ." He cleared his throat. *Goddamn, Pax is gonna cry, and then I'm gonna cry. Maybe that's okay. It's okay 'cause it's him.* "I'm just gonna miss you so fucking much."

Davis squeezed his eyes shut. Feeling that suspicious wetness seep through them. "I know. Me too. So much."

It was all he could say for a very long time.

But it really was okay, because this was Pax, and he'd never judge. Especially when he was right there with him. Davis knew when they finally parted, there'd be a damp spot on the shoulder of his t-shirt, and it was funny, because before meeting Pax, he thought he'd cried maybe once or twice in his entire life.

That terrible morning, for one. The worst morning of his whole life.

But he wasn't going to wallow in this pain, because it wasn't forever, now, it was fleeting, and the future was still stretching out in front of them, inviting and exciting with all its possibilities.

He was going to focus on that.

"It's gonna be okay," he said, finally pulling back, sure that Pax's damp eyes matched his own. "I'm gonna be back, and then we'll figure everything out. But I want you to remember one thing."

"You love me?" The corner of Pax's mouth quirked up in a smile.

"Well, that too, but mostly . . . *keep your hips loose,* okay?"

Pax laughed, the edges of it watery, but he was smiling with his whole face now. Exactly what Davis had hoped for.

The last thing he wanted to see before he left was Pax's smile.

"I'll try," Pax said. He let go of Davis, reluctantly, but he let go. "You go kick some ass and win a ring, okay?"

He pressed one last kiss to Pax's cheek. "They haven't hired me, yet."

"But they will." Pax sounded so fond. So sure. "'Cause you're freaking amazing, and they're not stupid."

Davis was right; the last thing he saw before leaving was Pax's smile, and he carried the warmth of it all the way to Los Angeles.

It was an irony, that was for fucking sure.

Davis didn't know why he hadn't put two and two together, but he hadn't remembered at all that the situation he was walking into was nearly identical to his own.

Nearly, because while nobody really knew that he was dating Pax, everyone on the planet knew that Sam Crawford and Heath Harris were together.

There on the sideline, Sam Crawford, QB1 for the Los Angeles Riptide, stood next to Heath Harris, the Riptide's quarterbacks coach, and while they weren't actually touching, they didn't need to. Just the way they stood, the way they talked, the looks they gave each other, it was clear they belonged to one another.

But then, they didn't need to touch to prove anything.

The whole world had seen them together on the Super Bowl victory stage three years ago, confetti swirling around them, as they'd held the Vince Lombardi Trophy between them—one the starter, one the backup—and blown the lid off the NFL when they'd kissed.

Now Heath was retired, and he was the coach, and Sam was the quarterback.

That wasn't the kind of image you could possibly stuff back into the bottle, so they'd gotten a bit of a free pass. Plus, Davis knew a lot of teams and their coaching staff considered the Riptide a bit too free and loose with their players anyway.

Allowing the quarterbacks coach to be in a relationship with the quarterback? That was just further evidence that Mark Rodriguez, the head coach of the Riptide, didn't have the kind of ironclad control they considered necessary to lead a championship team.

But then, they'd proved that wrong, several times now.

Heath jogged over now, still fit. He could probably take the field now; he was still in the prime of his athleticism. Davis knew it had been *his* choice to retire, though. He'd chosen to stay on the sidelines, unlike Davis.

"Abernathy, it's real good to see you," Heath said, extending a hand. "I'm so glad you could make it out here."

They shook. Harris' grip was just as firm as he remembered.

Heath had been a few years ahead of him in the draft, but they'd gravitated together at a few Pro Bowls, at the various NFL events they'd attended. Heath wasn't particularly sociable, and neither was he, but he'd always liked the guy.

He'd hoped it was mutual.

After the Condors had signed Taylor and destroyed his reputation in the process, Heath had been one of the few to speak up, to use his social media to say that he thought Davis' treatment was unfair. Considering that Heath rarely spoke up publicly anymore, this had been a major deal, and Davis had appreciated it a lot.

Heath had also reached out privately, but at that point, Davis was discovering just how few people actually gave a shit about him, and he'd already retreated into his own head, wallowing in his grief.

Still, he thought he hadn't been wrong about Heath's friendship.

He was here, wasn't he?

And, he'd just figured out, he was the only quarterback who'd been called to this tryout. Clearly Heath had stuck his neck out for him.

"I'm real glad to be here, to be honest," Davis said, chuckling. "And I know you had something to do with that, so thank you."

Heath raised an eyebrow. "I wanted a real solid backup for Sam, 'cause he's a fucking idiot, always throwing himself in harm's way, trying to make plays he shouldn't make, and God knows, if he gets injured, we need someone who can actually play."

Davis couldn't help but think of Pax, throwing that interception and going after the safety who'd picked him off. Putting himself in harm's way, just to stop the touchdown.

"I feel you there," he said emphatically.

"Yeah, I can definitely see some echoes of Sam in your QB in Miami. Paxton Kelly, right?"

Davis nodded.

There were more echoes than Heath could possibly know.

Davis thought again what a fucking irony this was. Of course he'd end up at the one team where the quarterback and the quarterbacks coach were in a relationship. Officially. With no hiding whatsoever.

"He's lookin' real good," Heath continued. "I was a little surprised you came out here."

"I wanted another chance, and I got it," Davis said. "I'm not gonna waste it."

Heath tilted his head, considering this. "That's why I like you, Abernathy. You've got that competitive fire."

He did, though he was less convinced that standing on the sidelines, and holding a clipboard, whether he was dressed or not, was going to quench it.

But they'd see.

"I'm ready," Davis said steadily.

"Yeah, I kinda figured you might be," Heath said, clapping him on the shoulder. "You get warmed up, and we'll go through some throws, okay?"

"Sure thing," Davis said, tossing a football from one hand to the other.

He'd done so much work actually *playing* in practice, practically becoming a third QB in the QB room instead of occupying the traditional coaching position, that he wasn't worried. He was in better shape now than he'd been last year, that was for sure.

He did his warmup, and it felt really good to be out here, on the field, not just as a coach, but as a *player*. Not in that weird quasi-position he'd occupied during the rest of the season.

Sam came over and said hello, said all the right things, a friendly smile on his face. Davis liked him—it was impossible not to, not when he was so nice, and also so impossibly talented—but he didn't really want to because it felt like a betrayal of Pax.

Pax was his quarterback. Not Sam Crawford.

Not anymore, not if you can do this, Davis reminded himself.

Coach Martinez, who Davis had a lot of respect for, walked over next, and said a lot of encouraging things, everything Davis had been wanting to hear.

But somehow it still didn't feel right, even after the practice was over, and he'd run not only some good drills, doing solid work with the ball and his footwork, but even a handful of the Riptide's simpler plays. Martinez had sent the playbook over yesterday and he'd spent the flight and the night before studying it. It was large and complex, but he'd gotten a decent grasp of some of the easier plays, and was gratified to know he could pick things up quick enough to at least run a facsimile of the Riptide's offense.

There was nothing wrong with Tristan or Carter Johnson, the two main receivers on the team, but it was another kind of experience to throw to Chase Riley, who could pluck even the wildest pass right out of the air.

"That was solid work out there today," Coach Martinez said, patting him on the back as he finished changing in the locker room. "You want to head over to the conference room and work on some plays after lunch? We're thinking one thirty. Give you a bit of a break."

Davis knew what tryouts were generally like. There was the physical component, of course, which he'd undeniably nailed earlier. He knew enough about coaches to tell, even when they were being cagey, that he'd exceeded even their high expectations as to his physical fitness, and his ability to still throw a ball really fucking well. But there was a mental component too—because the quarterback was the leader of the offense, and was not only responsible for running the plays, but making adjustments at the line to compensate for the defensive formations.

They were going to test his brain now.

Davis took a deep breath and then let it out. "I'll be there," he said.

"Okay, Heath'll show you where we're gonna meet up. Make sure you grab some food too, the cafeteria's good, Sam wouldn't stand for anything else," Coach Martinez said with a dry chuckle.

He ended up sitting in the cafeteria with Heath and Sam and Bran Phillips—Logan would probably pick his brain later, about every single thing Bran said, because he practically worshipped the longtime Pro Bowl center—and there was no denying it. It was a warm, friendly atmosphere, but with an undeniable focus not only on success and winning but on the idea that it didn't matter who you loved, acceptance was yours.

It was similar, Davis knew, to the Piranhas, and what they were trying to build. But Davis had to admit that as they finished up lunch, as welcoming as everyone was, and as nearly identical as the vibe was, it didn't feel like home.

Somehow, in the last few months, Miami had begun to feel that way, even though he hadn't realized it.

Still, Davis was determined to make the most of this chance, and he shook off the unease he felt, and he headed into the afternoon's meetings feeling confident and strong.

Especially after he texted Pax and said, **I think it's going really well. They're a good bunch here.**

Pax's reply had been the one that sealed the deal though: **I wouldn't want to lose you for anything less than the best,** he'd said, **and I think they might be up there, so I'll permit them to steal you away. Love you.**

For the next four hours, Davis broke down defensive tape, including giving a long analysis of how he'd helped Paxton prepare for the Condors game.

It was mentally exhausting, even though he'd been doing it every single week during the preseason and then the season, he didn't usually do it in four-hour chunks, and the questions didn't usually fly so fast and thick. And he thought as he leaned back in his chair, taking a quick five-minute break, finally, that this felt so different because it wasn't ever just him analyzing and breaking down the defense and suggesting plays to run, it was always a collaborative effort. Pax was always there. Jones, too, and he wasn't a total waste of space. And Beau, of course, and Randy, and naturally, Coach.

They all did it together. Despite that, Davis believed he'd done a pretty decent job of holding his own, but then came the last convo with Coach Martinez.

Heath hadn't come back from the break, and neither had the offensive coordinator. So it was just him and Coach Martinez—and Davis was pretty sure he knew what he wanted to discuss.

"You're an impressive player," Martinez said, leaning back in his chair, steepling his fingers in front of him. "Exceptional physical skills, and your mental abilities are even sharper than ever. You've learned a lot during the last year."

"Thanks," Davis said.

But he still knew what was coming.

It was inevitable.

Nobody was going to sign him without addressing the elephant in the room.

"And," Martinez continued, "last week's performance against the Condors was especially impressive, considering your . . . past with the team."

The one thing that Davis noticed that Martinez and Asa didn't have in common was their way of dealing with bullshit.

Martinez danced around it; but Asa never failed to cut right through it, like he didn't have the patience to even bother with it. Davis hadn't realized how similar that was to his own behavior until now. Until he was nearly unbearably tempted to stop pretending he didn't know what Martinez was about to ask about and just tell him what he wanted to know, flat out.

But he'd done so well so far, he knew it, and maybe being too blunt would be a strike against him. Maybe Martinez wouldn't like that. A player wouldn't talk that way, Davis realized, but a coach would.

You're thinkin' like a coach, not like a player, not anymore.

He ignored the voice.

"Pax is coming along really well and the team is gelling at the right time," Davis said. Not taking full responsibility because as far as he was concerned, sure, he owned a portion of that unbelievable victory, but it didn't really belong to him.

Martinez chuckled. "Anyone ever tell you you're too modest, Abernathy?"

"All the time, sir."

"I know a lot of us were concerned that you'd struggle with that particular opponent."

Mentally and emotionally, Martinez didn't say but undeniably meant, *not just with them as an opposing team on the field.*

"I didn't worry about it at all, to be honest," Davis said casually.

Like he still didn't know what Martinez was gearing up for.

Pretending he didn't was nearly killing him but he'd been working on his poker face longer than Pax had, and it was far better.

"I guess not," Martinez said. "No issues leading up? No issues during? No issues after?"

It was the innocuous word that Martinez used that broke him. *Issues.*

Like it was somehow too ugly to use the real ones.

Panic attacks.

"No, sir, I didn't have a panic attack before that game or during that game, and I certainly did not have one after," Davis said.

He hadn't been able to help it.

Martinez looked surprised. "Alright, well, I can't say we haven't been interested and watching from afar, 'cause we have. And what we've seen today . . . well, I'm not surprised, but I am, too."

"Thanks."

Really, it meant a hell of a lot more than that. That they'd been considering adding him for awhile, that at least they hadn't written him off, like everyone else. And that he'd shown up here, with nothing to lose, and done the very best that he could.

Why, then, did he feel so goddamn hollow inside?

This was supposed to be a real victory, and instead, it didn't feel like anything.

"Tomorrow, we'll pull in Phil Reynolds, he's the vice president of player personnel, and I'm sure he'll want to touch base with you."

That was as good as Martinez offering him the job.

Davis knew it, and yet when he left the conference room, the last thing he felt like was celebrating.

Still, it would be stupid not to properly, seriously consider what he was going to do.

Honestly, the more he thought about it, there was only one person to talk to about it.

He asked around, and got directed down, to the lower levels of the practice facility, to where the QB room was buried. The door was partially open.

Heath was sitting in there. Sam, too, and they were watching film of Pax playing against the Condors.

He knew the Piranhas weren't on the Riptide's schedule, so that meant only one thing: they considered them a threat for the playoffs, and *that,* more than anything else, actually made Davis want to smile. Made him want to fist-pump in triumph.

But he didn't.

"Hey, Harris," he said, poking his head in. "Thought even though it's late-ish, you might want to grab a beer, catch up?"

Heath and Sam exchanged glances, the wordless communication of a couple in almost perfect accord—and Davis' heart hurt, because he knew, if he and Pax had their kind of time, their kind of experience, it would end up being the same for them—and then Heath nodded.

"Sure," he said. "We're just finishing up. I'll meet you upstairs?"

"Sure thing," Davis said.

Chapter
Nineteen

Davis took the minute Heath had asked for to call Pax. It was after practice was over on the East Coast, and he should be able to catch him before he and Blake started breaking down the practice tape.

"Hey," he answered a little breathlessly. "It still going good?"

"Yeah," Davis said. Hesitated. He shouldn't be so unsure about this, but it was undeniable; he *was*. "I think they're gonna offer me the spot."

"Of course they are," Pax said confidently, breezily, like it wasn't cutting him inside, like it wasn't cutting *both* of them inside, like Davis knew it was. "You're fantastic and I'm just glad someone besides the Piranhas have finally figured that out."

That *did* feel good, there was no denying it. But there was another part of him that kept saying, *and?* Like, yeah, it *felt* good but what was the freaking point? He didn't want to stand on the sideline in LA and hold a clipboard for Sam Crawford, no matter how nice he was. He didn't want to break down plays with Heath, no matter how much he liked him.

He'd told himself at first that the reason this had felt so weird and off was because it was new, and he'd get used to it, and in time everything would be normal again, like it had been in Miami.

But Davis wasn't quite as sure it would anymore.

"Yeah, they did, apparently. How are things there? Practice goin' good?"

Davis could hear Pax's eye roll through the phone. "We're fine here. Why wouldn't we be?"

Because I'm not there and I'm not fine with it, and none of you should be fine with it either.

"No reason in particular."

"Worked on third-down conversions today, getting some really good timing down with Wade, positioning him on the field exactly where he needs to be to make the play and get the first down." Pax hesitated. "I know you told Beau to work on that."

He had. Nobody's game was perfect, even when you won thirty-eight to three against your division rival. He'd made a few notes and sent them over to Beau, before he'd started studying the Riptide's playbook.

It had been the least he could do, especially after what the Piranhas had done for him. When he'd sent it, he'd thought of it as a final thank-you to an organization that'd taken a chance on him when they didn't have to.

"I did," he admitted. And he wished, even while he told himself that it was stupid to even think about, that he'd been there to watch as Pax nailed down that timing with Wade.

Tristan was obviously the most exciting receiver on the team to watch, but Wade was bigger and stronger and could make plays with his body that seemed to defy physics.

Take advantage of that, Davis had written to Beau. *Don't let that talent go to waste.*

"Well, it was a damn good suggestion," Pax said warmly. He dropped his voice down a little. "And you were missed. Definitely."

Davis knew what he was saying. That it wasn't just the coaching staff who'd missed him, or the players at practice, but him, *Pax.* The man, not the quarterback.

He was suddenly swamped with a fierce longing to just *be* with Pax. To just stand next to him.

Of course, it was stupid to think that would be enough, because it had never really been enough, but right now, it would be better than nothing.

"You were missed too," Davis said softly. "That idiot Crawford can't throw a ball to save his life."

Pax laughed then. "You mean . . . Super Bowl-winning-quarterback Sam Crawford pales in comparison to my elite skills?"

"Yes." Of course it wasn't true—not that Pax was a slouch, but he just didn't have the experience Sam did. But if Davis had to choose a QB, the answer was a no-brainer.

He'd pick Pax, every single damn time.

"You sure those aren't my *other* elite skills you're thinking about?" Pax teased.

"Might be. You *are* a first-rate cuddler."

"Yeah, I actually had to turn the heat up last night 'cause I didn't happen to have a human furnace in bed with me," Pax said.

"Just wait til spring, you'll be glad to be rid of me," Davis joked weakly.

"Never," Pax said.

Davis almost opened his mouth to tell him he loved him, that he was sorry he was doing this, that he felt he *had* to do this, but out of the corner of his eye he saw Heath approaching.

"Hey, I gotta go," he said.

"Love you," Pax retorted very fondly, and hung up.

"All ready to go?" Heath said.

"Yeah, I was just making a quick call back to uh . . . well, to Pax."

It felt stupid to lie. He'd been Pax's coach. It wouldn't be unheard of for him to call him.

"Right," Heath said. "There's a little bar around the corner. We like going there, 'cause we don't get bothered. And they've got great tacos."

"Sounds good," Davis said and followed Heath out.

He hadn't been kidding—it was literally *right* around the corner from the Riptide practice facility—and when they walked in, Davis knew why they didn't get bothered. There was a big Riptide banner across one wall, and posters of the players everywhere. There was even one of Heath, arms crossed across his broad chest, his patented *fuck you* expression on his face, promising total annihilation if you didn't submit to the Riptide's dominance. There was Chase's face, beaming opposite Heath's. And in the place of honor, there was Sam, his blond hair cropped shorter than it was now, his blue eyes wide and a little bit naive, but he couldn't have possibly been, because sitting in his arms was the Vince Lombardi Trophy he'd won three years ago.

"Sam hates coming here," Heath said with a low chuckle as they took seats at a table off in the corner. "He says looking at his own face, ten times its regular size, kills his appetite."

"Ah," Davis said.

"But I like their tacos and the beer's cold. I don't mind that up there," Heath said gesturing to his poster. "Feels like a different man that's up there. Like an old version of me. A much unhappier version. Reminds me of how far I've come."

Heath was a lot happier now, that much was clear.

Davis had met both versions, and the first time he'd seen Heath, post-coming out, post-Super Bowl, he'd legitimately seemed like a different person.

Lighter, like he'd finally set down some of the burdens he'd been carrying around forever.

"You ever regret retiring?" Davis asked, even though he knew the answer.

Nobody could look at Heath now and think he had any regrets.

"Nope," Heath said, unsurprisingly. "And frankly, I work much harder now than I did then, being QB1, and I'm about a hundred times happier."

"'Cause of Sam?"

It was the question that Davis had really wanted to ask, but he'd been worried about asking it because Heath, while coming out in the most public way possible, was actually fairly low-key and private about his relationship.

Davis just didn't know if he wanted to go back to Miami so desperately because of Pax. Did he like coaching so much because it was Pax he was coaching?

What if he turned the Riptide down, thinking that coaching was his future and then he ended up coaching someplace else? Would that choice still feel like the right one?

"Well, obviously I like coaching Sam," Heath said, a small smile curling up the corner of his mouth. "Though he makes me crazy, half the time."

"Trust me, I sympathize," Davis added wryly.

Heath looked at him a lot more closely. It was only then Davis realized he'd waded right into the danger zone.

"But no . . ." Heath said slowly. "No, that's not only why I like coaching. I feel like I can see the field so much better from the sideline than I ever could from *on* the field, and it turns out that it's a view I like real well."

It was a view Davis had discovered he liked too.

The waitress appeared then, took their orders, and promised to be back with their beers.

Heath leaned back in his chair, crossed his arms over his chest, and looked over at Davis in a surprisingly close approximation of his poster on the wall. "You wanna tell me what this is about?" he asked.

"Uh . . . what do you mean?" Davis wasn't any good at playing dumb, and he did a fucking terrible job of it now.

"You don't really want this backup job."

"Of course I want it," Davis insisted, but the words felt hollow to him. Meaningless.

Heath shook his head. "I know what it looks like, a man going through the motions, doin' what he thinks he's supposed to be doin'. You forget, Abernathy, I did that forever. I know exactly how that feels."

"You do," Davis said. Not answering the question that Heath hadn't quite asked.

"And I can see it in you. Sure, you went through the motions pretty spectacularly today." He leaned in. "But I know when you're just goin' through the motions. You liked coaching. You *like* coaching."

"You're right, it's different seeing the field that way, from the sideline, than it is being in the middle of it," Davis said.

"But that's not all. Why'd you ask me about Sam?"

Why *had* he asked Heath about Sam? Had he secretly, desperately wanted Heath to guess what he was really asking about?

Maybe he had. Maybe what he needed to do was talk about this with someone who'd been there, who understood what he was going through.

And who else would know better than Heath Harris?

"I . . ." But it was hard, harder than Davis had anticipated to tell the truth.

The waitress re-appeared with their beers.

Heath tipped his bottle against Davis'. "You've got a look I recognize," he said. "You forget, I was *also* in love with someone I wasn't supposed to be in love with."

"Oh, I didn't forget," Davis said wryly.

"So you and Pax, huh?"

"Dawson's gonna string me up, when he finds out."

Heath raised an eyebrow. "When, not if?"

"I can't go back and coach for him and not tell him. I don't give a shit about anyone else knowing, but it doesn't seem right . . . paying back the chance he took on me, the faith he had, by lying. By continuing to lie."

"Asa Dawson's a fair guy, and a great coach," Heath said. "I can't say that it wouldn't work, because Sam and I make it work. Is it always easy? Course not. Sometimes I want to strangle him. Sometimes I think he's gonna yell my ears off. But we figure it out, 'cause in the end, nobody has my back like he does, and vice versa. We trust each other."

Davis didn't say anything, just toyed with the edge of the label peeling off his beer bottle.

"And, when you two are on the same page? There's nothing like it. It's symbiotic, in the best possible way. I saw that game against the Condors. Sam made me sit down and watch it. You think I guessed, probably, just now, but Sam guessed before I ever even considered the possibility."

"Pax and his stupid sense of honor," Davis grumbled.

"Yeah, course there was that, that sorta confirmed it, but it was the way he went out there and just fearlessly spat in their teeth. Sam said you don't feel that way, you don't play that way, unless you've reached a new level and he reached it pretty damn fast."

Heath shrugged, then continued. "Anyway, that's what Sam said. Didn't know if he was right, but then I saw you, lookin' at us, and I knew he was right. Like I said, I know what it's like to love the last person you're supposed to."

"Is he the last or is he the first?" Davis wondered. Not sure of the answer. But Heath's face broke into a wide grin.

"You're really gonna go back to Miami and just announce to Asa Dawson that you're in love with his quarterback, aren't you? That's fucking awesome."

"Or insane," Davis muttered, taking a sip of his beer.

"To answer your question, of course it's more satisfying that it's Sam I'm coaching. But I'd do it anyway."

"It was different, 'cause I didn't make the choice, I didn't ever have a choice," Davis said. "You had a choice."

Heath's expression softened and he leaned forward, elbows on the table. "Listen, I know it seems like I did, but I'd argue that I never had a choice in the matter. Our fate's what we make of it. Maybe it's time you make something of yours. Stop worrying about what you *should* do and worry about what you want to do. What you need to do."

Put that way, Davis' path suddenly felt very clear.

Crystal fucking clear.

"Thanks," Davis said. "I . . . I actually think I needed to hear that."

"Anytime you need the tough Heath Harris pep talk, you know where to come."

Their tacos arrived, and they ate in silence for a few minutes.

"I was sure you were gonna tell me I was making a mistake," Davis said, as their waitress dropped off a second round of beers.

Heath shot him a look. "Why? 'Cause if you were making one, then I've sure as hell been making one. Besides, you've got a solid head on your shoulders. If you went after Pax, it wasn't a fleeting thing. It was because it was important. What *we* want is important too, not just what the NFL wants. It's easy to forget, in the middle of the big machine chewing you up and spitting you out, that *you're* fucking important, too. As a person. Not just a player."

Davis glanced up at the poster of Sam with the Lombardi Trophy. "Is that why you came out at the Super Bowl?"

Heath's smile turned private. Tender. "Something like that," he said.

"You and Asa are too much alike," Davis said.

"I'm not surprised. He has unusual views. They kept him out of the NFL for a long time, until Rudy was too desperate for a winner, he didn't care how he got it. But I like what he's doin' out there, what all of y'all are doing. Why do you think you were our first call? Course we want someone decent out there holding the clipboard, especially if Sam continues to be an idiot and keeps doing stupid shit, but anyone can do that job."

"Sorry," Davis said.

'Cause he already knew what he was going to tell Phil and Coach Martinez when he met with them tomorrow morning.

Six months ago, he'd have jumped at this chance, it would have been everything he'd wanted. Finally, an opportunity to vindicate himself.

But in the last six months he'd changed, and more importantly, he'd learned that he got to pick whose opinion mattered. And anyone who'd bought the stupid line of shit the Condors had sold wasn't worth giving a crap about.

He knew the truth. Pax knew the truth. Asa and Beau Dawson knew the truth. Every single player on the Piranhas team knew the truth.

Those were the people who mattered to him—*his* people, his team—and as long as they understood what had really gone down, that was all that mattered.

He didn't need to exorcise his demons because the moment he turned his back on them, they were already gone.

"Well, can't say I'm real surprised," Heath said with a sigh. "But I'm glad for you. Really."

"Me too," Davis said, surprising himself.

"If it makes you feel any better, after what I saw today, you could take the field tomorrow as QB1," Heath said with a grin.

Davis quirked an eyebrow. "And so could you."

"Yeah, yeah, but why would I want to?" Heath said. "I'm having too much fun telling QB1 what to do."

Decision made, Davis wanted to fly out the next morning.

He'd spent too much time away from Miami already.

Too much time away from Pax.

But it meant something that Phil Reynolds, the VP of player personnel for the Riptide, and Coach Martinez, had thought of him and brought him out to try out.

It definitely meant something that they were intending to offer him the job.

But as Davis sat across from them the next morning, he only felt blindingly sure that he was making the right choice.

Like Heath had said last night, *when you know, you know.*

Before Phil could even go through the details of the offer, the contract sitting on the desk in front of him, Davis spoke up. "I really appreciate, more than you know, the chance you've given me," he said. "But I don't know if I'm interested in being QB1 anymore. Not interested in being QB2, either, it turns out."

Coach Martinez, who'd been a head coach in the NFL for over ten years, probably wasn't easily shocked. But his jaw dropped a little. "What?"

Davis shrugged. "I thought I needed this, and maybe I did, a little, but like I said, I really appreciate the opportunity to come out here and show you what I can still do. It reminded me too."

"I guess it did," Phil said with a reluctant sigh. He stood up and shook Davis' hand. "You're a damn good football player, Abernathy. We'd have loved to have you on the sidelines, and potentially under center, if anything happened to Sam. You know what we're trying to do here."

"Yeah, you're gonna win another ring," Davis said. He'd seen the way the team had gelled here, the way they were playing. It wasn't a matter of *if*, only a matter of *when*. "And we're gonna win one too, someday, and no offense, 'cause you've got a great thing going here, but I'm gonna win it with my boys in Miami."

Coach Martinez grinned and shook Davis' hand next. "I guess I should say good luck, then. And we'll see you in the playoffs."

"Goddamn, I hope so," Davis said and meant it.

To be the best, you had to beat the best.

And, no matter how much he liked everyone out here in LA, Davis had every intention of making sure the Piranhas *eventually* wiped the floor with them.

Maybe not this year.

Maybe not next year.

But *soon*.

"Thanks again," Davis said, standing up. "But it turns out that I've got somewhere I gotta be."

Pax was absolutely not sulking that he hadn't heard from Davis today.

He knew he was going to take the job. That wasn't even up for debate, especially if they were going to offer it to him—and why wouldn't they?

You're gonna have to get used to this. Driving home alone. Heading back to your empty condo, again. It sucks, but you're gonna get used to it, because as Davis likes to say, nobody likes a pouty QB1.

It was true, nobody did. The last two days when Pax had shown up at the practice facility, he could feel everyone let out a quiet breath of relief when he was normal. When he *pretended* he was normal. Because he wasn't quite normal, not deep down inside. He was trying, goddamn it, but losing Davis was more of a blow than most any of them realized. He hadn't just lost his coach, but his lover, his partner, his best friend, the person he adored more than any other.

You haven't lost me, not even close, Pax could hear Davis' wry voice reminding him. *Stop pouting. What did I say about pouty QB1s?*

He parked in his spot, and rode the elevator up to his floor, punching in the door code when he reached it.

And to his shock, the light was already on as he walked in, dropping his bag by the door.

Davis walked out of the kitchen, and that was absolutely a shit-eating grin on his face. "Hey," he said. "Surprise."

"Goddamn it," Pax said, and launched himself into Davis' arms. "What the hell are you doing back here?" He hugged him tightly. "Actually, don't answer that."

"Why not?" Davis pulled back. "You don't want to know?"

"I do, I really do, but I'm afraid . . ." Pax didn't want to say that hope was a painful thing. He didn't want to say that he was *glad* that they hadn't offered him the job after all, because that would be mean, and goddamn it, Davis had been through enough shit in his life.

But would he really be smiling that way if they hadn't given him the job? He'd be bummed, right?

Pax suddenly wasn't sure.

"I guess you'd better tell me," he continued.

"Damn straight," Davis teased. "Yeah, they gave me the job. A decent offer too, if I spied the details right, but I . . . I couldn't take it, Pax. I didn't want it, not really."

Pax had to fight to keep the encouragement on his face. "If it wasn't right for you, there's got to be another spot out there that is, and now that the Riptide took a chance, there's got to be others that will too . . ."

"It wasn't right, 'cause I've already found the spot that *is* right," Davis said. He reached up and cupped Pax's face in his hands. "It's here. It's with you. This is my place. Coaching you. Being with you. I don't want anything else. Not anymore. Not ever."

Relief flooded him in a dizzying rush. He pressed his body against Davis', not realizing how much he'd missed the warm insistent pressure of it until it was back. "God, I didn't want to think that it was, because it would hurt too much if it wasn't, but I'm really fucking glad you agree."

"I'm sorry I had to go out to LA to make sure," Davis murmured into his hair. "I'm sorry."

"Don't be, you needed to do it. You needed to know that you weren't a washed-up has-been." Pax had seen the pain in his eyes too many times to believe otherwise.

"Yeah, maybe, but the truth is their opinions don't matter the way they used to. I don't give a shit what people are saying about me. Just what you're saying about me." Pax had heard Davis confident, even in the last six months, but he'd never heard him like this. It wasn't even the same as it had been before the Condors had gotten rid of him, Pax thought he sounded even more settled, more grounded, and without a doubt, *happier*, too.

He'd wanted Davis' place to be with him, with the Piranhas, but now he knew, without a single doubt, that it was.

Reaching down he squeezed Davis' hand. "How about this? I love you. I want to be with you."

Davis grinned. "Best thing I ever heard. Now you wanna go cuddle on the couch and show me the third-down plays you're workin' on?"

Nothing had ever sounded better.

They went through all the practice footage, and Pax could finally admit to himself that even though they'd accomplished so much in the last two days, that it hadn't felt as good as it could've.

It hadn't felt quite right, because one of their pieces was missing.

"We're not as good without you," Pax murmured into his shoulder as they finished watching the last bit of the tape.

"I'm actually countin' on that," Davis said, and he took a deep breath, shifting Pax's body enough that he could feel it. "I want to do something, and I understand why you might not want to, but hear me out, okay?"

Davis sounded painfully serious, and Pax glanced away from the screen, back to his face. "What is it?"

"I want to tell Asa about us."

"But . . ." Pax stuttered. "What if . . ."

"I know," Davis said.

He didn't even have to say what could happen if Coach found out, what he could do about it, because Davis already knew. He could fire Davis. He couldn't really fire Pax, not now, not when he was playing so well.

"You're not really risking me," Pax said with a startled realization. "Not now you're not. Just you."

"And that's right," Davis said, "because I'm the one who wants to tell the truth. Who needs to tell the truth."

"Why?"

"Asa took a chance on me. It seems . . . wrong to pay him back by lying to him. Even by omission. Even if what we share is important enough that I was willing to do it before. Besides, there's something he wants. Something I can give him, now, especially considering that I know what I want."

"He wanted you to sign a contract, for multiple years," Pax said, further realization dawning. "And you're gonna do that."

"But . . . but only if he's okay with you and me," Davis said. With finality. Like this was the beginning *and* the end of the negotiation. "I don't need anyone else to know, though that might be easier. But he needs to know. We need to be able to live without living in fear, Pax. We can live privately. Or publicly. But we can't live in fear. You know that."

Pax nodded. He knew that. He'd been willing to do it before, because that was the only way he could have Davis, but the truth was . . . Davis was right.

"But I wanted to get your opinion first and well . . . your permission. I can't say one hundred percent for sure that if things go bad, it won't impact you."

"I wouldn't even want you to take all the risk," Pax said staunchly. "I love you, too. It's not just you in this. I'm in it, too."

Davis smiled softly, and pressed a kiss to his forehead. "God-damn, I love you."

"That's the only way this works," Pax insisted.

"Funny, that's what Heath sort of said, too."

"You talked to Heath about this?" Pax was surprised. Though, not really, when he thought about it. Who was the only other couple currently playing QB1 and also coaching QB1?

It was Heath Harris and Sam Crawford.

"Didn't mean to," Davis said wryly. "But it felt right. I hope that's okay with you."

"Of course. I get it. It's . . . well, it's a loaded situation."

That was the understatement of the century.

"But," he continued, "I agree with you. This is the right move. When are you gonna tell him?"

"No time like the present. Tomorrow morning."

"Not wasting any time, I see," Pax teased.

"When you know what you want, there's no point in waiting for anything else," Davis said.

And *goddamn*, Pax loved him, too.

Chapter Twenty

He and Pax drove in together, for the first time since the Condors game, and Davis was pleasantly surprised to see all the happy grins everywhere, and the players who actually came up and fist-bumped him, saying they were relieved he'd come back, after all.

It further cemented his belief that he'd made the right choice.

And, Davis thought as he approached Coach's office, he hoped he was making the right choice here, too.

No, it was right, he *knew* it was right, even if Coach didn't think so. *You're making the best choice for you* and *for Pax.*

He knocked on the doorframe and Coach glanced up.

They'd talked briefly, yesterday, before he'd left LA, to let him know that he wasn't going to be staying.

Asa had sounded surprised, but pleased, and said they'd talk more about it today.

"Oh, Davis, you're back," Asa said, standing up and, as Davis entered, they shook hands briefly before Davis took the chair in front of his desk. "I guess LA wasn't quite what you expected."

"Actually . . . it was a perfect job offer. Well, maybe not perfect. Perfect might've been if the contract was for QB1, but . . ."

"Sam Crawford, obviously," Asa said, a twinkle in his blue eyes.

"It was everything I thought I needed. Definitely everything I thought I wanted. I was their first choice and they were ready for me to sign on the dotted line." Davis hesitated. "But I didn't want to do it, in the end. I couldn't do it."

Asa didn't say anything, just sat back in his chair and watched him. There was a wary, watchful quality about him sometimes, it could be unnerving but Davis had mostly gotten used to it.

Except right now, when he had a monumental truth to disclose, and he felt a little like a particularly tasty bit of prey, being watched by a lion.

But, Davis reminded himself, *you have power here. You have something that Asa wants. You've got value.*

"I realized the right place for me to be is here, in Miami, on the sidelines, maybe getting our first divisional championship, maybe making it deep into the playoffs."

"And next year?"

Anyone who claimed Asa Dawson was just a dumb hick was just plain crazy. He was one of the smartest—and most intuitive—people that Davis had ever met.

"Yeah, about that . . . I'm willing to sign the contract. Three years, if you want it. My agent can hammer out the details with Roy Robinson, but I thought we could come to an unofficial agreement now. Today."

Asa didn't move. Didn't flinch. He was also a damn good negotiator.

Roy, who was the head of personnel for the Piranhas and handled all the contracts, including the staff contracts, could probably learn something from Asa.

"We can do that," Asa said.

Sebastian had told him once that facing Beau's father and telling him the truth about their relationship had been one of the hardest things he'd ever done. He'd been willing to put it all on the line for a future with Beau.

Davis was willing to do the same, but he realized that Sebastian hadn't been exaggerating how tough it was.

How nerve-wracking.

And he'd faced some of the best defenses in the NFL.

"Why don't you tell me what you want, Davis?" Asa's voice was mild, but there was an edge to it.

"Three years," he said, "with an option for two more. Same salary that the other assistants get."

Asa raised an eyebrow. "You don't want more? I know the Riptide were potentially ready to offer you a *lot* more, and that job wasn't all that different from this one, unless of course, if you ended up having to sub in for Crawford."

"Well, I do want more. Just . . . not money." Davis wiped his damp palms on his jeans and stood, belatedly realizing that he should have shut the door before this. He wanted Coach to know the truth about him and Pax, but he didn't know yet about anyone else.

Coming fully out would be complicated, especially considering who his relationship was with. Helen might have some ideas of how they could do it, but the last thing he needed right now was for rumors to start swirling like wild fire through the team, because there was nothing that would tip the media off faster. And once they knew? Well, the secret would be out.

He shut the door, and Davis felt the click of it resonate through him. When he turned around, Asa's eyebrows were lifted nearly to his hairline.

"What's going on, Davis?" he asked. He was upright now, leaning forward on his desk, no longer pretending to be only casually interested in the proceedings.

Door shut, Davis sat down again, and taking a deep breath, told *his* truth, finally.

"You asked me before if something was going on with me and Pax. I said no. I didn't lie, because at that point nothing was, because I was doing everything I could so it wouldn't. But here's the problem with that, sir. I'm in love with Pax, and he's in love with me, and I'm tired of pretending that isn't the case. I'm not asking for some big coming out celebration, or for anyone else on the team to know, but I want *you* to know. And I want your permission."

To say that Asa looked flabbergasted was an understatement, but Davis held his gaze.

"You get this idea from Harris?" he asked. He didn't sound mad. He didn't sound angry. He just sounded . . . resigned.

"No," he said. "But seeing him and Sam, of course it clarified some things."

"It would," Asa said dryly.

"You want me to sign this contract, and that's what I want too, honest to God, but I don't want to do it if I have to hide my relationship from everyone, including you, for the next three years," Davis said bluntly.

Asa didn't reply in words. He just sighed, and then stood, heading over to where a mini fridge was sitting underneath a credenza. He opened it and, to Davis' astonishment, took out two beers. With an expert flick of his wrist, he took the caps off and handed one to Davis, who took it with an incredulous look.

Asa settled back behind his desk and took a long drink of his beer.

"Sir, it's eight in the morning," Davis said cautiously. Not sure if he should say something—or if he should call Beau and tell him that his father had finally gone round the bend.

"Listen, Davis, someday you're going to be the coach of a football team—no, don't argue with me, you've got a coaching brain, I can see it, which is why I called you in the first place, not just 'cause the rest of the NFL are idiots who didn't see the real you—but someday, you're gonna be the head coach, and your players are gonna give you daily headaches, not just 'cause they won't listen to reason or to advice or plain just don't do what you tell them to do. No," Asa said, taking another drink and then leaning forward. "No, even worse, they're gonna *fall in love* and make your life hell."

Davis chuckled in spite of himself.

"I won't lie, it's not ideal, but . . ." Asa shrugged. "I suppose when I look back, I could see it coming. You two were always too close, but I thought, stupidly, that it might help Pax get his feet under him better. Make him more confident. Now, it did do that, so I can't say I was entirely wrong, but . . ." Asa gestured with his beer. "I did not expect it to go further than that. I suppose you can't promise that it'll be like Crawford and Harris."

"I don't think anyone can promise locker room harmony," Davis said carefully. "But I *can* promise that neither of us take this lightly. If it was just a fleeting thing, we'd get it out of our systems and you'd never know."

"Oh, that's reassuring," Asa said dryly. "Very reassuring."

"Just the truth," Davis said. "I'm not gonna sit here and lie to you."

"Well, clearly it's just not sex," Asa said. "That much I got from your very impassioned declaration. Full points for that, by the way."

"Thanks," Davis said, "I think?"

"I could give you the speech I'd give anyone else, but I think you already know about it, and you're already doin' your best not to let your relationship intrude onto the field," Asa said.

"Correct," Davis said. "Honestly, that's why it really began in the first place . . . we were fightin' so hard against it, it *did* start to intrude and we thought . . . maybe we should stop fightin' against each other and start fighting for each other instead."

Asa sighed and set his beer bottle down with a click. "I hate that I can actually see how much sense that makes. It was the game before the bye, wasn't it?"

There was no point in lying. "Yeah."

"You yelled at him on the sideline, and Beau told me he wasn't too nice to you, either."

"We worked through it."

"I'd say you did." Asa's tone was very wry.

He sighed then.

"Again, it's not ideal, but I also can't deny that you two have been real good for each other, and Pax is playing lights-out. Something is working here, and since it's impossible to say what, you have permission to do whatever you feel you need to do. *Outside this facility*, which I'm sure you understand, Davis."

"I do, sir," Davis said, fighting back a smile. He took a small sip of beer—because when Coach gives you a beer, even at 8 in the morning, you drink it.

"And I'm only doing this 'cause what else am I supposed to do? Be that asshole who listens to your declaration of love and tells you to forget it?" Asa shook his head. "I'm not gonna be the bad guy here, Davis. You know that."

"I do, sir." Davis couldn't stop his grin anymore. "But I promise, we're gonna be real circumspect."

Asa eyed him. "That is what Nicholson and Lewis keep telling me, and I promise you, circumspect is not the general outcome."

"We could've kept hiding it," Davis pointed out, "but neither of us wanted to. We wanted to tell you the truth, especially me, because I know you took a chance, calling me, and I didn't want to repay that trust with a lie."

"See, just when I want to be pissed off at you . . ." Asa trailed off. "And then you say that, and it's impossible."

"That's the idea," Davis said.

"Get out of here before I change my mind. And yes, three years. Option for two. Same salary as the other assistants. I'll let Roy know."

"And I'll talk to my agent."

"Good." Asa shot him a penetrating look. "This is a delicate situation, and if y'all want more than just telling me and expecting me to keep your secret, that's fine, but we approach it carefully. And with Helen's help."

"Agreed," Davis said. He reached out his hand, and Asa shook it firmly. "Thank you again. I'm real glad we could come to an agreement."

Asa smiled. "You know what? Me too."

And Davis thought as he left Coach's office, that he might actually mean that.

He found Pax making coffee in the little kitchenette outside the QB room.

"Hey," he said, not reaching out for him, the way he always wanted to, because the last thing he was going to do was break Coach's admonition literally five minutes after he'd given it.

Pax turned. "Oh, you're still alive," he teased. "And you're smiling. Must've gone well."

"Well, he's not *happy* about it, but he's grudgingly given his permission. And if we want more, like to come out to the entire team or even to the public, he says it's not impossible. But we'd need to be really strategic about it. Use Helen, etcetera."

"Someday," Pax said firmly. "But not yet. I'm good just with you and with knowing you're not gonna get fired for falling in love with me."

"That," Davis said with a big grin, "is not going to be happening. And it would've been pretty unfair, 'cause you were basically irresistible. How was I supposed to stop myself?"

"Truth," Pax said. He slid a cup of coffee towards Davis. "You wanna go watch some film?"

"Yeah. We've got a game to win," Davis said.

Pax knew he could've taken the field, no question, if Davis had stayed in LA.

He'd have worked, before the game, and after, to make sure that the Piranhas were in a position to win.

But he knew some of the shine would've been gone. He wouldn't have enjoyed it quite so much, if Davis wasn't there to offer pointed suggestions, to tell him he was being stupid, to just be able to look over to the sideline and know from his steady gaze that one person had his back, while he had the back of the whole rest of the team.

And it hadn't been a particularly easy game.

Coach had reminded the team several times, including in his pregame speech, that they couldn't let the euphoria of the Condors win the week before distract them. That winning *this* game was more important than anything they'd done last week.

But they'd felt sluggish, coming out of the gate. Their first two drives had ended just outside of Dylan's field goal range, and while they'd finally put together two touchdown drives, one late in the second quarter, and another in the beginning of the third, they'd unexpectedly been a struggle.

Pax was relieved that they'd spent some time working on third-down conversions this week, because Wade's skill and their intense preparation had saved both drives, multiple times.

Then, like everything wasn't hard enough, midway through the fourth quarter, Rob, the left tackle, had gone down with an ankle injury. It probably wasn't serious enough to keep him out next week, but it was enough to keep him on the sideline for the rest of the game.

That meant that the line was under siege, and Pax had spent half of this drive, which he'd intended to use to score a third touchdown, and win the game, putting them up by five, running for his fucking life.

"Okay," Pax said, huffing out a breath. He was not used to doing quite so much scrambling, and Coach Randy had been yelling in his headset for the last five minutes to make sure his hips stayed loose. "We ready for this play?"

"We're ready, boss," Logan said. Pax could see that his eyes were fiercely determined, through the visor of his helmet. He was having to take up a lot of the slack that the backup left tackle was leaving on the field.

Him *and* you, Pax thought. *You're the one who had to scramble for the last two first downs.*

The only silver lining to that was that he wasn't much of a runner, and the defense wasn't expecting it, so he'd managed to just slide past the first-down marker both times.

But now they knew he could, and they'd be watching for it. Davis had barked, during the last timeout, that there was no way he'd get away with it again.

"Wade, I need you to get open across the slant, make sure you hold the middle linebacker," Pax said, after he'd called out the play. "Open up Johnson for the catch and run."

Wade nodded. Pax knew he realized just how important it was to not only catch the ball, but to help someone else on the team catch it.

Not every player could be selfless like that, but Pax thought he'd ended up pretty lucky, 'cause the whole offense was willing to do whatever it took to move the ball. If that meant blocking and not catching, if that meant *pretending* like you were going to get the ball and not actually getting it, then they were cool with it.

He clapped his hands. "Let's get this done," he said.

It wasn't quite a two-minute drill, but Coach had already told him that he wanted him to score, no matter the time on the clock, and then leave the rest up to the defense.

They'd played well today, really gelling as a unit, and frankly, with Rob out, Pax knew if the offense managed to get into the end zone, that was exceeding expectations.

Still—that didn't mean he wasn't going to give it everything he had.

As they broke the huddle, he eyed the defense as they lined up. At second down with four yards to go, they were clearly expecting a run, which would be a conservative choice, but then Pax liked that they didn't always play conservative.

He called out the spike count, and felt the ball hit his hands perfectly on cue.

At least it had been Rob who'd gotten injured—and not Logan. Pax didn't know what he'd do without his trustworthy center.

The defense came for him, pushing hard at the left tackle spot, where the line was the most vulnerable, and Kenyon helped block, giving Pax just enough time to drop back, and scan the field, picking up as Johnson slid around the outside, Wade pulling the linebacker's attention away from him, and Pax threw the ball.

It was sad, Pax thought, as he watched Johnson snag the pass out of the air and turn up field, adding another three yards to the four they'd needed, that a seven-yard gain was something to celebrate today.

But, he reminded himself, it didn't matter how you won, as long as you won.

Kenyon got the ball on the next down, heading around the right side, both Wade and Tristan blocking for him, giving him an extra yard or two.

When they'd taken the field for this drive, Pax hadn't been particularly worried about the time they had left—certainly five minutes was enough time to move down the field and get the touchdown they needed to win—but with such slow, methodical bites, it was taking a lot longer.

They were down to only a minute and a half left and were still forty yards away, when Coach Dawson called a timeout, and Pax jogged over to the sideline.

Davis tossed him his bottle and he squirted some water into his mouth, swishing it around. "You need to step on it," he said.

Which Pax knew, of course.

"Yeah," he said. "We need to pull in a few two-minute drill plays. Take some bigger bites."

Davis looked skeptical. "You're barely making first downs as it is. The line's under constant harassment. I don't think we can go deep."

"Not deep," Pax corrected. "Deep-ish."

Davis still didn't look convinced. But Tristan spoke up. "We can try that thing that Wade did before, with Carter. He pulled the linebacker's attention just long enough to shake Carter loose."

"I like it," Davis said. "But it'd be even better if we swapped you and Wade. They're gonna be looking for you to go deep, with not much time on the clock. They're not looking for Wade to go deep. So we send him, instead. Everyone will think he's the decoy, but he's not."

"A variation of this play," Coach Randy called in through the headset, identifying one of the plays they'd worked on in practice this week. "But swap Tristan and Wade."

"Got it," Pax said. He met Tristan's gaze and then Wade's. They both nodded their agreement. "Okay, let's get it done."

This time when they broke the huddle and set up for the play, Pax could tell the defense expected a pass.

It only made sense—if the Piranhas tried to run the ball, it was likely they'd end up running out of time to score.

And Pax, well, he *really* wanted to score. He was tired of running around, trying to keep upright, and if they kicked a field goal, which Dylan *could* do, it would only tie the game, not get them the win.

He clapped and called out the snap count, leaning over and feeling the ball land in his hands. He dropped back, watching as the play unfolded past the offensive line, currently straining to hold back the defensive ends.

One of them broke free, and Pax had only a second to react, sidestepping around him, feeling him swish his arms around Pax's ankles, just barely avoiding the sack. He needed to give Wade another second to break loose and to get in position but then a second linebacker shot through the line, a delayed blitz, and Pax turned the other way, cleats digging into the turf as he barely kept his balance.

He was running from two players now, though he saw Logan chasing after them out of the corner of his eye.

One more fucking second, Pax swore, and then there was no time left. He could practically see the wild eyes of the second defensive end, the one that Logan hadn't been able to contain. He tossed the ball, arcing it over the player's head, and then he slammed him hard into the turf.

Pax felt the impact of the ground—which hurt—and then the impact of a two-hundred-seventy-five-pound defensive end landing squarely on top of him—which *really* hurt—but he craned his head around the guy's massive shoulders, and watched as Wade grabbed the pass, and turned up field, evading the safety and then the corner, taking what looked to be a really fucking good angle, and just barely managed to roll into the end zone.

Pax's head fell back to the turf.

The defensive end finally let up, but it was actually Logan who appeared in his field of vision with an extended hand.

"Fuck," Pax muttered. He was gonna need a real ice bath after that one. His ribs hurt, and he thought they might be bruised, but they weren't broken, because he could still breathe, even though it fucking hurt to do it.

"Sorry, boss," Logan said, even though he was grinning wildly, clearly pleased that they'd scored.

"Hey, if this was the only time I ended up on the turf . . ."

Logan shrugged. "We did our best."

"All we can do," Pax said.

But yeah, it fucking hurt to jog to the sideline.

"You okay?" Davis asked, as the defense took the field.

"Yeah," Pax said, and glanced around. He didn't see Coach. Where was Coach?

Davis was frowning, Pax realized, and it wasn't just because some enormous asshole had just tackled his butt to the ground.

That happened, more frequently than Pax wanted it to, because this was football.

But Coach always came around to where Pax sat, after a touchdown, sometimes only to give him a reassuring pat on the head.

"He's not here," Davis said. Still frowning.

"Where is he?" He realized now that Beau had his headset on, though he didn't always, and he was standing where Coach usually stood, right at the front of the sideline.

A bad sign.

"He went into the locker room, halfway through that drive. Nobody knows what's going on."

Pax felt a frisson of fear lance through him, which had nothing to do with the way the defense was trying to hold the opposing team back from scoring and making all that effort a moot point.

"What the hell," Pax said.

Davis just shrugged. But Pax could see the concern in his eyes. It was unmistakable.

The mood in the locker room after the game was excited—but surprisingly subdued.

Or unsurprisingly subdued, Davis thought, if your coach was missing and nobody had any idea what the hell was going on.

Finally, they were nearly changed, everyone dragging their feet, Davis knew, because they didn't want to leave before they found out what the heck had just happened, when Beau walked in, worry *and* relief in his eyes.

"Hey, y'all, I know you're concerned," he said, pulling out a chair and standing on it, just like his dad had, for so many games before this one. "I know you looked for Coach on the sidelines and didn't see him, and he hasn't been here to congratulate you on a hard-won victory, but I want to reassure you, first and foremost, Coach Dawson is gonna be just fine."

There was a palpable and swift release of tension throughout the room.

Coach Dawson had become the heart and soul of this team, and the last thing anyone wanted was to lose him—even temporarily.

"He had some chest pain, waited to get it checked out, but it got worse, so he had the medical staff take a look. He's been taken to the hospital—but only as a precaution," Beau said, and Davis believed him, because he knew Beau, and Beau would be a hell of a lot more upset, even if he tried to contain it, if things were more serious. "He's gonna be back next week, better than ever. I promise."

Beau hesitated, and gestured towards a staff member, who tossed him a ball. "I can't think of anyone I'd rather give this game ball to than our quarterback," he said, tossing it in Pax's direction. He caught it neatly, grinning. Maybe not as widely as Davis might have expected if the gift hadn't been prefaced by the announcement, but it was clear how much this meant to him.

"Pax," Beau continued, "never gives up on this team. Ever. He's the best leader I can possibly imagine for this team, and I know my dad feels the exact same way. In fact, he told me, just a minute ago, on the phone, that if I didn't give the game ball to Pax, I was crazy, so . . ." Beau smiled, and the tension in the room further relaxed. Coach wouldn't be saying stuff like that if he wasn't going to be fine. Davis knew it. And the rest of the players knew it too. "The game ball's yours, Pax. Thanks for being the quarterback we need, and for always havin' our backs."

When Beau got down and was headed over to the locker room door, Davis cornered him, lowering his voice. "Is he really gonna be okay?"

He was thinking of Asa's unusual behavior two days before, when he'd grabbed a beer from his mini fridge at 8 in the morning. *When you confessed something that made him so insane he had no choice to drink,* an annoying voice inside Davis' head reminded him. *This could be your fault. You drove him to a heart attack with your need to be honest.*

"He's going to be just fine," Beau said, and Davis could see the truth in his eyes. "Maybe he'll have to take it a bit easy this week, but they said they were very minor symptoms. Might have to change his diet and his sleeping habits." Beau rolled his eyes, which was the one thing that convinced Davis more than ever that

Asa really *would* be fine. "But then, we know I've been trying to get him to do that for ages. So maybe this was a good thing."

"He takes too much on his shoulders," Davis said quietly. "Maybe we can help lighten the load a bit."

"That's the idea," Beau said, and patted him on the shoulder. "I do know you signing that contract and being there for Pax in the future, that lightened the load already."

"I can do more," Davis said.

"I have a feeling," Beau pointed out wryly, "that if the doctors impose any kind of work and stress restrictions on him, we're *all* gonna be doin' a hell of a lot more. So hold that thought."

"Alright," Davis said.

"I gotta go to the hospital, check in with the doctors," Beau said. "You and Randy and Brett, you got the team, right?"

"We got them," Davis said. And realized, after Beau disappeared out the door, that he meant it.

He'd never really believed, not til now, that he was truly a coach, and not a player, but this moment, he felt the distinctive shift.

Pax headed towards him, Tristan following close on his heels. "Is everything really okay?" he asked.

"It's fine," Davis said. "I promise. This was more precautionary, truly, than anything else."

"Well, that's a first, for Coach," Tristan said, the seriousness evaporating out of his expression. "Him takin' care of himself."

"Well," Davis said, "I have a feeling that's gonna be happening a hell of a lot more, if any of us have a say in the matter."

Tristan grinned. "For damn sure it will be." He wandered off, leaving just Pax standing there.

"That was unreal, how you played today," Davis said. "In case you needed any more praise."

"No, but it's real nice to hear," Pax said, and for a second, he reached down, just brushing his fingers against Davis'. Not so anyone could see, but just the touch was enough. "Especially from you."

"I'm never gonna like seeing you get laid out like that," Davis said.

"No," Pax agreed. "But this is football, and I'd never want to do anything else."

With you, Davis saw the rest of the sentence shining in his eyes. Unsaid, but definitely not un-meant.

"Ditto," Davis said. And because he was feeling wild and a little bit dangerous, he mouthed the words, *love you too*.

Pax's answering smile was all he needed to know his message was received loud and clear—but not only that, was returned, wholeheartedly.

"Come on," Pax said. "I think you need to help me get ready for my post-game interview."

"Do I?" Davis asked innocently.

But the look Pax tossed him wasn't innocent at all. "Yep," he said. "Nobody puts me to work like you do."

"Just the way you like it," Davis teased.

He knew, nothing was ever going to be perfect. There were going to be days, just like Heath had told him, where he wanted to throttle Pax into next week. But the truth was, he wasn't ever going to want to do this without him.

Would he have wanted to be a coach without Pax? He didn't know the answer to that, and ultimately, Davis realized as he followed Pax out of the locker room, it didn't matter. Because it was both—the work *and* the man—that made him want to get up every morning. That helped him see each and every day like the blessing it was.

How could it be anything else, when they faced each one together?

Chapter Twenty-One

"I almost thought, we should cancel this," Sebastian said, leaning against the edge of the rooftop bar, "but then I thought, *fuck that noise,* Coach is fine, he's not dead, he's not even all that sick, so why should we cancel it? He'd kill me, anyway, if he found out. He's already embarrassed and humiliated enough that all anyone's talkin' about are a few little heart palpitations."

"He had a heart attack," Davis told Sebastian dryly. "He might like to dress it up in fancy language and try to minimize it by not saying the words, but he did. A tiny one, sure, but it was still a heart attack."

"Well, don't say that in his hearing, 'cause he gave Beau an earful yesterday," Sebastian said, lowering his voice. "They actually *argued* about it, and they never fight."

"Is he still mad that they're bringing in that guy?"

"Fighting mad," Sebastian confirmed. "I'd claim he's bein' stupid, 'cause at least he knows the guy, Beau said they worked together at Tennessee, and he's his godfather, so how much of a stranger could he be? But Coach's pissed, *still.*"

"He's a bit of a control freak," Davis conceded.

"No joke." Sebastian finished his drink and set it on the bar. "But I'm glad we did this anyway. Your boy keeps playin' like that, and we're just gonna keep winning. Having to throw these parties. I'm not sad about that."

"Me either," Davis said with a grin, glancing over to where Pax was chatting with Tristan and Kenyon.

"Beau told me that you turned the Riptide down for Crawford's backup spot." Sebastian hesitated. "That was real brave."

"No, it fucking wasn't," Davis said, chuckling. "It's braver to do this, to choose to do this, when I don't really know what I'm doing. I'm not really a coach."

"Not yet, maybe, but you're gettin' there," Sebastian argued. "I wasn't a safety either, was I? But now I am."

"Best damn safety in football," Davis said clanging his beer bottle with Sebastian's fresh drink.

"Besides," Sebastian asked with a conspiratorial grin, "isn't it damn fun destroyin' everyone's expectations?"

Davis couldn't argue with that one at all. It was unbelievably fun. He was enjoying the hell out of it, honestly.

It was a perfect, balmy evening, and even though it was late November, it was still Miami, which meant they were still out here enjoying Hibiscus' rooftop bar.

They'd celebrated here after the Piranhas' first win, and now it was a tradition that nobody seemed to want to quit.

Logan and Dylan were over in the corner, enjoying two beers and a plate of chicken wings.

Kenyon had come, the Thanksgiving they'd shared seeming to break down some of the walls he'd kept up between him and the rest of the team.

Beau was even here, and he was smiling and telling stories about how difficult of a patient his dad had turned out to be. Asa, *thank God*, Davis thought, was going to be just fine.

Crotchety and demanding and ornery but just fine.

But most importantly, Pax was here.

He turned to catch Davis' eyes as Kenyon drifted away to chat with Beau.

"Hey," he said, walking over. "You enjoying yourself?"

"Couldn't be happier," Davis said.

The music was going, a combination of pop and R&B hits, sprinkled in with a few more tropical-flavored numbers, because this was Miami and it wasn't ever going to forget its roots.

For a second, Davis just leaned against the bar and listened, his foot tapping against the floor to the beat.

"Isn't this . . ." Pax hesitated. "Isn't this the song we merengued to a few weeks back?"

Davis listened and it sure did sound awful familiar. Not many were on the dance floor, yet, it was still mostly empty, but a thought popped into his head and he couldn't shake it.

Then, he realized, he didn't *have* to shake it. He could do this. Nobody was here who knew them, besides the staff, and the players who were here had all been at that god-awful intervention weeks ago. They could do this and show everyone a little of what they liked to do every Wednesday night.

Maybe Floria's studio wasn't the only safe haven of inclusion they could enjoy.

He set down his beer on the bar and held out his hand towards Pax. "Let's dance," he said.

Pax's jaw dropped. "Are you serious?" he asked.

"Absolutely, one hundred percent, dead serious. Come on," he added with a little grin, "I think we should because we love doing it, but also . . . isn't it damn fun destroying everyone's expectations?"

Pax thought about this for a second and then a bright smile broke across his face. "Yes," he said, putting his hand into Davis' and then squeezing it hard. "Yes, it is."

They'd never done this before, and never in front of anyone who wasn't Floria, but somehow, it still felt natural to lead Pax to the dance floor, their fingers laced tightly together, and then they began to move just like they'd practiced so many times.

He could hear the whispers and the surprise around them, but he tuned it out, until all he could feel was the perfection of Pax's hand in his, the way his waist curved into his grip, the way their bodies moved as one body, hips twisting to the beat, the way the love of his life smiled when he turned him, pulling him back in so he'd be close, right where he belonged.

"You were right," Pax said as the song segued to the next. They didn't know this one, but Davis discovered that once you knew what the beat was and how to follow it with the steps, it wasn't actually that hard. Besides, he was having way too much fun to stop now.

He raised an eyebrow as he turned Pax again, flashier this time, and Pax pulled back to him, closer than ever. "I like to think I'm right a lot," Davis teased.

"It's a hell of a lot of fun destroying everyone's assumptions," Pax retorted.

Davis grinned. "Right?"

"Let's keep doing it," Pax said, twisting his hips in a particularly enticing way and Davis had to remind himself that *one*, this had been his idea from the very beginning, and also his idea tonight, and *two*, they were not at home, enjoying a little additional practice that could end in the bedroom, and *three*, they were definitely not in Floria's studio, and she wasn't here to yell at them if they got too close.

'Cause they were definitely pretty close now. Davis could see the light shining in Pax's sugar brown eyes, brighter than he'd ever seen it before. "I love you," he said.

"Is that a yes?"

"It's better than that," Davis said, "it's a promise."

Dying to read more about Coach's past and wondering if his old heartbreak can become a future HEA? You can read Coach's book, *Winning the Season* here.

To read a bonus scene about Coach and what he knew about Pax & Davis, AKA *Coach is smarter than y'all give him credit for,* click here.

INTERESTED IN READING MORE OF
BETH'S BOOKS?

CHECK OUT A FULL LIST OF TILES
BY SCANNING THE QR CODE
OR VISITING HER WEBSITE

WWW.BETHBOLDEN.COM/BOOKLIST

WANT TO FOLLOW BETH?

MAKE SURE YOU NEVER
MISS A RELEASE?

SCAN THE QR CODE BELOW
OR VISIT HER WEBSITE
FOR A SOCIAL MEDIA LIST,
NEWSLETTER SIGNUP,
AND SO MUCH MORE!

WWW.BETHBOLDEN.COM/ABOUT